The Mistletoe Mixtape

Twelve short stories to make you fall in love with Christmas, one song at a time

First published by The Christmas Collective
Email: thechristmascollective2021@gmail.com

First Edition

Cover design by Sarah Shard

Paperback Edition: October 2022
ISBN: 9798351375205

This anthology is dedicated to Christmas lovers all over the world with a special mention to those who remember creating their very own mixtapes filled with their favourite festive tunes.

Contents

Foreword

The Mistletoe Mixtape is the second anthology from The Christmas Collective. The collective was formed in 2021, following the "Christmas Love Story" competition hosted by Penguin Michael Joseph during 2020/2021. All the authors in this Anthology were shortlisted entrants and found each other on social media during the nail biting wait for the final announcement. Though we all knew there could only be one winner, every single person threw their support behind each other in the hopes that it would be a member of our community.

Once the competition was over, the momentum continued and twelve of us began working on a way to publish our stories. We knew we had something special in the close-knit group that we formed, and we weren't prepared to let that go. Our grassroots movement has flourished despite lockdown and the fact we are scattered across the U.K., Ireland and even one in Madrid!

At the end of 2021, three of our authors chose to take a break and we were thrilled when three other authors shortlisted for the same competition applied to take their places. This Anthology is the culmination of twelve people who chose collaboration over competition. It would have been easy for every one of us to lurk on the internet and go our separate ways after the competition ended, but we wanted something positive to come out of the journey we went on together. We are still on that journey, excited for what the future may hold if we continue to work together.

Our personal story is one of hope, perseverance, and the best of human nature – and the stories in each of our anthologies reflects all that and more.

With two anthologies under our belt, we hope you enjoy The Mistletoe Mixtape as much as you did for our debut collection, "More than Mistletoe".

Acknowledgements

We sincerely thank all our readers for their support. Every purchase makes us do a happy dance and our stories are just as much yours as they are ours. We hope you enjoy reading them as much as we have enjoyed creating them.

A Winter's Tale

Jenny Bromham

An ad popped up on my phone the other day: "Three Steps to De-stress. Step one, identify the source of the stress. Step two, identify what you can change. Step three, visualise your improved situation." The world's gone mindfulness crazy, but since age doesn't seem to be blessing me with extra wisdom, I'm more than happy to give it a go. I take a sip of my coffee and try to block out the café's Christmas music and the chatter from the other tables. So … Step one. The source of the stress? Can I say "Pete", or do I need to be more specific? It's the way he looks at me. Like just before I came here, and I asked him if we had any long-life milk, and he didn't answer, he just—

'Would you like some milk for that, Sarah?'

Garry towers over me offering a small jug. What a Godsend to be on friendly terms with the owner of a café which sells the world's greatest coffee.

'Thanks, but I'm having a black coffee moment,' I say.

Garry knows me well enough to understand what that means. Black coffee moments are becoming such a norm that I should replace "moment" with "day" … or "week" … or actually, "year". He smiles sympathetically, his laughter lines deepening with kindness and warmth, and he pulls out the chair beside me. 'Pete again?' he asks, sitting. Garry always looks like a giant in these chairs. 'What happened this time?'

'He left an empty milk bottle in the fridge, so I asked if we had any long-life, and he glared at me and stormed out.'

Garry nods. His customer care skills are so considered and patient. He's never too busy to make time to let me vent, he's always so careful not to pass judgement.

'We've been together for twenty-four years – he would've known the empty bottle would infuriate me. It's like he keeps trying to bait me into another argument.'

'Sounds like you were very cool, calm and collected.'

I feel the twitch of a smile. 'Not really. We never buy long-life.'

Garry puts a hand on my arm and gives it a squeeze, leaning towards me. 'Do you know, I don't think this is a black coffee moment. It's almost Christmas. If you've got problems, you need festive solutions. Wait one second.' He pushes back his chair and nips to the kitchen, returning with another small jug. 'Just don't tell the other customers,' he says, placing it next to my coffee before heading off to serve an old woman who's just walked in.

I peer into the jug. The liquid inside is pale brown instead of white. I give it a sniff and smile. Baileys. Is there a stronger word than "Godsend"? Whatever it is, Garry deserves it. The café isn't licensed so he's taking a risk serving me this, but now it's in front of me I know it's exactly what I need. "Three Steps to De-stress" can wait – for now, I'm taking a shortcut. I drink a little more coffee to free up some room in the cup, then pour in the Irish cream. Garry catches my eye as he hands the old woman her change. He grins.

My first Baileys of the season. I savour it as I watch the old woman making her way to the table by the Christmas tree. She eases her arms out of her white coat, revealing a bright red jumper which makes her lipstick and gold jewellery pop. As she settles against the twinkling backdrop of the tree, she becomes a Christmas card image of Mrs Claus. It's funny how the older I get, the more elderly my perception of "old" becomes. In films, Mrs Claus is usually cast as someone around my age, but now that I'm fifty-five, this festive eighty-something seems far more fitting.

'Good coffee?' Garry asks as he passes, carrying a tray of tea to Mrs Claus.

'The best.' I cradle the cup in both hands and drink, feeling calmer already. By the time I take the last mouthful, I'm humming along to "A Winter's Tale", remembering the night down at The Deer's Leap, when Pete got everyone singing along to this song. He can be so much fun. Maybe that's what we need – a party – something to organise together, something that'll make us laugh together.

Oh no! I must have been staring as I've been thinking, because Mrs Claus is smiling at me.

I smile back.

She beckons, and I look behind me in case I'm reading this situation totally wrong and there's someone there. No one. I point at myself, and she nods.

'Everything okay?' I ask.

'Everything's fine, thank you, dear. I was just wondering if you'd like your tea leaves read?' There's a sparkle in her blue eyes.

'Thanks, but I was drinking coffee, not tea.'

'I'm aware of that. But we could ask that handsome manager if he'll bring us another cup, and you can share my tea.'

I know I'm hesitating, but the Baileys has relaxed my brain and I can't think of a quick enough excuse why I can't join her. What the hell! Today's the first day I've considered mindfulness, it can be my first tea leaf reading too. 'Okay, thank you. I'll just clear my table.'

I bundle up my coat and bag, then take my incriminating cup and jug over to the counter.

'Can I grab a spare tea cup?' I ask Garry. 'I'm about to have my tea leaves read.'

'I didn't have you down as a fan of fortune-telling.' He smirks, carefully transferring a freshly-baked cake to a silver server.

'Neither did I. But until today, I didn't have myself down as a woman who picks fights by referencing long-life milk either. I think there's room for change, and fingers crossed, I'll find out I've got a happy ending with Pete, just around the corner.'

Garry crosses his fingers, just as the cake drops from the server. I refuse to see it as an omen.

As I settle at the table, Mrs Claus pours my tea, her hands remarkably steady.

'Now, dear, you need to frame a question about your future in your mind as you drink all the way down to the tea leaves. Then swirl the dregs three times and pass the cup to me.'

3

I lift the tea to my lips, and a single question bursts into my mind. Will I ever feel loved again? What? Where did that come from? A million memories rush forward presenting a parade of evidence: eye-rolls, snarky comments, silences, turned backs. Pete doesn't love me anymore. How has it taken me until now to see it? I meet Mrs Claus' eager eyes over the rim of the cup. What if she sees it too? It'll be announced, real, out there. I'm scared to drink more tea or pass the cup, but I robotically obey her instructions.

Mrs Claus smiles and taps my hand. 'Don't look so worried, dear. I wouldn't tell a bad fortune at Christmas – that's why I called you over, and not the poor chap sitting at the table by the door.'

I glance over at the man in question. I vaguely know him. Jed. He's part of Pete's cricket team. He looks absolutely fine, sipping coffee and laughing into his phone. I can't help but wonder if Mrs Claus is unstable. She's still smiling as she flips the cup into the saucer, twists it three times, then lifts it to peer inside.

'Oh, now, this is a lovely fortune. I knew it would be.' She holds out the cup for me to see inside. The tea leaves have mostly settled in two clumps at the base of the cup – I see nothing that implies "lovely".

'I'm going to ignore those stray leaves at the rim,' she says. 'The turmoil of the present is set to pass soon enough. What we want to focus on is that delightful formation at the bottom of your cup.' She looks at me, and when I don't respond, her smile widens. 'You've got a broken mince pie. True love will rise over a broken mince pie.'

Okay. She clearly is unstable. I give her a polite smile. 'So, I'm all set for a festive romance then?'

She nods. 'Oh yes. True love is so close, you could almost reach out and touch it. I'm delighted for you, dear.'

My phone pings, and as Mrs Claus' delighted gaze falls back to the depths of my cup, I take the chance to glance at the screen. It's Pete.
Sarah, we can't keep doing this. I'm leaving.

*

'You don't have to do this,' I say, following Pete as he struggles to pull a suitcase with one hand and carry a box of cricket awards and toys with the other. In fact, I should rephrase that – referring to his Star Wars models as "toys" is my equivalent to him referring to baking as my "little hobby". I don't know why we purposefully wind each other up. 'We can talk this through.' A trophy topples – the one with all the grooves that's a bugger to dust – and I reach to catch it. 'There are changes we can make … changes I can make.'

Pete pauses, balancing the box against the wall as I tuck the trophy back inside securely. It's on the tip of my tongue to ask him how a person gets to fifty-five but still can't pack to save their life. I've used the same line, but adjusted the age, since he was thirty.

'What – you're not going to say it?' He raises his eyebrows. When did those frown-lines get so deep?

'No, because then you'd ask me how I can get to fifty-five but still can't stop nagging.'

'You're right. I think we've said everything we have to say to each other too many times already.'

'But there are things we haven't said,' I say. 'In fact, I'm not sure we've really talked in years.'

'But we haven't missed each other, have we?'

There's no point denying it. We've filled our days, but not with each other. Where have those days, weeks, months, years gone since me and Pete were "Me and Pete"?

'Look, I'll make us a cup of tea and we can have a slice of that cranberry and walnut cake you made, and then I'll get going.' He leaves his baggage in the hall by the front door and heads into the kitchen. And I make my way to the living room. I snuggle the two armchairs up close to the fireplace and switch it on. We used to do this on winter evenings, a lifetime ago – close enough to hold hands, to pour each other wine. I check my hair in the mirror – still thick and thankfully still more strawberry blonde than grey. I check my teeth – no trapped food. I check my eyes – do I look like a woman whose life is falling apart?

Pete comes through with the tea and cake. I see him clock the armchairs, but he puts everything on the dining room table and takes a seat there. Outside, the snow is falling, and a robin is sheltering on the window ledge, looking in as though ready for the show to begin. I sit opposite Pete, moving the golden reindeer ornament along the table so I can reach the cake.

'Do you remember choosing this together?' I say.

'Yeah. We said we'd choose a special Christmas ornament together every year, but then the next Christmas you started choosing by yourself.'

'You should've said if you were bothered.' I look around the room, at all the decorations I've picked up over the years – the gnomes, and the

5

snowman lamp, the Santa wall stickers … 'I thought you weren't interested. You always say it's a load of tat.'

'It is; apart from the reindeer.'

There it is. Belittling my choices. If it was left to him, that reindeer would be the only ornament we own. 'Take it, if you like it so much.'

He shakes his head. 'I want a fresh start. In fact, I was thinking, you can keep most of our stuff. I'm quite excited to find out what my own taste is.'

His fingers trace a smile on one of the gingerbread men on the tablecloth, and suddenly I feel like they're all mocking me, they're on his side. He's excited. He's excited about leaving me. He takes a huge bite of his cake – my cake – and slurps tea into his mouth as if he's trying to dilute the taste. I hate it when he does that.

But what will this house be – what will I be – when he's not here to offend me about my cakes, to finish the last of the milk, to criticise my Christmas decorations? He's my family. He's part of me.

'Don't go,' I say. 'Please.'

'You know this is the right thing, for both of us.'

'But it's nearly Christmas.'

'That's no reason to draw this out.'

'But it's snowing.'

'I won't be driving far.'

We both sigh. This is exhausting.

'Where will you go?' I can't believe I haven't asked him already. I suppose I thought he'd change his mind.

'I'd rather not say. Just until after Christmas. I think it'll be easier to have a complete break for a week or so.'

Alarm bells are ringing. 'Are you leaving me for another woman?'

'No!'

'Or a man?' I think of the lovely Philip Schofield and his ex-wife.

'No!'

'You'd just rather be alone than with me, then?'

He holds my gaze. We both know the answer. He takes a final mouthful of cake and tea, then places his mug on the crumby plate.

'Don't worry, I'll clear that up,' I say, and he nods.

'I'll be off then. I'll pop back in a few days, just to pick up more bits, and if you really need me for anything, I'll have my phone.'

The emphasis on the "really" is loud and clear.

'It's okay. I'm sure I won't need to disturb you,' I say as we both stand at the same time.

6

'I'll see myself out.'

I sink back down into the chair. It feels wrong not to go to the door to mark this moment, but then, when was the last time I said goodbye to him on the doorstep and waved him off? I hear the latch click as he pulls the front door shut; the thuds of the boot and the car door; the revs of the engine and the crunch of tyres rolling away.

My hands are shaking too much to pick up my tea and my throat's too tight for cake. The robin looks on, as if the show's not over … maybe it's not. Didn't Mrs Claus say that the turmoil of the present is set to pass soon? I just need to calm down and figure out how to make that happen. What was step two of the "Three Steps to De-stress"? Identify what you can change.

I can change the house for Pete. I can change myself for Pete. But can I make him change his mind and love me again?

*

Oh! The doorbell! Pete's last text said he'd come and pick up more of his stuff on Christmas Eve – is it possible he's come sooner because he's missing me? Thank goodness I got ahead of myself, stripping back the Christmas decorations and ordering a life-sized Stormtrooper to stand by the front door. He's going to love it. I wonder if he'll notice I've dyed over my grey and had my eyelashes done too.

As quickly as my trembling fingers will allow, I pause "The Holiday" – one of my favourites, but Pete despises it – and put on the World Darts Championship. Pete usually watches it on his laptop, so he'll love seeing it on the telly.

I rush to the door and pull it back.

'Garry?' I hope my disappointment isn't too obvious.

In his thick winter layers, he looks even bigger than usual, his frame almost filling the doorway. His arms are folded against the cold, his cheeks flushed pink above the grey of his five o'clock shadow.

'I'm sorry to call round like this, it's just I've been worried about you. I heard a rumour Pete's moved out. I thought you might need a friend and perhaps a little extra of this.' He pulls a bottle of Baileys from inside his coat.

I should have known the gossip would be spreading. This suburb has all the nosiness of a small village with none of the charm. And what are they saying? "Moved out" sounds so final. Pete will be back once he sees the changes I've made.

'That's very sweet of you, Garry, but you shouldn't have worried. This is above and beyond the call of duty. Come in out the cold.' I open the door wider and Garry steps inside, shuffling snow onto the doormat, and suddenly I'm very aware that Pete's not here and that Garry is a man. The coffee shop is neutral ground – Garry's the owner, I'm his customer – but if the neighbours see this, they'll make all sorts of speculations.

Do you know what? Screw the lot of them. I shut the door behind him.

'Nice Stormtrooper,' he says, leaning on its helmet as he prises off his huge boots. 'Could do with a Santa hat and a bit of tinsel, though.'

'Only if I wanted an immediate divorce. Pete'd see that as the ultimate sacrilege!'

Garry blushes as he hangs his coat on the banister. 'Sorry – I didn't think.'

I put a hand on his arm to tell him not to worry, but immediately I lose focus. Garry's firm to the touch! I didn't think that was possible past fifty. I jerk my hand back, staring at the girth of his forearm through the sleeve of his blue jumper. I've got an unnerving compulsion to reach out and trace the muscle up to his bicep, to see if it's just as firm. My cheeks heat. What am I thinking? This is Garry. I'm a married woman. I reach for my wedding ring and force my eyes up from his arm.

'Don't be sorry. If it was down to me, I'd have that Stormtrooper decked up like a Christmas tree, but I'm trying to consider Pete first from now on … something I should've done a long time ago.'

Garry nods, then points towards the kitchen. He knows the way. He's been over a few times when I've baked the odd cake for the café. Apart from that, he generally keeps himself to himself. Sometimes I wonder if he has a secret life beyond the café and his son, Jonathan, but it's not my place to ask.

'Can I grab some glasses and some ice for us?' he asks.

I take the Baileys from him and shake my head. 'You've served me coffee most days for the last ten years. You're in my house – I want a chance to serve you. Take a seat.'

He looks like he's about to argue, so I point firmly to the living room. He slopes off, ducking his head to pass under the door frame. Two minutes later, I follow – the ice jingling festive rhythms against the glasses as I enter the room.

I stop. He's in Pete's armchair by the fireplace, where I left it. He's switched the fire on. He turns to me, smiling.

'I hope you don't mind. I love a cosy spot by the fire.'

I breathe. Pete's not here. He didn't want to sit in his armchair when he was here – he can't really mind Garry sitting in it now.

'I don't mind at all. It's a lovely idea.' I pass him a glass and sink into the chair beside him.

We clink glasses.

'To Christmas,' he says, and as we sip our Baileys, I'm suddenly worried. This is an alien scenario for us: we're both out of our café-owner / customer roles. How is this going to work?

As I flounder for something to say, Garry looks around.

'So, you haven't had time to get all the decorations up?'

I scan the room too. It does look horribly sparse. There are only blue and silver baubles left on the tree – I took the rest off in an attempt to make it look classy, rather than tatty, for Pete. The only other remaining item is Pete's reindeer on the bare dining room table.

'Pete's not a fan of living rooms that look like grottos, so I'm being discreetly festive this year. All part of the "Put Pete First" efforts.'

'That's what the new hair and make-up's about too?'

'You noticed!'

Garry nods. 'You look lovely – but then, you always do.'

'Thanks. I hope Pete has the same reaction.'

Garry nods again and I wonder if he'll offer an opinion on Pete now that we're out of role, instead of just listening to me vent, but instead, he changes the subject.

'Are you going to tell me what Edith saw in your tea leaves the other day?'

'Garry!' I gasp dramatically. 'You've just shattered my belief. Until now, she was Mrs Claus!'

Garry feigns despair with a hand to his forehead. 'I can't be responsible for shattering your belief.' His laughter lines deepen. 'What if I tell you her full name is Edith Claus?'

'Well, is it? What did it say on her cash card?' I give him an elaborately suspicious look.

'You're not catching me out with that question. She paid cash. But if she had used a card, it would almost certainly have been in the name of Edith Claus. I guarantee it.'

I laugh. 'How can you guarantee something that's only "almost certain"?'

'Christmas magic.' He grins and stretches out, his legs so long they almost reach the fireplace. I wonder if they'd feel as firm as his arm. No! I refuse to think about Garry's toned thighs. I take a gulp of Baileys. Where are these thoughts coming from?

'So, what did Edith Claus predict?

'Ah, she told me that true love would rise over a broken mince pie, so I'm all set for a festive romance. I just need Pete to realise that he's my leading man, then he can come over and smash all the mince pies he likes. It's quite apt, actually. He can't stand mince pies.'

'What?' Garry looks so appalled I can't help laughing.

'All the things I've moaned about over the years, and you've stayed totally neutral, but your mask finally slips because Pete hates mince pies!'

'I'm sorry but it's inconceivable. Mince pies are the meaning of Christmas!'

'Wait there.' I go to the sideboard and pull out my box of M&S luxury mince pies, holding them up for Garry to see. 'I don't bake them myself because of Pete, but every year I buy myself a box of these at the start of December and challenge myself to hold two back to have for supper on Christmas Day. I've got four left, so we could have a sneaky one with our Baileys.'

'Sarah, you're a woman after my own heart.' Garry grins as I nip off to grab two plates.

And then we sit, and we eat and drink in a pleasant, comfortable silence. I don't tell him, but I firmly approve of the length of time he leaves between bites and sips.

'Can I ask you a question?' I say, as we finish. 'Is there anyone … after your own heart? You've never mentioned anyone.'

Garry turns to face me: his features soft, no longer lit with humour. 'There's only been one woman since I moved here, but her heart wasn't free to give. She never really noticed me, anyway.'

'Well, that strikes Edith off the list. She was saying what a handsome man you are.' I'm smiling, but as I hear my own words, I see their truth. Garry's rough around the edges – not one for neat haircuts or close shaves – but he's beautiful, isn't he? Those deep, brown eyes. That jawline. Those lips. A warmth stirs in my stomach and spreads through my body, heating my cheeks once again. I'm drawn by his eyes, the way they flicker to my lips, and I—

He clears his throat and rises from the chair, the foil from his mince pie slipping to the floor.

'I'm sorry,' he says, stooping to pick it up. His face is as flushed as mine feels. 'I should get home.'

He strides to the door and pulls on his boots as I struggle up from my chair – my head is lighter than I expected.

'You don't have to go,' I say. 'It's been lovely … drinking Baileys by the fire … chatting … laughing.'

He opens the door and steps out into the snow.

'I didn't come here with intentions or expectations, Sarah – I want you to know that. I came here to see you're all right. That's all.'

'It's okay, Garry. I know.' I step towards him. He holds my gaze. My heart's beating furiously. It must be the Baileys … the luxury mince pie.

We both step back at the same time.

'Goodnight, Garry.'

'Goodnight, Sarah.'

I stand on the doorstep and wave as he walks away down the drive.

*

It's Christmas Eve. Pete came round earlier to collect more of his things. He stayed for a piece of cake. He didn't mention how I looked, or the Christmas decorations, but when he saw the Stormtrooper, he gave me a strange look. I couldn't tell if it was regret, affection, pity, or a mix of all three, but it gave me hope. It's got him thinking. He knows I'm changing.

But something else gave me hope too. Pete told me that Jed, from the cricket team, fell off a ladder yesterday, and broke both his legs. Edith's predictions really do come true! She knew Jed's Christmas fortune was a bad one. And she knew my fortune was good – that's why she chose me.

I sign my name on Jed's "Get well soon" card – it's the least I can do to make up for the fact that I'm secretly (and ashamedly) thrilled at his misfortune. I hesitate for a moment, and then add Pete's name too, smiling at the sight of our names side-by-side, as they always have been, as they should be.

I zip up my coat and open the door to walk to the post box. It's snowing again, thick white flakes falling fast to the ground. Pete's footprints have already disappeared beneath the crisp new carpet covering the drive.

He'd walked here earlier. Where were those footprints leading off to? He hasn't chosen to go far away. He could come back at any time. The thought energises me, and even though my breath burns hot in my chest, I trudge through the snow at high speed, blinking back the snowflakes and enjoying the frosted wind against my cheeks.

What was the third step of the "Steps to De-stress?". Visualise your improved situation. A final step and my worries will float away. I visualise. Pete and I are throwing that party I was thinking about. I've agreed to getting a bar, and even though it takes up a third of the living room, it's worth it to see him satisfied. His cricket friends are crowded around him, the music's turned up, and he's raising a pint and bursting into song. As I pass by, with my platter of fresh-baked nibbles, he slaps my bum like he used to when we were young. I make small talk with the other wives, and then I sit with a glass of wine in the armchair – now jammed up so tightly against the fireplace, I can no longer safely put the fire on – but I'm content to know Pete's happy, as I adjust the new Darth Vadar cushion behind my back.

A snowflake tickles my nose, drawing me back to the here and now. I ease the card under the tiny icicles in the mouth of the letterbox, as, in the distance, the church bells start to chime. Pete and I got married in that church. I wonder if he can hear the bells from wherever he is. Is he remembering our wedding day? Is he realising that he loves me after all, and he's made a mistake? Each chime is a countdown to Christmas, to the time when Pete will come back to me. When I get home, I'm going to put the box with the last two mince pies by the reindeer on the table. They've got to be visible if Pete's going to break them and make Edith's prediction come true. They're a sacrifice I'm willing to make.

*

I'm in the kitchen, adding more oil to the roasties, humming along to the radio, when it hits me. This Christmas Day, so far, has been strange, not because it's so different without Pete here, but because it's so similar. I got up early and spoke to Mum and my sister and nephews, as always. I poured myself a Buck's Fizz and spent the morning peeling and chopping, as always. The only difference is that I texted Pete a merry Christmas, instead of calling it through the door to the spare room.

Why do I still call it that? It's Pete's room, isn't it? It's been Pete's room for over five years.

I slide the loaded baking tray back into the oven and check my phone. Still no response from Pete, but there's a text from Garry.

Merry Christmas, Sarah. I hope your Christmas wishes come true.

That's nice. He's so lovely. I was worried things might be a bit strained between us after the other evening, but I've popped into the café twice since, and it's back to normal ... at least it is for him. I don't know what's wrong with me, but both times, I found it almost impossible not to keep looking at him, not to imagine the toned arms and the broad, hairy chest beneath his shirt. I need to stop thinking like this. I message him back.

No sign of Pete so far, but dinner's in the oven and the mince pies are out, ready to be smashed.

His response comes through almost immediately.

I'm here if you need me.

I know Garry never would have intended it, but his message zaps all the Christmas spirit out of me. He doesn't believe Edith's prediction is going to come true, does he? I take my Bucks Fizz through to the living room. The bare walls and the underdressed tree do nothing to comfort me. I look over at the reindeer standing alone on the dining room table. It looks so out of place without the gingerbread man tablecloth, the wall stickers, the snowman lamp. It looks so ... I don't know ... so lonely.

A sob heaves up through my chest, so powerful it hurts. I double over as a second wracks through me. My vision blurs, and a strangled moaning rises from my throat. I don't know where this is coming from, but it's like a dam has broken and I can't stop the flow. I don't like the living room like this on Christmas Day. I don't like the Darts Championship frozen on pause and ready to play on the television. I don't want a bar to fill a third of the living room. I don't want Darth Vadar cushions, or noisy parties. I don't want to cringe as Pete swills booze into each mouthful of the Christmas dinner that I've spent hours to preparing.

I don't want Pete.

I stride to the table, nose running, eyes streaming. I take a mince pie and tip it from the foil. I bite into it, crumbs falling, hands shaking, the taste exploding. This. This is what I want. I want to eat my mince pies. Pete's not getting anywhere near them.

I'm not sure if I'm having a breakdown, or if I'm experiencing a transcendental surge of Christmas spirit, but as I shove the rest of the mince pie in my mouth, I want to laugh. I'm going to make this room into the tackiest, most wonderful, Christmas grotto-style wonderland I've ever created. I drag the decorations from the cupboard under the stairs and set to work. Tinsel. Fairy-lights. Every bauble I own. It all comes out. The Stormtrooper is decked from head to toe, complete with Santa hat and reindeer antlers.

By the time I've finished, I'm exhausted and elated and … free.

I sit at the dining room table, with my wine glass filled and my plate piled high with both my portion and Pete's. I tuck in, pausing only to toast the robin when he hops onto the window ledge to catch up on the news.

'I've left him,' I say. 'It's over.'

*

Hugh Grant's telling me, yet again, how love is, actually, all around, when the doorbell rings.

'Edith, no! I don't want Pete to come back to me,' I say.

She's not here, but I've had another glass of wine, and my thoughts are wired directly to my lips. In fact, I'm a bit worried that means they're bypassing my brain – probably not a good time to talk to Pete. Maybe I could ignore the door. I'm sure Pete wouldn't be so ungracious as to let himself in.

The bell rings again, and I heave myself out of the chair. I've overeaten and overdrunk, and I feel happily enormous.

'I'll get back to you in a minute, Hugh,' I say, leaving the screen paused.

I pull back the front door.

'Garry!' He's wearing a red jumper with a fluffy snowman on the front and … a frown? 'What's the matter?'

'You didn't answer my messages. I needed to check you're okay.' His eyes dart past my shoulder. 'Is Pete here? I'll leave, I just want to know everything's fine.'

'Pete's not here. He hasn't been here for years … in his heart.' Did I just say that out loud?

Garry's frown deepens. 'Are you drunk?'

'I'm a touch tip-sy.' I hiccough. 'But it's because I'm happy. Come and see what I've done to the house.'

He hesitates, then comes inside, stepping so close to me, I can smell him. Soap and coffee and …

'Garry, you smell so good.' Did I say that out loud too?

He puts a hand on my waist and my breath catches, but instead of moving closer, he guides me to the living room. I'm stumbling, falling against him, but he supports me and leads me to the sofa.

'Have a sleep, Sarah,' he says. 'You'll feel better.'

I want to stay awake and sit in the armchair and drink with him by the fire, but before I can formulate the sentence, my eyes are closing, and the next thing I know, it's dark outside, my head is aching, and I smell coffee.

'How are you feeling?' Garry appears in front of me holding two steaming mugs. 'Is it a black coffee moment?'

'It's a black coffee moment in the best possible way.' I sit up slowly. 'I feel horrible and amazing at the same time. My head hurts, but I've left Pete. Please tell me it's still Christmas Day.'

'It's eight-fifteen, Christmas Day evening.'

'Thank God for that.' I reach for the coffee, but then spot the armchairs. Garry's already put the fire on. 'Shall we have these over there?'

He smiles and we move across.

'I love the decorations, by the way – especially the Stormtrooper. The whole place feels so much more ...' He looks around in search of a word.

'Christmassy?'

'I was going to say "Sarah". It's much more you.'

I look around. He's right. This is me. It's messy and tasteless and joyful. 'Do you know, I think that's the nicest compliment I've had in years.'

'As intended,' Garry says. His eyes are smiling. 'So, you're feeling okay about everything with Pete?'

'I am. He was right. We can't go on. We should have done this years ago. I think I got a bit overexcited when it sank in earlier. I ate his Christmas dinner for him, and I drank his share of the bottle of wine for him, too.'

'At least you lined your stomach well. And hopefully, you've still got room for that.' He points at my last mince pie, over on the table. 'It's part of your Christmas Day tradition, isn't it?'

I'm so lucky to have a friendly café-owner who listens so well. In fact, scrap that, Garry's come to my home to check on me on Christmas Day, I think this qualifies him as a friend.

'It is part of my tradition. But what about you? What do you usually do for Christmas? I'm guessing looking after drunk women isn't a regular thing?'

'No. This is a first. I always go over to Jonathan's for a festive fry-up and then I head home in the evening for turkey sandwiches, "Love, Actually" and mince pies. This year, I skipped the heading home part.'

That's his tradition? Okay, so the festive fry-up is questionable if it's replacing a full Christmas Dinner, but "Love, Actually", mince pies … I never knew we had so much in common.

'I'm truly grateful you missed the heading home bit. I'd have passed out and woken up on Boxing Day without ticking off my Christmas traditions,' I say. 'And, luckily, it sounds like our traditions merge beautifully.' The coffee's already kicking in and I stand up. 'As a thank you, I'm making the turkey sandwiches. You can turn the telly round so it's facing this way, and I think you'll find the film's there ready for you to press play.'

Five minutes later, I'm back. The armchairs are so close the arms are touching, and together they make a perfect surface for turkey sandwiches and the mince pie.

'I've never seen a man look so happy with a turkey sandwich,' I say, as Garry tucks in.

'It's nice to be noticed,' he says, and I remember his words from his last visit.

There was a woman he cared about. Someone who never noticed him. Was he talking about me?

He presses play and we watch the film, but for the first time ever, I'm finding it hard to focus on. Instead, I'm remembering all those times Garry's sat and listened to my problems, all the extra-large slices of cake, the kind top-ups on my coffee, the way he remembers all the little details, 'how did the dentist appointment go?', 'how's your mum's hip?'. He's been my confidante for all these years, and I thought it was just part of the service – the best café in the world. But I'm noticing him now. He takes the final bite of his sandwich, and I break the mince pie in half for us to share.

It's only as Garry's hand touches mine to take it that I realise what I've done.

'True love will rise over a broken mince pie,' I whisper.

'I … I haven't come with intentions or expectations, Sarah, same as last time. Please … please, don't think—' The way he's looking at me

… It's the way Pete once looked at me, long ago. He loves me, doesn't he? Garry loves me.

'But what if I have intentions or expectations?' I ask. 'What if I want something more?'

Garry moves his hand away, and for a heartbeat I think I've read this whole situation wrong, but he puts down the mince pie then reaches for my hand, threading his long fingers tightly through mine.

'Then I'd say, take your time, Sarah. Make sure you're certain. Because I've waited ten years for you, and I'm not going anywhere. My heart was yours a long time before you broke that mince pie.'

My heart is flapping like a teenager's, and I'm smiling so wide my face must be lined with a hundred wrinkles, but they're all happy wrinkles – I don't care! Garry guides my hand to his lips and presses a kiss to my fingers. My phone buzzes on the arm of the chair, and a message lights up on the screen. Pete.

Merry Christmas, Sarah.

I look up at Garry. Pete's absolutely right – it is a merry Christmas. I turn the phone over, burying the screen, and I know with the certainty of a million tea leaves that it's the first merry Christmas of many.

Jenny Bromham

White Christmas

Marianne Calver

It had once been the centre of her world, this house. A castle, a fortress, its weathered red bricks a deceptively bland disguise for the magic within. It hadn't altered in the three decades she had known it. It looked the same now as she always recalled it, even down to the rickety numbers on the front door that her mother still hoped to straighten up one day. No, it wasn't the house that had changed. Bianca stood at the end of the path, instinctively reaching for the rosemary bush that greeted guests there. The last time she had stood here, Felix was by her side. She pushed the memory away as she cupped her hand to her face and closing her eyes for a moment, breathed in the familiar, aromatic scent. Releasing the breath slowly, Bianca kept her eyes closed as she counted, forcing her shoulders down.

'What you doing?'

Bianca shrieked as her calming ritual was interrupted by a voice from above. Leaning out of the upstairs window, Lucia snorted with laughter.

'You coming in, or shall I leave you out there a bit longer?'

The impatient frown had only just begun to form on Bianca's face when the sound of her sister thudding exuberantly down the stairs forced an unwilling smile in its place. The front door was flung open with alarming force. Lucia stood, silhouetted in the warm glow from within, her arms outstretched and head tilted quizzically to one side.

'Come to me, Bambina!'

Bianca thought she saw a curtain twitch next door, so she hurried down the path before Lucia could cause any more of a scene.

'I'm two years older than you, when will you stop calling me Bambina?' she asked as she allowed herself to be drawn into a fierce embrace.

'Maybe next year. I missed you. And cheer up, it's Christmas; the most wonderful time of the year!'

'You think every day is the most wonderful time of the year.'

Lucia grinned unabashed, nodding to confirm that this was indeed the case.

Bianca sighed; she wasn't sure she could take the relentless optimism this year. Stepping into the hallway, she welcomed the warm air that brought with it the comforting smell of her mother's cooking. For a moment, she was five years old again. Maybe it would all be ok. So long as no one mentioned Felix, Bianca suddenly felt that she might actually enjoy it.

*

Bianca sat comfortably ensconced on the soft squashy sofa, Nonna's hand wrapped lightly in hers. She leant her head down towards her grandmother's and sighed. Her parents had been predictably delighted to see her. Her mother had caressed her hair and told her how well she looked. Her father had given her one of his famous tight squeezes, trying to lift her off the ground as he did, causing admonishments all round. 'Thinks he's 25,' her mother had muttered, shaking her head and hiding a smile. None of them had mentioned how long she had stayed away.

But Nonna was not so tactful.

'You should have come home sooner. Then you would not be carrying that big sigh around with you.' She nodded at her own wisdom.

'Nonna, I couldn't.'

'What was stopping you? Did the trains stop running? You could have walked back in an hour.'

'Don't be cross with me, Nonna.'

'If you stay away that long again, I might be dead next time you come back.'

'Don't say that!' Bianca shifted her body so that she could face her grandmother. 'You're going to live forever.' She lifted the frail hand to her lips and kissed it fiercely. The skin was so thin she could see the network of veins underneath; the knuckles were stiff and swollen.

Nonna gave a low chuckle. 'No one can live forever, Bianca. We can only hope to live a long life, and a good one.' She gave a sideways glance at her granddaughter.

'I'm trying, Nonna.'

'Pushing a cow won't get you milk.'

'Am I a cow in this scenario?' Bianca laughed, nudging Nonna lightly with her shoulder.

Lucia bounced into the room and settled herself in the armchair nearest them. 'Mum said dinner will be ready in half an hour.'

Nonna patted her hand. 'I must go and get ready for dinner. I want to look my best for Angelo.' Bianca was alarmed to see how slowly she stood from the sofa and shuffled from the room.

The warmth and contentment that had been creeping through her had rushed away at the mention of Angelo. Although she didn't want to consider the reason why, Bianca did not want to see her former friend. Waiting until Nonna had gone, she turned to Lucia. 'Why is Angelo coming for dinner?'

'Oh, he and Nonna have these little dates.' Lucia grinned, oblivious to her sister's discomfort. 'It's really cute! Nonna always puts on her make-up and then they sit and talk Italian to each other.'

'Why does it have to be him? Why don't you talk to her? I thought you were learning Italian?'

'I am, but there's only so many times I can ask her how she takes her coffee and does she have any pets. Angelo is fluent. They've always spoken it at home, you know that.'

'Okay, I get that, but why is he coming here now? I thought the Nevettis were going to Italy for Christmas this year?'

Lucia was irritatingly, but predictably, unclear of the details. It had always been this way: Bianca, organised, fastidious and careful; her sister flippant and wild. Lucia brooded briefly under Bianca's inquisition before deeming that enough time had been spent on it. Brightening, she leant conspiratorially towards Bianca. 'Anyway, it will be nice to see him, won't it? Maybe he'll bring the snoooow.'

Bianca flushed. 'Will you ever let me forget that?'

'Aw, don't be embarrassed! I like it. Nat brings my snow, don't you?' Lucia smiled at her wife as she entered the room.

'Oh, hi, Nat-Nat,' Bianca grinned. It was an endless source of amusement that Natalie had married into the Natale family, becoming, by choice Natalie Natale-Bell.

'I am the bringer of snow,' Nat agreed, planting a kiss on the top of Lucia's head and perching on the arm of her chair.

'Is it going to snow?' A deep voice at the doorway made them all jump.

Bianca's face, already pink, burned hot and red. She pushed her hair away from her face and neck in a vain attempt to cool down. Angelo! What was he doing sneaking in like that? The one consolation was that he seemed just as uncomfortable to see her there. He hovered in the doorway, partially hidden from view by the door. Bianca could just see his profile, his usually smooth skin dappled with stubble. It suited him, she acknowledged, before banishing the thought from her mind.

Lucia, unlike her sister, was thrilled with the situation and Bianca's stomach lurched as she noticed the unmistakable glint of mischief in her eyes.

'Oh, no, I don't think it's going to snow. It's just something we say in this family to describe a certain feeling. Bianca came up with it years ago, didn't you, Bambi – Bianca?'

Angelo raised his eyebrows and all three turned towards Bianca expectantly.

She felt her jaw tighten as she tried to suppress an exasperated sigh. At least now she was in control of the situation.

'Well, it's just that feeling, when you kiss someone.' Bianca found it suddenly impossible to lift her eyes. 'Sometimes, when you kiss someone, you get that excited feeling. Like when you walk to the window in the morning and see snow on the ground. Or when you're outside and the first few flakes of snow drift down. It's silly, really ...' She tailed off.

'I don't think it's silly,' Angelo said thoughtfully.

Bianca dared not look up in case their eyes met, and he somehow realised through osmosis that it was he for whom the phrase was first coined.

'I don't think it's silly either,' agreed Lucia. 'I like it.'

Bianca couldn't help thinking she was only saying that to make amends for landing her sister right in it with Angelo.

'Angelo, is that you?' Nonna's voice wavered in from the hallway.

'Maria! *Buonasera*!' Angelo disappeared from view. They could hear him talking to Nonna as he went. It was quite melodic, Bianca thought, before turning her thoughts to more pressing matters.

'Why did you do that?' she demanded of Lucia. 'Do you ever engage your brain before you speak?'

Lucia was nonplussed. 'Why is it a big deal? You kissed like, five hundred years ago. You didn't even date.'

'He was my First Kiss!' Bianca hissed. 'He was my best friend, and then, after that kiss, nothing. I don't like seeing him. I don't like talking to him, and I especially don't like having to explain to him about the snow.'

Lucia raised her hands, pushing away the negativity. It was clear she thought Bianca was overreacting.

'Bianca, you've always got on fine with him! What is this? You didn't have a problem last year.'

'Yes, but last year I was with Felix!'

The name hung in the air as Bianca silently cursed herself. Nat shifted uncomfortably and cast a glance at Lucia. Leaning forward in the chair Lucia opened her mouth to speak but Bianca raised a hand and looked away, the slightest shake of her head drawing an end to the conversation not yet started.

Sitting back in her chair, Bianca folded her arms and bit her lip. Maybe she was overreacting. It had been fifteen years since the kiss. Half her lifetime. Why couldn't she let it go? Maybe because it had been her first rejection. All of her romantic notions about love and friendship had evaporated the day he avoided her glance at school, walked past her in the lunch hall, turning his back on her to talk to Bobby McGrath instead. And okay, he had tried to speak to her after school, running after her down the street. Even now, her stomach swirled as she remembered cutting him off as he tried to explain. She couldn't bear to hear why they shouldn't be together.

Of course, it had all worked out for the best in the end. She hadn't sat home pining for him for too long. And it would be ridiculous to think that it would have been a long-term relationship, anyway. How many people were still with their first love?

These thoughts carried Bianca through dinner, and she was barely aware of the conversation going on around her. She moved the risotto absentmindedly around her plate, eating without really tasting. Occasionally she registered her mother glancing down the table at her, but thankfully, no one tried to coax her into conversation. She was roused from her reflections when Nat pushed her chair back from the table, and said, 'Well, Lu. I think it's time. Do you?'

Lucia's smile was unusually coy, and she gave a short laugh. 'Why do I feel nervous?'

Nat squeezed her hand in encouragement.

'Well, Bianca, this is an early Christmas present for you. I know how much you hate it when I call you Bambina. As of next June, we'll have a new Bambina. Or Bambino.'

The table erupted in jubilation. Bianca watched as if through a long lens as her parents stood and rushed round to Lucia and Natalie.

'Really? Is it really true?' their mother asked, tears shining in her eyes.

Lucia had produced a scan picture from somewhere and they huddled round to see.

'Federico, our first grandchild. Can you believe it?'

The words were like daggers to Bianca. They should have been for her. She was the oldest. She had always done everything right. Now, her life was crumbling while Lucia got everything she'd ever wanted.

Down at the other end of the table, Angelo and Nonna spoke rapid fire Italian, laughing warmly together. Bianca noticed his eyes flicker frequently over to her. They were laughing at her.

The picture was passed down to Nonna who held it with unsteady hands.

'Beautiful!' she said slowly. 'It is a miracle!' She smiled.

'We always thought Bianca would be first to have a child, didn't we? But no, it was you. A miracle!'

Bianca sat for a moment, too stunned to respond. Then, realising all eyes had turned towards her, she forced a smile to her lips. 'It is a miracle,' she agreed, hoping the hot tears that had flooded her eyes could pass for tears of joy. 'A wonderful Christmas miracle!' But the brief yet unmistakable arch of Lucia's eyebrow suggested that there was at least one person who didn't believe her.

*

In the sanctuary of her bedroom, Bianca allowed the tears to fall unchecked. How dare Angelo? Laughing at her misery, while he sat there like Mr Perfect. Urgh, the image of him sitting next to Nonna infuriated her. Even in her anger, a small part of her recognised how irrational it was, but having Angelo there as a witness to her failures was more than she could bear right now. What a mess.

For the second time that day, she was startled from her thoughts by Lucia, who flung the door open with a force that sent it bouncing on its hinges. She stood in the doorway, her mouth set in a straight line, hands clenched at her sides.

'Could you not be happy for us?' Her voice was low, but Bianca flinched at the uncharacteristic anger.

'I am happy,' she attempted, her voice wavering.

Lucia arched an eyebrow and gestured with her hand towards the tears still shining on Bianca's face. 'Looks like it.' She turned to go, then turned back. 'I get that you have a lot going on right now. I really do. But so do other people, you know. It's not all about you, Bianca. I know that's hard for you, but please, just try to be happy for us. For me. Can't you?'

'What is this? Is this pregnancy hormones making you mean?' she regretted it instantly, but the door had already slammed. Bianca called after her but Lucia was already stomping down the stairs.

'Let's just leave it for tonight, ok? I'll see you tomorrow,' she called as she left.

*

Bianca stayed in her bedroom for the rest of the evening. She couldn't face her parents. She had only been home for a few hours and had already caused an argument. Sitting on the bed, wrapped in her duvet, Bianca bristled as she thought about the implication of Lucia's words. Was she really so self-absorbed that she couldn't be happy for her own sister? She threw herself back on the bed to stare up at the ceiling and tried to avoid the answer. The shadows stretched across the room and were eventually eaten up by the night. Still, Bianca lay staring and thinking, looking for ways to lay the fault with Lucia, or Angelo, and finding none.

Eventually falling into a fitful sleep, she awoke the next morning, unrested and with a sense of dread sitting heavy on her chest. The cold winter sun streamed through the windows and shrill birdsong assaulted her ears. Bianca was just pulling the covers up over her head to shut out the day when her mother walked into the room. If Bianca had been hoping for some motherly comfort, she quickly realised she was to be sorely disappointed. Caterina Natale walked briskly to the side of the bed and pulled back the covers with a flourish.

'Enough moping,' she announced. 'If you leave it any later all the good trees will be gone.'

Bianca groaned and shivered as she groped for the duvet. 'Can't Dad go by himself?'

'Dad's not going.' Caterina pulled the duvet further off the bed. 'He has a bad back.'

Begrudgingly, Bianca pulled herself to a sitting position, 'What do you expect me to do? Carry the tree home myself?'

'Don't be ridiculous. Angelo is going to drive.'

Bianca fought the urge to scream into her pillow. Could this day get any worse?

*

Staring resolutely ahead, Bianca watched the sleet fall on the windscreen to melt and be pushed aside by the wipers, making room for the next barrage. Sleet had to be one of the worst types of weather. It was really just snow that couldn't quite be bothered. Half-arsed snow. Beside her, Angelo, perhaps sensing her mood, stayed silent. Instead, glancing at Bianca's fingers as they tapped impatiently on the dashboard, he reached across to turn on the radio. An implausibly jovial radio host blathered on about last-minute Christmas shopping. Leaning back into the car seat, Bianca closed her eyes and counted her breath on the exhalation, trying to stretch it to the count of seven. In for five, out for seven. Meanwhile, on the radio, Gail from Portsmouth was waxing lyrical about the joys of Christmas Eve.

'Eurgh.' The sound escaped before she could stop it.

'Eurgh?' The corner of Angelo's mouth twitched.

'Eurgh.' And then, sensing he was waiting for more of an explanation, 'It's just so twee, isn't it? Why does everyone feel they have to be happy at this time of the year?'

'Well, family? Friends? Nostalgia? The birth of our Lord?'

'It was a rhetorical question, Angelo.' She pursed her lips and felt suddenly like Nonna.

'I'm sure you used to love Christmas.'

Ignoring this, she blurted, 'What did you say to Nonna last night?' The question wouldn't wait any longer.

Angelo was bemused. 'What do you mean?'

'After Lucia made her big announcement, you were muttering away to Nonna and then she made that snipe about me. What did you say about me?'

'About you? Bianca, I didn't say anything about you. We were just celebrating the news. It's been a long, hard journey for Lucia and Nat to get here, you know.'

'She's my sister, of course I know!' Bianca snapped, uneasily realising that, in fact, she hadn't known. Lucia hadn't told her.

Angelo pulled the car into the car park of Firfield Christmas Tree Farm, but neither of them moved to get out. 'I don't think your Nonna meant to hurt you, Bianca.' He spoke without looking at her. 'She was excited about Lucia's news. She wasn't criticising you.'

Bianca opened the car door abruptly. 'So, you think I'm overreacting?' It was easier to channel her anger at Angelo than herself. She stepped out of the car, sinking her foot into an icy puddle. 'For goodness' sake!' She shouted up to the heavens.

'It's not beyond the realms of possibility,' Angelo said with a wry smile.

With as much dignity as she could muster, Bianca stormed on ahead, water seeping from her left shoe with every other step.

The Natale family had been coming to Firfields for their Christmas trees for as long as Bianca could remember, and it had barely changed in all that time. She and Lucia would bounce excitedly in the back of the car all the way there, then run around in a frenzy to find the best tree. As she approached the row of trees, Bianca slowed her pace and leaned forward to inhale the sharp, fresh smell. She laid a hand softly on one of the branches and then gave a gentle squeeze, just hard enough to know that it could hurt her if she let it. Turning her palm up, Bianca ran a finger over the indentations there.

'Are you ok?' Angelo took her hand with concern.

She snatched it awkwardly from his grasp. 'I just like to feel things.' She turned away to hide the flush that rose in her cheeks. Why did she always feel so foolish in front of Angelo these days?

'So, is this the one then?' he asked, one hand on the tree.

'You can't just pick the first one, Angelo!' Bianca said with a smile.

'Well …' He gestured around them. 'There aren't that many to choose from.'

'It's Christmas Eve! What do you expect?' She wandered along the feeble line of trees, left until last because they were too small, or too spindly, or had a bald patch on one side.

'You know, when I was growing up, I just thought it was our family tradition to get our Christmas tree on Christmas Eve. It added to the excitement.' She scuffed the ground with her foot, wondering why she was sharing this with Angelo. 'Then I realised.'

Raising her eyes to his face, she could see that he knew what she was about to say. 'You know why we did that?'

The slightest of nods confirmed it, but she found she wanted to say it anyway.

'It was the only way we could afford it. Wait until they were reduced. You know what my dad's like. He can charm anyone. He always managed to get an extra discount too.' She smiled at the memory. 'We got some lovely trees.' They stood side by side, contemplating the trees.

'I never felt poor, you know. I never felt like anything was missing in my life at all as a kid. We had everything we wanted. I know it sounds cheesy, but I had my family and you. I mean, not you, but your family and well, yes, and you too, of course.' Bianca's face burned as she grappled with her thoughts. 'The thing is, now I have money, I could buy a Christmas tree at full price.' She gave a small smile. 'But it's only now I feel my life is lacking.' She shook her head. 'I don't know what I'm saying. Ignore me. I'm silly ... overly nostalgic. Been listening to Gail from Portsmouth for too long.'

As she turned away, Angelo took her hand. 'That's the second time in two days that you've dismissed yourself as silly, Bianca.'

Turning back, she was surprised to see the concern on his face.

'What's going on? You stayed away for so long and now you're back, but it's like you're not really here. Like you're keeping yourself apart from us. You have some wall up that wasn't there before. Is this about Felix? I know he broke your heart but ...'

She pulled her hand gently from his and looked down at the ground between them. A tear hung perilously close to the edge of her lashes. 'It wasn't him. Felix didn't break my heart.' She forced herself to look at Angelo. 'It was me. I did the heart-breaking.'

'You broke Felix's heart?' Angelo sounded surprised.

Bianca nodded miserably, shivering as the cold crept from her wet foot up her leg.

'You're freezing. Let's get this tree and get you somewhere warm.'

They bought the tree in subdued silence and heaved it into the trailer with barely a word to each other. As they drove away, she realised she had to speak.

'Not home.'

'Not home?'

'Not yet. I can't go back yet. Can we go to yours?'

*

When all their friends had been renting plush flats in the city, Angelo had bought a small house on the edge of town. They had teased him at the time, but now Bianca could see the attraction. Simply furnished, and decorated with artwork that she knew Angelo would have spent years collecting, it felt cosy, rather than cramped, and in other circumstances Bianca imagined she would have felt quite at home.

Perched on the edge of the sofa, Bianca nursed the hot chocolate he had handed her.

'Do you want to talk about it?' he prompted.

She nodded, staring at the cream that was slowly melting into the chocolate.

'I don't know what to say.'

'What happened?'

'He proposed.'

'Felix proposed to you?'

'Is that such a surprise?'

'No, of course not. But then, why did you break up with him?'

'Well ...' She searched for the right words. 'There was no ... snow.'

'Didn't you break up in June? That hardly seems fair ... oh. Snow.' He gestured with his hand between the two of them.

'I didn't only have snow with you, you know!' She rolled her eyes and was pleased to see him shift uncomfortably on the other end of the sofa.

'Of course!' But then he brightened. 'But you did have snow with me?' He cleared his throat. 'Anyway, that's not what we're talking about. You and Felix.' He nodded for her to continue.

'It wasn't always that way. It used to be great. But we just, I don't know, we stopped being interested in each other, I guess. I could have said yes. It would have been easy. And it would have been fine. Fine ...' she tailed off. 'Is it wrong to want more than fine?' She raised her eyes to his and her breath caught.

'No, it's not wrong. Oh, careful!' He reached out to straighten her cup, his fingers brushing hers before he drew them quickly away. 'But why didn't you just tell everyone that? We thought you were heartbroken.'

'I was! It just wasn't Felix's fault, that's all. It was mine.'

'So, that's why you didn't tell your family? Because you thought it was your fault?'

'It was my fault! So, no, I didn't want to tell my family. I just, I suppose I was so busy dealing with my own disappointment, I couldn't face dealing with theirs too. I'm the one who always gets it right. How could I tell them I've got it so wrong?'

Angelo leaned forwards and took the cup from her, placing it on the coffee table so that he could take both her hands in his.

'Bianca, we love you. All the time. Not just when things are going well. You should have told us.'

'You love me, hey?' she teased. She wanted to embarrass him again, to draw the attention away from herself, but he didn't shift in his seat this time. He simply held her gaze and uttered one, stark word.

'Yes.'

'Ha!' Bianca withdrew her hands, laying them in her lap. 'Well. As a friend, right? You love me as a friend.'

He looked down, then back at her. 'Something like that.' That twitch of the lip again. Was he laughing at her? 'We should get that tree back to your folks.'

*

Caterina reached over Bianca's shoulder for the tomatoes, giving her arm a gentle squeeze as she did. 'This is nice.'

It was. When Bianca still lived at home, she and Caterina had cooked together most evenings. It was their special time, when they would dissect their days whilst chopping herbs and stirring sauces. This time they worked quietly, but the easy dance they had perfected all those years ago came back naturally. The freshly scrubbed clams bubbled on the stove, ready for the Spaghetti Allo Scoglio, potatoes scattered with rosemary and seabass nestled in a bed of tomatoes and garlic roasted in the oven. Tomorrow they would have the traditional British Christmas roast dinner, but today they embraced their Italian roots. The sound of chatter drifted down the hallway, punctuated regularly by bursts of laughter.

'Are you sure you don't want to join them?' Caterina nodded towards the living room, where Federico, Nonna and Angelo were decorating the tree. Bianca shook her head. She wanted to keep some distance between herself and Angelo.

Although it sounded like they were having fun, Bianca was aware of the missing voices. Lucia and Natalie had not yet arrived. She glanced anxiously at the door. What if they didn't come?

'They'll come.' Caterina read her mind. 'You know they're always late.'

As if on cue, the key sounded in the lock and Lucia appeared in the doorway. The glow from the streetlamp outside shone around her like a halo. She and Bianca stood frozen, eyes locked on each other. As children, Lucia had always been the first to apologise, the first to fix any fall outs but this time, Bianca knew it had to be her. After all, although it stung to admit it, Lucia hadn't done anything wrong.

'I'm sorry.'

Lucia's mouth dropped open. 'What?'

'I am sorry, Lucia. You were right. I was self-absorbed. I am self-absorbed, I guess.' Her face flushed at the admission, but a weight lifted from her shoulders, and she suddenly breathed more easily.

'Come here and hug me!'

Wrapped in the warmth of her sister's arms, Bianca's eyes blurred with tears and before she could stop it, a sob escaped from the depth of her chest, then another and another.

Rubbing her eyes, she fought to compose herself. 'I'm fine, I'm fine.' She responded to the concern on Lucia's face. 'Now, show me my niece or nephew!'

*

Bianca leant into the soft cushions on the sofa, drawing the cosy knitted blanket over her knees as she admired the Christmassy tableau before her. Caterina, Federico and Nat were adding the finishing touches to the tree with the occasional helpful advice from Nonna.

'You've too much gold clumped together there, look. Little baubles on the ends of branches, push the bigger ones right on, yes that's it.'

Lucia was hunched in the corner, frantically wrapping presents behind a barrier she had constructed from cushions. She paused occasionally for a mouthful of Pandoro and to admonish anyone who glanced her way.

'Don't look! Don't look! You'll spoil the surprise.'

'You know, you could wrap them upstairs, or even better, at your own home, if you didn't want people to see!' Bianca knew it was pointless to suggest this; Lucia had been wrapping her presents on Christmas Eve in front of the family since she had been old enough to buy them.

'Why are you trying to get rid of me? Do you want me to miss out on all of the fun?'

'You are the fun, Lu.' Bianca stood to walk over and hug her sister, prompting an indignant squeal from Lucia.

'Don't look! Stay there!'

Bianca laughed and sat back down, catching Angelo's eye as she did so. She dropped her eyes quickly but couldn't resist glancing up again. He was still looking at her, a playful smile on his lips, the flickering flames of the fire dancing in his eyes. She couldn't look away. Nonna impatiently tapped Angelo's arm, breaking the magic.

'Angelo, do you hear me? It is time for the star. Are you ready?'

'Shall I lift you up, Maria?' He made to put his hands on her plump waist, eliciting a happy chuckle from Nonna.

'Oh, you are a flirt, Angelo Nevetti!'

'And you love every minute of it, Nonna!' Bianca stood and put an arm around her grandmother. They gathered around the tree, Lucia piling cushions on the remaining unwrapped presents so that she could join them.

'Wish time!' she said, clapping her hands and bouncing on the balls of her feet. 'I have a really good one this year!'

Nonna held the star and pressed it to her chest, closing her eyes momentarily before passing it to Federico. Solemnly, they passed the star around the little group, Christmas music playing softly in the background. Bianca felt a lump in her throat as she watched the star pass from hand to hand, each person trusting it with their deepest wishes. When Angelo passed it to her, she held it carefully in both hands, wondering what to wish for. What did she really, truly hope for this year?

Handing it back, she shook her head. 'I have everything I want.'

'Awww,' said Caterina, whilst Lucia made retching noises at her side.

'Come now, Bianca. What is life without a dream?' prompted Nonna.

Nodding, Bianca laid her hand on the star as it sat in Angelo's hands, bowing her head. 'Okay.' Her voice was barely a whisper, and she was aware of her family's eyes on her. 'There.' she looked up with a smile, pushing the star and Angelo's hand away gently.

Angelo smiled and stepped towards the tree, stretching up to set the star on the highest branch.

Lucia whooped, and the rest of them clapped. Bianca remembered how strange Felix had found this tradition, admitting on their last Christmas together that he never made a wish, just held the star for a while and passed it on. She thought perhaps it was that confession that had signalled the start of the end for them.

'Now, time to hang the stockings and get to bed, or he won't come!' said Federico.

'Dad!' his daughters said in unison, although they both stepped forward to receive their stockings from their father, entwining their fingers and walking to the fireplace together as they had for as long as they could remember.

Lucia and Natalie were staying the night despite living just ten minutes away and Nonna was doing her best to persuade Angelo to stay too by offering him a pair of Federico's pyjamas to wear.

'Honestly Maria, I appreciate the offer, but I have some things to pick up from home. I promise I'll be back in time for breakfast.'

Bianca was surprised to find she was as disappointed as Nonna with this outcome and went to bed with an excitement bubbling in her stomach that had little to do with the prospect of a visit from Santa.

*

The bright white light of Christmas morning peeked playfully round the edges of her curtains and a cheerful robin sang a festive greeting. Bianca wriggled her toes and snuggled deeper under her covers, savouring the warmth and comfort. Gradually she became aware of another sound: the unmistakable tinkling of sleigh bells. She sat up with a grin. 'Dad!'

'He's been!' Federico called as he shook the hand bells he had bought at the school bazaar several decades previously and used once a year ever since.

'Dad!' Lucia was considerably less cheerful in the morning, much to Bianca's delight. They stumbled out of their bedrooms in various states of consciousness, the smell of turkey greeting them on the stairs.

'Happy Christmas! *Buon Natale*!'

Nat, who had been leading the way, stopped abruptly at the foot of the stairs, causing something of a pileup.

'Angelo! Blimey, you're early!'

'You could at least have turned up in your pyjamas! You're putting us all to shame,' Lucia admonished.

Angelo grinned as he undid his coat. 'This is way worse than pyjamas!' He opened his coat to reveal a Christmas jumper of lurid red and green; holly leaves, presents, robins and reindeers all vying for attention across his chest.

'Wow! That is truly hideous,' Lucia said. 'I hope you have something else to change into. I don't think I can bear to look at that all day.'

Bianca used the opportunity of the distraction to run upstairs and pull on some clothes, emerging as quickly as she could, looking slightly more presentable.

'Happy Christmas, Angelo!' She raised her cheek to receive his kiss, flushing at their closeness and wondering if she imagined him lingering there for slightly longer than necessary.

'Happy Christmas, Bianca.' She definitely hadn't imagined the softness in his voice. Had she? For a moment, it felt that they were the only two people there. Until Nonna bustled in, commandeering Angelo's attention for herself.

They bundled into the living room, talking over each other and laughing as they raced to see their Christmas stockings bulging at the fireplace. Bianca's eyes filled with tears. 'Mum, you are amazing!'

'You'd better check it's not coal!' joked Lucia.

Caterina wrapped her arms around her oldest daughter. 'I would never give you coal, Bambina.'

'Even if I deserved it?' Bianca couldn't stop her lip from wobbling.

'If you deserved it, I would give you coal, but you don't.'

The day passed in a blur of food, presents and games. Monopoly had been predictably fraught with Lucia attempting to make deals with everyone and Nonna forgetting to collect her rent. Ultimately, Federico won, bankrupting the rest of the family. 'Champion for four consecutive years!' he celebrated, clasping his hands above his head.

'What about last year when Felix won?' Bianca reminded him.

'We don't talk about that!'

'Does anyone fancy a walk?' asked Lucia. 'I want to work up the energy for another mince pie.'

Nonna opted for a nap and Federico and Caterina wanted to stay home and watch White Christmas, so the younger generation found themselves stepping out into the icy air. Lucia and Natalie set the pace, striding on ahead, but Bianca wanted to linger, admiring the frosted branches and the crunch of ice tipped grass underfoot. Angelo slowed his pace to walk with her. She could feel his eyes on her. Suddenly, he stopped walking.

'Bianca? I, er, I have a present for you.'

'Oh no! Angelo, I have nothing for you! I didn't know you were staying for Christmas.'

He raised a hand to placate her. 'It's only small. Don't worry. And I actually, well, I've had it for quite a while.' He looked sheepish.

'So, you're giving me a second-hand present?' she teased.

'Of course not! It's always been for you. I just didn't get to give it to you when I intended to, and then I thought you wouldn't like it, and now I think you might. So …' He held out a small square box wrapped with a silver bow. As she took it, he turned as if to leave.

'Don't you want to see me open it?'

He hesitated. 'I'm not sure I can.' The colour rose to his cheeks, and she somehow doubted it was because of the cold air.

As she untied the bow, he reverted to a safe distance. Putting the wrapping paper in her pocket, Bianca looked at the unexceptional brown box. Lifting the lid, she glanced at Angelo, who was shifting uneasily from foot to foot.

The winter light reflected on something inside the box – a glass dome. Carefully, she slid it from its box. The ornament fit perfectly in her hand; a white base decorated with silver swirls. Inside the globe, two figures stood entwined in an eternal embrace as delicate flakes of white and silver fluttered around them.

'What is this?' Her voice sounded strange, as though it belonged to someone else.

Angelo frowned, apparently confused. 'Well, it's a snow globe.'

Taking a step towards him, she struggled to conceal the hope in her voice as she asked, 'Why have you given me a snow globe, Angelo?'

With hesitant steps, he walked towards her. 'I bought it after we, after we kissed.' He could hardly raise his eyes to hers. 'But then, things didn't really go to plan, and I was scared, Bianca. I was fifteen. So were you. It couldn't have worked then, could it? I didn't know about the snow then, but I did know that there was something special between us. Well, I thought there was, anyway.' He looked at her, searching for affirmation. Bianca didn't trust herself to speak, so settled on a small nod.

'Bianca, I still think there's something special between us.'

Her stomach somersaulted. 'Angelo, I'm not who I was back then. If you're still in love with the girl you knew, well, she's gone. I'm not her.'

Angelo smiled. 'And do you think I'm just the same as I was then?' He gestured to himself, inviting her to judge.

Bianca looked at the man before her. 'Well, no. You're hairier now, for one thing.'

'Hairier?' he laughed. 'Fifteen years of personal development and you notice my hair.'

'I like your hair.'

He was so close now that she could feel the warmth of his breath on her face. She hardly dared to breathe lest she spoiled the moment.

He raised a hand, almost brushing a strand of hair from her face but stopping short.

'Angelo, so much has happened.'

'I know, I was there.'

'I thought we'd grow up together. Grow old together. But we only grew apart.' Her voice seemed to float away, a snowflake on the breeze.

Bianca reached out and held on to his coat to keep him there. 'Is it too late?' She shook her head and addressed his chest, unable to look at his face. 'It's not too late, is it?'

Finally daring to lift her face to him, she willed him to kiss her. Their eyes met as he leaned down towards her, and she had the briefest moment to notice that he smelled of pine trees before his lips found hers. The world spun as his fingers wound themselves through her hair, his heart pounding in the palm of her hand as she rested it on his chest. And then, she felt it; snow.

Marianne Calver

Sausage Rolls for Everyone

Bláithín O'Reilly Murphy

It's the most wonderful time of the year!

'We'd quite the stack of post today, they wouldn't fit in the box,' Binita said, placing the pile on the table. The handwriting on one of the envelopes caught Lynsey's attention. She reached out for it. It was Auntie's cursive. The postmark dated only three days ago. Lynsey moved her fingers across the lettering. Her Auntie had beautiful penmanship, an elegant scrolling cursive. She opened the envelope, half expecting to get the scent of her Auntie's house, but the envelope only produced a jolly Christmas card and a carefully folded note.

'You've gone as white as a *bhuta*, Lynsey – who died?' Binita asked.

'My Auntie.' Lynsey looked up at her flatmate Binita.

'Shit, sorry. I didn't think someone actually died,' Binita apologised.

'I got the call earlier. This is from her,' Lynsey said, holding up the festive card of five kittens wearing Santa hats for Binita to see.

'Cup of Darjeeling.' It was Binita's go to for everything, at least before 5pm in the day. 'What happened? Is this the auntie that came to visit you two years ago?' Binita added tea leaves to the infuser in the teapot rather than the tea cup infusers; this was definitely a teapot kind of situation.

Bl[a]ithín O'Reilly Murphy

'Yea, Auntie Maura. She was Mum's sister. I lived with her after my parents passed away,' Lynsey said, sitting down on the bar stool. It had been ten years since she was last home, and she hadn't thought about that part of her life in a long time.

'When did she die?' Binita asked.

'Two days ago; heart attack. She just collapsed in the kitchen. Her friend was with her.' Lynsey looked down at the Christmas card. It didn't seem real.

Binita poured the tea into a cup on a saucer she'd placed in front of Lynsey. Binita took tea very seriously. Tea was always served in a cup and saucer and always came with an accompaniment befitting the situation. Lynsey watched Binita as she opened one of the cupboards. She'd already started to buy the tins of Christmas biscuits; an Irish tradition Lynsey had brought with her and one which Binita had adopted wholeheartedly since they'd moved in together five years ago. She closed the press behind her, and instead, reached for a chair and went into her private stockpile on top of the press and took down a large box of Chocolate Kimberleys.

'I think we need something a little bit special, a little bit comforting for this kind of news,' she said as she took a knife to the side of the tin, slicing through the Sellotape that sealed it shut. Normally, Chocolate Kimberleys were reserved for Christmas Eve. She placed two on the side of Lynsey's saucer and two on her own, then left the box open between them which was unusual for Binita. "Everything in moderation" was a key motto of hers.

'So, Auntie Maura, may her soul achieve heaven. Will you be going home for the funeral?' Binita said, blowing on her tea before taking a sip.

Lynsey sat still, lost in her thoughts.

'Lynsey, are you ok?' Binita asked, full of concern. 'You're getting paler and paler!'

Lynsey took a breath. 'Yeah, I'm fine. Sorry. I just haven't been back in so long. And now, well, to go back and be the chief mourner, it feels all a little overwhelming.'

'Chief mourner?' Had she no other family?' Binita asked, as she bit into a biscuit.

'No, she never married. There was only herself and Mum and then, well, me.' Lynsey realised in that moment that now, it was just her. She was the last person in her family. Well, at least in the family that accepted her. She suddenly felt like she'd made the biggest mistake of her life, leaving Ireland all those years ago; because of a kiss. A forbidden love her family would never accept.

Blue Christmas

Lynsey stood in line at passport control at Cork Airport. She opened her passport and handed it across to the Garda. She waited for the raised eyebrow as he looked from her, to her name, to her passport. Travelling on an Irish passport with a name like Lynsey Singh and looking as Indian as her great grandmother always raised an eyebrow. But today all she got was a nod as he looked toward the passenger and called, 'Next!'

Lynsey placed her passport back in her bag and headed towards baggage reclaim. As she watched the luggage from her flight slowly travel around the carousel, she decided to take a taxi instead of the two buses that would take her to get from the airport to the little village of Ovens. As she exited into the Arrivals Hall, the sound of Christmas music filled the air and people ran forward to greet friends and family.

When she'd first arrived in Ireland, she was only seven and had attended her parents' cremation that morning. Auntie Maura had run forward and enveloped her in a massive hug when she came through those very doors. Lynsey closed her eyes and fought back the tears she'd been battling all morning. She'd have no one to do that for her now.

'Lynsey, Lynsey – over here, dear!' a voice called out to her from her left. She turned and stood wide-eyed, as a smiling, familiar face rushed towards her.

'Oh, thank God! I was terrified I missed you! C'mere to me, darling, how are ya?' And like it had only been a moment since she'd seen her last, Oona Walsh, her auntie's best friend, wrapped her in a hug. The tears fell then and didn't stop.

'Ah, pet, I know, I know. C'mere, an awful shock it was. Let it out there. You poor pet,' Oona said, her eyes glistening as she reached into her coat pocket and pulled out a wad of tissues.

Lynsey sobbed into Oona's arms and the two women stood there,crying in the midst of Cork International Airport, while passengers flocked home for Christmas, and familiar words from "It's the Most Wonderful Time of the Year" filled the air.

'Erm, Oona, are you vibrating?' Lynsey said, wiping her eyes.

'Oh Christ! I am! My timer, c'mon! The sausage rolls will be cremated if we don't get back soon!'

Lynsey laughed and shook her head. Oona hadn't changed a bit.

'How did you know I'd be on this flight?' Lynsey asked as she followed the petite, spritely woman out of the airport doors.

'Well, I didn't. I figured you'd be coming today or tomorrow, and there are only two flights a day. I was going to come up to each one. I figured you'd say no to the lift if I offered ya one on the phone, but not refuse me if I was here. And sure, here's the car, closer than any taxi.' She winked.

Oona was still driving the same maroon Nissan Micra she had been — possibly all her life — which she'd abandoned, with the indicators flashing on a double yellow line.

'Thank you, Oona. I do appreciate you coming,' Lynsey said, settling into the front passenger seat.

'You're welcome, pet. Couldn't have you coming home now on two buses. Besides, it's a two hour wait now in Cork City between buses. Scandalous!'

'I was going to take a taxi,' Lynsey said.

Oona whistled. 'A taxi from the airport? They're paying you well. Then again, as an Accountant you've probably done one of those profit / cost analysis things the bank is always talking about to me … probably makes more sense to spend on the taxi than wait the two hours, I expect. Time being money and all that?'

Lynsey smiled. For once, she hadn't actually thought of it like that — she just didn't want the hassle. Perhaps the Irish air was mellowing her already. Lynsey rolled down her window, hoping that more air might make her feel a little more together. As they drove out of the airport and on to Ovens, Lynsey wasn't sure what to expect. She'd been filled with regret for days now, but also the impossible fear that there was nothing she could do about that now.

'We'll just stop at mine so I can turn off the oven and then I'll drive you on to Maura's. I made up your bed for you, and I've put a few bits in the fridge,' Oona said as she sped on down the road, hopping the old car along the motorway.

'Thanks, Oona. Erm, where is Auntie Maura?' Lynsey had completely forgotten to ask.

'Sheehan's funeral home. They have her on ice. Just 'til you're home and the arrangements are made. Don't worry, they'll thaw her out lovely. It's amazing what they can do nowadays,' Oona said, rather impressed. 'We thought it best. Just to give you some time to get here and get up to speed on things.' Oona looked over at Lynsey.

As Lynsey nodded, Oona turned on the radio. She was glad of the distraction and to be alone with her own thoughts. This would be the second funeral she would attend and the second time she was a chief mourner. She was much older this time around, but the pain was no different. Again, she found herself completely alone and wondering what the hell was to become of her. Since deciding she would definitely come home and that she would stay in Ovens, she'd one big fear. Would *they* still be there? And if they were, how would she face them? Before she'd any real time to focus on what she might or might not say if they were, Oona was already pulling into her drive. The small cottage on the edge of the village looked much the same, except for its painted blue window sills and door, which Lynsey was pretty sure had always been a chocolate brown before.

'I'll just be a minute. I'll grab us some sausage rolls to have at Maura's while I'm taking them out of the oven,' Oona said as she darted from the car and into her house.

Lynsey was about to say that she was a vegetarian now, but Oona was already out of sight. The frilly net curtains that framed Oona's windows were white as the day they were hung, and Lynsey could see the outline of the Christmas tree in the sitting-room window. She'd helped decorate that tree every year when she'd lived with Maura. Oona always said it was because she was a short arse and needed Maura to do the upper half of the tree. Lynsey just loved the fact that she got to decorate two Christmas trees every year. Oona was already coming back around the side of the house with a Tupperware tub filled to the brim with sausage rolls. The smell of them brought back memories! She must have eaten hundreds, if not thousands, of them in her lifetime here.

'Take hold of that there for me now, while I drive. Pop the lid a little so they don't get soggy. I hate a soggy bottom,' Oona said as she sat back into the car and put it in reverse.

They could have literally walked to Auntie Maura's house from Oona's. It was only two doors down, but it meant walking back out onto the pathless main road, and Lynsey didn't fancy that with a rolling suitcase and a Tupperware of sausage rolls. And she was quite sure, she wouldn't be able to go back inside Auntie Maura's without Oona's support. As they passed by the house and around the back to park the car, Lynsey realised how much she'd missed this little hairy house.

The thatched cottage sat just feet back from the main road and had once been a gallery before her Auntie had gotten her hands on it. Now it was a home to the front, a veterinary practice in the middle and a cattery to the rear. It had combined all the loves of her Auntie's life, a little bit of rural history, working as a vet and caring for cats. Lynsey paused as she got out of the car. The place hadn't changed. She could still hear the familiar meows from the cattery until she realised she wasn't remembering them – there were actual cats still in there. She'd just assumed they would all have been rehomed elsewhere after her Auntie died. It was then the doors to the cattery opened, and the two people she'd run away from ten years ago emerged together. Lynsey turned in desperation for some intervention from Oona, but she was already walking towards the house.

Cat and James were both in deep conversation and hadn't seen her yet. Lynsey took a moment to study them. They both looked the same, older, of course, but there was no mistaking them. James was definitely more muscular than he'd been at nineteen, and his dark curly hair was still an envy of hers. The beard and moustache were new. At least new to her. He still gave her a thrill. Cat was taller, surprisingly. Lynsey glanced to see if she was wearing heels, but she was not. Her red hair was more of an auburn now, but still long and wavy. She'd never imagined she'd find them both here, together. Could they be a couple? As this thought floored her, they noticed her. Lynsey was rooted to the ground. She hadn't expected to see them both at the same time, at least not here, not so soon. She'd thought she'd have some time to prepare herself. They both walked towards her, crossing the yard that divided the cattery from the small garden at the back of the house. Lynsey wanted to run away so badly, but there was nowhere to go, and she knew she was going to have to face them, regardless.

'Lynsey, we're so sorry about Maura.' Cat engulfed Lynsey in a warm hug before getting her bearings.

Every sense in Lynsey's body stood on high alert. It had been years since she was this close to Cat, well, to anyone. Lynsey was afraid to take a breath. But Cat didn't release her tight grip and Lynsey was forced to breathe or pass out. The faint smell of lavender and sanitizer tickled her nose.

As Cat drew away, Lynsey stared into her eyes. They were as vibrant a green as they had been on *that* night. Today, not framed by the dark-winged eyeliner Cat had been famous for, the kohl had been replaced by an almost chocolate-brown wing that seemed to make her eyes wider and sparkle all the more.

Lynsey realised she still had her arms around Cat. Now that they were back there, she didn't want to remove them. The longing she'd suppressed all these years was still there. Lynsey drew her arms back slowly. Too long had passed and no one had said anything.

'Thanks,' Lynsey began, unsure of what else to say. She was still processing Cat saying "we're so sorry" as if speaking for them both was usual for her.

'Let's head in. I'm sure Oona has the kettle boiled, and she promised sausage rolls on her return.' It was James who spoke, squeezing Lynsey's arm as he passed. 'It's good to see you. Wish it was for a different reason.' He marched past towards the backdoor.

Lynsey turned to follow, and Cat fell into step with her.

'How's London?' Cat asked.

'Grand, you know,' was all Lynsey could think to say.

Cat nodded.

As they walked side by side, Lynsey noticed that both James and Cat were dressed in green scrubs.

'You both work here?' Lynsey asked.

'I do,' said Cat. 'I was Maura's veterinary nurse. James works at a practice in Cork City, but he's been helping out here the past few days. Just until you decide what's happening.'

It was Lynsey's turn to nod. She hadn't fully understood what inheriting from her Auntie meant. Cat stopped short of the back door and opened her mouth to say something. Lynsey looked at her expectantly.

'Ladies first,' Cat said, grimacing once the words were out.

Lynsey half smiled and wondered what it was that Cat hadn't said. She stepped over the threshold and the smell of home hit her. All thoughts of what Cat might and might not have said were lost as the smell of fresh baked bread, turf and lemon all fused together to bring her auntie back to life in a single scent. Tears sprang to her eyes. She looked around the kitchen where she'd spent so much of her life. She could feel the heat emanating from the Aga on her left. Oona had the kitchen table that dominated the centre of the room, laid with sandwiches, cakes, biscuits, and, of course, her famous sausage rolls. It was a spread Lynsey hadn't seen in a very long time, and it made her homesick for the years that she knew she'd never get back. James was at the kitchen press, lifting down mugs, while Oona was waiting for the kettle to whistle.

'Who do you want to drink out of today, Oona?' James asked as he shuffled cups around in the press.

'Oh, I'll take Fred if he's clean,' Oona replied. She turned to Lynsey. 'Come in pet, sit down.' Oona pulled out a chair, revealing a large Calico cat sleeping peacefully. She gently picked him up and placed him in one of the cushioned baskets that flanked the Aga. Lynsey walked over to where James was arranging mugs on the counter.

'They're all still here?' she asked, marvelling at all the familiar names she'd drunk out of in her youth.

'We've lost a few over the years and added to the collection as well,' Oona said, as Lynsey pulled out a mug with her own name on it.

'Oh my, my name is here?!' It was a question, a statement and a croak of emotion all at once.

'Yes. She finally found it. It wasn't long after she came back from her visit with you,' Oona began. 'We took a lovely little weekend trip to stay in

Bunratty Castle, and there in the gift shop you were. The owner said you'd been there for years. We couldn't quite believe it. Maura drank out of it every day.'

Lynsey closed her eyes and tears streamed down her face. 'I should have come home sooner.' She placed the cup in the centre of the table for Auntie Maura and took out Mabel – her old favourite.

Oona patted her hand. 'You're here now, pet. That's what matters. Here, have a sausage roll,' she said, popping two on a plate in front of her.

'Thanks, but I can't. I'm vegetarian,' Lynsey said, and for the first time, regretted that she was. The smell of them triggered all those memories of how truly delicious they were.

James spluttered his tea in his cup when she said this and looked sideways at Cat.

'Oh,' said Oona, 'Well, I did egg salad sandwiches, too. Those and the fairy cakes will see you right.' She loaded up a fresh plate and Lynsey smiled weakly at her.

A bell in the kitchen chimed and James and Cat stood up.

'We'll be back as soon as we're done with Mrs Cooney and her Tiddles,' James said, reaching across for a sausage roll.

Lynsey looked after them both as they left, still at odds as to how she felt seeing them both together.

'I'm glad I have you to myself, pet. How are you?' Tears welled in Oona's eyes.

Lynsey reached out for her hand.

'This is hard on you too, isn't it?' Her Auntie and Oona had always been so close, always popping in and out of each other's houses. Lynsey had probably spent as many nights sleeping here as she had in Oona's. As many dinners at her table as this one.

Oona nodded. 'But I want to hear about you, pet.'

Lynsey looked away. 'Honestly, Oona, I feel like I've messed everything up,' she began slowly. 'I ran away from home to a family who never wanted me. And I come back here after ten years and you're at the airport for me, prepared to come to the airport twice a day to give me a lift. You filled a table with all my favourite foods and through all this, you're grieving too. All the time I've been living in London, trying to get to know my dad's family again …' She stopped and looked down at her hands. 'I became a vegetarian for them, and they only invite me maybe twice a year. When my Dada died – my dad's father – they didn't even tell me until weeks later, by which time the cremation had taken place. I live four streets from them, but I'm not allowed to call without an invitation.' Lynsey reached into her coat pocket and placed a small bunch of keys on the table. 'I still have your backdoor key on my keychain. How did I get it all so wrong?' Lynsey lowered her head.

'I suppose you had your reasons to leave …' Oona said. It was both a statement and a question.

Lynsey looked at Oona, unsure if she would understand. That she'd left because of guilt and shame, because of a kiss – because she wanted to be much more. She could feel the blood rush to her cheeks with the memory.

The old landline phone, still perched and attached to the wall of the kitchen, rang, interrupting their thoughts. Oona stood up and answered it.

'Oh, hello, Fr Michael. Yes, yes, Lynsey has arrived. No, I haven't discussed anything with her. We're only in the door having the *tae*.' Oona nodded along with the conversation.

Lynsey allowed herself to remember more of that night, of that kiss, while Oona spoke with the priest. She'd never thought such feelings were possible. She'd never felt so alive, turned on or so sure of herself, and yet totally terrified at the same time.

'Is Oona on to the priest?' James asked as he came back into the kitchen and washed his hands at the kitchen sink.

Of course, she thought, it would be James who would catch her in the middle of such a memory. She blushed to her very core as his scrub shirt lifted, revealing a muscular stomach, while he reached for a towel to dry his hands. She remembered how she would trace the outline of his belly button while they lay in his bed. Lynsey nodded; it was all she could manage.

'Fr Michael would like us to go down to the Parish House at seven this evening to discuss some of the arrangements. Is that okay?' Oona said as she sat back down looking at Lynsey. 'Mrs Crowley has taken a turn and there's concern there'll be a need for two funerals in the one day. And that would be too much on Joe the sacristan. He just got the second knee done, and sure I'd never be able to do all the food for two funerals and attend them if they're both on together anyways.'

'No problem,' Lynsey said. She'd forgotten how tight knit and co-dependent the small village was.

'Tiddles is all checked into her luxury accommodation now.' Cat smiled as she came back into the kitchen. 'Would you like to see the new cattery, Lynsey? It was only finished in October.'

'Sure,' Lynsey said.

The thumping in her chest started as soon as she stood up. She followed Cat out across the short yard, staying a step or two behind her. She watched as Cat's hips swayed and how her long auburn hair swung ever so gently with the movement. Cat held the door open for Lynsey, but as Lynsey reached up instinctively to keep it open, their hands touched. Lynsey felt a spark immediately.

Just like the last time they touched.

She knew she should move her hand but she didn't. Their eyes met while their hands grazed. She opened her mouth, but only a tiny breath came out. Cat withdrew slowly and reached for the next door, which led into a small waiting area. Lynsey followed her through another door which led to a small passageway, where Cat stopped suddenly.

'Lynsey, I – I wanted to get you alone,' Cat began. There was little distance between them. Cat reached out but faltered and drew back. 'Lynsey, there is so much I want to say and talk to you about. So much I'm sorry for.'

Cat's eyes drew Lynsey in once more, and she found herself lost in them. Cat reached out again. This time, she tucked some stray hairs behind Lynsey's ear. She left her hand on the side of Lynsey's face, taking a step closer. Lynsey dared not move in case she spoiled the moment again. Cat lifted her lips to Lynsey's and when they met, their bodies melted into each other. Cat moved her hand around the back of Lynsey's neck and stroked it as they kissed. Lynsey moaned. Her hand moved up Cat's side, the soft, thin fabric of her scrubs allowing her to feel the lace of her bra as she grazed the contour of her breast. The delicate feel of the lace and the heat radiating from her body sent a thrill through Lynsey. Her thumb caressed Cat's nipple, and she pressed closer into Lynsey.

'Don't stop,' Cat whispered.

It was these words that brought Lynsey back to reality. She pulled back.

'Cat, I'm sorry. I can't. I want to, but I can't. Cat … I'm engaged,' Lynsey said, with tears in her eyes.

'Oh,' Cat said, stepping away. 'Sorry, Maura never said. I wouldn't have … if I'd known. I should probably go check on the cats.' Cat left abruptly through the door behind her, leaving Lynsey alone. She looked after her, wanting to follow, but she couldn't.

Lynsey walked back out of the cattery, suddenly exhausted. Oona was clearing the kitchen table when she went back in.

'Impressive, isn't it?' Oona said, as Lynsey walked through the door.

It took her a moment to realise she was talking about the cattery.

'It is.' Lynsey nodded, reaching for some dishes to bring to the sink.

'I'll do this, pet. Why don't you take a shower and have a rest?' Oona suggested.

'Actually, Oona, if you don't mind, I will do that. I'm just wrecked.'

'Of course, I don't mind. Plenty of hot water for you. I'll call you in a few hours. I'll rustle up a bit of dinner for us before we head up to Fr Michael's,' Oona said. 'And don't worry, I remember you saying you're a vegetarian,' she added, before Lynsey could remind her.

'Thank you. I'm really glad you're here,' Lynsey said, as she hugged Oona.

Lynsey took her bags down to her old room. As she reached the door, she stopped. She hadn't thought about this room in a long time. Would it be the same, or would Auntie Maura have redecorated since she left? Lynsey wasn't sure what to expect. Her hand rested on the door handle. *It's just a room Lynsey, what's stopping you from going in?* She pulled down on the handle, and pushed the door open, and stepped forward.

Lynsey smiled. It was exactly the same. She didn't know why this made her so happy. She walked in, closed the door and sat on the edge of her bed, placing her bags beside her. As she did, her bag fell open and Auntie Maura's letter that she'd sent with her Christmas card fell out. Lynsey had not been able to read it so far. She picked up the letter. It was written on her auntie's stationary, a crisp cream sheet folded in half. She carefully opened it in the knowledge that her Auntie Maura was the last person to touch it. When the words came into view, tears pricked Lynsey's eyes.

My Dearest Lynsey,

I was going to call, but I expect you might need some time to think about this, and so I thought it would be best to write. Would you come home and spend Christmas in Ireland? Your grandmother has sent word that she has arranged your marriage and so I expect it will be your last opportunity to visit with us for the holidays. It would be so lovely to finish decorating our tree together, because of course we did Oona's first! And the Carol Concert is on 16th – you know how I never miss it. It would be so nice to have you here; I've also tweaked my hot chocolate recipe – Cat introduced me to the most fabulous food influencer, and she has me buying up Lidl on the weekly!

It's not just Christmas though, there is much I would like to talk to you about and much I should have said all these years and well now, now it's important that we have these conversations before your wedding.

So, please, come home for cuddles, conversations, and Christmas?

Hugs & Kisses

Your Auntie Maura

Bláithín O'Reilly Murphy

Lynsey sat and stared at the letter. She hadn't realised Auntie Maura knew about the arranged marriage. She exhaled. *Why hadn't she told her herself?* Lynsey could see her reflection in the mirror opposite the bed. She stood up and walked over towards it. The reflection was older than the last time she had looked in this mirror, but sadly, the person was still exactly the same. She looked down at the letter in her hands. A realisation hit her. Lynsey left the bedroom and hurried back up to the kitchen, not noticing the new gallery wall of photos. Oona was sitting in a chair by the Aga. Lynsey realised it was Oona's chair. It always had been. And that her Auntie had a similar chair in Oona's house. Oona looked up from her book as Lynsey came into the room. She closed it and placed it on her lap. Lynsey sat on the edge of her Auntie's chair on the opposite side.

'Auntie sent me a letter. It arrived after she died. She asked me to come home this Christmas,' Lynsey began. She opened her mouth to continue and then stopped.

Oona swallowed.

'Was Auntie Maura a lesbian?' Lynsey asked, looking straight ahead.

'She was,' Oona said, looking in Lynsey's direction.

'Are you a lesbian?' Lynsey asked, this time, looking in Oona's direction.

'I am,' Oona answered.

Lynsey nodded.

'I'm to marry my second cousin from Delhi in the New Year. He's to arrive on the 20th,' Lynsey said.

'Maura said.'

'Did you know about this letter?' Lynsey asked, holding it outstretched towards Oona.

'I did. Your Auntie and I, well, we wanted to make sure that you knew you had options. That we were very happy for you, if the marriage is what you wanted, but if it wasn't, then that was okay too,' Oona said.

'Thank you,' Lynsey said quietly. 'Can I ask … when did you know?'

'About the arranged marriage? Maura told me once the letter arrived from your grandmother,' Oona replied.

'No, I don't mean that. I mean, when did you know you were a lesbian?'

'Ah! Well, I suppose I always wondered. But it wasn't until I was eighteen, when I met your Auntie Maura at a Dance, and I'd honestly never had as much fun in my life. Naïve me at the time, didn't even realise that you could fancy, or have feelings, for another woman, but it was the most natural thing in the world to me. And once I realised that I liked your Auntie much more than just a friend, that was it. She was the only one for me,' Oona said, with tears in her eyes.

48

'And you never felt guilty?' Lynsey asked.

'For being in love?'

'Yes, that you were in love with another woman?' Lynsey clarified.

'Oh, Lynsey. Have you been feeling guilty all this time?' Oona asked.

Lynsey looked at her, horrified. Her eyes widened and her hands gripped her knees. 'You knew? Did it show?' She bowed her head. 'I think it's why my Mami and family never accepted me.'

'Did you tell them?' Oona asked.

'No. I've never spoken about it,' Lynsey answered.

'To anyone?' Oona asked, surprised.

'No one.'

'That must have been lonely.'

'I've felt guilty and full of shame all this time,' Lynsey said.

'What's made you feel this way?' Oona asked.

Lynsey looked over to her. 'Because I can't decide.'

'What can't you decide?'

'Between men and women. I like them both. I mean, I'm attracted to them both,' Lynsey said with tears streaming down her cheeks.

'Who said you have to decide?' Oona said kindly. 'You can like and love them both.'

'You make it sound so simple.'

Oona smiled. 'I'm not suggesting that love is simple. But, simply put, you can be attracted to both men and women.'

Lynsey smiled weakly, wiping the tears from her face with her hands as she slipped into her Auntie's chair. 'How long have you known about me?'

'Ah, well. A while. I accidentally saw you and Cat kissing after your Debs.'

'Did you tell Auntie Maura?'

'I did, not immediately. It wasn't my business to. But after you left, well, everyone was a little surprised you did go, and so, I shared my theory with her,' Oona said.

'Your theory?'

'I suggested you might be struggling with your feelings for both James and Cat, a little like you struggled when Maura and I tried to tell you about our relationship.'

'You tried to tell me about your relationship? I don't remember that,' Lynsey said, wracking her memory.

'It was a long time ago. You'd only just arrived. You were very confused, and everything was so new to you …' Oona trailed off.

'I said something, didn't I? Something mean.' Lynsey had a flash of a memory. 'I'm sorry Oona, to you and Auntie.' Lynsey looked at her hands.

'My Mami said to me, as I was leaving for Ireland, not to become a *lesbian* like my Auntie. I didn't know what that meant at the time, but the implication that it was wrong is what I remember her trying to impart on me. I think that's stayed with me all this time, because I've always felt wrong.'

'Lynsey, pet, there is nothing wrong with who you are, or the way you feel,' Oona said, rising and walking over towards her. She stood in front of Lynsey. 'Your Auntie and I, well, I think we gave you too much time on this. We should have spoken to you long before now, long before you left. We never tried to hide the fact we were in a relationship from you, but I think we also didn't try hard enough to tell you either. And well, then you were gone. We'd always hoped to do it together. But here we are.' Oona's face and shoulders lowered.

Lynsey wondered what would have been if they had. Would she still be with James, or would she have been brave enough to be with Cat? Was she strong enough, like Oona and Maura? Perhaps now she'd never know.

'Do you want to go through with the arranged marriage?' Oona asked, pulling out a kitchen chair and pouring tea from the pot that had been brewing on the table. She handed a cup to Lynsey, who watched as Oona reached for the milk and poured a dollop into their cups. Lynsey looked down at the cup of tea. Until now, she didn't think she'd had a choice. Now she was afraid that she wasn't brave enough to make a choice.

All I want for Christmas is you.

In the two days Lynsey had been back in Ireland, a couple of things had become apparent. Her feelings for Cat were very intense. She could barely eat or sleep for thinking of her, which brought a whole new set of guilt when she should be grieving for Auntie. Also, if she chose Cat, or indeed anything else over her arranged marriage, she was kissing goodbye to any sort of relationship with her family in London, and India, for that matter. Her Mami had told her as much, in her own special way on the phone, both nights since she arrived in Ireland. Lynsey had never spoken to her Mami as frequently as she had since her Auntie's passing. Dev would arrive in London in four days' time and Lynsey was expected back in London tomorrow for the many preparations she would need to undertake before she met him, Mami decreed.

She had only one day left in Ireland. Today, December sixteenth, was Auntie Maura's funeral. Along with Auntie Maura, Lynsey felt like she was burying part of herself and any ties to Ireland or her Irishness. She wasn't

50

sure she was brave enough to do this, but she also wasn't sure she was brave enough to stand up for it, either. As she looked out the kitchen window, she could see Cat coming out of the cattery, holding a carrier. A young girl, about seven, hopped out of a parked car and ran up to Cat, a look of delight on her face. Lynsey was jealous. She couldn't remember when she'd last felt that sort of emotion. She watched as the girl skipped back to the car alongside Cat, who handed the carrier to her waiting mum. Cat waved them off and turned back towards the house. She didn't move then, seeing Lynsey looking in her direction. A longing passed between them, which gave Lynsey a physical ache. They hadn't spoken since their kiss, at least not alone.

'Has the kettle boiled, pet?' Oona said as she came into the kitchen.

Lynsey turned around. 'Oh, sorry, Oona, I forgot to hit the switch,' she said as she turned away from the window and moved over to the kettle.

'Don't worry, it's Mrs. Mooney's third cup. She won't die of thirst yet, more's the pity!' Oona said the last part under her breath.

Lynsey smiled. 'Still no love lost between you, then?'

'Oh, she's only here to see what sort of spread I've put on for the wake, so she can be down telling the knitting circle how it was lacking. All because I said her apple tart had a soggy bottom – you know how I don't like a soggy bottom – everyone knows it.' Oona stopped herself. 'Sorry, Lynsey, it's not the day for petty cat fights. I'm just a ball of emotion. It's lovely to have Maura home again, she'd be well chuffed with the turnout to the house, but, well, I can't believe it'll be the last time I'll see her in the sitting-room, even if she's laid out like the Queen of Sheba. She does look lovely though, doesn't she? So peaceful.'

Lynsey nodded.

'Fr Michael should be here soon, before Mr Sheehan comes to close the coffin. Would you like some time alone with her before they do? I can clear them lot out in here for you?' Oona offered.

'Yes, Oona, that would be nice. I'd like that.'

'No problem. Why don't you go in and get changed and I'll heat some sausage rolls? They'll follow their noses then.'

'Thank you, Oona,' she said, squeezing the woman's arm as she passed.

After she'd changed, Lynsey listened outside her bedroom door to see if she could make out if all the neighbours had indeed followed their noses down to the kitchen; from the sounds of it, they had. She walked down the hallway and paused at the sitting room door. Auntie Maura was laid out by the window, in the place of her favourite reading chair. It felt strange to think, but she looked so content. Lynsey went up to her. Her silver hair curled around her face. They had chosen a white pants suit for her to be buried in and she wore a silver locket. Inside were pictures of Oona, Lynsey, and Lynsey's mum, Kath.

'Auntie, I can't believe all the time I've missed. All the moments I will never get back with you. I'm sorry.' Lynsey's tears fell, hot and heavy. The saltiness made its way on to her lips and into her mouth. She didn't stop them or wipe them away. Some fell so heavy and far that they dropped onto the satin lining of the coffin.

'Ah, Lynsey, there you are, my child. Oona said you were having a moment. Can I join you?' asked Fr Michael.

'Come in, Father.'

'Tough day,' he said, patting her arm. 'She was some woman, your aunt. But sure, you knew that. Very proud of you, she was. Always telling us as you passed your exams and when you bought your flat. And sure, didn't she only try and suggest that we have a triathlon here after you took part in that one in London, but sure, Joe, the sacristan, was still on the waiting-list for the second knee so we had a bake sale instead. I judged the tarts. T'was a grand day. Your aunt sang, of course.' He looked off into the distance. 'Will be strange to have the Carol Concert today without her as compere, but you were right, she'd love to attend one last time. Having it as her funeral ceremony is fitting.'

'Thank you, Father. I think she'd really like it too. I know you were hesitant,' Lynsey said, glad she'd pushed for it in the end.

'To be honest, you reminded me so much of your aunt when you repeatedly asked, that well ...' He trailed off. 'She and I would often be at loggerheads. We'd very different approaches, but often our goals were the same. And to be fair, she was more often right – although I'd never let her know.' He laughed. 'Although, I suppose, I can't now,' he said faintly. 'Goodbye, old friend,' he said, blessing Maura. 'In your memory, I'll always fight for what I want. I'll leave you to it, Lynsey. Let me know when you're ready and we'll say the final prayers.'

'Thanks, Father.'

She looked back down at her Auntie. 'I wish I could be more like you, Auntie. I wish I was brave enough to go after what I want.'

*

It was only a two-minute drive to the church from Auntie Maura's, but it seemed like it was taking a good hour to get there. The village had turned out to line the route. While the sun shone low in the sky, a cold wind nipped at the mourners who stood solemnly on the roadside, and then joined the cortege as the hearse made its way slowly to the stone-faced church. Fr Michael was there to greet them, in his cheeriest of vestments, at Oona and Lynsey's request. As the parishioners filed into the church behind the coffin to the low hum of "Hallelujah", Oona smiled as they all took off their coats to reveal bright festive jumpers.

'Maura will be tickled pink with this service.' Oona beamed. 'Thank you for suggesting it,' she said, taking Lynsey's hand.

Lynsey looked around. There wasn't a space to be had in any pew but theirs. People lined the side aisles and filled the back of the church. Lynsey spotted Cat standing along the wall. She was dabbing tears from her eyes. Lynsey took a deep breath.

'Oona, I'll be right back,' she said, and left the pew and walked straight over to Cat.

'Cat, sit with us. Auntie would want it. I want you to,' Lynsey said, taking Cat's hand.

Cat nodded and followed her back to the front pew.

Oona sniffled as they joined her, and Lynsey reached out and held her hand with her free one.

'Dearly beloved,' Fr Michael began. 'We're gathered here today to celebrate the life of our wonderful friend, neighbour, Auntie, and, for some of us, so much more, Maura Crosby. Now, normally it would be Maura up here, leading us all today in our Carol Concert and I'm sure she's already telling me to move it along and get to the music ... so, without further ado, Mrs Murphy and the choir from The National School are going to lead us in "Silent Night".'

Lynsey tried her best to focus on the music, the words, the service, the kind words Fr Michael was saying about Auntie Maura. She knew there were readings and prayers too; she'd helped pick them. But she hadn't been this close, actually touching Cat in so long that her breathing, or the gentle movement of her hair as she sang, had Lynsey's full attention. They were still holding hands. Lynsey was scared if either one of them let go, the magic would break. Fr Michael's voice broke into her lustful thoughts of Cat and her touch, and she realised that very soon the magic would break. The service would be over and she'd have to let go of Cat's hand, as all of Ovens would take their turn to embrace her and offer their condolences.

Lynsey held her breath as Fr Michael began the end of the service

'Now, as we conclude today's service,' he said, 'Lynsey and Oona have asked me to invite you all to The Bar for some refreshments after the burial.

And so, we'll finish now with one of Maura's favourite songs, and given the day that's in it, I've given special permission for this one to be played.'

Lynsey let out the breath she'd been holding, leant closer to Cat and whispered. 'I'm not engaged anymore. I called off the arranged marriage this morning.'

Cat turned to look at her, surprise all over her face. They were mere centimetres from each other.

'I ran away from myself, and from you, all those years ago, but now I'm home,' Lynsey said, as the opening notes to the final song began. And as they played, Lynsey spoke the lyrics directly to cat: 'All I want for Christmas is you'. The congregation carried on with the song and Cat kissed her, right there, in the front pew and Lynsey kissed her right back.

Sausage Rolls for Everyone!

'T'was a grand service, Father,' said Mrs Crowley as she surveyed the spread in front of her. 'Nearly sorry I didn't go meself, I would have enjoyed that send off. Even if I would have shared it with Maura.'

Lynsey, Cat, Oona and Fr Michael nodded and smiled at her.

'Might hold on 'til next year, allow the choir to sharpen up on those melodies,' Mrs Crowley continued, 'But Oona, sausage rolls, there must be sausage at mine!'

'Oh Christ! Me sausage rolls!' Oona wailed, as she ran off towards The Bar's kitchen.

'Glad to see you two finally got your act together,' Mrs Crowley said pointedly to Lynsey and Cat. 'Your aunt would be happy,' she said, inspecting a ham and cheese sandwich. 'I've been waiting on the news since Mr Crowley saw you both shifting the face of each other after your debs. Cat had a face on her like a sheepdog left behind while his Master went to the mart after you went to London, Lynsey. Nice to see you finally smiling together.'

Lynsey and Cat smiled awkwardly.

'Here we are.' Oona arrived back with a mountain of sausage rolls that saved them from further scrutiny. 'Father, would you place them there on the table for me, so I don't have to lean over you?'

'Of course, Oona. Lynsey, sausage roll?' He offered her the plate as he went to put it down.

'No thank you, Father. I'm a vegetarian,' Lynsey said.

'What did she say, she's a Presbyterian now?' said Mrs Crowley as she reached for two.

'Don't worry, dear, you can have those – they're all vegetarian today.' Oona smiled at Lynsey.

'What's wrong with the sausage rolls – taste lovely to me?' Mrs Crowley asked as she popped the second into her mouth.

'Nothing, Mrs Crowley. I said sausage rolls for everyone!' replied Oona.

'Proper order,' Mrs Crowley said. 'Proper order!'

Bláithín O'Reilly Murphy

Carol of the Bells

Karl King

For once, it was snowing in London on Christmas Eve. It wasn't settling, but it did give the city a wintery and magical feel. The talk of a white Christmas could be heard on the streets around Covent Garden, as families and friends enjoyed the final few moments of Christmas shopping. It was fast approaching closing time and many of the shops had a single door closed, banning new customers from coming in, while letting the last few remaining stragglers pay and leave. Nick stepped up his pace, cutting through the tourists in the market square.

He took a left and ducked down a small, cobbled side street. There was a menagerie of small independent shops that felt like something out of a Dickensian novel. His memory of being a police constable walking the streets of London helped him to navigate his way. He missed the bustle of the city.

He was looking for a small shop that felt hidden from prying eyes, its front stepped back from the others, receding into the shadows, when he spotted it – an old-style swinging sign sticking out above the pedestrian's heads, the name "Bell Clocks" hand-painted on it. Above the sign sat a small clock, its face dirty with city grime, but Nick could see it still showed the correct time: three minutes to five. He slowed down and stopped, suddenly overcome at the thought of seeing the owner of Bell Clocks, Carol. The last time he had seen her was at her father's funeral in the summer. He'd seen, but not spoken to her. He hadn't the words to know what to say.

Nick stood in the middle of the street, jostled by other shoppers, staring at the second hand of the clock, stepping around the clock face. A sudden taste of regret entered his mouth. He should have come sooner. He hadn't been in London in nearly five years. He wasn't sure how Carol would react to his sudden appearance. He hoped well, but wasn't sure of that. The last five years had been tough, being alone in Scotland, with few friends of his age. He wanted Carol back in his life and this would be his first step towards that. His feet came back to life, and he walked cautiously towards the shop.

As he reached the front, he saw its windows were filled with large stick-on Christmas decorations, hiding the treasures inside. A "Closed" sign on the door swung as if someone had just locked up for the night. Nick kicked himself. Out of frustration, he rattled the door and, to his surprise, it opened.

As he entered, the tick of clocks enveloped his ears. It wasn't loud or overpowering, but it was there. He had been in this clock shop many times. The main lights were off, but there were Christmas fairy lights strewn around the clocks, different sets flashing at different times. Nick was suddenly reminded of how Christmas had been a special time for Carol and her father, Ted, they had both been mad for the Christmas spirit and decorations. They'd always turned their shop into their own little Christmas grotto, brightening up the dark streets of London.

'Dad?' a hopeful voice asked from the darkness to the back of the shop.

'Erm, no, sorry,' Nick replied. He felt awkward disturbing Carol's grief, which seemed to have momentarily suspended the reality of her father's death. 'It's, er, Nick.'

Carol came out from the back of the store. She was wearing worn denim dungarees over the top of a woolly, dark green jumper with loose-laced DM boots. She was still as beautiful as he remembered her. She had blonde hair, cut shorter than it had been at the funeral, blue eyes and a round, cute face with a button nose. He could see she had been crying, and noticed the moment she plastered on the smile that he knew and loved. She used the sleeve of her jumper to quickly wipe a tear away, as if she had an eyelash tickling her.

'Nick! Nick Mingun, do my eyes deceive me? Surely not?' Carol took a step forward, looking at him, and pulled him in for a hug. She was shorter than him and her head hit his chest, her arms squeezing him. The embrace felt slightly odd, but still somehow right. He hadn't held her for so long. The sweet scent of her signature perfume rose into his senses, bringing a flood of memories back to him. The longing for this embrace to be more than it was ached at his heart. He hated the fact their friendship had overtaken any chance for his feelings to be truly realised.

After a few seconds she released him.

'You haven't changed a bit!' Carol said, tapping his arms and stroking his black hair as she took him in. Nick looked back into her piercing blue eyes. He wished he could read her true thoughts; did she really think he'd hardly changed? He knew he had. He'd matured at the very least.

'You have,' he said awkwardly. 'I mean, your hair, it's shorter than when I last saw you.'

'Couldn't be bothered with the long hair. Too much faff in the morning.' Carol touched the back of her head, putting her fingers through her bob of blonde curls. 'How's all up in Balmoral, then?'

Of all the things Nick wished to talk about, it certainly wasn't where he'd been hiding in plain sight. 'It's okay. Her Royal Highness is hardly ever there, apart from the summer,' he explained. 'The rest of the time, it's pretty quiet.'

'Oh right, is it lonely up there?' Carol asked as she picked up a watch and started winding it up. 'You should have invited me up. I could have kept you company.' She held his gaze. If only she knew that he'd wanted, no, needed, the distance between them to give his heart a fighting chance to get over her. Although it hadn't worked, had it?

'Not really, it's peaceful,' Nick said, deflecting her longing for an invite. 'I liked the solitude. We do get the occasional crazy turning up that we need to deal with.'

'Such as?' Carol raised an eyebrow, putting the watch down. 'Obviously don't tell me if you can't. I understand that there's all that confidentiality stuff.'

'I'll tell you one story,' Nick said as he stifled a laugh just thinking about it. He had missed exchanging stories with Carol. They used to laugh until weak.

'Go on …' Carol said, her face lit with interest.

'Well …' Nick started, 'we had some lad driving around the other day in an old ambulance. This lad decided the Balmoral grounds were the perfect place to, how do I say it, go for a number two.'

'He did not! Where did he get the ambulance from?' Carol asked with a wry laugh.

'It was supposedly an old film production prop.'

'That's hilarious. And what did he do with the ...' Carol asked cautiously.

'Wrapped it in a bag and took it with him. There was no way I was going to clean it up. We christened him "The Balmoral Poo-er".'

Carol half-heartedly laughed. Thankfully, the background ticking sound of the clocks grew louder and whirled suddenly, as they all began to chime five o'clock. The building vibrated and the panes of thin glass in the windows looked like they were going to shake out of their frames, as if a train were hurtling past outside. There was no way to continue the discussion above the dings and dongs. Once the cacophony finally subdued, with a grandfather clock taking its time to chime its last bong, Nick broke the silence.

'The shop's still here then. I was worried it might have been gone.'

'Yeah.' Carol shrugged. 'I had been thinking about selling it. Never quite got around to it. Saying that, I've actually been looking at a few jobs.' She showed him a newspaper. Scribbles of red pen circled a few job adverts.

'You should do it, make the leap. What's keeping you here?' Nick asked.

'Nothing, I mean, maybe I will. Anyhow, what are you doing here?' Carol asked, quite obviously changing the subject.

'I'm looking for a gift, I suppose,' Nick said, looking around for inspiration.

'And there I was, thinking you were back to see me.'

Nick felt his face flush. Was she joking, or being serious?

'Um, no, I mean, of course, but no,' Nick stuttered. This was the bit he had rehearsed in his head; he had come up with a reason for why he was popping in. He composed himself. 'Alan, he's the clockmaker in Balmoral. He's retiring, and I wondered if you had anything as a gift for him.'

Carol thought for a while. 'Wait here.' She ran out to the back of the shop and, after about twenty seconds, she returned, holding a frame. She handed it to Nick.

'Well?' she asked, as Nick inspected it. The frame was A4 in size, with a battered, slightly rusty cog in its centre. A small plaque at the bottom stated:

A Piece of Time.
Certified cog from the Elizabeth Tower Clock.
Removed and replaced during 2021 refurbishment of Big Ben.

'It's perfect,' Nick said, putting it down on the side. 'How much?'

'Shall we say fifty?' Carol asked.

'You sure? I thought it would be a lot more,' Nick said, shocked, taking the money out of his wallet.

'It should, but "mates' rates", as they say,' Carol said nonchalantly.

Beyond the ticking of the clocks, if Nick listened hard enough, he could hear his heart crack a little. Always mates, friends.

'And to be honest, it would be an honour to supply a royal clockmaker with a retirement gift.' Carol took the frame and put it into a paper bag. 'So, where are you for Christmas? Back up there?'

'Nah, down here, covering shifts tonight and tomorrow night at Westminster. It's not like I have anyone in either place to have Christmas with.'

'Nick, that's sad!' Carol's face dropped, her bright blue eyes staring at him. 'Well, I have no one either, this year. If you want to, you're always welcome to join me tomorrow.'

Nick weighed the situation – he hadn't expected this proposal. 'I'm not sure you want me there on Christmas Day. You must have forgotten how much of a Scrooge I am at Christmas.'

'I prefer to think of you as a Grinch.' Carol smiled. 'Stealing Christmas for everyone else, but deep down, I know it's not all bad. I'd love to have you there. I could find my Madonna outfit for old time's sake.'

It was one of those moments where in a film, if Nick was drinking water, he'd have spat it all out in a spray of laughter. 'Oh God, I remember that outfit – you wore it when we met a decade ago?'

'Yes,' replied Carol, as Nick thought back to when they met.

He was a constable in the Parliamentary and Diplomatic Police Force, or PaDP for short. It was Christmas Eve, and he had been stationed at a sentry box protecting the Palace of Westminster. Carol had appeared at his window dressed like Madonna from the early 80s. The only difference was that Madonna had brown eyes, and she had piercing blue ones. A section of her long, blonde hair curled on top of her head; the rest sprayed out in all directions. She wore a black dress, which Nick could only have described as turning into a tutu around her hips. She had blown his breath away.

'But it was your eighteenth, wasn't it?' He remembered her telling him that she had been out in London celebrating her birthday, which would actually be on Christmas Day. 'You were helping your dad with fixing the clock. Seemed a strange thing to do on your eighteenth!'

Carol looked at Nick oddly, and he immediately regretted this questioning, but surprisingly, she gave an answer.

'It was special for my dad. It meant a lot to him for me to be there. And to be honest, it meant a lot for me to be there with him, too. I was only there for ten minutes. I think I spent more time on my eighteenth talking to you!'

Nick chuckled. 'You wouldn't leave me alone'

'And yet, it was you who asked for my number.' Carol pushed her fringe back.

'Best question I ever asked, in my opinion,' Nick said. There was a silence. Nick hadn't really left Carol anywhere to go with that statement. 'Look, can I let you know about tomorrow later, see how work goes tonight?'

'Sure, of course, no hurry. I mean, it's only tomorrow, but you're always welcome.' Carol fretted as she took Al's present back out of the bag and wrapped it in Christmas paper. 'You wanted this wrapped, yes? It should be wrapped, and I know you won't do it.'

Nick was unsure if she was hurt by his answer to her Christmas Day invitation. 'I'm actually very good at wrapping, but look, you have it done now.'

'I don't think I have ever seen you wrap anything! I certainly haven't received anything wrapped,' Carol said as she pushed the last bit of Sellotape on the paper. 'Just give me some warning if you do decide to come over, so I can tidy up, ay?' She looked up. 'What are you smirking at?'

Nick wasn't sure that he *was* smirking, but he thought about the perfectly wrapped gift he had in the bag for her. But now didn't feel quite right to give it to her.

'I'm not! But sure, I'll give you warning if I can make it,' Nick said. He could see her eyes were still ever so slightly bloodshot. He took a small breath. 'Are you alright? I mean, really?'

'Yes! Of course,' Carol said chirpily. 'Why wouldn't I be? It's Christmas.'

'It's just,' Nick paused, 'I know it's the first Christmas since …'

'Since Dad died. I'm a twenty-eight-year-old woman. I can cope,' Carol said, choking up.

'Can you though?' Nick asked sympathetically.

'I—' Carol started, but faltered at the thought. 'Nope, I'm not sure, but look, I'll get through it.' Her eyes watered; Nick took her in his arms.

'I can't do a father's hug, but I've been told I'm the next best thing,' Nick said, Carol's head tucked in under his chin, her ear to his chest.

'And who told you that now?' Carol asked as she cut through the tears. 'How many orphaned women have you cuddled?'

Nick looked down and saw a small smile appear as she, in turn, looked up. 'Well, you are only my first, I think, but surely, I have a hundred percent success rate in that case?'

'A hundred percent.' Carol gave a small hiccup of a laugh. 'Thank you for coming. I think I needed to have a cry, have a laugh. I'm not quite sure which!'

'Probably both,' Nick said as she slid out of his arms, putting her hands on his shoulders.

'Your dad's funeral was lovely. You did a great job. He would have been proud.'

'You were there?' Carol asked, 'I thought I saw you, but I couldn't find you. Thought I'd imagined it.'

'I was there. I saw the Elizabeth Tower Cake. I didn't realise funerals had cakes, but it somehow seemed fitting!' Nick smiled, knowing this was proof he was there.

'Why didn't you talk to me?' Carol asked.

'Because ...' Nick started, the truth being that he hadn't spoken to her for so long, he'd been afraid it would open that Pandora's Box of feelings again. Yet, in reality, that decision had certainly been a factor in his being there now. 'Because I was silly not to. I just didn't want to draw away from Ted's day, turning up like some ghost of the past. Silly I know. I wish I had.'

'I wish you had too, but I am glad you're here now. What else have you been doing while down here?' Carol asked, as she tapped his shoulders and swung her arms back down.

'Finishing off my shopping, of course! I wanted to give you this.'

'What is it?' Carol asked as she took it from him.

'Open it and find out. I'd never forget it's your birthday, and I suppose, Merry Christmas.' Nick chuckled.

Carol looked at it. Half of the wrapping was blue birthday paper, the other half red Christmas paper. It was small enough; it fitted perfectly into her hand.

'Now I know why you were smirking earlier. This wrapping is a strong nine out of ten.' Carol turned it in her hand.

'Told you I could wrap.'

'Could and would are very different things, as you very well know.' Carol eyed Nick with suspicion and carefully unwrapped the gift. A small snow globe was revealed. She held it close-up and examined the picture inside it. It was a picture of her and Nick, with Ted in between them, all three broadly smiling. Carol gave it a small shake and started to cry again, as she wrapped her arms around Nick's neck, squeezing him tight.

'I've missed you,' she whispered.

'I've missed you too,' Nick replied quietly.

Carol let her arms drop and wiped her tears once again on her sleeve.

'I feel really bad,' she said. 'I haven't got you anything for Christmas.'

'I don't need anything. I really don't. Seeing you smile is enough.'

Carol smiled weakly and pointed down at his bag. 'Who else you been buying for then?'

Nick quickly answered, 'Oh, that's a Nintendo Switch. For Holly.'

'Your niece? Wasn't she born the night we met?'

'Yep, another Christmas Day baby, like you. Holly will be ten this Christmas.' Lying about Holly's true identity never got easier. When Nick had secretly agreed to help his cousin and her girlfriend to have a baby, he hadn't realised how painful it would be to deny that he was Holly's father every time he spoke about her. 'I'm aiming for top uncle points this year.'

'I'm sure you'll win that. It's a big present from an uncle,' Carol said.

Nick wasn't a hundred percent convinced she could not tell he was lying.

'Right. I best get back to my digs. Got to shower before work tonight,' he said, quickly turning towards the door.

'Your present for Al!' Carol picked it up off the side and held it out to him. 'Well, I'll see you tonight then.'

'Tonight?' asked Nick, taking Al's present. 'What do you mean?'

'I mean,' Carol stuttered and then paused. 'Well, did you not know the East clock is broken? I've been called in to fix it. I was just about to head in now, actually.'

Nick's eyebrow gave the involuntary twitch of a police officer who didn't believe what he was being told. Of the three Christmas Eve nights he had worked since they met, there had always been a broken clock face, or at least, so it seemed. Nick thought better than to bring it up.

'Oh, okay. Well, I'll see you tonight then.'

'Yep, see you tonight, I guess,' Carol said, and she walked towards the door, pulling it open to let him out. She gave him a kiss on the cheek. 'Get back safe. You're always welcome tomorrow. You know that?'

'Yes, yes, I do,' Nick said dreamily. He had a warmth in his heart and smiled as he left. Carol shut the door, leaving him outside in the cold air. He turned back, but she had already gone. He could still feel her kiss on his face. He didn't dare touch it in case the feeling was lost. Tightening his scarf and giving his jacket zip a little pull up, he put his head down against the wind and snow, and walked away from a past he wished could be changed into a present.

*

The snow was falling thicker, beginning to settle on anything it could. Nick arrived at work, just as he saw Carol disappear into the bottom of the Elizabeth Tower to work on the clock. He felt a stab of pain in his heart that she hadn't waited to greet him. With his face long, he went into the main building and got changed from his civvies into his uniform. He looked at his watch: 18:58. He wandered towards the same sentry box he had started his career in, over a decade ago. As he neared the box, the small blue door swung open, revealing his ex-mentor, Bill.

'You're a sight for sore eyes,' Bill said, with the gruff Northern Irish accent he hadn't lost even after four decades of living in London. He examined Nick up and down. 'They been feeding you well up there?'

'Balmoral's been treating me well. You could say that – these MetVests are getting tighter, I swear.' Nick tugged at his body protector.

'Suppose I should be bowing to you – Sergeant now, aren't yous?' Bill asked, not one for being shy.

'Not at all, Bill! Well, yes, I am a Sergeant,' Nick explained. 'But tonight, I'm just a PC, taking the overtime!'

'Well, nice to have yous back.' Bill reached a hand out and Nick grabbed it, each squeezing the other.

'Good to be here. Anything to report?'

'Devil-a-bit, you should be in for a quiet night. Especially in this weather. Drunks don't do the cold.' Bill laughed to himself as he packed up his small lunch box and coffee flask. Nick kicked himself for forgetting his own. 'Oh, and that clock lass is in.'

'Yeah, Carol, I saw her go in,' Nick replied, wishing again that she'd waited to see him.

'Didn't ye have a thing for her once?' Bill asked as he picked up the newspaper on the desk.

Nick felt his face drop. Were his feelings for Carol common knowledge?

'You wouldn't do me a favour and leave that paper?' he asked, letting Bill's question float and vanish.

'Course. You still do the crosswords?' Bill handed him the paper.

'You've a strong memory in there, Bill, but no, not had the time, really. We have a lot of land to patrol up in the Gorms.'

'No Scottish lass by you up there?' Bill asked, a man of a thousand questions.

'No, Bill. No Scottish lass,' Nick replied, not that it had been for want of trying. He'd been on a few dates but hadn't really had a connection with anyone. No one had been able to take his mind off Carol.

'Well, enjoy tonight.' Bill tapped Nick's shoulder as he passed. 'And when you're on your break, take that lass a coffee if she's still up there. She was asking after yous, when you'd be in and on a break. That sorta of thing.'

'Right.' Nick's face broke into a smile, and his heart lifted. 'Will do. Have a good night, Bill.'

'Happy Christmas,' Bill said as he walked back into the main building.

Nick placed the paper on the small desk and scooted into the box. He settled himself on the tall stool, excited at the thought he might see Carol again. Especially as she had been asking for him. Hopefully, the thought of seeing her on his break would make the first part of his shift fly by.

*

Just before midnight, Nick had finished the crossword – in record time for him. It turned out to be Christmas themed, and he could guess most of the answers by the letters he had in place.

There was a sharp tap at the door that made him jump. Nick swung it open to find Luke, another officer, standing there.

'Break time!' Luke said chirpily. He was still young, about nineteen, twenty-one at a push. He reminded Nick of himself when he'd first started.

'Oh, right,' Nick said, unfolding himself from the booth. 'Gasping for a coffee. Do they have that shoddy vending machine still?'

'They have a Nespresso thing in there now. Was a gift from the Prime Minister, I heard.' Luke nestled his way into the box, and Nick set off towards the building.

He found the break room quite quickly. It had hardly changed. The walls were still a pale blue; the room was windowless, with the florescent strip lights casting a clinical feel across the room. The carpet was made of alternating dark and light grey carpet tiles. He walked over to the kitchenette area, where he found the large silver Nespresso machine, Luke had mentioned. It looked completely out of place in this worn-out room. Nick had a small one at home, but it only had two buttons on top. This thing looked a little more complicated. He examined it and pressed some buttons hopefully. The machine started whirring, hissing, and spitting as if it was a Willy Wonka Machine.

'Shit,' Nick cursed as coffee poured out. He'd forgotten the cup! He grabbed one from the side and slid it under the dribbling run of coffee and steaming milk.

As the cup filled, the bells of the Elizabeth Tower began to toll. He looked up, hoping he hadn't missed Carol. If she was still up there, the noise must be deafening for her. As the bells rang their last peel before Big Ben struck, there was an explosion of blisteringly bright white light that blasted through the room. Nick covered his head with his arms. It felt like the light had come through the ceiling, like the shockwave of an explosion. After a second, he lowered his arms. There was nothing. No noise, no debris, no smoke. Nothing had changed. What had just happened? Was it an electrical issue? All the lights still worked, and the explosion had come from above him. It was then he thought of Carol.

Without looking back, Nick ran out of the break room, along empty corridors and into the tower. He paused, debating whether to take the lift, but thought better of it. He raced up the three hundred and thirty-four stairs. Everything was silent, everything was still in place. There was no burning smell, no rubble. It all looked normal. Confused, Nick slowed, momentarily wondering if he had imagined the light explosion. Of course, he hadn't. He kept running. He had to be sure Carol was safe. Reaching the top, Nick looked to see if there was anything out of place. No change, no damage. Wiping sweat from his brow, he shouted.

'Hello! Carol! Are you there? Are you okay?'

'Hello!' Carol's voice nervously shouted back from up a small staircase. Nick let out an audible sigh. The relief of knowing she was okay was almost euphoric.

'Carol, thank God! I'm coming up!'

Taking the final couple of steps, he entered the large belfry. He spotted Carol standing beneath the criss-crossed beams, her expression shocked.

'Are you okay?' he asked, rushing towards her. 'I saw a bright light. It flashed past me. Did you see anything?'

'Ah, yes,' Carol replied, pushing her hair behind her ear as she turned to face him. It felt like she was waiting for him to elaborate.

The door behind him slammed shut, making him jump, but Carol stood there calmly.

'How are you here?' she asked, this time with concern, like how you would ask a relative of a car crash victim how their family member was doing in hospital.

What a strange question. What could she mean by that? Being a policeman, Nick wasn't used to being asked questions about his whereabouts – it was very much the other way round.

'I was in the break room making us coffee, then suddenly there was a giant flash of light. I raced upstairs to see if you were okay, and well …'

'I'm sorry, but you shouldn't be here.' Carol glance nervously at him, then she looked over towards the bells. Nick hadn't noticed it before, his attention on Carol, but there was something strange about the place. The large bells of the tower were in shadow, silhouetted by a tiny silver bell which hung in the middle of them. It shone brightly, as if there was a large, bright light pointing at it. It swayed gently, ringing a musical but almost inaudible *ding, dong, ding, dong.*

'What's that?' he asked, completely mesmerised.

'You can see the bell?' Carol asked. 'Can you hear it?'

'Yes, of course. It's bright enough.' Nick laughed. 'And I suppose I can just about hear a ringing.'

His gaze fell back to Carol, who was still calm. 'Carol, what's going on? What's that bell about?'

She took a deep breath. Nick's intuition was always suspicious when someone took a deep breath. Was he about to be spun a lie, or an inconceivable truth? At this moment in time, he couldn't decide which one he would have preferred.

'You haven't looked outside, have you?' Carol asked.

'Ummmm, no.' Another strange question. 'What's going on? Should I?'

'Perhaps, but …' Carol gave his arm a squeeze. 'Just promise you won't freak out.'

'Freak out? Why? What's out there?' Nick looked across the room to the window. 'There's nothing out there. It's still snowing'

'Move closer to the edge,' Carol said cautiously. He caught a quiver in her voice. 'Take a look down.'

Nick edged towards the open edge. He looked out, across the city. Everything stood perfectly still. Not a car moved, although that wasn't a complete surprise in London. The people looked like tiny ants, but ants that were suspended in motion. The noise, or more the lack of it beyond the ringing of the tiny bell, suddenly hit him.

'Is this some sort of 3D picture on the inside?' Nick tried to come up with a logical solution.

'Nope, not quite,' Carol said.

He moved around the tower, looking out every window, trying to focus on the smallest of details. And every time he spotted nothing but stillness, not a thing moved. Even the smallest of waves usually found on the tidal Thames were still. The snow that fell from the sky hovered. He tried to put his hand out and touch it, to see if it was real, but he couldn't reach it. He looked at the sky and saw a seagull mid-flight, floating still and silent above London. He scoured all sides of the tower and came back to Carol, who was laying out what looked like a picnic.

'What. Is. Going. On?' Nick asked.

'Of course, you were born on Christmas Day too,' Carol said, as if that was relevant.

'What?' Nick fought to control his voice. 'London has become a sculpture park. There's not a single movement out there, and you're reminding me it's my birthday!'

'Well, yes.'

'It's like time has frozen!'

'Held,' Carol corrected.

'Held?' This was more of an answer than Nick believed she wanted to give away. He waited. He wasn't going to let this one go. If time was held, then he had all day to wait for her to explain.

'I've held time,' Carol explained. 'For Father Christmas.'

'For … Father Christmas?' Nick tried to compute what she'd just said.

'Yes. I have the power to hold time, so Father Christmas can get around all the children.'

Nick shook his head. He'd heard some strange things while being a police officer, but a twenty-eight-year-old woman professing to stop time fir Father Christmas to drop presents was possibly the strangest. Stranger than The Balmoral Poo-er. Yet, there was something about Carol's demeanour that came across as if she was telling the sincere.

'But Father Christmas isn't real. Christmas magic is not real!' he blurted.

Carol breathed out deeply. 'You don't believe, do you? And yet here you are. You have a gift, and you really have no idea how lucky and special you are. Of course, Father Christmas is real! Who do you think you got your presents off when you were young?'

Nick was taken aback, and unsure how to react, how to answer.

'My mum, of course! It's what she said, anyhow. But having a birthday on Christmas Day makes it hard to know what's for which occasion,' Nick tried to explain. He thought back to when he was young. It was never just his birthday, or just Christmas, like every other child who was born on the other 364 days of the year.

'Your mum claimed to give you all your presents?' asked Carol, sounding upset and accusatory.

Karl King

'Yeah, I didn't get many. She and my stepdad couldn't afford much,' Nick explained. He didn't like to see Carol upset, but he wasn't sure how to react to the fact that she was possibly accusing his parents of something … he wasn't even sure what. 'To be honest, I try to work every Christmas. It becomes neither a birthday nor a Christmas then.'

'Nick, Father Christmas is real. This …' Carol waved her hands around, '… is real. Please believe me!'

'I don't get what this – ' Nick waved his hands mockingly, but, realising how rude he looked, he dropped them quickly, '– actually is. Why is no one moving? Why are we able to?'

Carol took his hand. 'Let me explain … or, try to.'

Nick felt her hand in his. She was so close to him.

'I've held time,' she said. 'Everyone in the U.K.,– apart from you and I – that is, is paused in time. It doesn't move forward or back. It allows Father Christmas to deliver his presents to all the children in the U.K. without being seen, without trying to get around the world in twenty-four hours. Now, to hold time, I must hit a magic bell.' Carol pointed to the shining, silver bell. 'There's a bell like that one in every capital city, all over the world. We call them the Christmas Bells. Ringing them puts a sort of stop on time.'

'Right.' Nick let go of her hand and rubbed his eyebrows with the heel of his palms, then raced his fingers through his hair. 'Let's go with the idea this is true, because quite frankly, I can't think of any other reasonable explanation at the moment. Although I'm certainly not saying I believe in Santa.'

'Father Christmas. "Santa" is a marketing tool. Never call Father Christmas, "Santa"!' Carol said pointedly.

'Right, so I'm not saying I believe in, well, him, but let's go with the idea that I believe you. Why you? How do you wield this power? Are you some sort of Hermione Granger?'

'I wish I was! No, it's not really magic. It's hereditary. You must be from a long line of Christmas-born children, too. My father, grandfather, great grandfather, great-great grandfather, great-great-great grandmother – you get the idea – were all born on Christmas Day. They were, and now, I am, what are called Bellringers.'

'Bellringers? But how does this, or even that, work?' Nick asked, pointing all around and then directly at the Christmas bell.

'Work?' Carol released her hands as Nick stared down at them. 'I don't know. I really don't know the science of it. It just happens. It happened for my father when he did it, and it works for me.'

70

'I still don't get it. I must be dreaming.' Nick sat down on a stone lip and Carol sat next to him. She slid her hands around his right bicep, gripping it tight, and nestled into him. He so wanted to kiss her – none of this mattered. Before he could act, she kissed him on the cheek.

'You're not dreaming. This is all real, I promise you,' she whispered.

He could still feel her kiss from earlier. That was the second time she had kissed his cheek. Could it mean something? He wondered and hoped. No, it wasn't worth overthinking.

Nick forced himself to collect his thoughts, to think like a logical policeman. 'So, if this isn't a dream, then it would mean Father Christmas is real and you can somehow stop time.'

'Well, yes. It's not a dream,' Carol said.

'It's quite a bit to take in.' Nick fidgeted, his bum going numb on the cold stone.

'Nick, I wouldn't lie to you. Okay, perhaps I've hidden this from you since we met, but can you understand why?'

'I can, I think.' The hardest part was believing this was all for Father Christmas. He believed in magic more than the man with the beard.

Carol gave a tight-lipped smile, like she knew he needed time to process it, and it struck Nick that even though everything was different, strange, or just plain odd, she wasn't. His brain was fighting to understand this magical world, but his heart had already accepted it, because this was Carol. He would always accept her for who she was.

'Was your mother born on Christmas Day by any chance?' Carol asked, breaking his train of thought.

'No, May. Why?' Nick replied. He really didn't want to get onto his parents again. He'd fallen out with them long ago.

'I wonder, was your father born on Christmas Day? Do you have any contact with him at all – I know you don't get on,' quizzed Carol.

'No, none. I'm not even sure he's still alive. What does it matter?' Nick held his gaze on her.

'Because you're here, awake, and not held in time like everyone else. It's something special.' Carol paused and stood to look out of the window, absentmindedly winding up the watch on her wrist. Nick noticed that the hands didn't move, no matter how much she turned it.

'Carol, I just think you're special,' Nick said without thinking. He stood quickly, turning away, flustered. 'I should go and get some coffees.'

He rushed to the door and tried to pull it open. It wouldn't budge. He tried again. 'The door's locked or jammed. I think it's stuck.'

'It's locked,' Carol explained. 'You see, this is now a safe space for Father Christmas to take a break if he needs. The door automatically locks so that no one can get in or out. Come sit, I have coffee here. Let's use this time to catch up.' She ferreted in a large backpack and pulled out a flask. She hugged it close to her, as if it were a hot water bottle.

Nick gave the door one last yank for good measure. It didn't move a millimetre. It was like it was made of stone, embedded into the walls of the building.

'That's a good idea. I'd really like that until Santa, I mean, Father Christmas, turns up.' Nick turned towards Carol.

'He won't come,' said Carol. 'Or at least, if he does, you won't be able to see him. Only those who truly believe in him can see him. Saying that, I've only met him once. He prefers to stop in Dublin before his trip across the Atlantic. He thinks the whisky is better there, although I'm sure you've a few nice scotches up there in Scotland.'

'One or two, that could be said! So, who unlocks the door then?' Nick asked as he walked over to Carol. There was something that felt normal about it … no, not normal, but like it was meant to be. He and she were meant to be there, just the two of them.

'It does so automatically. It'll be a few real hours,' Carol said calmly. 'Come, sit, drink some coffee.'

Nick sighed and took a seat on the blanket. She poured a cup of coffee from the flask.

'Earlier, you said I was special. What did you mean by that?' Carol asked.

'Well, all this, you made it happen, of course you're special!' Nick hoped this answer would quell any further questioning.

'Oh, right,' Carol said, handing him the cup.

'Do you know,' Carol said absentmindedly, as she finished her sip of coffee and watched Nick do the same. 'I may be special as you put it, but all this is quite a curse.'

'A curse, how?' Nick asked. It seemed like a neat trick to him.

'Nick, have you ever noticed that I've hardly any friends, and I've never had a boyfriend? How could I explain this to anyone?' Carol said exasperatedly.

'Doesn't mean anything. You're beautiful and funny and intelligent, Carol,' Nick said, his mouth and feelings running away with him. 'That's what really makes you special. One night a year should not dictate your whole life. I certainly know it wouldn't have dictated your father's life. He was a blast, he lived life to the full.'

'I couldn't tell anyone though, could I? Who would really believe me?' Carol threw her arms into the air and mocked looking around for this fictional person.

'I believe you.' Nick pointed his thumb at his chest. 'Now I've seen this, how could I not?'

'I wish you had before. I wish you had always believed in Christmas. I just wish you could have had the joy of growing up believing in Father Christmas. I knew you didn't believe, that's why I couldn't let myself, you know ... You and your siblings missed out on Christmas, and it just makes me so sad.'

'I don't have any siblings,' Nick replied. 'I thought you knew I was an only child.'

'Then, who's Holly?' Carol asked,

'Holly? Holly is ...' Nick trailed off.

'You said earlier that she was your niece. How can you have a niece without any brothers or sisters?' Carol stood up and walked a few steps away. 'I've been honest with you, but I think you're not telling me something here.'

'Holly is ...' a lump filled Nick's throat. She was right. She'd been honest with him. Was it Carol's secret alone that had stopped them being together, or had his secret about Holly been part of it too?

Carol had only been eighteen when they'd met. He hadn't wanted to scare her off by telling her he was about to become a father. And anyway, he'd promised his cousin he'd keep his true relationship to Holly hidden. He stood up to face Carol. Secrets and lies had kept them apart for too long.

'Holly is my daughter,' he said, with a tone of pride and care. 'Well, biologically, anyhow.'

'You have a daughter?' the pitch in Carol's voice increased. 'Holly's your daughter?'

'Yes.' Nick dropped his head.

'I've known you for a decade, and you never told me?'

'You never told me about all this!' Nick said, half-heartedly throwing his arms in the air. 'It was a family secret, like yours.'

Carol's lip quivered, and Nick tried to take her hand. Initially, she flinched, but then let her hand be held by his. She turned to him. She blinked slowly and deliberately.

'I'm ready to listen,' she said. 'Tell me.'

Nick took a deep breath. 'Yes, I have a biological daughter. But, to her, I'm just, Nick.'

'She doesn't know you're her father?' Carol asked, her hand coming away from her mouth.

'No, I promised her mums I'd never tell her. I play the role of her uncle, but I love her as a father,' Nick said, not sure whether his chest felt lighter with relief at telling Carol, or heavier with sadness.

'It must be difficult. You don't regret being the donor, do you?' Carol asked, holding his gaze.

'Of course not; she means too much. There may come a day where she finds out that there was a donor involved, and the donor was me. I ready myself every year as she gets older and wiser. I may not be the perfect father, but I want to try to be, if, or when, the time comes. I just want to be the best father I can be.'

Nick felt as if he'd mentally taken five rounds with Mike Tyson. Today's revelations had been a lot to take in and to let out.

She squeezed his hand. 'You *are* a brilliant father; I can hear it in you. You will *always* be a brilliant father because I know you will always be there for Holly. My father was a brilliant father because he was there for me.'

Carol released his hands and rummaged in her bag. She pulled out the snow globe he had given her and gave it a small shake, placing it into her outstretched palm in front of Nick.

'Dad always liked you,' Carol said, small snow pieces whirling past their faces in the globe's water.

'I always liked him, too.' Nick smiled as he took the globe out of Carol's hand and gave it a little shake. He thought about when the picture was taken. It was during the summer, about seven years previous. Ted had joined them on what should have been a Club 18-30's style holiday in Magaluf. Ted had stayed out longer, woke earlier, and certainly drank more than the two in their early twenties.

'He was always so much fun, so full of energy,' Nick said, a smile on his face. Ted was in his late sixties then, but he was always young at heart. Nick now realised why. It was because he had always believed in Christmas, believed in that most childish of feelings. It had kept his soul young.

'He not only liked you, but he also thought you were good for me,' Carol said, the words laden with implication.

'Then why didn't we ever … Why did you never …?' Nick fumbled.

'Because we met when I was young. I mean, look at us in that picture!' Carol pointed her arm towards the globe. 'Also, you didn't believe. If you had believed, I know things would have been very different for both of us.'

'I do now. How could I not?' implored Nick.

'Do you?' Carol rubbed her head. 'Because if I believed you did, then I could believe in us. But I'm not sure I can. For thirty years you've not believed. I'm not sure that's going to change tonight.'

Nick suddenly placed the snow globe in Carol's hands. He looked out towards the frozen sky. 'He's out there, right?'

'Who?' Carol asked.

'Father Christmas, of course. Only a true believer can see Father Christmas, right? That's what you told me.' Nick strode to the other windows of the belfry.

'Yes,' Carol said.

'Well, I'll prove I believe and then you must believe in me, in us. I'm going to find him, spot him out there.'

Nick sped from window to window, trying to find any sign of him.

He paused by one of the windows, looking out deeply. Something moved out there.

'Is that him? There?' Nick muttered to himself, unsure if it was a trick of the light or even a trick of his mind, so wanting to prove his belief. There was a dancing silver light that bounced gently. It was surrounded by a rainbow effect, like spilt diesel on water, swirling around. It had to be him!

'Carol, I think I have him,' Nick said, the excitement welling up inside him – a feeling he'd never quite experienced but had heard of, a feeling felt by every small child when they wake up on Christmas morning – a tickle in his stomach, a thumping heart.

Carol came running around the belfry, and stood in front of Nick, peering out of the window.

'That's him, right?' Nick asked nervously.

'That's him, alright!' Carol confirmed. 'Good spot.'

Nick put his arms around her shoulders. They used to do this as friends when they went out on night-time walks together. They would go up to Greenwich Park Viewpoint and look out over the city. They would either be putting the world to rights, or saying nothing, depending on their moods that day.

Carol rested her head on Nick's upper arm.

'See, I've proven I believe in him! Do you think you could possibly believe in me?' Nick asked.

'Nick, I believe you. I could even believe in us, perhaps.'

Nick was waiting for a "but", but it didn't come. Carol turned into him, bringing them even closer – their faces a mirror of joy. She stroked his face gently, and his hands wandered to rest on the small of her back. He hesitated to make the first move, still unsure of the moment, but Carol took the lead. Her head tilted upward slightly, and their eyes met before their lips touched. Nick closed his eyes, not believing his luck had changed after a decade of loving Carol from afar. *Sometimes, the best things do come to those who wait.* The weight on his chest lifted as they pulled away, and surveyed each other, taking in the shift from friends to lovers.

Carol slid her hands into his. 'I have fought us having a relationship since we met. These secrets never allowed our friendship to turn into something more. But do you know what my biggest secret is?'

Nick wasn't sure he had the energy for any more secrets. 'Not a clue!'

Carol grinned. 'It's that I want to be with you.'

Nick's eyebrows raised. 'Want to know my biggest secret?'

'Sure, why not? For the day that's in it,' Carol replied.

'I've been in love with you for ten years,' Nick said. 'I want to be in love with you forever.'

'I love you too, Nick,' replied Carol

'I never want us to be apart again,' Nick said, his heart so full it felt it could burst. 'Even if that means I have to leave Balmoral and move back to London, I'll do it. Whatever it takes.'

Carol dropped Nick's hands and went over to her bag. Her face lit up as she pulled a newspaper out, jittering with excitement.

'Look,' she said as she rifled through the pages. 'Look here.' She pointed to the ads page, turning to Nick. 'It's meant to be'.

He took the pages from her shaking hands and read:

Wanted: Full time Clockmaker based in Scottish Highlands Estate.

'I wonder if this is Alan's job.' Nick asked the world more than Carol. 'The colleague I bought the cog for; he's retiring at the end of January.'

'This could be at Balmoral?' Carol asked, taking the paper back.

'Could be,' Nick said, reading it again. Hope flooded through him.

'It's fate. It must be. I mean, I was looking at a change of jobs. The shop's not the same anymore, and as they say, a change is as good as a rest,' Carol said, the smile broad on her face.

Suddenly, there was a click from the door. The flash of light seemed to travel in reverse, like it was being sucked out of the bell. It flashed past and the small silver bell dimmed and then faded out from sight, like it was never there.

'And that's it,' said Carol. 'Another Christmas delivery is over.'

'But Carol, if you were to take the job, what about the Christmas Bell?' Nick asked.

'Well,' Carol said thoughtfully. 'I'll still have to keep an eye on the Elizabeth Tower, and make sure to come and fix it every Christmas – at least until I can train another young Bellringer ...'

Nick chuckled and kissed her. 'I suppose I better get back to work.'

'Haven't you got a thirty-minute break? You only started about five minutes ago.'

Nick checked his watch. She was right. He'd only been on his break for five minutes, even though he had been with Carol for hours. He kissed her once again, delighting in the fact he now could.

'Happy Birthday, Nick.'

'Happy Christmas, Carol.'

It felt so right; he always knew he was meant to be with Carol Bell, his Carol of the Bells.

Karl King

Twelve Days of Christmas

Cici Maxwell

Gemma made her way down from her apartment where she lived over her jewellery shop. Hopping over a snow mound, she rushed into the shop — she had a commission to finish, the only commission she'd gotten this winter. She flicked on the Christmas lights around the window frame and glanced outside at the leaden sky. The forecast predicted another storm, and just like clockwork, Al's snowplough chugged by. Gemma waved at the cheery old man behind the wheel before getting back to work.

  Pacing her shop, Gemma saw nothing but frayed carpets and dusty surfaces. Her shop was just as it had been when she had inherited it from her father. Nothing had changed at all. She'd been up to The White Gold Resort, where her best friend Allie worked, to take a look at her competition. The jewellery shop in the lobby had marble floors and gleaming glass displays. It was ostentatious, but that's what customers wanted these days, she thought, glitz and glamour. Gemma sighed. Her phone buzzed in her pocket, dragging her away from her thoughts. It was Allie:

- *Hey Gems, have you heard from Jake yet?*
- *Hey Allie! First – happy birthday! Second, no. Have you?*
- *Of course, he always texts me in the morning. I'm just worried about you two.*
- *It's going to be ok.*
- *Is it though? You guys have been best friends since…*
- *… since we were born, I know. I'll call him, I promise.*
- *You still on for tonight?*
- *Yes. Is there a dress code?*
- *No snow boots! Gems – this is a fancy schmanzy spot, I tell ya! Gotta go. Big wigs are here … think they're going off-piste this morning! I can snoop!*
- *Be safe, my little spy friend!*

Laughing, Gemma put her phone back in her pocket. It was Allie's thirty-seventh birthday, and they were meeting up at the resort for cocktails in the bar before they retired to Gemma's apartment for a home cooked meal. Neither one of them could afford dinner at the expensive Two Turtle Doves, the resort's Michelin Star restaurant.

Gemma made her way to her workshop at the back of the shop, the commission on her mind. It was an unusual request for not one, but five of her gold rings – the domed ones with celestial engravings, and dotted with tiny sapphires of all shades. Gemma opened the safe. Her hands shook as she placed the gemstones to one side; she didn't hold a lot in stock these days so the safe was pretty empty. This particular client had supplied the gems personally, saying that they were family heirlooms. Gemma closed her eyes. She had inherited a family heirloom too: Sapphire Springs.

Sapphire Springs was a tiny ghost town Northeast of Gold Mountain Ridge founded by Gemma's relatives in 1854. It sat on the edge of forty acres and had once boasted a post office, a saloon, a laundry house and a freshwater spring. Someone found a sapphire in the dirt and mining began in earnest, but they found nothing more. The town's population dwindled after that, and most of the residents moved to Gold Mountain Ridge where gold had been found. Her other best friend, Jake, was always telling her she needed to file the deeds properly, that she'd lose them if she wasn't more careful, but so far, she'd been fine. He'd grumble at her if he knew that they were shoved in the drawer in the bedside locker. She could hear his voice telling her a locker wasn't much good, that at least her safe was fireproof.

Opening her eyes, she pushed his voice away – Jake had been a getting a little too close lately, and what was worse, she liked it. But right now, she didn't need him meddling in her imagination. She set to work.

It was lunchtime before she sat back, stretched, and admired the ring she was working on. Even rough and in need of polishing, she knew it was one of her finest pieces. It gleamed under the lamp – the sapphires sparkling and glimmering – and urged her to try it on. The only finger it fit neatly was her wedding ring finger. It sat next to her tiny engagement ring, outshining it completely. Uncomfortable, Gemma took off both rings and laid them on the workbench in front of her.

Matt had proposed to her in the middle of a snowstorm. They'd been snowed in for days, and the power was out. They were running low on candles so had blown them out and were content to stay warm, curled up in front of the stove. He'd been antsy, unused to being indoors. The storm was the worst the county had seen in over twenty years. Temperatures had dropped and the wind was cutting. He had no choice but to stay in. On the third day, he'd gone out to his apartment to pick up a few things and had returned with the ring and a promise to love her forever if she'd be his. He moved in that weekend and Gemma hadn't taken the ring off since – until now.

She stood up and rubbed her back. Wrapping up, she locked up the shop and made her way down the street and around the corner to Pears' and Partridge's Grocery and Sundries store on Main Street. Cream, garlic, shallots, mushrooms, pappardelle, and a bottle of white wine went into her basket. Gemma's hand hovered over a tub of salted caramel ice cream, another of Allie's favourite foods.

'Go on, get it!' A voice from behind made her turn around, a huge smile on her face.

'I would if I could,' Gemma said. 'But the rent on the shop and the apartment is due tomorrow, and business has been slow.'

Lizzie Pears frowned. She shoved her hands deep into the pockets of her old jeans. 'It's this snow … no one expected so much of it. The only people coming into town are staying up at the hotel, and I haven't seen hide nor hair of any one of them.' Lizzie sighed. 'So much for the promises the Big Shots made. We should have asked for a formal agreement instead of taking their word that tourists would bring some commerce to the town.'

'Have you seen the sign?' Gemma asked. Her forehead creased. 'They've ignored the town's actual name – it's as if they're saying that Gold Mountain Ridge is a part of their resort.'

She'd seen the newly erected sign as she drove back into town the night before. *Welcome to The White Gold Resort* it said in all its obnoxious glory. The town's official welcome sign was dwarfed by it; snow flocked and weather beaten. The words *Welcome to Gold Mountain Ridge, Pop. 2,537* were faded and almost illegible.

'I heard all about it from Jake,' Lizzie said. Her eyebrows flew up. 'He's furious. Says he's going to go down there with a chainsaw and take it out. You can't let him do that, Gemma. He'll get locked up!'

'I'll try,' Gemma said. 'But you know Jake Sheridan. Once he gets an idea into his head, there's little to stop him from doing it.'

'You have to try,' Lizzie said. 'Promise me. He's a good man, just a little … passionate.'

'That's a nice way of saying bull-headed,' Gemma said. 'I can't promise anything. We're not really on speaking terms right now.'

'Oh,' Lizzie said with a frown. 'But you're still friends?'

Gemma nodded. 'I suppose we are.'

'Now, grab that tub of ice cream. It's on the house,' Lizzie said.

Taking Gemma's basket, she strode towards the checkout. 'Come on, I want to lock up. I'm closing early on account of the storm. They say it's gonna be a whopper.'

Gemma looked back at the ice cream, hesitated, then took a small tub.

'I'll pay you back,' she said to Lizzie as she followed her to the checkout.

'Don't sweat the small stuff – it's just a tub of ice cream.' Lizzie smiled. 'I popped a cake in for Allie – wish her a happy birthday from me.'

Gemma shook her head. There were no secrets in this town, except for the biggest of them all. What had happened to Matt Drummer five years ago? Gemma could still see his smile and his blue eyes; she could hear his laugh as he nudged her awake with a coffee, calling her a sleepy head and brushing away her groans. She longed to run her hands through his long messy hair, to see him scratch his beard while he pondered over maps and planned trails. Matt's disappearance had baffled everyone. She knew that everyone thought he was dead, that he'd gotten lost in the mountains, but that didn't make sense to Gemma. He had to be alive. He knew every inch of the mountains surrounding Gold Mountain Ridge, could tell the weather without a forecast, and had loved her more than anyone ever had.

The sky had darkened drastically since she'd arrived at the store. Although it was just after lunch, it was as dark as dusk. The town was almost deserted. Gemma's eyes tracked up the wide street towards the mountains to where The White Gold Resort perched. The hotel was spectacular, all white concrete and stone, with double height windows overlooking the slopes and mountains. It supplied jobs for the locals, for which many were grateful. Despite that, Gemma bristled and turned away from the bright lights of the hotel. Allie, for all her hard work, was paid minimum wage, and there was little chance of a pay rise.

Across the road, the Lords & Ladies Bar was the only establishment in the town with life inside. Golden light spilled from the windows out onto the snow; the Christmas tree, bedecked in tinsel and flashing red and gold lights, twinkled in the back. Jake was behind the bar, looking far too damn fine for someone who'd made Gemma cry so hard she'd needed a cool cloth to calm her face down. He was wearing another one of his flannel shirts and an old pair of jeans that hugged his lean hips nicely. Gemma took in his tanned forearms and his easy smile. He almost looked happy, but she knew better.

She flicked her hair back from her face and wondered what would have happened if she'd fallen for Jake and not Matt. Life with Jake would be something. He was romantic and passionate. You'd never be bored, but he'd never been one to settle down, always flirting with any woman who crossed his path. Except for Gemma. He'd never flirted with her ... until twelve days ago, when he'd kissed her and possibly ruined their friendship.

Maybe she should have kissed him back. But that would have changed their lives forever. It would mean letting Matt go, and it was too soon for that. All the same, her cheeks flushed as she remembered the softness of his lips against hers. His voice drifted back to her: *We only get one life, and I've waited too long to tell you – I've always loved you, Gem. I ... I know you loved him, and I know you still think of him, but Gem, he's gone ... Please Gem, love me.*

The flush turned from embarrassment to shame as she remembered how she'd spurned his simple proclamation of love; how she'd accused him of hating Matt, that he was thrilled that Matt was gone. The words she'd said in anger and pain twisted inside her. With all her heart, she hoped Jake would forget them, but he'd listened to her and hadn't spoken to her since the kiss. Gemma watched him wiping down the counter and chatting with Vanessa, who'd been mad about Jake since he'd taken her to prom. His words had stung. There was an element of truth in them, and that hurt. It was easier to exist without love, easier to stay safe if her heart was protected. It was easier to think that Matt might come back, and they'd start their lives exactly where they'd left off. But it was getting more difficult to keep the faith as each year passed by and Matt remained missing.

She bit her lip. She shouldn't have said those things to him. He would never hurt her, she knew that. Would Jake forgive her? If she walked across the street, right up to the bar counter and said sorry to him, would he let her back in? Gemma wished with all her heart that she could take back that argument, but she couldn't; and now he was smiling and joking with

Vanessa, who was loving the attention, and Jake seemed happy in her company. It was too late. Gemma turned away as it began to snow.

A man walking down the street from the direction of The Four Calling Birds phone store caught her attention. He turned towards the bar. She peered through the snow, her heart pounding and her mouth dried up. It was him! Jake was wrong! He was back! That was the way he walked, the way he flicked his hair from his eyes. Hell, it was even the way he checked his watch. She took a step and raised her hand to wave just as the man stepped into the light coming from the bar. She dropped her hand. It wasn't Matt. The man's hair was too corporate. Matt would never have cut his hair. And his jaw was weak and close shaven, nothing like Matt's bushy beard. He looked softer too, as if he spent too much time behind a desk. Gemma swallowed. Jake was right: he was probably never coming back. Jake looked up as the man walked into the bar. His gaze turned from the man and rested on Gemma for a moment. He looked away as if he hadn't seen her and served the man. Gemma felt the prickle of tears.

Gathering up her bags, she turned towards her apartment on Swan Street. There was no point in moping, not today. Allie deserved happy Gemma, not stuck-in-the-past Gemma. As she approached her shop, Gemma could see it was in darkness, as was her apartment above it. The power had gone out. Gemma dashed inside as snow flurries spun in the air. The open plan apartment above the shop was still warm. The wood-burning stove glowed with tired embers that quickly lit the logs Gemma added to it. The Christmas tree lights were off, and the bags she carried suddenly seemed heavier. Damn this storm. The room always felt warmer when the tree was lit. She went into the tiny, but spotless, kitchenette and unpacked her groceries.

Her phone buzzed. It was Allie again.

- *Gems. You need to get up here.*
- *Allie, what's up? Are you ok?*
- *I'm fine but ... no time to explain – get up here! You need to see this.*

*

Allie waved frantically at her from a side door as Gemma reached the resort.

'What's going on?' she asked. Her cold fingers fumbled over her coat buttons. Her face began to thaw as she breathlessly followed Allie down a long service corridor.

'Hurry up!' Allie said. 'We don't have a lot of time – in there – the room on the right.'

'Al, what's going on?' Gemma looked around. They were in a large conference room. The table was huge, and down the far end lay a scattering of documents and plans.

'Now,' Allie began. 'Don't get mad, but I asked Jake to come too.'

'You what?' Gemma spun around.

'He told me about what happened between you two, the kiss,' Allie said simply.

Gemma scrunched up her face and shook her head.

'I asked him to come because he loves you,' Allie said. 'When we were seven, he told me he was going to marry you. When we were twelve, he said he was in love with you. Matt moved to town just as Jake was going to ask you to be his plus one to my wedding – you fell for Matt and Jake never stood a chance.'

Gemma's heart pounded. Jake had told Allie he loved her ... if only he'd told *her* all those years ago, then things might've been different.

Allie shrugged. 'He's always loved you.'

'Allie, what am I going to do?'

'You're going to behave yourself and not break his heart any more than it already has been.' Allie took a long look at Gemma. 'Because we're going to need him for this.' She pointed down the room to the documents that were scattered across the end of the boardroom table. There was an ordnance map on the top of them all, with the boundaries of a patch of land highlighted.

Gemma winced. Jake was heartbroken? She wished again that she'd kissed him back instead of lashing out so cruelly. With a heavy heart, she walked down the room. Reaching out, she swivelled a document around and pointed to the ordnance map.

'This,' Gemma said, 'this is my land.'

Allie nodded. She pulled a document out from under the plans. 'And this is what they plan on doing.'

Gemma looked down. The artist's impression of the plans showed a glamourous building surrounded by a number of smaller, spectacular log cabins, set in the bend of the river. The accompanying paperwork listed luxurious amenities, one being a visit to the abandoned ghost town and mines of Sapphire Springs where guests could pan for gold or even search for sapphires. Gemma swallowed.

'They can't do this,' she said. 'Not without my permission.'

'I thought so too,' Allie said. 'But I found this – it says that if the person who owns the land doesn't turn up by Christmas Eve, then the land is up for sale, and they've already pre-empted an offer on it.'

'This is crazy. Everyone knows it's my land!' Gemma searched through the rest of the papers. 'They can't get away with this! All I have to do is to tell them that I'm here, and it belongs to me. Look – the deadline is in twelve days.'

'Gems, the date on that letter is ten days ago,' Allie said. 'The deadline is tomorrow.'

'Close of business on Christmas Eve.' Gemma read the letter and shook her head.

There was a knock at the door.

'Hey.' Jake came in, shaking snow from his hair.

Allie hurried over to him. 'Come in, quick. Close the door.'

Jake hugged Allie and looked over at Gemma.

'I'm sorry,' he began. 'That night ... I shouldn't have – '

'Not now.' Allie raised her hand. 'We have bigger fish to fry.' She gestured at the plans spread out on the conference table. Jake picked up the plans. He frowned and picked up a page with the words "Purchase of Land Agreement" in red on the top.

'No one nearby is selling land as far as I know,' he said. He leaned down over the map, his fingers tracing the river.

Gemma took in the smattering of grey at his temples. They were getting old. Too old to be fighting like children. He looked up, right into her eyes, and her stomach squeezed.

'Where have they in mind?' he said.

Gemma whispered. 'Sapphire Springs.'

'No.' Jake dropped the artist's impression on the table. Allie nodded.

'It says it here, on the plans.' Allie pointed. 'And there's nowhere else around with that in its name, so unless they've magic-ed up a new Sapphire Springs, it's the one and only Sapphire Springs that we know belongs to our Gems.'

'You need to tell them that,' Jake said. 'Tell them you're not selling – you're not selling, right?'

'No! I'm not. That's where Matt and I were going to live.' Gemma stood up. She walked around the conference room, her head in her hands. Jake's eyes never left her.

'Matt was obsessed with striking lucky out there,' Gemma said, avoiding Jakes piercing gaze. 'Those last six months before he went ... he spent all his free time searching the mines and panning.' She shook her head. 'My patience was wearing thin. He kept going back out there. Said he wanted to find something I could use for my wedding ring.'

'You never told me,' Allie said. She took Gemma's hand and squeezed it.

'You'd enough going on with Tim leaving you. You didn't need my griping,' Gemma said. 'One day, I went with Matt. He showed me where he'd been searching. We had a picnic, poked around the old saloon and the post office. They were falling down in places, but we had fun. We talked about building a house. I figured we'd maybe give a few guided tours, that kind of thing. We were going to pick them up from where my property borders the resort and taking them hiking and fishing.'

'Show me exactly where your property borders the resort.' Jake was all business.

'It's somewhere along where the river bends,' Gemma said. 'In fact, the river is mostly on my property but swings into the Resort for a bit and back out again before Gold Mountain Ridge.'

'Down near where the new tree plantation has gone in?' Jake asked.

Gemma got up. 'Want me to show you on the map?'

'Sure.' Jake shifted closer to her. She could smell the apple shampoo he used. If she wanted to, she could touch his cheek and say she was sorry, that he was right. That she cared for him too, only she couldn't stop loving Matt as well.

'I'm sure it's here,' Gemma said, pointing to the spot on the map that Jake's fingers had traced earlier. 'I need to compare this map to the deeds. The deeds clearly state the land markers.'

'You still have the deeds?' Jake asked.

Gemma nodded. 'Yes, they're with Matt's things.' She winced as a shot of pain flashed across Jake's face.

'We need to see them,' Allie said. 'Come on – we've no time to lose.' She opened the door and beckoned them to follow her.

'Allie, thank you,' Gemma said. 'If it wasn't for you …'

'Shhh, it's nothing,' Allie said. She pointed down the service corridor. 'You may as well go out the front door. Take this corridor right to the end, and the second door on the right will lead you into the lobby.'

'Aren't you coming?' Gemma grabbed her friend's hand.

'I can't stay MIA – I'll meet you at yours in half an hour,' Allie said.

Gemma looked at Jake. He gave her a tight smile, pulled his hat on, and held out his hand to her. Gemma closed her coat and pulled her hood tight around her face. She looked at his hand, and her fingers tingled with longing. Allie's words came back to her. Gemma felt a hot blush spread across her face. All this time he was patiently allowing her to be herself, and she'd failed to see him for who he was. Her throat constricted. She slipped her hand into his; it was warm, a little rough, but when he closed his fingers around hers all she could think about was what it would be like to have him touch her in other places too. She followed him down the corridor. Her footsteps echoed on the tiled floor and they began to run.

'Wait!' Jake slowed as they came to the second door. 'We don't want to draw attention to ourselves.'

Gemma nodded.

'It'll be ok,' he said. 'Just walk through the lobby as if we're guests.'

'We don't look like guests,' Gemma said. 'This coat is at least ten years old.'

'It doesn't matter,' Jake said. 'What matters is that we walk through that lobby as if we own it – do you hear? Head up. We go out that front door, down that hill and we find those documents before it's too late.'

'What if it's already too late?'

'It's never too late,' Jake said, his expression soft and tender. 'I promise you; it'll be ok.'

'Jake?'

'Yes?' He stopped peering through the porthole in the door and turned to face her. He looked tired, she realised, as if he hadn't been sleeping well for a while.

'I'm sorry,' she said. 'I didn't mean those things I said.'

'I know.' Jake's face softened. 'Come on, we'll talk later.' He took her hand again and opened the door. Gemma walked with him across the lobby, her hand in his, her thoughts slipping every so often to how strong his grip felt. She couldn't shake how right it felt to be with him, to be holding his hand and wanting to hold him closer. They reached the main door without anyone paying them any attention, and the doorman opened the door with a smile. Gemma pulled her scarf up around her face.

'It's blowing up a blizzard,' the doorman said without really looking at them. 'Are you sure you want to go out there?'

Gemma nodded from the depths of her scarf and followed Jake outside. The wind was howling now. Snow whipped down. Visibility was pretty poor.

'We can make it,' Jake shouted over the wind. 'Come on, hold onto me.' Gemma grabbed hold of his arm tightly and bent her head. Freezing and shivering, they stumbled down the resort driveway and eventually tumbled through her front door.

'Oh my God!' Gemma's teeth chattered. 'I'm so cold. Are you okay?'

Jake nodded, his eyebrows and stubble heavy with snow. He wiped his hand over his face and shook off his jacket. Gemma longed to touch him again, but he stepped back and pulled off his boots before taking the stairs, two at a time. Upstairs, he poked the stove, adding kindling to get it going again. The power was back; the Christmas tree lights twinkled in the corner of the room making the space warm and cosy. Gemma stood in the doorway and watched him for a minute. It was good to see him here again, almost normal. She could get used to this. He glanced up at her.

'Jake,' Gemma began. 'We need to talk.'

Jake stood up and wiped his hands on the back of his jeans. He looked perfectly at home. Gemma's eyes lingered on his jeans, wondering how it would feel to take them off him, to lie naked with him in front of the stove. Jake cleared his throat and took a step towards her. His eyes never left her face.

'I didn't think we'd get the chance to be alone together again,' he said. 'You okay with this?'

'Yes. Very much so.' Gemma nodded; her mouth suddenly dry. She watched him move closer, his face soft, a gentle smile on his lips. He was so close that he could touch her if he wanted to, but he didn't, he let her make the first move. She didn't realise she had reached for him until she heard his quick intake of breath.

'I, Jake...' Gemma breathed as she looked into his eyes.

Downstairs, the apartment door banged. Allie's voice carried up the stairs. 'We're not in Kansas anymore! That's some storm. Be right up!' Jake's face fell as Gemma stepped away from him. Allie ran up the stairs, stopping when she saw Jake and Gemma.

'What?' she asked. 'What did I miss – did you find the deeds?'

'Nothing – we've found nothing,' Jake replied. His eyes flickered away from Gemma's.

'I'll just check in the bedroom,' Gemma stammered and hurried off.

She walked around the side of the bed that she still thought of as Matt's, to his bedside locker where he'd kept the deeds to Sapphire Springs. Gemma breathed in and opened the bottom drawer. She shuffled through the contents, then pulled the drawer out completely. The deeds weren't there. She tipped the drawer onto the bed. Nothing. She opened the other drawer. Again nothing. She searched the cavity but only found a Christmas card she'd sent him one year. There was nothing behind the locker, nothing under the bed. Gemma stood in front of the upended locker; fistfuls of her shirt held tight in her hands. Where were the deeds? They were all she had to prove she owned that land. Her throat tightened. He must have left them somewhere else. Maybe they were in the filing box. Maybe he'd left them on the top shelf in the closet.

Gemma stumbled to the closet and flung open the door. She dragged the dressing table stool over and clambered up. The top shelf was empty except for an old t-shirt balled up at the back. Stretching in, she caught hold of it by her fingertips and pulled it towards her. Dust flew up into the air and she sneezed. There was nothing beneath it. Nothing at all. Climbing down, she opened the other side of the closet, the side where Matt's clothes still hung. Desperately, she rifled through the pockets and sleeves of every piece, unearthing nothing. In desperation, she tossed through his boots and trainers. Still nothing. A sob broke from her. Allie and Jake ran into the room.

'Gems!' Allie ran to her. 'Are you ok?' She sank to her knees beside Gemma, who was fumbling around in the bottom of the closet. Jake stood in the doorway, transfixed by Matt's clothes still in the wardrobe, the pile of Matt's things in a heap on the bed, the Christmas card. He shook his head, then moved into the room.

'It's gone.' Gemma sat back on her heels. She rubbed her eyes. 'I can't find it. It's not here. I've checked all the usual places, all the places he'd put things down by mistake, but he wouldn't put that down by mistake. It was too important, he knew that.' Gemma leaned on Allie as she stood up. 'The deeds aren't here. I was sure they were. I never checked for them. He always kept them safe in his locker. Oh my God. They're gone. I have nothing ...'

'They must be here,' Jake said. 'Maybe he put them away somewhere else.'

'Where!?' Gemma cried out. 'You tell me where, because I *know* he always had them right here! He knew how important they were to me – he'd never put them somewhere else.' She covered her face in her hands and began to cry. Gemma raised her head and tugged her shirt up on her shoulders. 'I need those deeds. I can't prove anything without them.'

'Can't you get a copy from the registry?' Allie asked.

'I tried before. They didn't have a record of it, but said that my deeds were all I'd ever need to prove it was mine.' Gemma sank down onto the bed. 'I meant to make copies ...'

'And you didn't?' Allie sat down next to her.

Gemma shook her head. 'I didn't. Oh, Allie, I'm so sorry. It's your birthday and somehow, it's all about me again.'

'Stop,' Allie said. 'It's okay ... if only we'd found out sooner. I didn't realise what was going on and I should have. The suits were down so often, they were all over the place. There was a contractor in, but I thought they were going to expand the hotel, not create a whole new resort.'

'You weren't to know.' Gemma wrapped her arms around her friend and held her tight.

She could hear Matt in her head as sure as if he was in the room with her: 'There can't be just one sapphire. That doesn't make any sense, Gem. There's gotta be more down there.' His obsessiveness hadn't been healthy, and had almost torn their relationship apart. He'd disappear searching for days on end. The last time he'd gone out and not come home had, ironically, been to go to the store and not to Sapphire Springs. Just like that, he'd vanished. It took a lot of convincing people that he was missing, and it was only when he was twelve days gone that they'd begun searching for him. No one found anything. There wasn't even an eyewitness to say they'd passed him on the street.

Allie sat back and sniffed. Gemma reached for the box of tissues on her bedside locker. 'Allie ... where's Jake?'

The doorway was empty.

Gemma frowned. She checked the living room, then slipped down the stairs, but there was no sign of Jake. Opening the door, Gemma leaned out to see if he was outside. While the wind had died down, it was still stormy and snow was falling thickly, but Gemma could see faint footprints leading away from her door. She slipped her boots on quickly and ran out onto the sidewalk, calling out his name.

'What's going on?' Allie appeared in the doorway.

Gemma ran back to the door and stamped the snow from her boots. 'Jake's gone, Al, he left.'

Allie scrunched up her nose. 'Come on, he's messing with us.' She stepped outside, her hands on her hips, and hollered, 'Jake Gibson Sheridan. You get back here right now.' She listened to the street. 'D'ya hear me? Quit fooling around!'

'He's not there,' Gemma called to her. 'Come in out of the cold.'

'Jake,' Allie shouted. Her voice echoed back to her. 'This isn't funny, Jake!'

Gemma bit her lip. 'Allie,' she called. 'Stop. He's probably had to go back to the bar for something.'

Allie stomped back inside. 'Well, he could have told us.' She ran back upstairs. Gemma stood in the doorway for a moment longer, peering both ways down the street. It wasn't like Jake to just disappear. Slowly, she climbed the stairs to find Allie with her head stuck in the refrigerator.

'I need a coffee,' Allie said in her matter-of-fact tone. 'We'll search the apartment afterwards, that's about all we can do.'

Gemma nodded and picked up the kettle. Jake would be back; he was never gone too long. She filled the kettle as Allie went to look out the window.

'It's really storming out there,' she said. 'I hope Jake is alright. Remember when he got locked up in jail, and we bailed him out?'

Gemma laughed. 'Jim Piper stole his bike from outside Pears' and Partridges' and Jake punched him in the stomach. What were we – twelve?'

'Yeah, about that age.' Allie hawed on the window and drew a heart in it.

'I'll never forget the look on his face when he was dragged up the station steps,' Gemma laughed.

'Well, Jim's dad was the Sherriff, and how brave you were, going in and demanding his release,' Allie said. 'Sherriff Piper's face when you slapped your hand on the counter and told him he was abusing his power ... you should have been a lawyer, Gems, not a jeweller.'

'Someone had to keep the family business going,' Gemma said. 'The chances of me being anything else was slim to none.' She paused to add a log to the stove. 'Al?'

'Yup.'

'What if he doesn't come back?'

Allie turned away from the window. 'What? Of course he'll come back. What makes you think he wouldn't?'

'Cos Matt ... he ... left the same way. Just went out to pick up dinner.' Gemma scratched her forearm. 'What if it the same thing happens to Jake?'

Allie stared at Gemma. 'It's not gonna happen,' she said. 'He's Jake. He's never gone long.'

'Yeah,' Gemma smiled. 'It's Jake. And it's not the same.'

'No,' agreed Allie. 'It's not the same. It's very different.'

Gemma gave a tiny nod. 'Different.' Allie turned on the radio to Christmas FM. Music was exactly what they needed to keep their minds off things.

'Gems,' Allie called over a rowdy version of "The Twelve Days of Christmas". 'I wonder if Matt left the deeds in the safe. Maybe he put them in it and forgot to tell you.'

Gemma leaned against the kitchenette counter. She didn't want to tell Allie that she never gave Matt the code to the safe, something told her to keep her business separate. She looked over at Allie's hopeful face, and sighed.

'It would be unusual for him to use the safe,' Gemma admitted. 'I never gave him access to it.'

'Oh,' Allie said with a slight frown. 'Right, yeah that makes sense.'

'I added cream.' Gemma placed a mug of coffee before her friend.

'Oh yum,' Allie said appreciatively. 'I'll have some of my birthday cake too – I saw it in the fridge.'

'Is nothing sacred?' Gemma asked. She pulled the cake from the fridge and cut them each a slice. She handed Allie a fork.

Allie took a huge mouthful and sighed happily. 'This is so good. Is it from Lizzie's? Thought so – you wouldn't get anything this delicious up at the Two Turtle Doves, I'm telling you. Hey, did I tell you I saw Ben and J-lo in there a few weeks ago?'

'You didn't tell me.' Gemma eyeballed her friend.

'Confidentiality clause,' Allie said. 'I can't go telling everyone when a very famous celeb is dining up at the resort now, can I?'

'I'm not everyone,' Gemma said. 'You should've told me!'

'Honestly, I couldn't; they really did make us sign a clause.' Allie's nose wrinkled. 'They wanted to go hiking. I didn't take them for the hiking type. They said they wanted to see the sunset from Twelve Drummers Ridge. Turned out they wanted a five-course meal up there.'

'No one goes up to Drummers Ridge, and definitely not at sunset,' Gemma said. 'It's lethal after dark. Did anyone tell them that?'

'That's how they wound up in the restaurant.' Allie raised her eyebrows.

'Matt was convinced that there were mine shafts leading from Sapphire Springs to the Drummer mines,' Gemma said. 'Said that if there was anything to be found, it'd be in those shafts.'

'I heard him say that to Jake once,' Allie said. 'He thought that the way in was through Drummers Ridge. Jake didn't pay him much heed.'

'He really didn't like Matt.'

'No, he didn't. But it didn't stop him searching for him.' Allie pointed her fork at Gemma.

Gemma nodded. She sucked in her bottom lip. 'Matt didn't like Jake either. He said that he felt as if Jake was peering right into him.'

'Whoa, that's uncomfortable.' Allie leaned back.

Gemma frowned. 'Al, did you like Matt?'

'Why would you ask me such a thing?' Allie said.

'That's a no, then.'

'It's not a no, per se, just … well, I wasn't sure of him.'

'Did you and Jake talk about him?' Gemma looked down at her slice of Red Velvet.

'No.' Allie took a bite of her cake. 'Well, sometimes, but then we made a pact not to. Jake said it was up to you to decide who you loved and we should support you.'

'Oh.' Gemma laid her fork down. 'Allie. I wish you'd said something.'

'And risk our friendship? Not on your nelly.' Allie shrugged. 'I'm sure you had your doubts about him.'

'No,' Gemma said. 'Maybe I'm a bad judge of character.'

'Maybe.' Allie ran her finger around her plate, scooping up buttercream.

'I just wish I knew what happened, you know,' Gemma said. 'I keep seeing Matt everywhere, at silly times and at places I know he'd never be.'

'I know!' Allie said. 'I did a double take yesterday at one of the suits who'd just arrived. I was sure it was Matt; you know, he had the swagger and there was just something in the way he held himself that made me think that maybe it was him.'

'I thought I saw him in town at lunchtime.' Gemma sat up. 'I almost called out to him.'

'I'm sorry, Gems,' Allie said. She sat back and looked away before continuing. 'I know how hard and lonely this is, but you have to be the one to make it better. You can't keep living like this. You need to move on.'

'Allie,' Gemma said tightly.

'It has to be said,' Allie continued. 'Gems, you've put your life on hold. You should've gone places. Applied for a bank loan for the business. *You* should've made a business plan for Sapphire Springs, you know. You could've done that without Matt. Instead, you've sat here and wasted years of your life, not to mention Jake —'

'Stop, Allie. You're walking a fine line,' Gemma said. Her hands shook, so she sat on them.

'I love you, Gems. It's really tough to see you alone.'

'Did Jake put you up to this?' Gemma stood up. She stalked into the kitchenette and dumped her plate in the sink.

'No! Of course he didn't,' Allie said. She followed Gemma. 'He'd never do that. And you know it. The only person who ever put you up to things was Matt. There. It had to be said. If you'd listened to Jake you'd still have those deeds.'

'What's that supposed to mean?' Gemma spun around, her hands on her hips.

'You trusted them to Matt's care.' Allie was deliberately slow.

'Allie.'

'You shouldn't have.'

'Well, I did.' Gemma flared. 'You didn't know him.'

'You're right, I didn't. But it wasn't because I didn't try,' Allie said. 'He wasn't interested in knowing me. It was always you. It was always Sapphire Springs.' Allie twisted her hands together. She stepped back. 'He chased you from the moment he found out about you and Sapphire Springs. And you fell for him the moment he smiled at you.'

'What are you saying? That he was after me for the land?' Gemma snorted.

'No!' Allie said, raising her hands. 'Yes! Sometimes I felt that way. Okay, so yes, I thought he was a creep and you couldn't see that all he wanted was your land. He didn't care about anything else. You can't deny that. Deep down, I think you didn't trust him any more than I did. You just went along with the fairy tale he spun you about living off the land and building a business together.'

'Let it all out, Allie!' Gemma blazed.

'There's a reason why you let him have the property deeds – you thought they were useless, you told me that yourself, but you never gave him the code to your safe. When you think about it – all those years ago, you actually had something to lock away – your land – and now the chances are, it's gone and you've lost it for good.'

'Allie. You're so far across the line …'

A rumble of thunder broke right above them making them both shake. There was a searing flash of lightning. The Christmas lights flickered, the radio crackled, then the power went. Gemma looked at Allie. The silence was as loud as the thunder. In the firelight, she saw tears on Allie's face. She wiped tears from her own and said, 'Get out of my house.'

'Of course,' Allie said quietly. 'I knew you'd say that.'

Gemma turned away and leant over the counter. Outside, the snow was falling faster, whipped by a forceful wind. She turned around to call Allie back, but she was gone. Gemma sank to the floor. Hugging her knees to her chest, she cried until her chest hurt and her eyes stung. Then she dragged herself to her room.

The bed was still piled with Matt's things. She grabbed a corner of the quilt and yanked it. The quilt slid towards her; Matt's things tumbled, but stayed in the middle of the bed. She took her pillow and the quilt and curled up on the couch by the stove. Allie's words played on her mind. Matt had been hard to love at times. He'd always pushed her out of her comfort zone. He said it was a good thing. As for his obsession with Sapphire Springs, well, she'd gone along always thinking he'd eventually realise there was nothing there but dust and tumbleweeds. If she'd had her way, she'd have sold that land years ago when the bigwigs at the resort had first approached her about it. The things she could have done with the money. She could have furthered her education, gained accreditation, but Matt always insisted she hold out. Maybe if she'd sold it then, he'd still be here with her.

Gemma's head pounded. Wincing, she pulled the quilt over her head and tried to fall asleep.

*

It was the power coming back on that woke Gemma. The radio blared out yet another version of "The Twelve Days of Christmas". She slapped it off with a grumble, then sat up and squinted; she'd forgotten to close the drapes. Rubbing her face, she realised that she had to find the deeds fast, and it was going to be a long day of searching without Jake and Allie to help.

Picking up her phone, she saw that she'd seven missed calls, three from Jake, three from Allie and one from the Sherriff's office. Her voicemail pinged. Brushing hair back from her face, she pressed "call" to listen to her voicemail.

'Gem, it's me, Jake. I'm at the Sherriff's office. I need you to bail me out. Gem, please. This is important and we don't have much time. I've found …' There was a muffled sound and then the call was cut off.

Gemma rolled her eyes. Typical Jake. He was the only person who could manage a disappearance and getting arrested in twenty-four hours. Well, at least she knew where he was. She hauled herself up from the sofa, grimacing as her muscles protested. Pulling on her boots, she listened to her voicemail again. Jake sounded concerned. He would though, he was in jail. All the same, it was Christmas Eve. She couldn't leave him locked up, and in return for her bailing him out, he could help her find the deeds.

Grunting, Gemma went downstairs. Overnight, the storm had blown away, leaving the bluest sky she'd seen in days. As she hurried along Main Street a cavalcade of shiny blue-black four-wheel drives cruised past, carrying the suits from the resort, she assumed. She stared in as they went by, catching the profile of the man she had seen outside Jake's bar yesterday. There was just something about him that made her think of Matt. The jeep pulled up at the town's one set of traffic lights and Gemma took a good look at him. He turned to face her and her breath caught under her ribs. She swallowed. The man's eye was black and swollen, his lip cut. His eyes met hers for a brief second. He blinked, then turned away. Gemma quickly lowered her head and strode on. She turned the corner and hurried up the steps into Gold Mountain Ridge's police department.

Jim Piper was behind the counter. He smiled and tipped his hat as she came in.

'Looking for trouble, Gemma?' He gave her a lazy smile and tweaked the tiny Christmas tree on the counter beside him.

'How'd you guess?' Gemma leaned on the counter. 'How much?' She pulled out her purse.

'I'm afraid you won't bail him out,' Jim said. 'He punched one of those money men up at the resort. They're pressing charges. Bail is set high. Over a thousand.'

'What?' Gemma grasped the counter. She closed her purse. 'Jim … you're kidding me.'

'Wish I was,' Jim said. 'Do you want to talk to him? He said to ask you, but said that you'd most likely say no.'

'Oh, for the love of God.' Gemma pinched the bridge of her nose. 'Okay. I'll talk to him.'

'Come on.' Jim lifted the counter up for her.

Gemma followed him to the cell. Jake was sitting on a bench, his fist bandaged and his jacket torn. He looked up at Gemma and shook his head.

'I wasn't sure you'd come,' he said. He got up from the bench. 'Can you bail me?'

'I can't,' Gemma said. 'I haven't enough money. They're pressing charges. What did you do?'

'I punched the guy who's stealing your land.' Jake grasped the bars. His knuckles went white. 'I need to get out of here.'

'Hey, calm down,' Jim said. 'No need to get riled up.'

'They're planning on stealing Sapphire Springs, Jim,' Jake snapped. 'Now I know the concept of stealing isn't something new to you. You get what I'm saying here … they're stealing Sapphire Springs right out from under Gemma's nose.'

'Is this true?' Jim turned to Gemma.

She nodded, her throat tight. She turned back to Jake, placing her hands over his on the bars as if she could measure the truth in his answer through his touch.

'Is it … is it *him*?' Her eyes widened as she looked at him, searching his for an answer, hoping he'd say it wasn't. He lowered his head, then raised it to look right at her.

'I want to say it isn't, but …'

'Oh.' Gemma staggered backwards, her hands slipping from Jake's. 'So it is him.'

Jake nodded. Gemma bent double; her arms wrapped tight around her. She leaned back against the wall.

'For crying out loud, Jim,' Jake said. 'Open this gate!'

Jim nodded and quickly let Jake out. He rushed to Gemma, pulling her into his arms, shushing her tears and smoothing back her hair.

'Gem, it'll be ok,' he said quickly. He held her gently. 'Look at me, I'll stop this.'

'Let me go, Jake.' Gemma shook his hands from her. 'I need to go to him. I need to see him. Matt …' She turned to Jim. 'Can you give me a ride?'

'That'd be a gross misuse of …' Jim began. 'Hold up – this is Matt? Screw it. C'mon.'

'Gem – '

Gemma heard Jake calling her, but she was already out the door. She climbed into Jim's four-wheel drive and pointed towards the resort. She heard Jake call her again, but she barely glanced his way. She didn't look back until they were turning the corner. Jake stood alone outside the station, his shoulders slouched and his face pale. She turned away. Matt was back! After all these years, he was back! She leaned forward, willing Jim to put his foot down while he stubbornly kept within the speed limits.

They pulled up at the resort's main entrance. Through the huge windows, Gemma could see a large group of suited men chatting. She leapt from Jim's jeep and ran into the lobby. Allie was behind the reception desk, waving her over.

'Jake called me,' she whispered. 'I can't believe it.'

'Neither can I,' Gemma whispered back. Her eyes shone. 'I knew he wasn't dead.'

Allie looked at her friend, her forehead crinkled with concern. 'Gems, you know what's going on here, don't you?'

Gemma looked around the lobby. 'He's not here. Where is he?'

The lobby was filled with people. The business men were gathered around a guide who was handing out warm outerwear.

'I'd say he's outside,' Allie said, referring to the computer screen. 'They're going to on a tour. Some have left already.'

'Where have they gone?' Gemma gripped the desk.

Allie scanned the screen.

'Twelve Drummers Ridge,' Allie said. 'Gems … be careful.'

'I know what I'm doing,' Gemma said.

Gemma flew back out the door, calling to Jim, who was driving down the hill. He drove on and didn't notice her waving. She cursed him. Spinning around, she saw one of the dark cars unattended. The engine was idling. Hurrying to it, she slipped in behind the wheel and pulled away without looking back. She turned off before the resort gate and drove down along the trail towards the bend in the river, where it turned from the resort back onto her land. The hike to the ridge would be tough in the snow, but she'd done it before and she could do it again. She pulled the car in alongside the others and jumped out, then ran towards the trail. Voices to her left made her stop. She turned towards the boathouse where you could rent fishing equipment in the summer. She listened. Her breath stilled.

'The border is here,' a deep voice said. 'And it turns back at the bend.'

Gemma's head whipped around. Matt's voice was unmistakable. She breathed out hard, her breath clouding in front of her. Slowly, she made her way to the boat house. The wood creaked gently as she stepped onto the dock, but no one paid any attention. She huddled by the door and watched them. There was a group of five men. One held a well-worn map in his hands. Gemma recognised the man with the black eye from the car that had passed her earlier. He was the same man she'd seen outside Jake's bar yesterday. Her throat closed up. He looked so different from how she'd imagined he'd look now. Gone was his lean, lanky frame and his slightly scruffy beard and long hair. Gone was his tan, his easy smile. His loose jeans and t-shirt had been replaced by a dark, well-fitting suit. She checked his left hand; his ring finger was bare.

'And what about this Gemma Hawkes I've been hearing about?' One of the suits said. 'Someone said she owns this land we're all talking about.'

'Only until five o'clock.' Matt chuckled. 'And without the deeds, she can't claim anything.'

'Doesn't she have the deeds?' the suit asked.

'No,' Matt said with a wink. 'She does not. Gentlemen, let me put your fears to rest.' He patted his chest. 'You have nothing to worry about. This is a project very close to my heart.'

The men laughed, Matt with them. Gemma gasped.

'You!' she said as she stepped forward. 'How could you?'

Matt's face paled. He stared at her; his mouth open. Then he smiled and laughed.

'Ne'er a dull moment around here,' he said to the suits. 'May I introduce Ms Gemma Hawkes. A nobody from the middle of nowhere with no aspirations and no money.'

'I had ... have aspirations.' Gemma advanced on him. 'And you stole them from me. Give them back. Now.'

'Give what back, exactly?' Matt smirked.

'My deeds.' Gemma poked him in the chest. 'The ones you've got so close to your heart.'

'Whoa!' Matt raised his hands. 'I don't know what you're talking about.'

Gemma looked at him. She stared straight into his eyes. He looked away from her uncomfortably.

'Matt,' she said softly, quietly. 'I dreamt of you, you know. All these years, I wished for you to come back. Now you're here in front of me and I don't know who you are. What happened?' She laid her hand on his chest. 'Didn't you ever think of me?'

He laid his hand on hers. Gemma shook. His touch was warm and so familiar. He'd touched her like that so many times before. She longed for him to hold her as he used to. Tears pricked the back of her eyes and she blinked them away. She moved closer to him. He took her hand and held it tightly before removing it from his chest.

'Matt,' she whispered. 'You're a lying, stealing, son of a bitch. I'll never forgive you.' She drew back her hand, balled it into a fist, and smashed it into his face. He staggered backwards and fell over.

'That land is mine,' she said. 'And you'll have to kill me to get it.'

Gemma launched herself at Matt, bowling them both over until she was sitting astride him. He raised his hands to protect himself from her blows. Yanking his jacket open, she searched for the deeds in his inside pocket. But they weren't there. Screeching, she began to hit him again. It took three of the men to haul her off him, the other helped Matt to his feet.

'You're stone mad.' He spit blood out of his mouth. 'What the hell do you think you're doing?'

'I won't let you win!' Gemma howled. She turned and snarled at the men holding her back. 'Let me GO!'

'Let her go!' Sherriff Jim Piper hurried across the snow and onto the dock. 'Take your hands off her now.'

The men reluctantly let Gemma go, and she shrugged them off with a grimace. Jim nodded to Gemma to join him. He turned to Matt.

'I believe you are in possession of stolen property,' he drawled.

Matt grinned. 'I am not.' He held open his jacket. 'Search me if you like.'

'If you insist,' Jim said.

'Oh, I do,' Matt sniggered. 'You'll find nothing on me.'

Jim searched Matt's pockets and coat lining. He turned to face Gemma.

'Sorry, Gemma.' He shook his head. 'There's nothing there.'

'Like I said.' Matt pulled his jacket back on. 'Now, if you don't mind, get the hell out of here.'

Gemma staggered backwards, stumbling over the snow as she made her way to Jim's jeep. Jim helped her up and closed the car door behind her. She kept her eyes trained on Matt as he turned his back on her. Jim slid in beside her.

'Thanks, Jim,' she said. 'I don't know what would've happened if you hadn't turned up.'

'You put yourself in a bit of danger,' he said. 'Allie called me the minute you'd left.'

Tears rolled quietly down Gemma's cheeks. 'I've messed it all up. I've lost everything.' She glanced at the clock on the dashboard. It was four o'clock.

In one hour, Sapphire Springs would be lost. She'd balled it up with Allie, screaming at her for justifiably calling out her bad behaviour, and picked a serious fight with the man she'd once loved with all her heart. Matt would probably press charges for making a fool out of him. She couldn't prove he had the deeds, so didn't have anything against him. And Jake? She'd left him standing in the middle of the road while she'd run to a man who'd stabbed her in the back, and who would do it again without conscience.

Jake, who'd always been there for her no matter what, who'd listened to her talk about her hopes and dreams, how she'd make the most amazing jewellery, how much she loved Matt, how many babies she wanted to have with him. It must've broken his heart to listen to her all that time. She'd never guessed the depth of his feelings for her, just taken his friendship for granted. He'd forgiven her a lot of things, but somehow, she didn't think he'd forgive her for running from him and back into the arms of the man who couldn't care less for her.

Allie was waiting for her at her hotel reception with a blanket and a brandy.

'Here, drink. Knock it back,' she instructed. 'Good, now, come on. Let's get you warm. You're shivering.'

'Allie, I'm so sorry,' Gemma started. Allie shushed her and led her to a quiet spot in the lobby near the Christmas tree.

'It's okay, doesn't matter,' she said. 'We move on from here. Let me sort those cuts.'

Gemma touched her face. She had small grazes across her cheek. She leaned back on the cushions and closed her eyes.

'You were right all this time,' she said. 'I should've gotten up and done something with my life and not wasted it waiting around for that ass to come back.'

'Yeah, for sure,' Allie said. She dabbed a warm cloth against Gemma's face. 'From what I hear, Matt looks worse than you.'

'Well, Jake is responsible for that.' Gemma groaned. 'Ouch. That stings.'

'Did someone say my name?'

Gemma opened her eyes and sat up. 'Jake?'

'That's me.' Jake stood before her. His boots were caked with snow, his face red and his hair windswept. 'You ran off before I could tell you. I – '

'No! Jake, stop!' Gemma jumped up. 'Don't say it.' She took his hands. They were freezing. Frowning, she looked up at him. 'Why are you covered in snow?'

'Because I followed you on foot.' He grinned at her. 'And you were like a bobcat – you definitely learned how to right hook from me.'

'You saw?' Gemma gasped. 'Where were you?'

'Oh, I saw!' Jake laughed. 'I went off track, thinking I'd be quicker, but ended up stuck in the snow. I caught the tail end of you punching that jerk in the nose and Jim turning up. You and Jim were gone before I got down the hill to you.'

'Oh.' Gemma blushed. 'I didn't see you. I'm sorry. Jake. I really am so sorry.'

'It's nothing.' Jake looked down at her. He let go of her hands. 'I'll give you some space.'

'No!' Gemma cried out. 'Don't. Don't ever give me any space at all — invade my space!'

Jake looked sideways at her.

'Finally,' Allie clapped her hands. 'Finally, you've come to your senses!'

'Allie!' Gemma glared at her. She turned to Jake and took his hands again.

'Jake, I don't know how to prove how sorry I am, for all the years wasted, for taking you for granted, for not seeing you for who you are. I was so selfish and devoted to my misery, yes, devoted. And you never made me feel bad for it. I regret all the time I've wasted not being with you, because if you're still up for it … I'd like to try us out for a while?'

Jake opened his mouth.

'Touching speech,' Matt drawled.

Bruised and bloody, he stood in the lobby, a huge smirk on his face. 'It give me the utmost please to tell you to your face that those five gold rings … that commission … was from me – one for every year I had to wait for this moment. And those sapphires, guess where they came from – they are all you're gonna get from the land you thought was barren and empty.' He pulled out his phone and tapped it. 'Look at that – in five minutes, Sapphire Springs won't be yours any longer. And heads up – I was right all those years ago. I always knew I was, especially when the hotel tried to buy you out. That's when I knew I could take it all, but you – you only gave me the map. You kept those deeds close right up until the end. I had to propose to you to get you to trust me – how sad is that?'

'What!?' Gemma stared at him. Her voice got louder. 'I'll kill you!'

Across the lobby, people looked up at them. A few moved closer.

'Now, that's a threat.' Matt raised his eyebrows at her and nodded. 'And you're all witnesses.' He spoke to the small group around him.

'Well, then they're also witnesses to this.' Jake stepped forward. He held up an old, yellowed and tattered document. Matt's face dropped. Jake raised his voice, it carried across the lobby to everyone there, including the Christmas carollers who were setting up in the corner, the investors, the legal team and the hotel owners.

'I suggest you guys get over here because this document belongs to Gemma Hawkes. This is proof that she is the sole owner of Sapphire Springs and the forty acres surrounding it. And I will not allow anyone to say otherwise.'

The clock flicked to five o'clock. Matt's phone beeped. His face fell. He staggered back, furiously pressing buttons on his phone to stop the beeping. Jim Piper swiftly took the phone from him and pressed the stop button. He placed a hand on Matt's shoulder and shook out his handcuffs.

Allie nudged Gemma, who turned to face Jake. She ran to his arms. 'How?'

'I was reminded of something Matt said to me once: that if there was anything to be found, that it'd be found in Drummer Mines, so I put two and two together and it added up. I found the deeds in an old tin tucked away right inside the entrance.' Jake pulled Gemma closer. 'Then I confronted him because, well, I couldn't help it. Punched him hard and got locked up.'

'You went up to the mines, last night, in that storm?' She shuddered thinking of how dangerous that was. 'You should have told me!' Gemma looked up at him, her arms tight around his waist.

'I tried but you didn't listen.' Jake looked tenderly down at her.

Gemma buried her head against his chest. She squeezed him tightly and peered over her shoulder as Jim led Matt out to his jeep.

'Jake, I'm …'

'Shhhhh,' he said, his lips already on hers. 'It's just us, now.'

Gemma nodded. 'Just us,' she whispered and finally kissed him back as the carollers sang the "Twelve Days of Christmas."

Cici Maxwell

Under the Mistletoe

Hayley-Jenifer Brennan

Why don't you just come home?

I blinked at the bright light of my phone screen – my best friend's name, dotted with the little green circle that lets you know they're online.

It wasn't my first year living across the world and away from my family, but it had certainly felt like the loneliest so far. I had moved to South Korea when I was twenty-three and, at twenty-nine, still single and now missing the best friend who had come here with me, my heart felt about as cold as the icy temperatures outside my office window.

[Rose is typing …]
It's the best thing I ever did.

I sighed. Yes, maybe it was, but she had her own business to grow and a husband to show off to everyone, and I had six years of English Camp teaching experience and very little else to show for my time here. I couldn't even speak Korean fluently. Pressure was building in my temples as my eyes threatened tears. I'd been feeling so emotional and lonely lately, but there was nobody left here for me to talk to, and I didn't want to worry anyone back home.

I did my best to hold in the exhausted, drawn-out sigh that stewed in the pit of my stomach. Maybe Rose was right. I didn't necessarily *want* to go home, but there wasn't any reason for me to stay, either.

'Excuse me, Jihoon …'

My gaze tracked the voice to the other side of the office.

'… could you …'

'No.'

I rolled my eyes at the bane of my existence – Mister Ji-hoon Kang. The only son of our school's director was (supposed to be) working off his debt for crashing a car that his Dear Daddy had bought him for his thirtieth birthday. What he was actually doing was nothing. Well, nothing other than doubling my workload. I choked down a growl that formed at the back of my throat at the mere thought of him.

'… Paige?' Yura, the marketing manager, turned to look at me with apologetic eyes and I could already tell where this was going.

I chewed on the inside of my cheek, throwing my auburn hair over my shoulder in an attempt to look ready. 'Yes, Yura?'

Jihoon looked up from his phone and caught my eye. Behind Yura, as she walked towards me, he shook his head slowly as he mouthed the words "say no".

I ignored him and gave Yura what I hoped was a welcoming smile.

'I know you're already busy,' Yura said, folding and unfolding a piece of paper in her hands as she made her way to my desk. 'But we've got a booking for a Christmas Day camp.'

I blinked.

'Of course we have,' I muttered. I didn't even know we were offering a Christmas Day camp which, as head of Curriculum Development, would've been nice to be informed of. I worked mostly with foreigners, and we had been more or less promised that we'd be off for Christmas Day. The pit of my stomach twisted at the idea of having to pick who would have to work it, because I knew that Jihoon wouldn't do the honours.

'I can't believe a school actually booked for Christmas Day,' I said.

'Well …' Yura's voice trailed off. 'It's not really a school.' She bit her lip and outstretched her hand, the piece of paper she'd been fiddling with begging for me to take it from her.

I scanned down through the English translation. '*Four* kids? We're running a whole day's camp for *four kids*?' I knew my voice sounded more accusatory than she deserved, but I couldn't help it. '*Who* booked this?'

I heard a scoff from the other side of the room and threw daggers at the perpetrator.

'I'll bet it was my dad,' Jihoon said acidly, not looking up from his phone. 'We just *looooove* Christmas in our house.'

'This doesn't make any sense …' I pushed my seat back, standing up a little too hastily, and my desk shook. The computer monitor wobbled and my cup of tea sploshed. I shimmied my way out from behind the unsteady slab of wood and around Yura. On my mission to stride angrily to the door, my foot caught on some extension cables that were covered in bulky plastic and masking-taped to the floor.

'Every damn time,' I mumbled, catching myself and allowing a frustrated exhale to fill my nostrils.

Jihoon glanced up again from his phone and cocked a lazy eyebrow. 'Mind your step,' he drawled.

'Mind your business,' I shot back.

He shrugged and went back to clicking at his phone screen. His computer monitors weren't even switched on, and his legs were thrown up on his desk as though he were on a relaxing holiday in the sun. His half-finished iced Americano sat, leaving a ring, on top of the marketing reports I had asked him to sign over a week ago. I should've got the job as Team Lead – Lord knows I'd worked hard enough to earn it. I hated him for his attitude, his work ethic and his spoiled behaviour, but mostly I hated him for getting the position I'd wanted without so much as blinking an eye. I didn't look at him as I walked past his desk.

Director Kang's office was next to ours. I sucked in a deep breath and went to knock on the door, but a hand around my wrist stopped my knuckles from connecting with the wood.

'Dad's in a bad mood,' Jihoon said, uncurling his fingers. 'I'd leave it if I were you. Just pick a couple of teachers that you don't like, and I'll tell them they have to work it.'

I scoffed. *Of course,* that would be his approach.

'We can't pay the teachers, the lunch staff, the camp counsellors, and the security guards for four children for six hours. Plus, we haven't budgeted for the materials. We're already in a deficit for this quarter – it literally does not make sense to run this camp. *You* might not understand money, but your dad is a businessman. He will.'

'Three hours and lunchtime,' Jihoon said, nodding at the piece of paper in my hands.

I glanced down at it and, sure enough, it only had three of the six lessons circled. I cursed under my breath at having overlooked that. 'That makes even less sense,' I muttered.

'I told you—' Jihoon eyed the door and lowered his voice. '—he's in a bad mood. That's probably why he booked the camp in the first place.'

'What did you do this time?' I asked without thinking.

Jihoon scoffed. 'While I appreciate that you automatically assume that it's my fault, today it's on my sister.'

'Your sister?'

'Older sister,' he said. 'She's supposed to be taking over this company when Dad retires next year, but she's decided to move to the States with her fiancé. He's a—' Jihoon looked me up and down. '—*foreigner*.'

'Ooh, the *devil*,' I mocked.

'He is in Dad's eyes,' Jihoon said. 'Guess who's the only child left to take over this business, now?'

'Oh.' Suddenly, it wasn't so funny anymore.

Jihoon's expression darkened into the sourpuss he usually wore around the school.

'Anyway,' he said. 'Don't go in now. You'll only make it worse.'

I cleared my throat. 'Thanks for coming out here to let me know,' I said as kindly as I could muster. 'I appreciate it.'

Jihoon looked affronted. 'I didn't come out here to help you,' he said quickly. 'You just happened to be about to poke the dragon when I walked past.' He folded his arms in a defensive manner. 'I've had enough of his shit for one day,' he said, cocking his head towards the door. He moved away then, tugging his *Comme Des Garcons* cardigan around his frame. 'I was just on my way to get coffee,' he said, already turning his back to me.

I thought about the half-finished Americano on his desk.

'I see,' I said. 'Well … thanks anyway.'

I watched him walk away for a few seconds, wondering how much his cardigan cost, and then contemplating what him being director would mean for my job, for the team, and for the students who loved to come here. I went to turn back to the office, but the door opened abruptly, and Director Kang stared at me like I'd murdered his favourite cat.

'You've been standing out here for a while,' he said gruffly. 'What do you want?'

*

I would never have admitted it aloud, but Jihoon was right. Talking to Director Kang had been an immeasurably bad decision, and I was still reeling from the earful I'd got about contract renewals, budget cuts and lazy children when I tried to make my way back into the office. The door beeped to signal that my key card had been declined.

'Ugh!' I sighed, resting my head against the door. My key card did this every so often and I'd have to bring it down to the security office at the camp entrance to get it recalibrated. 'Great.' All the teachers were in class, so there was nobody there to let me in if I knocked.

'I did warn you.' Jihoon's singsong voice came from behind me, but I didn't turn around. He stretched his arm over my shoulder and pressed his key card up against the reader. He smelled expensive.

The machine decided he was allowed to enter, and the door clicked open. I mumbled my thanks and made my way down through the scattered office chairs and baskets of various school supplies towards my cramped desk.

'Whose Christmas have you decided to ruin?' Jihoon asked, dropping down into his chair with a thud and placing his new iced Americano next to the old one. 'I vote Kevin. I hate that guy.'

'Kevin?' I didn't mask my confusion. 'Kevin is lovely.'

'Smug prick corrected my grammar once,' Jihoon complained. *'It's "fewer" than, not "less" than,'* he mocked. 'It's conversational, you pretentious ass.'

I let out a laugh. 'Well,' I said. 'He *is* an English teacher.'

'An English teacher? He teaches soccer to five-year-olds.' Jihoon folded his arms. 'And he's always hovering around you – it's weird. He's weird.'

'He's just friendly.' I smiled. 'And helpful. He always asks me if I need a hand.'

'Whatever. I vote Kevin.'

I flopped into my chair and clicked at the mouse to reignite my monitor.

'Actually, I'm not going to schedule anyone; I'm just going to do it myself. It's only three classes.'

He rolled his eyes. 'You're not a martyr for doing extra work,' Jihoon scolded. 'It's silly.'

'It's fine.' I inhaled to quell my bubbling rage. 'It'll save money only having to pay one teacher's holiday wages. Plus, I figure I can do a cooking class with them, and they can eat what we make. That way, we don't need lunch or cleaning staff either.' I cracked my neck. 'Now, I just need to figure out a way to translate for them so that I don't need the Korean staff, and that will just leave security.'

There was silence for a few moments before Jihoon spoke again. 'Mr. Kim needs the money – he'd be happy with the holiday wage.'

'The security guard?'

'Yeah.' Jihoon sniffed. 'That's why he does all those extra shifts. The man practically lives here.'

'How do you—' I was interrupted by Jihoon's phone going off. He answered, left the office, and I didn't see him again for the rest of the morning.

*

In the end, I decided not to even bother telling the teachers about the Christmas Day classes because I figured it wouldn't matter if I was the one teaching them, anyway. Somehow, still, word managed to zip around the office and suddenly people were giving me sympathetic head tilts and little pats on the shoulder.

'Next year you can take the time off to spend with your boyfriend,' one of the Korean teachers said, balling her hand into a fist. 'Fighting!'

I nodded, plastering on a smile. 'I hope so!' I sounded a little too bright, even to myself.

'You're single this year again?' she asked.

'I'm single every year,' I said, shrugging. 'I'm used to it.'

'We should do Secret Santa!' Nayla, one of the foreign teachers, tapped her desk excitedly. 'Nothing expensive, just something to cheer up those of us who don't have significant others to swap gifts with.' She gave me a knowing look. 'I feel your pain.'

'I'm not—' I started to scoff out a denial but a chorus of 'oh yes!' and 'that would be so much fun!' rippled through the office and the next thing I knew we were all gathered around to pull names from a hat.

'Don't put my name in there,' said a voice from behind me, and I stiffened.

'I didn't,' I stated, shaking the hat, and used the motion to try and shake the goosebumps off my skin.

'Aw, come on, Jihoon!' Nayla pouted. 'You're no fun.'

Jihoon didn't say anything else. He just sat back in his chair and clicked away at his phone again. I shook my head.

Nayla looked over my shoulder at Jihoon, then looked at me, and narrowed her eyes. 'Okay,' she said, but added nothing else.

We had all picked names out of the hat by the time the bell rang to signal the teachers' next classes. Suddenly, it was just me and Jihoon left in the office. I hated when it was just us – even though we rarely spoke – because his mere presence made me nervous in a way that nobody else's did.

I pulled a little bag of decorations out from under my desk. I'd bought a few bits for the classroom, the kitchen and the reception, and then one or two small things to try and brighten up the office. Christmas away from home could be lonely and not entirely festive, especially in a country where Christmas was mostly a "couple's holiday".

'You should really learn to say no.' Jihoon didn't even look up from his phone. 'In the five months I've been here, I don't think I've ever heard you tell anyone other than me to piss off.'

My eyes widened. 'I have never told you to—'

'You're so courteous to everyone else,' he said, sucking at his teeth like a petulant child. 'Why are you always so cold with me? You don't even greet me in the mornings.'

I snorted. 'You don't greet me, either.'

'Don't you know Korean culture?' he asked. 'You've been here long enough to know that you should show respect to your seniors.' He looked up then, a glint of something playful in his eye. 'You should greet me first. I'm your manager.'

'You're definitely not,' I scoffed. 'I've never seen you manage anything other than getting yourself a cup of coffee.'

He shrugged, a cheeky grin tugging at the corners of his lips. 'Who says I'm not doing something important?'

I noticed, for the first time, that he had a small scar just above his upper lip on the left side. I cleared my throat. 'That stack of papers I gave you to sign over a week ago,' I told him bluntly.

Jihoon's gaze wandered to the stack and then back to me. 'You do know that signing those will mean marketing will be allowed to change any classes according to a school's demands without having to inform you first? Materials and all.'

I felt my stomach flip. Yura hadn't told me that part; she just said that they were the new marketing reports for the next year.

'I ... I didn't know that ...' I admitted.

'I take it that the marketing team didn't translate the Korean bits for you?'

'Well, they told me—'

'It also says that they can increase the intake from eight to fourteen teams up to an hour before arrival.'

I shut my eyes, trying not to panic. 'Is everyone in this place trying to make me quit?' I said it more to myself than to him.

'Anyway, don't worry about it.' He shrugged. 'I haven't signed them, and I won't.'

'Thanks,' I mumbled.

He blew a raspberry. 'Please, I'm only doing it to annoy my dad,' he replied, looking back down at his phone.

'Oh.' I turned to leave, the little bag of decorations in my hand, then stopped. 'Are you sure you don't want me to include you for the Secret Santa? It would be a nice way to get to know the team ...'

He laughed, but it was empty. 'Absolutely not,' he said. 'I hate Christmas.' I nodded and let the door click closed behind me.

*

I was putting up the last few decorations in the office when I heard the yelling. I couldn't make out what the director and Jihoon were arguing about, but I glanced up at the clock to make sure the teachers wouldn't be back from class any time soon to hear it. I placed a little knock-off "Frozen" snow-globe on my desk, and then stuck some tape to the underside of the fake mistletoe I'd bought for the office doorframe. I wasn't sure if mistletoe was as big a tradition in Korea as it was at home, but I thought it would be a nice conversation starter either way.

As I balanced on an uneven desk chair to reach the top of the doorframe, I heard Jihoon's voice yell something in Korean and then suddenly switch to English.

'It's not like I have any intention of staying here,' he shouted. 'I speak fluent English. I could go *anywhere*.'

The director yelled back at him in Korean, but I didn't have the skills to translate it. Jihoon shot something in retort, and I picked out two words I understood: 'not' and 'dream'. We were all very aware that being here was *not* Jihoon's dream. Some of us wished that he wasn't here at all.

Suddenly, the door flew open, and I teetered on the chair with surprise, grabbing the doorframe for support. Jihoon huffed past, steadying the chair, and briefly looking at me before the mistletoe became unstuck from the frame and kamikazed itself down in front of his feet. He picked it up and tossed it into the wastepaper bin next to the door. The director's door slammed shut, startling me back to reality.

'Hey!' I called after Jihoon, jumping down from the chair. 'You've no right to do that!' I pulled the mistletoe decoration out of the bin. It had some pencil shavings on it, but it was relatively unscathed.

'It's my office,' Jihoon muttered, throwing his jacket around his shoulders. 'I can do what I want, and I *don't want* Christmas decorations all over it.'

'It's not *your* office,' I said. 'It's *our* office.'

'No.' Jihoon shot daggers at me. 'Not that you speak Korean, but that's what the argument you were just eavesdropping on was about. This place …' he outstretched his arms, '… all mine. Woohoo.'

'You know, it's fine for you,' I said, irritated that he'd called me out on my lacking Korean skills, even though I knew deep down that he was right. 'Korea is your home. But for the ESL teachers, it's nice to put up some decorations or play Secret Santa, or listen to Christmas songs because we *miss* our homes. We *miss* our families.'

'Then leave,' Jihoon said, stuffing his phone into his pocket.

I didn't mean to, but I let out a soft whimper as my eyes filled with tears. Jihoon's head snapped up, and he froze.

'I …' he started. 'I didn't mean to make you cry … You don't have to leave …'

The world swam around me in slow motion for a second as I tried to swallow down the lump in my throat. It was the first time I'd ever seen Jihoon look at me with concern. His dark eyes narrowed as his eyebrows hovered in a knit at the bridge of his nose.

'It's not your fault.' My voice caught, and my legs buckled underneath me. My bum smacked against the seat of the wonky office chair with a thud. 'I'm just overwhelmed, lonely and I *can't* go home.' I waved a hand dismissively. 'I'll be fine.' I sucked in a breath and wiped my eye with my palm. 'I just need a minute.'

'Why can't you go home?' Jihoon asked, still unmoving. 'Are you a criminal or something?'

I couldn't help but laugh at the irony of that, but only a hollow sound came out. It sounded insincere, even to me. It was the first time anyone had asked me anything about my life in a long time and I couldn't help the word vomit that escaped my lips.

'I came here because when I finished college, I didn't know what I wanted to do,' I told him. 'I worked for a couple of years at home doing jobs that I hated, and watching my friends all become lawyers, or accountants, or whatever.' I shook my head. 'They've always known what they wanted out of life. I've never had a brain that functions like that, so I thought, if I wasn't in the country, it could at least *look* like I was doing something cool. I'd have something to talk to them about when I visited home instead of just looking like a loser who is nearly thirty, and still doesn't know what she wants to be when she grows up.' I shrugged, looking up at him. 'I've been applying for jobs back home for the last two years, but I'm not qualified to do anything. I'm not even qualified to teach ESL, because I'd have to do another degree that I can't afford.' I flicked at the mistletoe's leaves with my nail. The office felt eerily silent, other than the roaring of my computer down the back. 'I'm too old now to start at the very beginning and not be embarrassed when I can't afford to do the same things my friends can. So, I …' I glanced down at my desk. 'I stay here.'

The computer rumbled, the clock ticked, and Jihoon said nothing. I felt my face heat up, mortified that I'd just shared my innermost feelings with my arch nemesis. I took a deep breath and threw the mistletoe back into the wastepaper bin. I pulled myself up and shook myself out.

'I guess I thought that adding a few decorations to the office would make me feel less … shit.' I sniffed, wiping under my nose with the back of my wrist. 'Sorry, it won't happen again.'

There was another long silence as Jihoon studied me, but never moved. I gave him a second and then cleared my throat, the awkwardness too uncomfortable to dwell in any longer. I shouldn't have overshared like that – what was I thinking?

'We don't celebrate Christmas in our house,' Jihoon said, finally. His voice was small and soft, and it caught me off guard.

Jihoon exhaled through his nose, his hands moving to pick at his nails, but he stayed securely behind his desk like the barricade of a man at war.

'My parents sent me to all the best schools, but all of those schools were abroad. They were in countries where people *do* celebrate Christmas.' He rolled his eyes. 'And, as you can imagine, I was surrounded by kids who came from very rich families.'

The tick of the clock was the only sound for a few moments and I assumed that was the end of the story until he let out a disheartened, shaky snort.

'I still remember the first year I was away, and I learned about Santa,' Jihoon said, not looking at me but instead focusing on his nails. 'I was six and the teacher asked my class to write our Christmas lists as part of one a project.' His eyes glassed over as though he were trapped in the memory. 'I wanted a yellow remote control race car that I saw advertised on the cover of some catalogue.'

He finally looked at me and I felt afraid to even breathe in case he changed his mind and finished his story there.

'Christmas Day came and went,' he continued. 'And then all the other kids came back the next week with their toys from Santa. They said that I must've been naughty, and that's why he didn't come.' He half laughed. 'I was six. I believed them.'

In my already fragile state, I teared up again and pressed my sleeve into the corner of my eye to stop myself from crying.

'Anyway,' he said, letting the moment wash over him. 'I later realised that I'd been pretty good all year, but I still hadn't gotten a present. So, I figured that I might as well just be naughty if that was the case.' He shrugged, his usual smug demeanour returning. 'Been naughty ever since, as I'm sure you've heard.'

He moved around his desk and towards me. He outstretched his hand and gave me an awkward pat on the shoulder.

'Your decorations are kind of cute,' he said. 'But the mistletoe is silly, and you know that everyone — probably other than Kevin — will hate it.' He arched an eyebrow. 'Because nobody in here wants to kiss anyone else, right?'

He was right. I sighed.

'Right,' I agreed. 'Sorry about your race car.'

'It's okay.' He cocked his head. 'I used my dad's money to buy myself a real one for my birthday last year.'

I rolled my eyes. 'Yeah.' I scoffed. 'Which you then crashed.'

'Actually,' he said, lowering his voice. 'I didn't crash it. My sister did.'

Before I had the chance to voice my surprise, the bell rang, and he walked out.

*

I picked Christy, the office fashionista, out of the hat for Secret Santa. The low budget made it very difficult for me to find something for her that didn't look tacky or thoughtless. I wandered through the streets of the tourist shopping district, hoping to find something cute at one of the many stalls that lined the area but, nothing had caught my eye.

I was also distracted. I kept thinking about Jihoon's admission that he hadn't crashed the car that he was working to pay off. If that was the case, then why hadn't he ratted his sister out? Why was he showing up every day to a place he hated just to keep pretending like it had been his fault?

I was mulling over how I could possibly bring it up again when a pair of earmuffs on a children's toy stand grabbed my attention. They were pink and fluffy and had a little USB charger so that they could be heated. They were perfect for Christy. Just the right amount of fun and practical while also being so gaudy that they might actually be considered Instagram fashionable.

'Excuse me?' I asked the older man, who was slurping down a bowl of ramen. 'How much for these?'

'For you?' He gave me a half-toothless smile. 'Twenty.'

'Hmm …' I mulled it over. The limit was ten dollars but, if I could get them down to fifteen, I could cheat a little bit. 'How about fifteen?'

'No, no.' He shook his head. 'USB heated. Twenty dollars.'

I sighed, going to bow and walk away when a toy on the top shelf behind him twinkled in my peripheral vision. A bright yellow remote control race car.

I couldn't.

Could I?

The man's gaze followed mine, and he wiggled a finger at me. 'If you buy this – ' he pointed to the race car. 'I will give you the earmuffs for fifteen.'

I chewed at my lip. 'How much for the race car?' I asked, not really considering it.

'Ten.'

I blinked. 'Really?'

'Really.' He grinned. 'Kids these days want to control them with their iPads, or watches, or whatever. This is just a remote-control car.' He shrugged. 'Ten dollars. And for these – ' he tapped the earmuffs with his gloved finger, '– then, fifteen.'

I stared up at the race car, asking for some kind of divine intervention to talk me out of it. Jihoon and I were not friends. This would be weird, right? In the time I'd been haggling, I talked myself in and out of it a hundred times. No, I thought. Bad idea. Weird.

'Okay,' the man said as though I were holding him at gunpoint. 'Earmuffs for *ten* dollars with the car.'

'Deal.' I heard myself say.

*

I wandered up the stairs and towards the office on Christmas Eve morning with a steaming mug of tea in one hand and my phone in the other. I was multitasking – triple checking the schedule for the following morning, and also texting my family and friends at home to wish them happy holidays in case I forgot the next day, with all the chaos that four kids, who were special enough to have their own camp, would bring. Christy's present was tucked into the paper bag that hung on my arm, alongside the race car. I hadn't decided whether I was giving it to Jihoon. I didn't want to make an ass of myself, but his story had left me surprisingly touched.

I was glad when my key card decided to be gracious that morning as it beeped to signal I was granted permission to enter. I was startled to see Jihoon there before me, standing at his desk and scribbling something with fixated ferocity. I turned, so as not to interrupt him, and couldn't help the gasp that escaped me. The room was covered in decorations and fairy lights. They twinkled like stars, casting a soft glow throughout the office, and I noticed that he had picked mostly blues, whites, and mints – my favourite colours.

'You like it?' Jihoon asked. 'I thought about what you said and figured the teachers should have at least one day to feel festive.'

'I love it.' My voice came out as a whisper. 'You even got real "Frozen" decorations.'

'Yeah, no offence, but the knock-off Olaf in the snow-globe is terrifying.'

I nodded, taking in all the decorations. 'It's, um, it's nice to see you on time for once,' I remarked, unsure of what else to say.

'I came early to decorate the office and the classroom for the kids coming tomorrow.' He said it so nonchalantly that my brain took a couple of seconds to register it while I was staring at the sparkling fairy lights.

I spun on my heel when I finally processed what he had said. 'You did? For the kids?'

'Yeah.' He looked up from what he was writing and cocked an eyebrow. 'Yours were pathetic.'

I scoffed, unsurprised at the sudden wave of disappointment I felt.

'Great,' I said. 'Thanks.'

There was a long pause as I made my way to my desk, but I felt his eyes on the back of my head the entire time as I walked.

'What?' he said after a moment. 'That's it?'

'I'm sorry?' I placed my things down on my desk and turned to look at him, not bothering to cover my confusion. It was too early for this.

'I just insulted your decorations. Normally you fight me for much less.' He looked just as confused as I felt.

'I'm not in the mood today,' I said, a pang of loneliness hitting me when my gaze fell on a wrapped gift he had sitting on his desk. I missed home today more than usual.

'Did I do something wrong?' He asked. 'I mean, aside from existing in the same space as you?'

I sighed, giving in. 'My decorations were fine.'

'Oh, well, it's no fun now.' He folded his arms. 'You're just placating me.'

The office smelled damp, and I knew it was cold, but the disappointment, loneliness and now irritation warmed me from the inside.

'No,' I said. 'I mean it. My decorations were fine. The kids won't even notice – they'll be too busy running around the place.'

'I didn't even realise you had put *up* decorations. They were so pathetic,' he said smugly.

Fury boiled in my jaw, and I stomped down the office, ready to give him a piece of my mind for constantly demeaning my work and just straight-up not doing his. I was so focused on getting there that I didn't even make my usual trip over the taped down cables. When I arrived at his desk, I took a deep breath and angled my chin up, ready to let five months of frustration out on him at once, but the glint in his eyes stopped me dead.

'Wait …' I shook my head, realisation smacking me like a sledgehammer. 'You actually enjoy annoying me?'

117

His eyebrows floated into his hairline. 'You think I stick around the office for the coffee?'

'Are you …' I stopped. 'Where did that come from?' I eyed the mistletoe that hung on the doorframe. 'I thought I threw that out last week …'

'I rescued it,' Jihoon said, a sheepish blush creeping across his cheeks. 'I felt bad for calling it silly, so I kept it in my drawer until I put it back up this morning.' He cleared his throat and stood up straighter. 'Maybe Kevin would like it after all.'

I pursed my lips. What was his deal with Kevin?

'Anyway.' Jihoon folded the card he'd been writing and stuck it into the ribbon around the present. 'I'm going to get lost before the teachers get here.' He clinched the gift under his arm and stepped around his desk. 'As you might recall, Santa presents are kind of traumatic for me. Santa's a bigger prick than Kevin.' He said it jokingly, but a part of me wondered if he was hiding honesty in his humour.

'Who is your gift for?' I asked, deciding to be nosy. 'Your girlfriend?' I felt my face heat up. 'Or boyfriend?' I added quickly.

'I'm very single,' Jihoon said. 'But if that's your way of asking me out, you're going to have to do better.' He nodded to the office. 'I decorated a whole room for you.'

I couldn't help my face as it contorted into disgust. '*Please*,' I scoffed. 'You annoy me enough as a co-worker. I imagine you're ten times worse as a boyfriend.'

'Imagine me as your boyfriend often, do you?'

'Literally never.'

Jihoon shrugged and strode past me, his gift making a little tinkling sound as he did.

'It's for Mr. Kim, the security guard,' he said, beeping open the door. 'I don't know if you've noticed—' he lowered his voice to a whisper, but it dripped with sarcasm. '—but the man is here, like, *all* the time.' He finished in an accent that mimicked Nayla's.

'I'm surprised *you* noticed,' I shot at him. 'Considering you're barely here when you're supposed to be.'

'Hey, I've been pretty good these past few weeks,' Jihoon said. 'Besides, I've got places to be, parents to disappoint – you know how it is.'

'Still, it's nice of you to get him a gift.' I made my way towards the coffee maker, switching it on so that it would be hot when the teachers arrived.

'Well …' Jihoon's voice was light. 'I figured I *had* to, since you guys left him out of Secret Santa.'

My mouth fell open, but no sound came out. We had?

'I'm not as bad as you seemed to have convinced yourself I am,' Jihoon said with a cheeky grin, but there was an honesty in his tone that I wasn't used to.

'I don't think you're bad,' I admitted. 'I just think you're lazy. I would've worked really hard if I'd got your job.'

He seemed taken aback and stayed silent for a second, his brow furrowing as he mulled over my words. 'You wanted this position?' he asked finally.

'Of course I did,' I said.

'But you don't speak Korean.' He nodded in the direction of the director's office and the marketing office. 'They'd eat you alive.'

'Well, then,' I said, my mind racing as it dissected that information. 'I could do with a hand sometimes.'

'Deal,' he said. He dawdled at the door for a second before giving me a half-bow half-nod hybrid and left the office.

'Oh, Jihoon!' I called after him, stepping towards the door, suddenly realising that I probably wouldn't see him now until after New Year's.

He spun around, the gift tinkling as he did so. 'Mmm?'

He was closer to me than I'd expected, his face barely more than a few inches from mine. I watched him catch his breath.

'S-sorry,' he said, but he didn't step back.

'Happy – uh ...' my brain buffered. 'Merry, um, merry Christmas.' I didn't step back either.

He smiled, the lines around his eyes crinkling. 'Merry Christmas, Paige.'

I noticed he had a little freckle under his right eye and another one on the tip of his nose. We stayed like that for a moment, studying each other. Jihoon's gaze wandered up and mine followed. The mistletoe he had rescued hung between us at a perfect position: either mocking us or egging us on, with its little plastic leaves, as we stood in silence.

I waited for him to say something sarcastic, but he didn't. I waited to hear myself say something sarcastic, but I didn't. Jihoon tilted slightly forward as though he were going to kiss me on the cheek and my heartbeat sped up. My mind battled to try and pre-empt how I should react.

But I never got there.

'—I don't really understand why we have to come in on Christmas Eve when we don't even have any students.' Christy's voice came from around the corner and Jihoon jumped back as though I had bitten him.

'Uh, anyway,' he said, clearing his throat. 'Merry Christmas.'

'Yeah.' I blinked rapidly, hastily manoeuvring my way back over to the coffee machine.

'Morning, Hoonie.' Christy made no bones about Jihoon being her senior staff member. Christy made no bones about anything. 'Ugh, what's with the mistletoe? Gross.'

'Oh,' Jihoon said. 'I put that up. I thought it was a western tradition.'

I let my gaze meet his. He gave me a small smile and left the building without so much as another word.

*

The Secret Santa exchange was mostly cute and uneventful, with everyone enjoying their gifts and singing along to some Christmas music, until Director Kang popped his head in the door and told everyone they could go home early, acting like he was the best boss ever, despite the fact he made us all come in just to do nothing in the first place. Derek was my Secret Santa, much to Kevin's chagrin, and had given me little moon and star magnets to put on my fridge. I loved them.

I spent Christmas Eve dinner alone in my apartment, eating pasta, and watching "Home Alone" as I replayed the moment under the mistletoe over and over. And over. My mind wandered as I drifted into a restless sleep, my brain fixating on every single thing Jihoon and I had ever said to each other. "I'm not as bad as you seemed to have convinced yourself I am," his voice reminded me.

~

When we first met, I'd bowed respectfully and said "hello" in formal Korean. He'd replied to me in informal Korean and I immediately took a dislike to him. I never called anyone out on anything, but something about the way he smirked at me and the cocky glint in his eye made me snap. I asked why he would speak to me informally just then – we weren't friends. He didn't reply.

The day Director Kang let it slip that I had said he shouldn't let his kids get away with crashing cars that he'd paid for, a shadowy look crossed Jihoon's face and he asked me why I would get involved with family politics that didn't concern me. I said that I had just been chatting with his father and I didn't expect anything to come of it – least of all this. He asked me why I was even discussing these things with his father in the first place. I said that Director Kang and I were friendly.

'But you speak formally to him,' Jihoon had said. 'You're not friends.'

I didn't reply.

~

I thought about when I had tripped over the taped-down wires in front of Jihoon for the first time.

'Mind your step,' Jihoon said.

'Thanks,' I replied.

'I don't want you falling onto my desk and knocking my coffee everywhere. That's expensive coffee,' he said.

I rolled my eyes.

~

Jihoon was almost always late. He would show up every day just before lunch and then go on his lunch break as his first act of the day. He'd come back from lunch later than everyone else and sit at his desk, clicking away at his phone, his computer well and truly turned off.

'Nice to see you on time for once,' I said, the first time he'd shown up before noon.

'Thanks,' he replied.

'You might actually do something useful today, instead of using up oxygen for something you could've done at home,' I said.

Jihoon rolled his eyes.

~

'First thing I'm going to do when he leaves is throw a party,' I mumbled once to Nayla.

Jihoon looked back over his shoulder at me. 'First thing I'm going to do when my sister takes over is have her fire you,' he said. 'Then *I'll* throw a party.'

'Fine,' I said, not having a decent comeback to something that might be probable.

'Fine,' he mimicked.

'Fine!' I huffed.

'Fine!' He grinned.

~

Right before my alarm woke me from my unrest, I thought about the glint in his eye and the cheeky smile that would follow whenever we argued. My eyelids fluttered open to the sound of Britney's "Work, Bitch" ringing in my ears and I wasn't entirely sure I hated Jihoon Kang anymore.

*

I was zoned out when I walked into the office on Christmas morning. My brain was somewhere between sleep – or lack thereof – and running through the schedule for the day, making sure I hadn't forgotten anything.

'Morning.' Jihoon greeted me when I walked past him.

'Morning,' I said, not realising until I was already at my desk that he was even there. And that he'd greeted me first. When I turned back to question him, he was holding the race car and staring at me with all the gleeful delight of a child.

'O-oh ...' *Shit.*

Panic welled up inside my chest. I'd left it on his desk, thinking that I'd have time between today and New Year's to decide whether to leave it there or not. He wasn't supposed to be here. My brain scrambled to think of something to say.

'Looks like Santa didn't forget you this year—' My laugh was tinged with awkward embarrassment, '—you must've been relatively good.'

'Well,' Jihoon started, flipping open the battery hatch and smiling when he saw that I'd already put batteries in it. 'I'm glad *someone* noticed my efforts.' He pushed the forward button on the remote and the wheels on the upside-down car spun to life. 'Why'd you get me this?' he asked, not looking at me. 'Is it because I put some Christmas lights up? Because, really, that was nothing.'

'Who says it was me?' I could hear my voice shaking and I prayed it wasn't as obvious to him as it was to me that I was completely freaking out.

'I mean, considering you're the only person I've ever told ... aside from my therapist ...' His chuckle was light. 'It's a pretty safe bet to guess. Especially because the only thing he ever gives me is the bill.'

'Right, well,' I stalled, blowing air out through my nose. 'I figured since you "Hunger Games'd" this job for your sister ...'

'Subtle way of asking why I did it.' He scoffed, arching an eyebrow. 'I've actually got a gift for you, too.'

This piqued my interest. 'Oh?' I scanned his desk for something either wrapped or shiny. 'What is it?'

'It's me.'

I felt my face fall and my heart thud against my chest. 'What?'

'N-not in a lawsuit kind of way,' he added, quickly. 'I'm here to take your classes today so that you can have the day off to ... spend with your boyfriend?' His nose wrinkled. 'Or Kevin, I suppose.'

'I appreciate the gesture,' I said. 'But you can't teach.'

'They're making sandwiches, right?' he asked. 'I can do that. Then we can watch a Christmas movie or something.'

'That's really sweet of you.' I smiled. 'But their parents would definitely complain if all they did was make sandwiches and watch a Christmas movie.'

'What kind of parents send their kids to school on Christmas Day, anyway?'

'Probably the same kind who send their kids to fancy schools overseas, but then don't get them a yellow race car for Christmas.' I winced. Maybe that was too harsh. I tapped my knuckle against my desk.

'You're definitely right.' Jihoon sighed. 'The worst kind of parents.' He dragged his finger across the wheels and their little motor squealed. 'I do love it, though. Thank you.'

'Don't let your sister crash this one,' I said. 'The insurance is already through the roof.' I wanted to pat myself on the back for sounding so casual when, internally, I was like a warzone.

We stood in amicable silence for the first time ever, until I decided it was probably time to go get the kitchen set up.

'I'm going to prepare the sandwiches and cookie dough,' I said. 'I really do appreciate you coming all the way here, though. Thank you.' I took a deep breath. 'Truth is, I offered to work today because I would prefer to be here, bitching about my job, martyring myself, and hanging out with ten-year-olds, than to be sitting alone in my apartment and commenting on Facebook statuses that say "I SAID YES!" or "BABY'S FIRST CHRISTMAS!", you know?'

'Trust me,' Jihoon said. 'I get it. I really didn't want to be at home today – Christmas is a point of contention in our house – so my present was a bit selfish, not even going to lie about it.' He placed the race car on his desk with gentle hands, as though it were made of glass. 'Come on, I'll help you set up.'

We made small talk while we turned on the heating in the classroom and kitchen and gathered the ingredients for the sandwiches and cookies. I was in the middle of preparing some spare dough in case the kids' dough went wrong when Jihoon pottered through the door of the kitchen with two Styrofoam cups of hot chocolate.

'I was wondering where you'd disappeared off to,' I said.

'The 7-Eleven is the only place open.' He placed one down in front of me. 'I figured their hot chocolate might be better than their crappy coffee.' He grimaced. 'I tried mine on the way back and I was wrong, but you can give it a go.'

'Thanks,' I said. 'I actually prefer tea and hot chocolate to coffee, so good call.'

'I did wonder why I never see you drinking coffee,' he said casually.

'You noticed that?'

'I notice a lot of things about you.' Jihoon studied me as though he was about to say something more, but chose instead to look over my head, out the window, and into the distance. He then stared at his cup for a few seconds before clearing his throat. 'My sister is getting married to a foreigner,' he said, a pained weight to his tone.

'I remember.' I didn't look up from the bowl of dough. 'Your dad thinks he's the devil.'

'She doesn't love him.'

That caught my attention. I looked up; my hands still squished into the dough.

'What?'

'She had this boyfriend before – he's the son of the Haneul Sek CEO.'

My mouth formed an 'o'. 'So, he's like … *rich* rich, then?'

Jihoon nodded. 'In Korean, we call them *chaebols*. Mom and Dad liked him, but I never did.'

I nodded, but didn't say anything.

'He ended up having an arranged marriage to some other rich heiress – someone much richer and more powerful than Dad.' Jihoon shook his head. 'My sister was so heartbroken that she left the country for a year and that's how she met David, her fiancé. David is …' Jihoon searched my eyes. 'He's *fine*. But, more importantly, he's wealthy and American, and Ji-hyeon doesn't want to be here anymore. Dad expects too much of her and all her friends still run in the same circles as her ex and his new wife.'

I nodded again. The dough was getting warm and sticky in the heat from my hands, but I didn't move.

'Ji-hyeon has always had her life together but then she got a call from that ex, saying he wanted to meet her – that he missed her – and she went. She took my car so that hers wouldn't be recognised if any of their friends were in the area and saw his car near it. You know how people talk …'
Jihoon clicked his tongue.

'Anyway, long story short, he made a pass at her and she refused. She took off, but she wasn't concentrating and crashed into a wall. She would've been arrested for the damages because she'd been drinking with him. Not a lot, but … enough. Enough that she'd be denied her visa for the States.' Jihoon's brow furrowed.

'She called me, so I asked a friend to drop me off and pick her up. We swapped, and then I called the police.' He fidgeted with his cup sleeve. 'Moving to the States is the only way she'll get out of running this place. I figured Dad wouldn't have me take it over – given my track record – and that he'd just sell it. Looks like I was wrong.'

'I'm going to pretend that you didn't just admit fraud and drink driving to me,' I said, finally pulling my hands out of the bowl. 'Because I probably would've done the same for my sister.'

'You have a sister?'

'A younger one,' I said. 'I miss her.' I dropped my gaze. 'You're different than I thought,' I admitted.

My phone buzzed. It was Mr. Kim, the security guard, letting me know that the kids had arrived. I covered the bowl in cling film and stuck it into the fridge.

'So …' I pursed my lips, unsure of how to continue the conversation. 'Do you want a crash course in Camp Teaching?' I threw a smile at Jihoon.

'Sure,' he said, stretching out his shoulders and neck. 'I think I got this.'

*

Neither Jihoon nor I got anything other than a splitting headache. From the second the parents dropped the kids off at the door, they were screaming and crying and running around, tearing things down.

'I can see now why their parents wanted to get rid of them for the day,' I whispered, instantly regretting giving them *any* food substances when a slice of tomato flew past my head. 'I say we hype them up on sugar right before we hand them back as punishment to the parents for doing this to us.'

Jihoon's laugh rumbled deep in his chest. 'I like that plan,' he said, picking up the tomato slice and tossing it into the bin. 'Cleaning up is going to be fun. How do you *do* this every day?'

'It's actually pretty great when the students aren't …' I pressed my lips together. 'Spoiled, little rich kids.'

'Aha.' Jihoon nudged me with his shoulder. 'Funny.'

'Teacher, is that your boyfriend?' one of the students asked.

I opened my mouth to respond but was cut off when Jihoon's phone vibrated, and he cheered quietly.

'You're going to like this,' he told me. 'I made amends with an old foe for you.'

'Excuse me?' I couldn't even begin to decipher what he could possibly mean by that.

'Okay, everyone!' Jihoon shoved the phone into his pocket and clapped his hands. 'Santa's here!'

I spun to stare at him. 'Santa?'

'Hey,' he said. 'Even spoiled, little rich kids need Santa in their lives.'

I couldn't argue with that.

*

Trying to wrangle a bunch of ten-year-olds who don't speak the same language as you is difficult, even at the best of times. But these kids were wild, dosed up on Christmas cookies, and very unimpressed by the lessons I'd prepared. I was beginning to think this was some sort of divine punishment for a sin I'd not yet committed. I was about to give up and just let them trash the place when a voice from the doorway brought with it a fascinated lull.

'Ho, ho, ho!'

I bit back a flabbergasted laugh when I realised the man in the Santa suit was none other than Jihoon. I'd half expected him to just pay someone to be Santa – because that seemed like the sane thing to do – but this I hadn't anticipated at all.

'I heard there were some kids here who haven't had get their presents yet!' Jihoon shook a red, fluffy bag and the boxes inside it bumped off each other.

One of the kids muttered something in Korean and Jihoon tutted.

'This place is a mess,' he said. 'Nobody is getting anything until this kitchen is cleaner than it was when you arrived.'

None of the kids moved and one of them mumbled the word I recognised as being Korean for "what?"

Jihoon sighed and repeated himself in Korean and suddenly the room was a flurry of excitement and, to my surprise, tidying-up.

Once the kitchen was spick and span, Jihoon rallied the troops into the classroom he had decorated. I had to admit that his decorations were nicer than mine, but I'd never tell him that, even under duress.

'Who wants to go first?' Jihoon asked. 'What about ...' He scanned the kids, and they all blinked up at him expectantly. 'Erik?'

The smallest boy – the one who had started the food flinging fiesta – ran forward and sprung into the air, landing on Jihoon's lap. Jihoon winced, and I covered a chuckle with my hand.

'What do I have here for you, Erik?' Jihoon's voice was jolly and deep, and he pulled out a parcel, handing it to the little black-haired boy. 'Can you tell me what this is in English?'

'Umm ...'

'Puh ... puh ...' Jihoon prompted. 'Present,' he finished when Erik didn't guess it. 'Can you say it with me?'

I smiled, softening towards Jihoon as I watched him with the kids. He got each kid to say the word 'present' before he gave it to them and then waited for them to open it before he called the next kid up. Erik got a soccer ball, Jay got a teddy bear, Stella got a colouring book and two packets of crayons, and Jenny got a set of toy trains.

I would have to ask Jihoon later how he had known exactly what each of them wanted.

Jihoon played soccer with Erik while I coloured with Stella. I heard him say 'goal' over and over again until Erik was finally shouting 'goal' every time he kicked the ball past Jihoon. I saw the delight in Jihoon's eyes when Erik remembered the word.

When the time came to clean up and send the kids home, I packed the trains and then turned to help Stella tidy her crayons up.

'Hmm,' I said, counting them. 'It seems you've lost one.' I gave Stella a smile and pointed to the pack in her hands. 'This one has less crayons in it.'

'Fewer,' Jihoon corrected me without missing a beat, before gasping at himself and then cursing under his breath. '*Kevin*,' he snarled.

I let out a loud laugh and Stella looked at me like I was insane.

'It's a weird feeling,' I said, knowing she wouldn't understand. 'When you don't like someone and then you start to feel like you do. Sometimes you just have to laugh about it.' I moved some hair out of her eyes. 'Maybe someday you'll get it.' I blinked, shaking my head and expelling the thought. I'd unpack that later, I figured.

I looked over my shoulder at Jihoon, who was nonchalantly trying to pull a wedgie from his Santa suit trousers. I chewed my cheeks to stop myself from smiling. I suddenly couldn't believe it had taken me this long to see Jihoon as a real person and not just an inconvenience. I let my hair fall in front of my face and turned my attention back to Stella, when Jihoon caught my eye and his cheeks reddened from being caught in the act of wedgie removal. My smile escaped.

I was ready to fall face-first into my bed by the time we waved the kids off and wandered back up to the office. Because Santa had been such a huge success, the parents promised they would send the kids back again next Christmas as though they were doing us a huge service. I made a mental note to have absolutely quit by then.

'Hey,' I said, loitering at my desk instead of just grabbing my things and going home. 'Thanks for coming today. And for all your help.'

'I had fun,' Jihoon replied. 'Much more than if I'd been at home. *And* I got a race car.'

'How did you organise the Santa suit so quickly?' I asked, smiling as he took off the beard and laid it out on his desk with care.

'I have a few friends who are actors, and now I owe one of them a lot of money ...' his laugh was light. '... but it was worth it to see how happy it made the kids. I gave Santa a pretty hard time all these years, but he's not so bad.'

'You know ...' my tone was coy, '... you're also not the worst trainee teacher I've ever seen. You've got potential.'

Jihoon tapped his fingers against the back of his phone rhythmically. 'I have to admit,' he said, 'I surprised myself with how much I enjoyed it. There's something so joyful about watching a kid learn English from you – even if it's just one word and even if it's through games. I'll have to apologise to Kevin.' He shook his head. 'Any chance I could be a teacher instead of the manager?'

'You'll have to talk to HR about that,' I said.

'How do I get into HR's good books?' he asked.

'Well,' I said, giving him a smile. 'You're looking at her.'

Jihoon smiled back. 'I know,' he said. 'How am I doing?'

I felt my cheeks heat. 'Pretty good.' I nodded, dropping my gaze.

The little motor of the race car whirled to life as it tried to make its way over to me, only to get stuck on the cables.

'I'll get it,' I said, but we both made it to the race car at the same time. The mistletoe was taped to the top of it.

I wrinkled my nose up at it. 'Why is the mistletoe taped to your car?'

'Christy didn't seem to like it on the door,' Jihoon said, releasing the car from its masking tape prison. 'Plus, I didn't want to take any chances that you'd kiss Kevin.'

'I'd never—' I started, but then stopped and glanced up.

We were both crouched down at the cables and Jihoon was staring at me with a soft hopefulness, a red tint creeping up his cheeks.

'There's a note ...' He nodded to the car. 'I was trying to be romantic, but those cables ...'

'Every damn time,' I mumbled, picking up the note from the hood of the car.

'Meet me under the mistletoe?'

I read the words twice and then eyed the race car. 'It's going to be difficult to fit in that car,' I said. 'But I'll try.'

Jihoon rolled his eyes. 'You're so pedantic,' he said, grabbing the mistletoe and standing up, holding his hand out for mine.

I took it and he helped me up, his thumb grazing over my knuckles as I stood. My heart thumped in my chest, and I was afraid to look at him in case my face gave away my nerves. Instead, I stared at my hand in his; the way his tan skin looked against mine, the tiny freckles dotted across his fingers, his nails bitten around the edges. The movement of his other arm, as he held the mistletoe over our heads, caught my attention and I went to look at it too, but my eyes locked with his.

'Can I kiss you?' he asked gently.

I held my breath so I wouldn't gulp out my reply. I tried to steady my voice as the word formed on my tongue.

'Yes.' I whispered.

He squeezed a little on my hand as he pulled me closer, my shoulder connecting with his. The arm that was holding the mistletoe dropped so that his hand landed on my other shoulder, then trailed down onto my waist. The hairs on my arms tingled as goosebumps zinged all over my body. His fingers nudged my waist, bringing us closer, so that our noses touched, and I wrapped my arms around his neck, feeling his breath on my face. He closed the gap, pressing his lips against mine. His kiss was tentative and careful, and I felt the mistletoe brush against my cheek as he let it go and it fell to the floor.

After a moment, he pulled back, leaving me frazzled.

'Happy … uh,' I blinked. 'Merry … um. Merry Christmas,' I said.

'Merry Christmas, Paige,' he whispered.

I searched his eyes for the cheeky glint that I was so used to, finally understanding that it had always been aimed at me and wasn't just his general state of being. I flashed him what I hoped was an equally cheeky grin and pulled him back in for our second kiss.

Hayley-Jenifer Brennan

Dominick the Donkey

Donna Gowland

'You got any plans for Christmas?'

Justin stretched back nonchalantly, forming triangles with his arms, giving Sam the faintest hint of his divine aftershave and the hidden curve of his biceps. It was enough to catch her off guard. Her mouth went dry, and her pulse started racing. This was it. This was the moment she'd waited for, when she'd finally get an invitation to the secret VIP event they sponsored. Could she even pretend that she hadn't dreamt of this moment ever since she'd started working for him, and lusting after him, six years ago?

Her mind rolled out the scene as she'd pictured it: a quaint cottage snowed into the middle of nowhere; a front door ringed with a wreath of holly and mistletoe; Justin's lips meeting hers in front of a blazing log fire; and a glorious Christmas tree sparkling its approval from the corner of the room. Perhaps he'd be wearing a Christmas jumper, but, if her imagination had its way, he wouldn't even be wearing that for very long. Sam sighed loudly, and the sound of Justin's cough brought her back to attention.

'Well, Sam, are you free?'

Sam scoured his gaze for the slightest glimmer of hope and expectation, but he was looking at her with the bemused urgency that accompanied a request she hadn't quite understood or was taking too long to answer.

'It's just that I know you don't have children, or a partner, and you always kind of tag along to other people's Christmases,' Justin continued.

Sam's Christmas spirit sank to the floor. Angry tears sprang unexpectedly to her eyes, and she held on to the walnut table to keep herself upright, even though his words ripped through her. The table's highly polished surface reflected her sad, pale face back at her – why had she thought he might be interested in her? People like her never got a happily ever after, so the chances of a Christmas miracle were even fewer and farther between. No, that face staring back at her was a ghost with nothing but memories of Christmases past. She'd been a fool to hope that she might have a future.

'I don't tag onto – I go to my sister's house – which is actually half mine …'

Her cheeks flushed; why was she attempting to justify herself to him? What difference did any of it make to him? None. She bit her lip, desperate to stop the emotion overwhelming her.

'It's just, we sponsor a charity event – we always have – it's good publicity but an absolute ball-ache. You'd get there on Christmas Eve, show your face at the event, travel back Boxing Day. All on company expenses, of course. You would be doing me a massive, massive *personal* favour.'

He tilted his face and Sam was mesmerised by his large blue eyes: oceanic pools that drew her in, and made saying anything other than "yes" impossible. Sam pursed her lips into reluctant acceptance and Justin clapped his hands together, smiling like a superhero who'd just saved a city.

'We'll pay for your train tickets and accommodation. You'll only have to show your face at the event, smile and shake hands with a few people – be the face of the company – and the rest of the time would be your own.'

She'd been half-right then. Justin *had* been thinking of Sam spending Christmas in a ramshackle, middle-of-nowhere town; he'd just never intended to go with her. Sam cast her gaze towards the city streets below their offices. The sky over Covent Garden was darkening, and a sea of stars waved through the winter skyline, suspended at the end of crystal ropes like trapeze artists. Crowds scuttled past like ants under the golden streetlamps, huddled in their coats. Sam sighed as she pictured couples holding hands, snuggled in their affection. A shiver ran through her. She pulled the documents tightly to her.

'So, whereabouts am I going?'

*

Sam had her eyes closed and her hands clenched for the entire journey; but thanks to the taxi-driver's constant narrative, she hadn't missed a beat of the hazardous journey. Justin had told her it was a stone's throw from the local train station, but the "stone" turned out to be a hill – and one that was almost impossible to climb. The hum of Christmas songs from the intermittent radio added nothing to the scene. When she finally opened her eyes, Sam felt like she'd been beamed onto another planet, one with nothing but snow-covered hills, and a darkness that stuck to her throat like treacle; the sky didn't *seem* to be the colour of mud, it was mud.

'Welcome to Wales.' The taxi driver chuckled.

Sam gulped. 'Right,' was all she could think of saying. She scrambled in her purse for a tip.

'The village centre is over there.' He pointed into the distance, past a grim field where a single yellow light quivered. 'I'll take your things to the castle, but I can't drive you there because the bridge is closed.'

'Closed?' Sam stammered, wondering how a bridge could be closed on Christmas Eve. The taxi driver nodded, making the briefest of eye contact in the rear-view mirror. 'Digger's going to pick you up.'

'A digger?' Sam's mind desperately tried to keep up with all these changes, but failed spectacularly. 'A digger is taking me to the event?' She sighed. 'And are you still collecting me from the hotel on …?'

She wasn't certain of anything anymore; she still didn't really know why she was here or what the event was. Justin had been irritatingly vague about it all. Her heart sank at the thought of how desperate he'd been to get her out of the way.

'I'm collecting you on Boxing Day. I've got another appointment, so I'm going to have to let you out now. Digger should be here soon.' The taxi driver turned to her, his face creased into an unconvincing attempt at a sympathetic smile. Sam looked out of the window. Even the trees were shivering. 'It's only a couple of fields to the village hall. You'll be there in no time. If Digger doesn't show, start walking.'

Sam's cheeks burned. Had he suggested walking? In these boots? If she'd known she was walking hills, she wouldn't have worn her best designer boots.

'So, I'm going down there, where that light is?' she gulped.

'That's right. It's just down the hill and over the field.'

'Down the hill?' A wave of panic flushed through her. 'Can't you drive me to the bottom of it?' She pleaded. 'Can't I get to the castle and then go to the village hall?'

'Wrong direction, I'm afraid. It's a maze down there, but the bridge will be open again after the show.'

The blood rushed to her ears, and a determination to show him she didn't need his help, or anyone else's, gripped Sam. What type of place had Justin dragged her to and what did he mean by "show"? She'd seen "The Wicker Man" and she was ready to run at the first glimpse of animal heads and floral headpieces – even in these boots.

'No, I'll manage.' She steadied herself to step out into the darkness and shuffled down the seat towards the door, ready to propel herself out as if jumping out of a plane.

'Well, if you're sure …'

The taxi moved off before she'd even closed the door and the surprise movement shoved her forward. A signpost halted her fall, and she clung to it with gratitude.

'Thanks for the tip!'

The taxi driver waved at her as he drove past, taking all her possessions with him except the clothes she was wearing, and a mobile phone that was about as much use as a brick. If there wasn't any electricity around here, then there sure as sheep wouldn't be any Wi-Fi. On cue, a lone sheep bleated a welcome. Or was it a warning? Sam couldn't tell.

She surveyed the land in front of her – a downhill walk, then a hop over a field; that was what he'd said, wasn't it? Surely it couldn't be that difficult, could it? Her teeth chattered but Sam didn't mind, she was grateful for the anything that might warm her up. When she went to prise herself away from the signpost, her palm was reluctant to move. She twisted it, desperate for the heat to return to her blue fingers, until it finally came away, the friction from holding onto it burning her palm. Sam winced, shook her hand, and blew on it, then looked around in the darkness. How could it be so dark? It wasn't even mid-afternoon.

Why hadn't Justin warned her about this?

'You okay there? Are you lost?'

A stentorian voice shouted across the misty darkness.

She resisted the temptation to twirl around, aware that any sudden movement might tempt the delicate arrangement of her feet on the patchy terrain.

'I … er … I've got to go to the Light Festival … in the village, but the taxi driver left me here, and I've got to get down there and up there, and I haven't got a clue where I'm going. I'm waiting for a digger?' The words spewed out of her mouth before she could stop them.

'Not a digger. Digger. That's me. I'm going to the Light Festival too. Everyone else is already there. I'm late, as always. You ready?'

A man stepped out of the shadows, and Sam caught the scent of his light, fresh aftershave. It was clean and functional, nothing like the thick, musky one that entered the room before Justin did. What was the better option here? she mused, freezing to death on the top of a slope; being eaten alive by sheep or wolves – or whatever else roamed the darkness – or getting a lift with a man she didn't know, to a place she couldn't name? There was no way of raising an S.O.S here, no three words to tell anyone of her location apart from the three words "I AM LOST," which wouldn't be much use to anyone.

'The taxi driver said you can't get to the castle by car. Can you get there by car? Why is it so difficult to get anywhere around here …?'

What was it with her word vomit? The words flew out before she could stop them. Talk about looking a gift horse in the mouth. 'I'm sorry …' she added, hoping that he wouldn't retract his offer.

'No bother, Dave's right, you can't get there by taxi if the bridge is closed, but you can get to town by quad bike.'

'Quad bike?' Sam's stomach somersaulted.

'It's quicker, and safer, than walking. And it's our field, so, at least we won't get told off by the farmer. Here.'

A torchlight flickered on; the yellow glow looked sickly against the landscape, streaking anything it landed on with an eggy glow. The man turned it around the field, then on to himself. Sam gulped, willing herself to remember all his features in case she needed to give the police an accurate description later.

'I'm Digger,' he said, repeating his earlier confirmation of the same.

He held the torch to the side of his face; his features were haloed beneath it. Everything about him was the opposite of Justin: his hair was black, thick, and unruly, like a bramble bush; his eyebrows were dark caterpillars framing his square face, and his eyes perfectly matched the depth of the dark landscape that engulfed them. Something in the openness of his face, and the kindness in his eyes, put Sam at ease. She could almost forget that she was about to get on a quad bike to go down a hill and over a field – at least she wouldn't be able to see where they were going this time.

'Come on.'

Digger flashed the torch at his arm and gestured for Sam to link arms with him. As she complied, she felt a sense of peace that she hadn't felt for a long time, as if something, somewhere, were slotting into place; but that was ridiculous. He was a stranger, helping her out, that was all, and she … she was there to show her face at an event and then get the first train out of there on Boxing Day.

'I'm Sam,' she said as they walked towards the bike, nestled in a shed that stood out like a ramshackle cardboard box on the horizon.

'Well, Sam, I hope you enjoy the Living Nativity. It's a big deal around here.' Digger smiled as he passed her a helmet. 'Here, put this on.'

Even through the darkness, Sam could see the mud splattered across it. Or, at least, she hoped it was mud. Her mind raced. No Christmas songs or carols were rolling through her mind, just an unfamiliar chant that she'd never sang before and couldn't imagine she'd ever need to sing again. It went something like this – *Please don't let him be a serial killer, please don't let him be a serial killer, please don't let him be a serial killer.*

*

The village green shimmered like a sweet wrapper. Everywhere Sam looked, there were candles and garlands of lights frosting every tree and bush, adorning every surface. She had either opened her eyes in the right place, or she'd landed in heaven, just in time for Christmas Eve. A warm aroma of cinnamon and spices pricked her nostrils – this was heaven, but definitely the living kind.

'See. I didn't kill us, did I?' Digger turned to face her; his curls were wet with frost that made the golden lights slide off them in thick strips. He looked like an angel. He'd certainly saved her a trip or two.

'The castle – where I presume you're staying, it's where everyone stays – is just over there.'

Sam gasped. A tall gothic castle towered over the village like a giant. Even from this distance, Sam could see the blazing Christmas lights and lush decorations on the door and in every window; if it were that opulent from the outside, she could only imagine the luxury inside. Her heart soared. It wouldn't be such a bad Christmas, after all.

'Digger, I see you've met our city friend.'

Sam squinted; she vaguely recognized the man striding towards them but couldn't quite place him.

'Told you it was easy to get down the hill!'

'You could have given her a lift, Dave,' Digger jostled at Dave light heartedly.

The laugh cinched it. The taxi driver. Annoyance swirled in her chest. If he'd known where she was going and that he was going to the same place, why on earth put her through all that? She looked down at her boots and jeans: mud, snow, and flecks of dead grass from ankle to kneecap. The boots had perished, but at least she was alive. No thanks to Dave.

'And miss out on the fun, no chance. Well, she's here safely now, isn't she?'

Sam pouted. Though she wanted to give Dave a piece of her mind, she reminded herself that she was here as an ambassador for the brand, and she had a job to do, same as everyone else – including Dave.

'I've got to speak to the mayor.' She quickly scanned past the rows of people decked out in wintry coats, hats and scarves, all brandishing candles and brightly coloured lanterns.

'I've got to get into costume, so I'll leave you to it.' Digger replied.

'Get into costume?' Sam asked.

'Yes, I'm in the Living Nativity. I've got the lead.' A proud smile spread across Digger's face.

'Oh, yes, Digger, who are you playing, the donkey?' Dave laughed.

'No, we've borrowed Mr. McGregor's rescue donkey, Dominick, for that.'

Keen to get it over with, Sam coughed before speaking. 'I'd better find the mayor, please excuse me,' Sam smiled sweetly at Dave, who burst into uproarious laughter again, so much so he could hardly speak. Sam felt the eyes of the entire village boring into her. Dave held out his hand.

'I *am* the mayor, the taxi driver, and the village dogsbody. It's nice to meet you again.'

*

The villagers assembled around a giant Christmas tree which lived anonymously next to the unassuming white chapel, but came alive and brought the community together at Christmas. It reached into the skyline, stretching out as high as the church's spire, and its golden star looked like it was neck-and-neck with the weathervane in an imaginary race. The tree was decked with scarves of tinsel, sprigs of fresh mistletoe, holly and ivy and tear shaped crystals that shimmered.

Sam held a mug of mulled wine and a homemade mince pie that a kindly woman with sparkling eyes had handed her wordlessly. For a minute, she'd wondered what the catch would be, then had the realisation that there wasn't one. Kindness and magic infused the air and Sam relaxed. She could not see why it was so important for a representative from the firm to be here, or even why they sponsored a small village event in the middle of nowhere. Still, everyone had been welcoming and their mince pies were something else. The choir started singing carols, the sweet voices adding to the general feeling of serenity. Sam didn't feel like a stranger here. She had the overwhelming sensation of being exactly where she was supposed to be.

The carol singing was swiftly replaced by a brass band. As the trumpets started their B flat verse of "In the Bleak Midwinter" her mind travelled back to her childhood and their annual Christmas shopping trip with her parents. This had been her father's favourite tradition. Every year after her father's death, she and her mother had made a pilgrimage of it. They had listened to the song holding hands, aware of his absence, which gripped their hearts. As the years went by, Sam had seen the song as a symbol of him, a way to remember him. Now that her mother was gone too, Sam placed them both in the song and imagined them listening to it together somewhere.

She felt a tap on her shoulder.

'Sam, Sam … I need your help!'

Digger's voice, soft and pleading, made her turn.

'Why? What is the matter? Oh, my …'

The sight of Digger made her jaw drop in disbelief. She had never seen a full-grown man dressed as a nativity Joseph before. Was that … a green and white teacloth on his head?

'There's a sick bug going around. It's taken down Mary and all the W.I. You're the last woman standing, I'm afraid. You're going to have to stand in … Please.'

'Me?' she squealed, incredulous. Finding her voice, she added, 'I can't act!'

'If you can shove a cushion up your front, put on the blue dress and headpiece, and rub your back, you can do it! If you say no, we're going to have a seventy-year-old or a seven-year-old Mary, and either of those would just be wrong.'

They separated from the crowd, aware of the disapproving glances they were getting for disturbing the brass band. It was only when they had moved to the side of the tree, away from everyone else, that she realized he was holding her hand.

'Please, Sam, you're our only hope.'

Her mind flashed back to Justin, how he would turn on the charm when he wanted something. Digger had none of that self-awareness, the only expression that flashed across his face was desperation.

'Please.' He continued. 'I helped you when you needed it. If you had broken a leg getting over that stile or rolling down that hill, you wouldn't be happy, would you?'

'No, Digger, you're right, I wouldn't be,' she conceded, rolling her eyes at his exaggerated example. With a reluctant sigh she said, 'Okay, I will be Mary … what do I have to do?'

'You will? Oh, bless you.'

Digger put an arm around her shoulder, hugged her to him, and kissed her on the cheek. When he moved his lips away, the space felt cold. Sam's stomach flipped as if she were a shaken-up snow globe. They stared at each other in mutual confusion. Sam thought a spark fizzed between them, and had an overwhelming urge to kiss him on the lips. But that was ridiculous and inappropriate – she was about to have another man's child, after all.

'Come on, quickly. You don't have long to learn the lines. We need to get you into costume.'

'Is it a better costume than yours?'

'It's got a newer teacloth, if that's what you're asking.'

Sam put her arm around Digger's waist, and they strode off together, past the crowd listening to the band playing 'Lonely This Christmas.' At that precise moment in time, Sam felt anything but lonely.

*

'So, you know your positions? Where you go? How you walk the donkey?' The director wiped his forehead. For an amateur production in a small Welsh village, they were taking it seriously. It was, Sam learned as she put the blue dress over her head and the cushion around her stomach, the highlight of the Living Nativity. At least she had finally discovered why she was here; the firm sponsored the Living Nativity every year, but this year they had been told that the boss was coming so they'd gone all out to make sure it was better than ever. Sam's nerves doubled at the thought that Justin could still turn up, especially now she had been roped in for a reluctant Mary.

'… And I won't even tell you the trouble we had in finding a real donkey! Sheep? Coming out of our ears. Horses even, but donkeys? Here? No.' A ruddy-cheeked villager spoke.

'Alwyn, I told you it would be fine.' Digger soothed. 'It's going to be great, and there's no pressure from the company because she *is* the representative, and there's no sign of Justin.' He turned to Sam and said pointedly, 'and you're going to go back and tell them how wonderful it all is, aren't you, Sam?'

Now that she was decked out in her Virgin Mary costume, a religious serenity passed over her. Sam nodded meekly in response.

'See! She's already miles better than the last one.' Digger clapped his hands together. 'Right, someone get Dominick and then we're ready to roll.'

An orchestral version of "Silent Night" piped through unseen speakers, and Digger held the donkey's reins in one hand, and put his other hand on the curve of Sam's spine. Everywhere he touched generated electricity which buzzed around her. He smiled at her, and when she smiled back, Sam felt as though an invisible force was weaving them together. If that was acting, he had the combined skills of Richard Burton and Michael Sheen – with a good dollop of a young Tom Jones on the side. Why weren't there more men like this in London? Perhaps if there had been, or she'd noticed them, she wouldn't have wasted so much time on Justin. Looking at Digger made it harder to picture Justin's face, as if he were in the rear-view mirror of her life and she was accelerating away. Sam had always thought that only the streets of London were paved with gold. She had to admit that there was more than a shimmer here, too.

The first of the four points successfully navigated, Sam congratulated herself on remembering her few lines and standing in the right place at the right time. GCSE Drama had finally come in useful. As they walked through the glistening village, it opened like a shell, each stage lovingly created and beautifully painted. By the time they reached the third inn and the penultimate point of the play, the familiarity between her and Digger felt like a tentative intimacy that was growing with each step. Even the night sky joined in; their audience multiplied a thousand times by the blanket of stars that swelled the skyline. An owl, cutting a swarth of creamy white into the night sky, temporarily stole the show and made the (easily distracted) boy playing the innkeeper momentarily forget his lines. The crowd laughed, the boy smiled too, said his lines perfectly, and the show continued to its final stage.

When they reached it, Sam gasped. It was a large, painted stable, rich with reds and golds. Everything was handmade and perfect. The manger for the baby was made from local reeds, painstakingly woven from willow. The lights that shivered above the heads of the cast matched those that lined the village, and even the blue of the blanket matched her costume. The colour made her think of Justin for a moment, his blue eyes proving harder to forget than she'd thought.

She looked at Digger. His features came into focus and Justin disintegrated into fog. The lights and music quietened; this was the part where she was supposed to give birth. There was a five-minute break in the action, where the spotlight would fall on the casting of a star into the night sky, symbolising the Star of David.

'If I don't do this now, I don't think I ever will ...'

Digger shuffled his feet in front of her as she tried to disengage the cushion from the dress. The baby doll that was currently hidden behind a hay bale was waiting for its starring moment.

'What's the matter, Digger?'

His face crumpled; his brows tightly knitted together under the teacloth. He couldn't be losing his nerve now, they were over the hard part. All they had to do now was welcome the three wise men, sing "Away in a Manger" and then they were home free.

'Can you help me with this cushion? I think it's a bit stuck.' Sam giggled.

Digger inhaled. 'It's stuck in the zip, sorry. I think I'm going to have to pull it away.'

His hands were on her back, moving along the cushion before finding the join in the zip. Sam's breath quickened; she closed her eyes.

'Nearly there. Hold on. I'm going to pull it, get ready, on three – one, two ...'

He pulled at the cushion, which came free and landed on the ground seconds before they did. She was in his arms, and it felt like the only place to be.

'Can I kiss you? I think I'm going to explode if I don't ...' Digger blurted, before shaking his head and pulling back. 'No, I'm sorry ... I –' He levered himself up and turned away.

Sam rushed to him, pausing for a heartbeat to look into his deep, earnest eyes before crushing her mouth to his in a kiss that made her head swim and her heart feel like she was shooting up into the sky. Just then, the white star's beam shot back at them, and the crowd saw them kissing, whooped, and clapped. Fireworks went off from behind the castle, puncturing the sky with shards of neon rainbows. The donkey seemed to give its approval brayed in bellowing brays, but then –

'The donkey's collapsed.' A voice shouted.

The wise man carrying the gold dropped his gold coins to the floor and Sam and Digger pulled apart, racing back to the donkey, who was panting on the straw.

'What's wrong with it?' Sam's voice was a whisper.

'I think she is going into foal …' Digger scratched his temples and turned to Dave. 'I thought you said it was called Dominick?'

'It is!' Dave cried. 'But old McGregor's only had it a few hours, and his eyesight isn't what it was – I didn't think we'd need to do a DNA test on it!'

'What do we do?' Sam's heart was pounding, her head thick with the guilt of her own uselessness in this situation. 'Do we get towels, hot water?'

'It's not Call the Midwife.' Dave tutted, moving past her to get a better look at the donkey. 'Donkeys know what to do, same as humans. We leave her to it and help if she gets in any trouble.'

'Switch that enormous light off,' Digger shielded his eyes as he called to the stage crew. 'She'll want a bit of privacy.'

'What do I do? What do we do?'

Alongside Sam's growing sense of panic was a secret annoyance that her starring moment with Digger had been overshadowed by the Donkey. Talk about stealing the spotlight!

'Not a lot we can do here; we're all as helpful – or as useless – as one another in this situation.' Digger chewed his lip. 'What I mean to say is: we're all farmers, so any of us can help or hinder as much as the other and poor Daisy here's got enough of an audience.'

'Have you just re-named the donkey?' Sam smiled.

'Can't be calling her Dominick now, can we?' Their eyes met and they hovered in awkward anticipation of each other's next move. Digger broke the silence. 'I don't know about you, but I could do with another mulled wine. Shall we sneak back to the village hall?'

'Will it still be open?'

'Open?' Digger raised his eyebrows. 'We never lock it. Come on.'

They rushed away, the ends of their costumes flapping in the early evening sky like a festive Batman and Robin. It really was a different world here. As far away from London as the moon from the stars. But Sam felt at home. Even though she'd only been here for a couple of hours, the thought of leaving on Boxing Day – and never seeing Digger again – made her heart ache.

'I suppose you work in the head office in London?' He asked, as they sat on a hay-bale next to the Christmas tree.

'Yes, I do.' Sam nodded. She didn't even want to think about it now. 'And I'll be going back on Boxing Day, but I'd rather not think about that, now. I'd rather spend time with you.'

That silenced him, and he grinned from ear to ear.

'Well, I suppose we'd better not waste all our time talking …'

He stroked her face, and Sam kissed him. The night sky and all its stars swam around her head as she lost herself in the moment. It seemed to last forever.

'It's beautiful here, isn't it?' Sam sighed, once they'd stopped kissing. 'I never knew places like this existed. I've always lived and holidayed in cities.'

'You've never been to Wales before?' A splash of colour dotted his cheeks, and Digger laughed. 'You've been missing out.'

'Yes.' She laughed too. 'I'm starting to think that way myself.'

'Do you think I could come to London and take you out?'

'Take me out? What are you, a hitman?'

'Oh, heavens no, I don't mean like that. I mean, I could take you to dinner, to a show – whatever you city types do for enjoyment.'

'We do the same as everyone else. There's just more of it there.' Sam blushed at the thought of a date with Digger. Of all the things they could get up to. 'Have you, er, been to London?'

'Yes.' Digger sniffed. 'Many times. My brother lives there.'

'Oh, that's good.' Sam felt herself beaming. She was trying – and failing – to play it cool, but the prospect of seeing him again made her fizzy with excitement. 'Should we swap numbers, or social media, or something?'

'Social media?' Digger slapped his hand on his knee. 'I don't do social media! I have a phone number, but I don't have my phone with me – no pockets in this costume.'

Sam felt the fabric of her Mary dress. No pockets on hers either. The phones were back in the changing room at the village school. She shivered, feeling the chance for happiness slipping away as she tried to grasp it with both hands.

'Are you cold?' Digger looked at her. The moonlight shadowed his cheekbones; his face was perfect. She'd never wanted to kiss anyone more in her entire life. He moved closer to her. 'Shall I put my arms around you? Keep you warm.'

Sam nodded, and Digger wrapped her up in his arms. Now it felt like the moon was shining on them. It was them against the darkness. Nothing else mattered in the world.

'Digger?' she asked, scuffing her feet on the frosty ground beneath them. 'Do you think it would be okay if I kissed you again?' She smirked; it had sounded much better coming from him.

'Well, I don't know …' he flapped the teacloth behind his ear. 'I mean, technically I'm married to Mary, but I don't think she'll mind, do you?'

Sam smiled and cupped his head in her hands. When she brought her lips to his skin, she noticed the veins in his neck twitching like a frog's legs. She

143

was sure he felt it too – this powerful energy between them, this attraction. It made everything she'd felt for Justin seem childish in comparison. She was thankful that Justin had never given her the time of day. If he had, she may never have come here – never have met Digger.

They kissed until the bells pealed for midnight and a light layer of snow fell like confetti around them, frosting their lips as they parted.

'We completely forgot about Daisy. Should we go and check on her?' Sam asked, getting up from the seat.

'I'm sure Daisy's in safe hands.' Digger wrapped his arm around her, and they walked back to the Nativity. The midnight sky was quiet and calm, all was still and even. A crowd of locals sat around the front of the stage, where Daisy was licking the newly born foal who nestled snuggly to her.

'Is it okay? Is everyone okay?' Sam whispered.

'She's fine. They both are. She's had a baby boy. We've called him Dominick and we've renamed her Mary.' An elderly lady with twinkly eyes smiled up at Sam. Digger pulled her closer to him.

'Don't worry, Digger. Daisy can be her middle name.' Sam whispered to him. They giggled and Digger kissed the side of her head.

'Right, now you two lovebirds have graced us with your presence, can we finish the Living Nativity?' the lady said to Digger. 'We don't want your brother cutting off our money because we didn't finish the story.'

'Your brother?' Sam frowned. 'What's your brother got to do with it?'

'Didn't you know? Hasn't he ever mentioned me?' Digger shook his head. 'Sounds like Justin – far too wrapped up in himself to be concerned with anything that's happening here.'

'You're *Justin's* brother?' Sam shrieked, slumping down on a hay-bale as the words swam around her head.

'Twin brother.' Digger continued. 'You wouldn't believe it, would you? He's got all the blonde heartthrob looks and business brain and I've got … this!'

Digger stretched out his arms. The snow fell into his palms and into his hair, flickers of white melting into the dark curls.

'I've never envied Justin's life before – he can keep his rat race,' Digger continued. 'I've always been happy here, but now …' He paused, a twinkle in his eye. 'I'll admit I'm jealous he's worked with you for years, while I've only known you for a couple of hours.'

'You're Justin's brother,' Sam repeated. 'I can't believe it.'

'Does it change anything?' Digger asked, his forehead creased with concern. 'It doesn't change anything for me, Sam. The way I feel about you has nothing to do with my brother.'

'I just … would never have known it,' she said, her head and heart frantically trying to join her thoughts together.

'I know I don't have his money or fancy ways.' Digger bit his lip.

'No, but you have kindness, beauty, and modesty …' Sam smiled, taking his hand. 'And that, if you'll forgive my saying, is something that Justin definitely lacks.'

'So, you don't mind? It doesn't bother you?'

'Not a bit.' Sam shook her head fiercely. 'It doesn't bother me if it doesn't bother you. It isn't as though I work for you, is it?'

Digger edged closer to her. Sam loved that they'd fallen into this easy rhythm; they had their own shorthand, and it seemed so natural; unlike anything she'd experienced before.

'I mean, he has an ancillary office here in Bethlehem, so you could always work here if things go well.' He smiled. Digger's eyes shone with the same optimism as hers, and Sam had no doubt they were on the same page.

'Come back with me to the castle. Let's spend Christmas Day together and see how we get on,' Sam whispered in his ear.

Digger stepped back to look at her, scanning her face as if checking to see that he'd fully understood what she was saying. Sam smiled and nodded her head.

'So, this really *is* a living nativity.' Sam laughed. 'We're in Bethlehem. We've got a donkey called Mary, a plastic baby Jesus, three wise men and a fake Joseph …'

'Well, actually.' Digger took off the teacloth and scratched his head. 'My real name's Joseph. Digger's a childhood nickname because I was obsessed with diggers.'

Sam wrapped her arms around him, covering his face with kisses.

'Well, it looks like we've got the full set. Merry Christmas, Joseph!'

Donna Gowland

Walking in a Winter Wonderland

S.L. Robinson

Walking in a Winter Wonderland

It's the night before Christmas Eve, and time has frozen. Lying on the floor is a black box. This box, which tumbled to the ground so lightly — completely defying its metaphorical gravity — has changed the course of the night. Scratch that; it has changed the course of the rest of my life.

I pick it up with shaking hands, scared I'll damage it. I crack it open and relish the satisfaction of the stiff material yielding to my curiosity. Inside rests a huge solitaire ruby set upon a thick platinum band, inlaid with diamonds. It's not my choice of ring, but the lettering on the box says *Deliciae Diamonds*, and I feel obliged to put aside my misgivings when a quick google shows the astronomical amount my boyfriend, Damian, has paid for it.

Really, I couldn't care less about the ring; it's more about what it represents. After years of being the proverbial rabbit's foot for every man

S.L. Robinson

I've had the misfortune of dating, someone has finally chosen *me* to settle down with. I, Lucky Charm, am getting married and with it, shedding my cursed last name (ironic, right?) to become Mrs Lucky Wiener.

Yes, I realise it's not much better.

I try not to listen to the little voice that says it's too soon, we've only been dating a few months and that if Damian really knew me, he'd know I'd hate such a flashy display of jewellery. At the very least he might have picked an emerald, given that it's my favourite colour. My excitement wins over in the end, and quashes the voice; at this point, I'd accept being battered by red flags as I waltz down the aisle if it means I get my happy ending.

Don't judge me. I'd like to see anyone else survive the hundreds of dates and failed relationships I have, and still believe there's a chance at love – even after the universe craps all over you. *Every. Single. Time.*

I can't resist plucking the ring from its cushion and jamming it onto my finger. Despite my best efforts, it won't slide all the way down, but that's what resizing is for, right? I twist the band off and wedge it back into its box. Then, I carefully re-pack the contents of Damian's suitcase to how it was before I prised it open to hide his presents. I eye those presents with pity now: novelty socks and a framed photo of me as a sexy Santa are clearly no match to the ring, but, I reason, I'll have plenty of time to make it up to him as his fiancé.

I carefully place the ring back in the pocket it fell from, zip the suitcase up and carefully stand it in its original position. Then, I call my family and friends and squeal my adrenaline out as I dance around my cottage. Congratulatory messages pour in, and every buzz of my phone sends thrills through me. I need Damian to hurry home from his "nip to the shop" so we can celebrate in style.

I change into my sexiest underwear, draping myself in a sheer chiffon robe, and poise myself on the couch for his return. The illusion is broken when I have to answer the door.

'Damn girl, you look fine.' Damian whistles when I fling the door open, and strike a pose for him.

'Oh, stop!' I giggle, pulling him in for a deep kiss.

He leaves the bags on the floor, and by the time we reach the bedroom, we are both naked. Him, tanned and chiselled to the bone, every inch as divinely sculpted as Michelangelo's "David" (but far more impressive in the trouser department), and me … not too shabby either, despite the food baby I've been carrying since dinner.

After, we lie under the covers, tangled up in each other's limbs, panting from the exertion of our quickie. The fairy lights on the garlands hanging off the beams above us twinkle slowly, lending the room a romantic golden hue.

'I wish you didn't have to go to Chicago,' I say, a little disappointed now that he hasn't planned his trip home to include his newly betrothed.

'I know babe, me too. I'll be back soon enough.'

Damian pulls me closer to him and I nestle into his chest. I decide I can't wait any longer. Like Liv in "Bride Wars", I must have my proposal, and I must have it *now*.

'Damian?' I start, coyly.

'Yeah, babe?'

I can barely get the words out. I shift so I can see him, propping up on my elbow to gaze down into his chocolate brown eyes.

'I found the ring.'

His face drains of colour. I've never seen that happen before — you read about it and you think it's not a real thing, or perhaps it is, but reserved for terrible news like someone dying or finding out they have a severe illness. Damian's skin *actually* turns grey at my words, and I know right then I've screwed up, stealing his chance at a perfect proposal.

'I'm so sorry, it was an accident!' I hastily explain. 'I was putting your presents in your suitcase and the ring just fell out when I opened it.'

He sits up and runs his hands through his hair. He looks visibly distressed — his perfect face wearing a painful grimace.

'Lucky, I–'

He won't look at me, and my euphoria is fading fast. How could I have misjudged this so badly?

'I'm going to say "yes",' I blurt, grabbing his hand.

He finally looks at me, and I swear there is fear in his eyes. I falter, but only momentarily.

'I want to be your wife; it would be an honour.'

Without a word, Damian jumps out of bed and pulls his boxers on, his back turned to me the whole time. He paces from the room, leaving me dazed and confused. Maybe he's going to get the ring to salvage a proposal out of my ruination? I kick myself for my impatience while he clunks around downstairs.

I hear his heavy footfall up the stairs and perk up, ready to right this egregious wrong. However, when he bursts into the room, he's fully clothed and shamefaced. My gut instinct kicks in, and I know now that this will not be my happily ever after moment.

'Lucky, I'm so sorry,' he starts, gingerly perching himself on the end of the bed. 'I don't know how to say this …'

I stay silent, forcing him to continue.

'That ring isn't for you.' He's squirming as he says this, but I don't care. If he's going to do this to me, he deserves the discomfort. 'Being with you has been amazing. It really has. But it made me realise who I'm in love with. There's a girl back home—'

I pull the covers around me, suddenly intensely vulnerable in my naked post-shag state.

'Get out,' I choke, strangled by my anger and confusion. I don't want to hear anything else. 'GET OUT! And take your stupid ring with you.'

I grab the nearest object from my bed stand and start blindly throwing things in his direction. Anything to get him to leave.

'Fine! But just so you know, I would have asked you if she said "no". But you've ruined that for yourself now.'

A furious rage overtakes me, and I fly down the stairs behind him. As he grabs his suitcase, I spot the remnants of our curry dinner and launch them at him. The chicken korma settles over him in a satisfying *splat!* coating his Armani suit in congealed yellow sauce. Victory is mine.

'You're crazy!' he throws at me as he hurries out, slamming the door behind him.

My breath comes out in ragged pants, slowing in the quiet night as devastation crashes over me. What was he thinking? How could he have set me up like this? Why — *why?!* — on earth did he sleep with me if he knew he was leaving to propose to someone else?

My boyfriends have always found The One after me, going right back to primary school, when my five-minute boyfriend Ben dumped me for Jessica P, and married her on the field at lunch-time while I cried into my sandwiches (they repeated that ceremony twenty years later. Sickeningly cute). But at least the others had the grace to let the relationship end before moving on to their bliss.

This is an all-time low.

No more! I promise myself. The curse ends here; I am done with love, done with romance, and done with everything that comes along with both.

I realise I am still naked when the torrent of tears rushing down my face drips onto my bare chest. The mirror behind me shows a curly-haired, wild-eyed mess and, full of self-pity, I tramp upstairs. I eschew my sexy robe for my comforting fleece onesie and drink myself into oblivion while watching "Bridget Jones's Diary". I howl along when dear Brij sings "All by Myself" and I am sure some far-off wolves hear me, and return a howl of solidarity with my wounded pride.

That could just be the wine, though.

Sleigh Bell Lane

Christmas Day arrives two days later, and I am miserable and all alone. My phone is off after the embarrassment of having to backpedal the engagement news, and I've taken my decorations down. *Screw the holidays!* There's no redemption for this year.

I flick through the roster of scheduled Christmas television, vindictively jabbing the buttons on my remote every time the screen has the gall to show me a happy couple. It seems love is in the air this year because I can't bloody escape it! I land on the Hallmark channel and decide to give in. If I'm going to be forced to watch romance films, I'm going to watch the cheesiest ones possible and ridicule the characters from the safety of my couch.

I fill my glass to the brim with a dusty bottle of mulled wine I found languishing in the back of my cupboard, and settle in as one film ends and the next begins.

"A Walk in Wonderland" is on and a small part of me is begrudgingly happy. I've watched this film every year since I was a teenager: a couple going through a rough time overcome their problems through a series of mishaps that take place in the North Pole. It's an older movie, reminiscent of "The Wizard of Oz" where the couple are in black and white before entering the beautiful colours of Wonderland. Completely naff, but they get their fated happy ending, and the actors aren't awful.

When the film starts, I immediately notice something is different. The couple have changed; the husband isn't wearing his wide, boxy suit, and the wife doesn't have her big Russian hat on. Before I can focus my thoughts, the film's title looms large on the screen, growing bigger until it completely obscures the town behind it. I try to turn down the roar of the choral soundtrack as it fills the room, but the remote doesn't work.

What the hell?

I rub my eyes in disbelief, because now something bat-shit-crazy is happening. The film's title has bloomed past the wide-screen frame, projecting into the room like a neon sign. The television morphs into a black void which spreads across the wall, and something with a stripy head and razor-sharp ears pokes out from the centre, birthing itself into my living room like a Christmas nightmare.

The head slowly lifts to show a baby elf, with a wide smile and enormous round eyes. The elf extends his tiny gloved hand, beckoning me to join him. If horror films have taught me anything, it's that you should run screaming from events like this, but he's so cute and those big baleful eyes are hypnotic.

It appears I've lost my mind.

Either that, or this is a hallucination brought on by the expired wine I've been drinking. But … why not engage with it? Surely anything my mind can create can't be as poor as my current reality?

Screw it!

I rise from the couch and the black void swirls with bright colours, presenting a gingerbread door, adorned with gumdrops and a frosted window. The door is ajar from its candy cane frame and the baby elf peeks out from the crack, jumping up and down, gleefully motioning for me to join him.

I feel like Lucy about to enter Narnia.

In a few steps, I reach the elf and take his hand, noticing how cool to the touch it is. The door swings open and the last of my rationale deserts me.

One more step, and I tumble down a snowy hill.

Disorienting as this is, it doesn't hurt. The snow is soft as marshmallows and I land at the foot of the hill with a satisfying FLUMP! Startled, I shuffle around to stand, but my hands can't find a purchase in the powdery snow, and it takes a few minutes of mighty effort. Once I'm upright, I shake the snow off my onesie, except … it's not a onesie any more.

Now, I'm wearing a plaid dress that comes down to my knees, thick tights and winter boots. On my hands are a pair of mittens, matching a scarf around my neck. I've a long dark coat with trim fur layered over the dress, and when I reach up to my tangled mess of curls, I feel a 1940s victory roll and a tamed ponytail of ringlets.

I take in the surroundings: my fall has landed me before a path of sparkling white stones, lit up by the bulbous moon above. A forest of huge silver trees lines the path. When a breeze rustles through them, I realise their leaves are actually thousands of tiny bells ringing faintly. This must be a lucid dream, I decide. Everything is so exquisitely detailed and lifelike. A wooden sign next to the path creaks for my attention.

Welcome to Sleigh Bell Lane! the looping letters read.

I start down the path, and for the first time since Damian left, I feel happy. The trees and their bell song urge me forward. Ice sculptures of huge snowflakes glitter around me, slowly rotating as if perpetually falling from the sky.

The path curves, and a new sound joins me in the night. I strain to listen. Are those … footsteps?

As soon as I know I'm not alone, the bells stop jingling. The silence amplifies the footsteps drawing closer, and in my periphery, I pick up movement to the left of me. Heart racing, I stand frozen on the path until I work up the courage to look.

Across from me, a man on a white path of his own mirrors my statuesque pose, staring at me like a deer caught in headlights.

Goodbye, Bluebird

Neither of us move as we size each other up.

He's wearing a tweed suit and knee-length overcoat, leather shoes and a felt hat. In one hand he holds a wooden pipe, and it's with this he eventually breaks our stalemate to salute me. I wave back warily, and both of us walk forward at the same time. We come face-to-face when our respective paths join to form a singular road leading out of the lane.

'Hi?' My voice rises with uncertainty to form a question.

'Hello.' He nods back. His face is kind and plain, but his bespectacled eyes betray some caution.

We stand here, shuffling our feet in the cold, puffing out clouds of white air. Two awkward people unsure of how to proceed.

Well, if this is my dream, I've no reason to fear, right?

'I'm L–' I cut myself off. Wary of inviting ridicule over my name, I decide to reinvent myself. 'I'm Elle.'

'Mike,' he replies shortly.

'Okay, Mike. You have any idea what's going on, or where we are?'

'Nope. I was just watching the telly when …' he laughs, shaking his head at the absurdity of what I know happened next.

'A baby elf waved you into this world?'

He nods, and we dissolve into peals of laughter.

We eventually calm ourselves, wiping the tears from our eyes, and I feel brave enough to ask, 'So, what *do* you think is happening?'

'Some sort of dream or–'

'Delusion?' I quip. 'Well, it's nice to have company on the descent to madness!'

The awkward silence returns and, eager to dispel it, I wave to the path before us.

'Shall we?'

Mike strides forward and together, we head to the edge of the forest, into a huge snowy clearing. Billions of stars dazzle brightly over a landscape of rolling white hills in every direction. In the near distance, the lights of a village stand out and we tramp towards it. With each step, the village reveals more of itself to us. Tiny cottages lit by rainbow lights, and gigantic fir trees cluster in front of a grand old building. A nagging sense of familiarity tugs at my memory.

Mike lets out a strangled yelp. 'What the—'

A swarm of birds surrounds us. They dart back and forth in a frenzy, twittering and chirping as their wings brush over us.

'Eeeeee!' I squeal, protecting my head with my arms and stamping about.

'Just stand still,' Mike calls out calmly, reaching out to me through the melee.

His hand finds my arm and grips it firmly, and I'm surprised at how quickly this grounds me. I'm glad of it, because once I'm still, the dance of the birds becomes intricate and gentle. They soar and swoop in perfect formation, singing sweetly in harmony. After a few minutes, they take their dance further afield, leaving us astounded in their wake.

'What was that?' I ask incredulously.

'Shh.' Mike holds a finger up for quiet.

He removes his hat and cocks his head to the side, alert like a meerkat in the wild. A lock of slicked-back hair falls loosely over his face and a twinge of attraction goes through me. He's not as plain as I initially thought …

Nope, nope. Absolutely not! I shake my head, dislodging the thought before it can settle. I'm done with that nonsense!

'D'you hear that?' Mike says, oblivious to my musings. 'Come on.'

He pulls me, and suddenly, we're running through the snow. We stop just as soon as we've started, and he drops to the floor to examine something. Puzzled, I come around him and notice a tiny bluebird flailing on the ground. The poor thing weakly flutters a bent wing and chirrups sadly.

'He's injured.' Mike tenderly scoops the bird in his gloved hands, cradling it like a baby. Without looking at me, he says, 'Give me your scarf.'

He makes a bundle with my scarf and his hat, and another twinge of attraction pulls at me. I can't help it; I've always been a sucker for a man holding a tiny animal. It seems my subconscious is testing my recent promise to stay single.

'We'll take him to the village,' Mike murmurs, still focused on the bird. 'We can get help there.'

That nagging familiarity returns, and I pause to consider it while he paces to the village. I can feel the cogs in my brain working overtime, the further away he gets.

'Hey, hold on,' I shout, catching up. 'I think I know this. I think I know where we are.'

Mike stops in his tracks.

'You do?'

'Yeah, it's the North Pole–'

'No, it isn't,' he scoffs, and resumes walking. 'Mountain bluebirds aren't native to the North Pole, they're native to North America.'

'What are you, a bird expert?' I reply tartly.

'The correct term is ornithologist.' He smirks, raising an eyebrow sardonically. 'And yes, I am. That's why I'm sure we're not in the North Pole. Also, the North Pole is uninhabitable. Definitely not host to a village like that.'

His patronising tone irritates me, squashing my attraction to him.

'Look, in the movie, Fred and Belle get lost and the first thing they come across is an injured bluebird. They save the bird by taking it to a village *in the North Pole.*'

'What movie?' Mike laughs like a parent disabusing a child of a silly daydream.

'The movie — *this movie* — ' I gesture around us. '"A Walk in Wonderland". And, I know what's going to happen next. When we get to the village we'll be invited to a party.'

Mike rolls his eyes instead of answering, and I swear I could punch him right there for his smarminess.

'Listen, this is my dream or delusion–'

'Ha!' Mike interrupts. 'If this is your dream, why am I here? And why is this bird injured? You'd think if it was about you, we'd be doing something requiring your expertise — whatever that is.'

It's good logic, but I can't back down now.

'Because my brain is testing my resolve,' I theorise. 'And the recent promise I made myself.'

'Which was?'

'That I'm done with love and I'm staying single.'

'Bold of you to assume I'm attracted to you,' Mike retorts, and I flush despite the cold.

'I — no — what I mean is that my brain is trying to tell me not to give up on love. You're just the random person it chose for the message. That's why you're so beige,' I fire at him. 'You're an amalgamation of every other man on the planet, rolled into one inoffensive character.'

Mike shakes his head, seemingly amused.

'I could say the same about my brain, sending me on some magical quest to find romance. And, while I won't be as unkind to label you "beige", you're definitely not my type. Maybe you're just here to be my annoying guide – like Donkey and Shrek.'

Oh, hell no! Even in my own fantasy, I can't escape the curse?

'No way! I'm not helping you on your magical quest to find The One,' I huff. 'In fact, once we find some help, we can part ways and you can find her yourself.'

'Relax,' Mike drawls condescendingly. 'I don't believe we're sharing a fantasy, nor do I believe in The One, especially when–'

He cuts off as we reach the village square, where (just as I predicted), a jolly party rages around an immense Christmas tree decorated in red, green and gold. Before I can ask him to finish his sentence, a snowman bounces over to us. His costume is so realistic it sparkles like actual snow in the moonlight.

'Wow, you look amazing.' I smile, resisting the urge to reach out and touch him.

'Why thank you, miss,' he says, doffing his top hat. 'And who might you two wanderers be?'

I blink away the tiredness overwhelming my eyes; his coal stone mouth moves exactly like a real mouth.

'I'm Mike, and this is Elle.' Mike offers up the bundle containing the bluebird. 'Is there a vet centre anywhere? We found an injured bird.'

The snowman wrinkles his carrot nose and furrows his brow.

'Here at the North Pole, we can supply anything you need,' he trills.

'I told you!' I nudge Mike, who shrugs my smugness away.

'Let our elves take care of that for you, and you can enjoy the party! In fact, we have a special event that you two would be perfect for,' the snowman announces loudly.

A faction of elves bears the bluebird away, holding the bundle high above their heads like pallbearers.

'Now, come with me.' The snowman grabs Mike and me with his stick hands and pulls us around the tree. There, a candy cane altar bedecked in red and gold ribbon awaits us. 'Let's get you into costume for tonight's event. This really is perfect timing — you'll both do nicely!'

The remaining elves squeal with delight, rushing over one another to grab at us.

'Oh, no, we can't!' we shout in alarm, as their tiny yet effectual hands pull and push at us. The elves multiply into a terrifying swarm, each elf more excited than the last to get at us. Mike and I desperately cast about for an escape.

'Over there!'

I nod to the only street not blocked by our stripy captors. He takes my hand and we tear away from the village square, leaving behind the bemused snowman and his elves. After a few minutes, we reach a grand stable filled with fresh hay and twelve majestic reindeer, each housed behind a beautiful gate bearing their name.

'I think the coast is clear,' Mike says, checking behind us.

The reindeer grunt and sniff at us, but they warm up considerably when we find a bag of fresh apples to feed them with.

The run has exhilarated and exhausted me in equal measure.

'God, I am absolutely knackered,' I say through a yawn, which Mike catches after me.

'Here.' He arranges some hay into a nest. 'We can lie on this.'

I'm too tired to object to sleeping on the floor, but when I settle in to the nest, it's warm and cosy, cushioning us from the stone underneath. My last thought before sleep overtakes me is that this has been one of the best dreams I've ever had.

*

I wake to a snuffle in my ear, and something wet licking my cheek. It tickles and I come to in the stable, laughing my fatigue away as a reindeer nudges me awake. A warm blanket falls off me as I sit up, and there's a delicious smell in the air. I wipe the sleep out of my eyes, and Mike hands me a delicate silver cup filled with thick, hot chocolate.

I must admit, I'm glad I'm still here.

'How long were we out?' I ask, sipping the luxurious drink. It tastes like childhood and presents and magic all in one.

'About twelve hours — you missed the end of the party!'

The snowman's jolly voice startles me, but not Mike, and I realise they've been waiting for me to wake up. He bounces over with a tray laden down with food, which jumps every time he does.

'Eat up, now. Your bluebird is fully healed and ready for release! He wants to say goodbye to you both before he goes.'

'Bluebirds don't talk,' Mike says matter-of-factly.

'How can you stick to your real-world knowledge when there is a literal snowman serving us breakfast?' I tease.

He doesn't answer. I assume he isn't quite ready to commit to the insanity, like I have.

We practically inhale everything on the tray — muffins, pancakes, pastries and sugar cookies. The reindeer whinny, their big brown eyes glued to our

157

food, and we gladly share our bounty with them. Once we've eaten our fill, the snowman opens the reindeer gates. While most return to their enclosures, two trot over to us, allowing us to bury our heads in their soft pelts.

'These will be your steeds,' the snowman tells us. 'Cupid for the lady, and Vixen for the gentleman. Climb aboard, don't be shy, and hold on tight!'

We scrabble onto their backs and take hold of the reins. The cords are made of hundreds of strands of gold thread, tightly woven together, and there are golden bells hanging from the saddles, which twinkle with every movement.

'On, Cupid!' the snowman roars, lightly slapping the behind of my reindeer. 'On, Vixen!'

With a jerk, we're off. The reindeer's hooves thunder through the village as Mike and I hold on for dear life. It takes me a moment to realise we are rising through the sky, and sheer joy overwhelms me as the wind whips over us. The village spreads out beneath us like a picturesque card, and beside us, the snowman glides through the air.

'This is *MENTaaalll*!' Mike cries, his voice dropping in terror as the reindeer suddenly dive forward to the ground.

We speed toward a grassy meadow so fast that a collision seems certain. I close my eyes, but just before the moment of impact, we stop and settle gently on the grass. We alight ungracefully, but Mike more so than me. He looks green around the gills.

'I hope we get to do that again!' I say, stroking Cupid.

'Speak for yourself,' Mike replies shortly, but he perks up the longer his feet are on the ground.

'Here he is, here he is!' The snowman swoops down, followed by our bluebird.

He flits around us, his bright plumage more vivid than the blue sky. Mike holds out a finger, and the bluebird perches on it, dipping his beak lightly. Mike's face is full of wonder, and he uses his other hand to stroke the bird and his wings. In the distance, we spot a group of bluebirds making their way over, and after another flutter around us both, our bird darts away to join them. We wave goodbye as he reaches the group and they start their synchronised dance, complete once again.

'How lovely,' the snowman says behind us, and we turn to see him melted on the ground, his coal stone features arranged in a smile on the grass.

Parson Brown

'What now?' Mike groans.

'Don't worry yourself, dear man,' the snowman says from his puddle. 'It's just the afternoon sun. Happens all the time in this part of the Pole.'

'Is there anything we can do to help?' I ask, fighting my mirth at Mike's puzzled face.

'Over that hill, you'll find plenty of snow. Rebuild me and I'll be good to go,' the snowman says.

We gather the stones and carrot into his hat, and Mike brings his scarf and stick hands.

'Shall we fly?' I ask, scoping out the distance to the hill. 'It's probably about a mile away.'

Mike blanches at the suggestion.

'No! Let's walk and maybe we can fly on the way back?'

I give Cupid's reins a little tug to start toward the hill.

'I'd have thought a bird expert would enjoy flying.'

Mike shakes his head. 'I've always had terrible travel sickness. I hate flying. Pity all the good birds are in exotic places — I've spent hours with my head in a bag on those flights!'

I can feel myself warming to Mike, so I ask, 'What drew you to birds?' hoping his answer will be so boring, it will dampen my enthusiasm for him.

'I was a real nature nerd as a kid. We lived on a farm in Surrey, so there was no shortage of animals and birds that would come to be fed.' The reindeer perk up at the word "fed," and we give them some apples to munch on.

'I remember one year, there was a pair of magpies that would come to visit every day without fail,' Mike continues. 'They would bring shiny little things for me in return for food. My mum would say that because there were two of them, they would always bring me joy. Birds have fascinated me ever since — they really are intelligent creatures – and, I guess my mum was right, because I've always loved my job and the birds still bring me joy.'

Damn it, he's good.

'How about you?' he asks. 'What do you do?'

'Nothing as passionate as your career,' I sigh. 'I'm a Project Manager in a travel firm. Sometimes, I get to go abroad and do conferences, which are fun. But mostly, it's figuring out how to sell over-inflated luxury packages to people with more money than sense.'

'Why do you do it?'

'I sort of fell into it after Uni — it pays well and I get to travel. I was saving up for my dream home and figured I'd move on after I bought it. But I've been in my cottage for a while now and I'm still working there …' I trail off into a shrug.

'What would your dream job be?'

This, at least, is an easy answer.

'I'd love to have a little shop selling handmade things. I make all sorts of knick-knacks for friends and family and they always say I could do it if I put my mind to it.'

'What's stopping you?'

I hate being probed like this. If this is a dream, then clearly my love life isn't the only unhappy area my subconscious wants me to address.

'I guess I'm worried that if I turn my hobby into a job, I'll hate it. Or I'll fail, and then be so miserable I'll never want to create again.'

'Valid concerns,' Mike agrees. 'But you'll never have the chance to love your job and make money while you're doing it if you never give it a shot.'

'Insightful.' I roll my eyes. I've heard this a million times before now. 'It's not like I haven't thought about it, it's just … I'm thirty-five, and not much in my life has gone the way I thought it would by now — especially in the romance department. I don't think I can handle putting myself through any more failures.'

Mike murmurs in agreement, but I get the feeling he doesn't want this part of the conversation to continue. That suits me fine. We climb up the hill in relative silence, struggling with our breath as we gain on its peak.

'Wow! What a view,' I wheeze, when we reach the top.

The summit of the hill literally takes my breath away and we pause to take in the glorious sight below us. Islands of ice and snow fracture off into a blue sea, as the sun, weaker now as the afternoon draws in, overlooks it all. We scrabble to the nearest bank and set about rebuilding the snowman, starting with his head. As soon as we arrange his face, he wrinkles his nose as though fighting off a sneeze.

'Thank you, thank you,' he greets us. 'Parson Brown at your service! Now, when you make the rest of me, be as generous as you can. A snowman is only worth his salt if his proportions are large.'

Mike and I laugh, and pile mounds of snow into two huge balls. I'm almost done rolling another layer onto the snowman's midriff when —

THUD!

Cold, powdery ice slides down the nape of my neck and back. I spin around to see Mike bent double, laughing at my shock. My surprise quickly turns to revenge, and I mount a swift offensive on him.

'Argh!' Mike shouts through the barrage. With no landmarks to hide behind, he's an easy target. 'How are you so good at this?'

'Netball M.V.P every year in high school and Uni.'
I land another ball squarely in his face.
'Okay, I surrender!' he calls, waving his arms.
I'm too hyped up to stop.
I stoop to form another ball, but before I can stand, he tackles me around my waist, and we topple onto the floor. We lie there, catching our breath through fits of laughter. Without thinking, we simultaneously turn and our prop ourselves up to face one another. Mike's glasses are skewed slightly, and I'm endeared to him when he fixes them in place on the crook of his nose. I notice his eyes for the first time; a cool grey to match our wintry scene, and completely focused on me. He reaches out, and I hold my breath as he grazes my temple to push back some stray curls from my face. His fingers linger there, and an undeniable moment passes between us.
I cough to break the tension and roll away from him. I'm not ready to be hurt again.
'We better finish the snowman before it gets dark,' I mutter, refusing to meet his gaze.
'Sure.' The deflation in his voice is palpable.
Still, he's a good sport about it and we make light-hearted talk while we finish our work. He tells me about his favourite birds and the exotic places he's studied at. I tell him about my favourite things to make, and how my cottage is my pride and joy — painted emerald green against the original Tudor features, which pissed off more than a few of my neighbours.
'You two work well together,' says the snowman when we're done, revering his lower half like someone who's just found the perfect pair of jeans for their bum. 'Are you sure you don't know each other?'
'We're getting there,' Mike replies, with a twinkle in his eyes.

Conspiring by the fire

We return to the village by flight despite Mike's protests. The night draws in, sending streaks of pink and orange shooting across the twilight sky. The elves run around making preparations for another night of partying, and this, the snowman tells us, they will do until New Year's Day, when the preparations for next Christmas begin.
'You can freshen up here.' The snowman shows us to a gingerbread house. 'There are clean clothes set out for you and a fire to warm you up. We'll come and get you when the party starts.'
He ushers us in and closes the door behind us. The gingerbread house is small and cosy, and a roaring fire fills it with the smell of baking biscuits.

The downstairs is an open plan room which functions as a kitchen and sitting room. A squashy couch sits in front of the fire, and there are two plates of sandwiches and mince pies, with a note that says: *Turkey dinner at 8pm sharp, enjoy your snacks!* A vat of peppermint hot chocolate hangs on a little copper stand, and after we've washed and changed our clothes, we snuggle into the couch, basking in the fire's warmth.

We enjoy ourselves in comfortable silence for a little while, watching the crackling flames twist and turn into different shapes. A thought pops in to my head and I break the quiet.

'Mike?'

'Hm?' he replies drowsily.

'Yesterday, when we were talking about what all this could be, you said you "didn't believe in The One, especially when …". What were you going to say?'

Mike sighs heavily. A shadow passes over his face, and I kick myself for prying. It's a few minutes before he answers, staring resolutely ahead into the fire.

'I was going to say "especially when you've already had The One".' His voice is quiet and mournful.

'I'm sorry — ' Christ, I'm mortified. 'You don't have to explain.'

'No, it's okay.' He breaks his trance and gives me a half-smile. 'I should talk about it, but I don't.'

The pregnant pause as he finds his next words has me braced for a bombshell.

'I was married once.'

Whoomph, there it is! I don't know why this makes my heart sink into my stomach, but it does.

'She passed away a few years ago.'

His grief at uttering these words is tangible.

'I'm so sorry.' My hand finds his and I squeeze it gently. Tears fall from my eyes, and to my surprise, this makes him chuckle.

'Why are *you* crying?' he asks, brushing a tear away from my cheek.

'You had it,' I wail. 'You found that person you were going to stay with forever and the universe took her away from you. It's so unfair.'

I know this can't be helping him, but it's just so sad. I suppose this is my subconscious telling me that there will always be someone who's had it worse than me, but does the lesson have to be this painful?

'Ignore me,' I blubber. 'It probably wouldn't affect me so much if I wasn't so hung up on my own misery.'

'What's that old saying, hmm? Misery loves company! Tell me about it,' Mike coaxes.

I know I have to tell him the truth after he's been so open with me, and shame shoots through me when I remember I've deceived him from the beginning.

'Well … for starters, my name isn't "Elle".' Mike's eyebrows shoot up his forehead, but he doesn't interrupt. 'It's Lucky.'

He looks confused. 'That's not so bad–'

'Lucky Charm.' I wince saying it out loud. 'That's my full name.'

'Ahh.' He connects the dots. 'And you hate this because …?'

'It's a curse. My name is a curse.'

'Oh, come on, you can't possibly believe that,' Mike laughs. I give him a withering stare and he grimaces.

'Every man I have ever dated has always — and I mean without fail — found the love of their life after dating me. I'm actually known around my village for it. My last boyfriend chose someone else while we were still dating. I feel like next time, all it will take is one look at me, and they'll find their soulmate somewhere else!'

Mike lets me blow off steam without interruption.

'And, then you … you tell me you found someone in this melting pot of loneliness, but you didn't even get the chance to grow old together before it was taken away. What's the point? Why do we bother looking for love when it hurts this much?'

Mike's face is full of sympathy as he nods in agreement.

'I thought I was done with all the first dates and heartbreak,' he says. 'I can honestly say I was the happiest I've ever been when I was with Mel. It's been over five years, and I still can't bring myself to "get back out there". I don't think I could be that lucky — sorry — to find that kind of connection again.'

'Do you think that's why we're here?' I ask quietly. 'Some big conspiracy to get us to believe in love again?'

I am painfully aware of the implication of this question and hold my breath for his answer.

'In the realm of things possible since I walked into my television?' he chuckles, rubbing his cheek. 'Yeah, I'll say that could be the reason.'

'You know what we should do,' I say, perking up. 'We should try to find each other in the real world once the dream — or whatever this is — is over. And then we would know that the universe is giving us a sign, right?'

A playful look crosses Mike's face.

'I feel like there's a more immediate way to find out if the universe wants us to be together.' His voice drips with suggestion.

'And that would be?' I ask, half-wary, half-excited.

'All fairy tales have true love's kiss, right? If the universe wants us to be together, I don't know … maybe there'll be some sparks flying when we kiss?'

'Well, I have always known if a guy was right for me based on how he kisses,' I reason.

'No offence, Elle — Lucky — but if your gut instinct could tell by kisses alone, you wouldn't have ended up with all those idiots,' Mike teases.

I can't argue with that logic.

'Okay, then.' I nudge him playfully with my shoulder. 'Kiss me.'

He leans into me. I close my eyes and hold my breath, heart thudding in my chest.

There's only a hair-width distance between our lips, when a loud knock at the door interrupts us.

Parson Brown, Again

We break apart in frustration, and I jump up to answer the door.

'Party time!' the snowman shouts as soon as I open it.

A small cannon explodes, and the elf holding it gives a raucous shriek as confetti settles in my hair.

'Okay, we'll be out now,' I say, beckoning to Mike.

We don our coats and shuffle out into the cold, our unfinished business lingering between us. Night has fallen, and the square is lit up by fairy lights of every colour, strung from one building to the next. The Christmas tree has been frosted and decorated with silver, green and blue ornaments. The previous night's altar is also different — now, two silver trees, wrapped in green and blue ribbons, intertwine to form an arch. Mike catches me staring at it, and I blush.

It's so hard to escape the romance of this place!

'I love the colours,' I say lamely, 'the green especially.'

We're led to a vast table laden with every type of Christmas food you can imagine. An enormous golden turkey takes precedence in the centre, and trimmings of roast potatoes, vegetables and stuffing fill every other space. Each plate has its own golden gravy boat in the shape of a sleigh and delicate, matching cutlery.

'Elves! Tonight, we are joined by our esteemed human friends for our feast,' the snowman booms. Cheers erupt from all around us. 'Before we eat, let us pull our crackers!'

A basket of crackers comes around, and the elves whoop and holler. When everyone has one, we take turns pulling them apart. Inside are small silver crowns inlaid with jewels. Mine has emeralds and jade stones all around it. Mike's crown is similar, with jewels of aquamarine and sapphire.

'You look like Prince Charming,' I tease.

'And you look every inch a princess,' he flirts back.

The feast officially begins, and we eat until the thought of another plate makes us feel sick. When we've finished our second helping of dessert (a mountainous flaming brandy cake with lashings of amaretto cream), our plates magically disappear.

'Wishbone, wishbone!' The snowman comes bounding round to us. 'The guests must have the honour of the wishbone.'

He hands us the golden bone, and on the count of three, we pull. It snaps in my favour.

'Make a wish, Lucky,' Mike murmurs under the applause of the crowd.

I pause for a moment. If there's even the slightest chance any of this is real, then I don't want to waste this opportunity.

I wish for us to meet in the real world. I keep my eyes closed for a few seconds, hoping the magic is real.

When I open them, Mike asks, 'What did you wish for?'

'Can't tell you that,' I say conspiratorially. 'Might break the juju.'

The rest of the evening passes in a blur of games and dancing, and Mike and I revel in it. At midnight, a trumpet sounds and the snowman addresses us all.

'And now for tonight's most sacred tradition: I need two volunteers for the "Meeting of the Years" ceremony,' he declares.

The elves nudge each other and throw suggestive looks at Mike and me.

The snowman must sense our apprehension as he adds, 'Let it be known that Lady Luck shines brightly on all those who volunteer.'

'What do you think?' Mike asks ruefully. 'I have to think his use of the word "luck" is a pun well-intended.'

I roll my eyes, but the romantic in me is well and truly alive.

'I'm in,' I say firmly.

Mike lifts our hands into the air, and the crowd cheer us.

'To the altar!' the snowman orders, and we walk around the tree, played out by a brass band.

By the time we reach the silver arch, I'm wearing a long green gown, with a gossamer skirt decorated with snowflakes. An elf hands me a bouquet of roses dyed to match the colours of the altar, and a lift of my dress reveals crystal heels. The crown on my head is still there, but now it's attached to a veil that cascades down my shoulders to join the train of the dress. Mike is wearing a suit of brilliant blue, with a top hat and tails.

'*Now,* you look like a princess.' Mike's eyes light up and I get a twinge of sadness. It feels like an ending is upon us, and I don't want the night to end.

'I wish we could stay here,' I murmur, as we step up to the altar where the snowman is waiting for us.

'Me too,' Mike replies sincerely.

'People of the North Pole,' the snowman states grandly. 'We are here on this second night of the ceremony, to mark the joining of two years: the past and the present. We hope for love, joy and peace for all that will come, and understanding and acceptance of all that has been.'

Mike and I share a look of knowing as we hold hands. Regardless of what happens next, I know that both of us will carry this message forward when we go our separate ways.

The snowman drapes our hands with a black cloth. 'This black signifies all that has been. May you wash away any past strife while taking any lessons forward with you.' He gives me a wink, then places a white cloth over our hands. 'May you both start the year afresh, with hearts open to anything that may come your way.' This, he says to Mike, whose face is serious.

'And now, if you will, a union of the lips,' the snowman says, causing the elves to snicker.

This time, when we lean in, our lips meet. The kiss feels like coming home after a long trip; it's new and familiar at the same time, and as Mike pulls me closer to him, I know I'm ready to fall again.

Suddenly, the ground shifts beneath us, and I open my eyes to see Wonderland crumbling.

'Don't let go,' Mike calls as we're swept up in a swirling snow flurry.

I hold on tightly, but our fingers slip apart. For a moment, time stops, and both of us are suspended in mid-air. Our eyes briefly lock onto each other before we're pulled into oblivion, and my heart skips a beat, knowing I'll never forget him.

Unafraid to Face our New Plans

I come to on the couch, back in my onesie. The film is almost finished; Fred and Belle (returned to their usual selves) are kissing in an avalanche of snow. I turn the television off and marvel at the silence. The black screen stays within its frame and there's no sign of the baby elf. What I wouldn't give to see his little head again!

I sit like this for a long time, contemplating everything I've just dreamed. Yes, that's the rational (if disappointing) explanation — a magical, lucid, crazy dream reminding me that love is still possible. Still, Mike's face has imprinted on my memory, and I grieve his fictional state. I'm sure there's a real Mike somewhere out there for me, but he can wait.

I pull my laptop out and write a brief email to my boss.

> Hi Sharon,
> Hope you're enjoying the holidays! Please take this email as my formal notice to quit.
> Lucky

Though Wonderland might have been a dream, there's no reason I can't follow through in other ways, and I don't want to lose this momentum while I have it. I work into the early morning hours, drafting a business plan for my shop, which I affectionately call "Lucky's Charms". I'm done hating my name; it's time to harness its power for me!

The next day, I resolve to see my family and shrug off the embarrassment I've been running from. After all, it's not my fault Damian turned out to be an actual wiener. I'm almost ready to leave when a knock at the door startles me. Is that music I can hear? I open the door, and Kylie Minogue's "I Should Be So Lucky" blares out from a speaker on the ground. It's a little on the nose but perfect for the moment, considering who's standing there.

'Mike?' My voice is so high-pitched it could wake all the dogs in a ten-mile radius. 'What are you doing here? You're real? How did you find me?'

I fire the questions rapidly, unable to think straight as reality and fantasy collide.

Mike lowers the music and takes my hand.

'I couldn't stop thinking about you after I woke up. I knew I had to at least *try* to find you.'

'But how did you?' I'm pinching myself so hard I think I'll break skin, willing my brain to wake me up if this isn't happening.

'It's the strangest thing.' Mike looks bashful. 'I got in my car, and it was like I knew exactly where to come.'

'Oh, my God!' I gasp. 'The wish!'

'I knew I was in the right place when I saw the green walls.' He laughs, then turns serious and drops to one knee. Now, I really am going to lose my mind. 'Lucky, I never thought I'd want to put myself out there again.

But, seeing you in that forest … I knew straight away that something had changed.' He pulls out a Haribo ring from his pocket: it's green. 'Will you make me the happiest man in the world and agree to date me while we figure out this craziness?'

'My favourite colour,' I whisper. I can't believe Mike remembered such a minute detail from our time together.

'It's just a placeholder,' he says sheepishly. 'I promise I'll get you a better ring one day.'

I'm beyond ecstatic and pull him up for a kiss. It's perfect, again.

'Is that a "yes"?' We pull apart, and he strokes my cheek.

'Absolutely,' I reply, knowing my curse has finally lifted.

Stay Another Day

Sarah Shard

'Happy endings aren't real. There is no Prince Charming waiting to rescue you. And don't even try the frog thing. Trust me, a frog is just a frog, and when you kiss them, they are still a frog.'

'Auntie Holly, you kissed a frog?' The little girl with perfect blonde curls peeping from underneath her plastic birthday crown giggled at the thought.

'Oh, Jodie, my precious little girl. Auntie Holly has kissed lots of frogs.' Julia, Holly's sister, interrupted her impromptu, uninvited, anti-fairy-tale storytelling session. 'Now, it's your birthday party and your friends are waiting for you to play pass the parcel. Come on, go find Daddy.'

The little girl jumped off Holly's lap and ran into the front room to continue her birthday celebrations.

Holly shouted after her niece, 'Remember, no kissing until you're thirty. And not even then.'

'Holly, she's four years old. For the love of God, let her believe in fairy-tale for a few more years.'

Holly rolled her eyes at her sister's plea before reaching into her handbag and pulling out a plastic glass of wine with a foil lid. She managed to pull back half the lid before Julia snatched it away.

'Hey, that's mine!' barked Holly.

'I have been up since four a.m. baking two dozen princess cupcakes, one dozen minion cupcakes because Spencer refuses to touch anything girly, and I have had to cater for gluten-free, dairy-free, sugar-free and I have done all that alcohol-free. So, unless you can trump that, then this is mine.'

'Okay, like that, is it? I have spent months in a cottage in the middle of nowhere trying to push through my writer's block when all I seem to have done so far is prove that I couldn't find inspiration if you hit me in the face with it!'

Both women paused before Julia scoffed. 'Nope. Spending months alone in a country cottage sounds like bliss to every parent, so not a chance. This wine is mine!'

The sisters sunk deep into the sofa, the kicking off of their shoes and the putting up of their feet on the footstool perfectly synchronised.

'I gotta be heading soon, anyway. I'm not the best at driving through country lanes during the day. Don't want to do it in the dark.'

'So, you really haven't written anything yet? Isn't Christmas Land as festive as you thought?'

'Cringleton, not Christmas Land. And yes, it's totally as festive as you would imagine. It's just not sparking anything.' A fed-up Holly lay her head on her sister's shoulder.

'No hot elves, then? No dishy teachers doing nativity plays in the church hall?'

'Nope and nope.'

'I think you need to ask Santa for a man to put some mistle in your toe.' Julia laughed at her own joke.

Holly, however, looked at her sister with sheer confusion.

'What? That's funny. Mistle … toe, like camel toe.' Holly shook her head and covered her face with a cushion, trying to hide her embarrassment and laughter. Julia downed the last of the wine and sat on the edge of the sofa, trying to compose herself.

'Mummy, does Auntie Holly really have camel's toes?' Giggled the little blond-haired boy with yellow and blue icing around his mouth as he jumped up from behind the sofa. Both women burst out laughing, at which the slightly confused little boy ran off back to the cake table. When Julia eventually calmed down, she stumbled to her feet.

'That Merlot went straight to my head.'

'Wow! I haven't laughed that much in months.'

'Me neither, but it's time to be the responsible parent again and time for you to drive back to Christmas Land.'

'Fine. Can I take a princess and a minion back with me then? Cupcake, that is, not your children.'

'Please feel free to take the kids or cupcakes.'

After a few rounds of air kisses and sticky-fingered hugs, Holly left the party, and London, far behind, as she set off for the long drive back to Cringleton village.

*

The following morning, Holly looked around the cottage which had been her home from home for nearly three months. She'd thought her decision to rent a quaint cottage in a village known for its Christmas traditions would be the perfect inspiration for her second romance novel, but the almost blank screen reflected the emptiness of her mind. So far, she had written and deleted thirty-five opening lines. The current line, which had managed to survive more than two days, read:

> It was December in the village of Cringleton, where Christmas abounded around every corner and ...

As she stared at the screen, she became distracted by voices outside. The cottage was on the edge of the village, so hearing voices was unusual, unless it was Graham, the gardener, but he tended to pop round later in the afternoons and seemed mostly content to chat to himself.

If he did holler in Holly's direction, it was usually, 'How's thee lass? Written that book yet?' She usually just smiled and waved back, not wanting to vocalise her writer's block beyond confiding in Alexa.

Holly peeped out of the small window that overlooked the garden and driveway, but couldn't see anyone. She felt sure she recognised the female voice but couldn't make out the identity of the male voice. Giving up on trying to figure it out, she checked the door was locked and took the keys upstairs with her. Maybe a shower would help to get some inspiration flowing. She switched on the shower, sitting on the edge of the bath as she waited for the water to get warm. The problem was that, since the release of her debut novel, "Wake up to Love, Daisy May", Holly's belief in romance had all but disappeared. The experience of becoming the face of debut romance had shone a spotlight on the void of true love and magic in her own life. Popping her head out of the bathroom door, she called out, 'Alexa, play some Christmas music. I need to find some festive spirit.'

'Here is a channel you might like. Playing "Stay Another Day" by East 17.'

'Oh, God, no. I don't need a sad song. Screw this! Alexa, play me a song I can sing to.'

'Okay, playing "I Will Survive" by Gloria Gaynor, on repeat.'

'Why not? Come on, Gloria. We got this.' Holly stepped into the shower before belting out the chorus as if she was duetting on stage at Wembley.

Three renditions later, just as she was about to launch into another final chorus, the water temperature plummeted. Holly let out an almighty scream as the freezing water hit her skin. Every hair stood to attention, and even her soul seemed to shiver. Fumbling to switch off the torturous water, she stepped out and grabbed her dressing gown, enveloping herself like a pig in a blanket.

Wrapping her hair in a towel, she turned towards the door but paused with bated breath as she heard one of the voices from earlier. This time, it sounded a lot closer.

The ornate brass door handle started to turn slowly. In her mind, she was screaming, but she dared not make a noise. She grabbed a bottle of talc to arm herself. 'Who is it? I've got a weapon and I'm not afraid to use it!'

'Whoa. Pull in your horns, ma'am. You're the one screaming. Are you alright?' said a male voice in a broad American accent.

'What? No, I di–' Holly paused, realising she *had* just screamed. 'Well, that was just the water. I mean … What the hell are you doing in my house?'

'Well, ma'am, it's actually my house. So, I could ask y'all the same question.'

'What?'

'It would be easier to explain face-to-face. Are y'all decent in there?'

'What?' Holly shook her head in a state of confusion-meets-panic, mistakenly putting her hand on the heated towel rail. 'Arghh!' she screamed out in pain, throwing her arm in the air, which knocked her off balance, making her slip on the wet floor.

She screamed again, and the door opened. Before she could protest, she fell backwards and her dressing gown flew open just as the man barged in. In a split second of sheer panic, Holly threw the bottle at him. On impact with the rim of his black Stetson, the bottle of talc exploded, covering him entirely in shimmering white powder.

Holly landed on the sink. Luckily, her dressing gown had landed in a way that covered most of her.

'What happened? Are you okay?' he asked, covering his eyes to protect her dignity.

'Who are you and what do you want?' she blurted whilst looking around to find her next weapon of choice: a toilet roll.

He peaked out through his fingers to see what was going on.

'Please, not the paper, too.' He raised his hands in the air and closed his eyes. 'I surrender. I never knew you British girls were so violent.'

'Don't move. I know Tai chi!' Holly threatened.

'Hey, I'm sorry. If a lady screams, I try to help. That's all this is. Now, is there any chance you can ask Gloria to pipe down so we can talk?'

'Oh, yeah. Alexa, music off.' As the music stopped, the stranger lowered his hands and slowly opened his eyes, one at a time.

He carefully removed his talc-covered hat to reveal thick, dark brown hair which had been flattened on top but curled out at the edges by the rim of his hat. His white-dusted eyelashes revealed the deepest blue eyes that glistened in a heaven-sent, fallen snow kind of way. Suddenly, Holly became acutely aware of her nudity beneath her sparkly unicorn dressing gown, and his close presence. His tall, dark, very handsome and – to top off her dream book-boyfriend checklist – American cowboy presence.

Her legs turned to jelly and her face reddened. Steadying herself on the sink, she couldn't take her eyes off his every movement. She gulped, lost in lustful thoughts, wondering if he was the inspiration she had been looking for.

'Ma'am?' She didn't respond, but still stared at him. 'Ma'am?' He waved his hand in front of her, but still, she didn't react. 'Ma'am, are you okay?'

As she felt his hand touch her shoulder, she snapped out of her dream and back into reality. 'Shit! Sorry ... Yes ... Sorry. Who are you?'

'Tyler.' He lifted his hat, tipped it, and got a second dusting of talc.

She couldn't help but giggle, partly as it was a genuinely funny moment, but mostly because she felt like a schoolgirl who'd just been touched by her secret crush.

He shook his head but smiled. 'Okay, can we start over?'

'That'd probably be the best idea, but may I get dressed first, please? Kinda feeling naked right now. I mean, exposed. I mean ...'

He laughed as she squirmed in embarrassment, pulling her dressing gown as tight as she could and covering her face with the toilet roll to hide what she was sure were the reddest of red cheeks.

'I'll wait downstairs.' He seemed to be trying to hide his amusement as he backed out of the room, closing the door. But it was no use. She heard him laughing.

She looked at herself in the mirror. 'Holly-bloody-Hope, you've just talc-bombed a cowboy!'

*

Holly had just pulled on her jumper but switched to something a little less frumpy when she heard a knock at the front door. She had been contemplating popping on some lipstick, which was unusual for her, but instead went for a quick swipe of lip gloss. She ran down the stairs of the cottage and managed to just make it to the door before Tyler. It was Betty, the lady from whom Holly thought she was renting the cottage.

'Oh Holly, there you are. I'm so sorry, but there's been a little confusion. It seems the owner's nephew is here earlier than we expected.' Betty's gaze slipped past Holly and over her shoulder. 'Oh, Tyler, there you are. I was just explaining the mix-up, but it seems you two have already met.'

'Well, not really. Just in the shower. I mean, I was just in the shower, and he came in.'

'Well, I never. That might be how you do things in America, but that is not acceptable in Cringleton.' The small, plump lady stepped inside as she grabbed an aerosol bottle from her bum bag. She held up the pepper spray inches from Tyler's eyes, holding her other arm in front of Holly to protect her.

Tyler jumped back. 'Whoa, hold your damn horses there. It is not like that, and I didn't do … that. I was waiting for you to show me inside, but you were talking on your cell when I heard a scream.' He looked at Holly with pleading eyes and raised eyebrows. 'Please, tell her! You screamed, I had a key, so I let myself in and shot upstairs to help who I thought was a damsel in bloody distress.'

'Holly, is this correct?' whispered Betty.

Holly looked at Tyler, who still had some traces of talc on his plaid shirt and a smattering above his top lip, just to the side of what she expected could be the perfect smile.

She sighed. 'So, yes. I did scream, BUT I am no damsel in distress. The water was cold, that's all.'

Keeping her pepper spray poised for action, Betty squinted at Tyler, then looked back and forth between them.

Tyler spoke first. 'Betty, please put that damn thing down and tell me what this woman is doing in my house. The lawyer told me he'd let you know the cottage was being sold and that I'd be here to sign the papers and sort it out.'

'Yes, he did, but the email said you'd be here in January, not December.'

'That's impossible. We agreed we'd let the current tenant stay until December 1st, which was three weeks ago. I'm sorry, Miss, but you have had more than enough time to move out.'

'I don't understand,' said Holly. 'YOU own Ivy Cottage? I thought the owner was an old lady.'

She stepped forward and put her hand on Betty's arm to lower it. She obliged and put the bottle back in her bag. Betty then proceeded to take out her phone, flicked through some stuff for a few seconds and then thrust the phone in front of him.

'Here, it says you will be arriving on the 12th of January.'

'No, Ma'am, that's the 1st of December. In America, we write the dates with the month first then the day, not the other way around.'

'Well, that's just silly. How was I to know the date wasn't in English?' She looked towards Holly, who sat down on the sofa, deflated. 'Oh, I'm so sorry, Holly. I was looking after the place while the sale went through. I thought you'd be gone by the time he came, so there wasn't any point in telling you.'

There was a moment of awkward silence. Tyler was looking at the women, seemingly waiting for one of them to say something. He eventually broke the silence. 'Look, I guess I can find somewhere else in the village for tonight. That gives you one night to pack up.'

'Holly? I know you wanted to spend Christmas here, but tonight's the candle walk. That will be good inspiration for the book, won't it? And maybe you can find a room somewhere. I think the pub is fully booked over Christmas, but I can ask around for you.'

'It's fine. It's not like I'd managed to write much here, anyway.'

'Write?' interrupted Tyler.

'Oh, Holly's a famous author,' said Betty proudly. 'She's been staying here to write about Cringleton at Christmas, haven't you, Holly?'

'Well, not famous, but yes, I'm an author,' said Holly. 'I needed to write a Christmas romance and London wasn't giving me any inspiring ideas. So, here I am.'

'Wow, impressive. I hope Ivy Cottage helped.'

'Not really, but that's not the cottage's fault. Okay, well. Everything happens for a reason, or so I've heard.' Holly paused as she noticed Tyler smile. 'What?'

'That saying reminds me of someone, that's all.'

She smiled back. 'Someone special, I hope.' There was a moment of silence as they smiled at each other before Betty coughed, reminding them of her presence. 'I'd better get myself packed up and, well, if I can't find anything around here, then I guess I'll just go back to London.'

'That's the spirit, love. I'll see if there's anything in the village, so don't give up yet. Righty-ho, I need to sort out the brass band for later. I don't know how your auntie did all this in her eighties, God rest her soul.' Betty made the sign of the cross and headed towards the door. 'Tyler, is there anything else you need from me?'

'Erm, if you could just direct me to the nearest hotel.'

'Oh yes, we can try The George. Come on then, don't dawdle. Holly, I'll see you later? We start around seven outside the church.'

After her unexpected visitors had left, Holly slouched back on the sofa and looked around at the talc that seemed to be everywhere. 'Well, Alexa. Guess I should pack.'

'I'm sorry. I don't understand.'

'Okay, Alexa, play "I Will Survive".'

'Playing "I Will Survive" by Gloria Gaynor.'

*

Holly looked around the aged pine four-poster bed with lace drapes that delicately hung from each corner. The white bed cover with its lace trim was perfectly in keeping with the atmosphere of the cottage.

'Oh, beautiful, perfect bedroom. You held so much promise when I first arrived,' she whispered as she patted the headboard. 'Now, I have one more night and then, who knows where I will go next?'

She smiled as she gazed out of the window, which overlooked the wild but perfect country garden. She recalled fondly how Graham had pointed out the abundance of lavender, witch hazel, sweet box, and yew trees, which she had mistaken for her namesake, holly. Her stories tended to take place in fictitious villages, but Cringleton totally hit the mark. Unfortunately, she had failed to be inspired by it.

Holly zipped up her second case and dragged it down the slightly winding staircase. She had been so caught up in packing all afternoon; she hadn't realised how late, and dark outside, it was. As she set her case next to the other, in the little nook under the stairs, her phone pinged. It was a reminder that the candle walk was due to start. She quickly grabbed her coat, put her boots on, and made her way out of the tiny front door.

As she walked down the path to the driveway, she noticed a second car parked next to hers that she didn't recognise. There was a hanger on the rear-view mirror with rental company details on it.

With her torch in hand, she walked down the long lane towards the centre of the village. It wasn't long before others came out from their houses and there were a number of people walking in the same direction. When they reached the front of the church, Holly was amazed to see that everyone in the village, and probably the surrounding villages too, had come out for this event.

'Holly! Holly! Over here!' shouted Betty from behind the little tent where a large group from the Women's Institute was handing out candles.

'Hi, Betty. Great turnout. It's amazing.'

'Not as many as last year, but at least the rain has held off so far. Get yourself a candle and we'll start in about fifteen minutes. Just follow the crowd when the church bells ring. We'll all walk in that direction, up through the village. There are little tents like this dotted around with hot drinks.'

'Oh, okay. Sounds great. Did you …'

'No, no, no. Not that one,' shouted Betty at two women who were carrying a table from inside the church. 'Sorry, love. If you want something doing, you have to do it yourself round here. I'll speak to you tomorrow.' She was gone before Holly could even finish her question.

Holly hadn't made any friends in the village but had become a familiar face, so she smiled and nodded at people she knew. She found herself a little gap in the crowd, which she hoped was likely to be near the sides so she could grab a hot drink to warm her up.

'Hey, hot chocolate for Holly?' The voice had a newly familiar American accent.

'Oh, hello. Thank you so much. That's so kind of you.' Holly shivered as she took the white paper cup from Tyler's hands.

'Well, you looked as cold as I feel, so thought I'd grab us a hot drink while I could.' They smiled at each other shyly before both turning away and awkwardly taking a sip of their drinks.

'Do you have a place to stay yet?' Tyler asked.

'No, I'm hoping Betty has some good news if I can catch her later or in the morning. If not, I might try to book into The George for a night or two.'

'Oh, that place is fully booked. They ain't got a room free until next year.'

'Oh, really? Did you find somewhere for tonight?'

'Erm, yeah. I'll be fine.'

'I'm sure you will be. Sorry, I guess we haven't been formally introduced even though I'm staying in your bed, I mean, house,' said Holly, feeling embarrassed.

'Tyler Fleming, but most people call me "Ty".' He held out his hand but quickly realised Holly was holding a candle in one and a drink in the other. 'Sorry, we can shake it later. I mean shake on it. Sorry, shake hands. Jetlag must be hitting me hard.'

Holly giggled before continuing the introduction. 'Well, Ty, my name is Holly Hope.'

'It's nice to meet you, Holly. It all makes sense now.'

'What?'

'How you ended up at my auntie's cottage. Her name was Hope, and she always believed that everything happens for a reason. Kinda like you said earlier. You reminded me of her.'

The conversation was interrupted by an elderly man with a candle. 'Light?'

'Oh, no. Sorry, I don't smoke,' replied Holly, which seemed to tickle Tyler.

'Oh, no, dear. I meant; do you want me to light your candle?'

An embarrassed Holly held out the tall white candle which had a paper cup round the bottom to collect the wax. 'Thank you.' As the man carried on lighting other candles, Holly turned to Tyler. 'Stop laughing. How was I to know?'

'Well, I ain't no rocket scientist, darling, but if someone is looking for a light, they usually don't have a lit candle in their hand.'

'Whatever.' Holly shoved him with her elbow and for a moment felt a fluttering in her stomach. She noticed that when he smiled, his eyes smiled too. Although he no longer had his Stetson on, his hair remained the same shape.

As the church bell began ringing, they were carried along with the crowd. The brass band was at the front, leading the way. The first song began, and the crowd started to sing.

Ty bent down towards Holly and whispered, 'No one told me we had to sing.'

'Me neither. I thought it was a silent walk.'

The woman in front turned round and hissed, 'Sing, don't talk.'

'Sorry, Ma'am. She isn't from these parts.' Tyler nudged into Holly as the woman gave her a look of disgust. He was desperately trying to stifle a giggle; Holly pursed her lips as she looked at him with widened eyes.

The walk through the village felt inspiring to Holly. She observed details of the buildings that she hadn't noticed during the weeks she had been there. The holly and ivy that were intertwined around the sign hanging outside the pub. The paper snowflakes stuck to the windows in the bookshop, just above the display which had Holly Hope books front and centre. The mistletoe hanging in the middle of the entrance to the café.

Young and old alike sang Christmas carols in a perfectly out-of-pitch-and-sync but beautiful sort of way. Holly and Tyler weren't taking part, but absorbed the atmosphere. The crowd slowed to a stop. Everyone stood in silence for a moment before a single voice started singing "Silent Night".

With each line of the song, a few more people joined in, but the band remained silent. Holly felt goosebumps throughout her body. She looked at the tall, handsome man next to her and smiled.

'This is awesome,' he whispered.

'I know. I've got goosebumps.'

'Me too.'

As the singing came to a close, everyone blew out their burned-down candles, but the band started to play again. This time, it was just as background music, not for singalong purposes. Holly blew out her candle, and when there was an opening in the crowd, pushed her way towards a bin at the side. She threw away her empty cup and candle. Tyler copied her, then slipped his cold hand into hers. He led her through the crowd towards the edge of a quiet side street.

It had been so long since any man had held her hand that Holly surprised herself by not even flinching. She just followed his lead without hesitation. When they were alone, he let go of her hand and her heart sank.

'So?' she asked without planning the rest of the question.

'It was getting crowded around the trash can. Didn't want to be in the way in case it turned into a Black Friday kinda rush to throw away garbage.'

'Well, if they fear the wrath of Betty, then you might be right,' giggled Holly. 'I guess I should get back to the cottage to enjoy my last night.'

'Yeah. I'm sure you'll find somewhere else to stay.'

'Oh, I'm not worried. Everything happens for a reason, remember?'

'Yes, it does,' he agreed. He put his hands in his pockets, but lifted his elbow out and nodded his head for her to link. She obliged. They waited in silence for a few moments before walking back through the village, arm in arm.

As they walked up the lane to the cottage, Holly carried her torch to light the way. 'Guess that's your hire car, then?'

'Yeah, there didn't seem to be anywhere else to park.'

'Well, thanks again for the hot chocolate. Really hit the spot.'

'You're welcome. Always like to hit the spot.' Holly's eyes widened, and Tyler covered his face to hide his embarrassment. 'I should go. Goodnight, Holly Hope.'

'Night, Tyler Fleming.'

Holly opened the garden gate and made her way along the cobbled path to the little arch in front of the cottage door. Once inside, Holly locked the door and then fell back against it with a smile so wide her cheek muscles ached. Holly looked at her hand, recalling how strong Tyler's had felt in hers. She walked up the stairs in a daze. How unexpectedly magical the evening had been. Reaching the main bedroom, she saw her notebook, which she had left next to her bed. The notebook's cover had the words, "Just a girl dreaming up her next book-boyfriend" on it and she picked it up, grabbed a pen and frantically started making notes.

Christmas Wishes & Mistletoe Kisses

Every love story has a beginning, middle and, if you are as unlucky in love as Ivy Berry, then they definitely have an end – just not always happy ones. Christmas in Cringleton was always magical, but not for Ivy, which is why she had successfully avoided them for ten years. However, the passing of her aunt had forced her to return and face the ghosts of her Christmas past. This year, a new face in the village may just be the one to turn Ivy from frozen to—

The sound of a car horn abruptly halted Holly's flow. She jumped up and as she got to the bedroom window, she saw a light inside the rental car. She pulled her boots back on and ran downstairs. Grabbing her torch and forgetting how cold it was, she opened the door and shone her light on the car.

'Who's there?' she called.

No reply. She stepped onto the path and slowly walked towards the driveway. As she got close, she cautiously approached the passenger door and knocked on the window.

'Hello?'

Someone shifted in the car before opening the door. 'It's only me. No more powder, please.'

Stepping back, Holly watched as Tyler emerged. His hair was even messier, and he squinted at her with one eye closed, blinded by the light of her torch.

'Sorry.' She lowered the torch. 'I thought someone had broken in. Were you sleeping?'

'Yeah. Sorry if the horn woke you. There weren't any rooms, so I figured I could crash in the car for a night. I've slept in worse places.'

Holly shone the light inside the car and saw the front seat was fully reclined and a coat had been thrown on the other seat, which she assumed was his attempt at a blanket. 'Why don't you come inside?'

'No, Ma'am. I'm okay here. I've already disrupted your stay. I couldn't ruin your last night in the cottage.'

'It's okay. You wouldn't be ruining anything. It would be nice not to have to sleep alone for once.'

He said nothing, but waited for Holly to correct herself.

'You know I don't mean it like that. Blooming heck, I really have to watch everything I say with you cowboys, don't I?'

'If you really don't mind, I can crash on the sofa.'

'There are two bedrooms, so no sofa surfing required. Come on. I'll make you a brew 'cause you must be freezing.' She made her way back to the cottage as Tyler grabbed his keys and a bag from the boot and followed.

Once inside, she showed him to the spare bedroom and left him to sort himself out. When he came back downstairs, she had made a hot chocolate for him and was sitting on the sofa, waiting.

'Oh, thanks,' he said, sitting next to her. As he got comfy, his hand accidentally brushed against hers. He pulled away, smiling. 'Sorry, this is a really small sofa.'

'Yeah, it's definitely what I would call a snuggle sofa.'

'Snuggle sofa? That's a new one on me.'

'You know what I mean,' said Holly. 'It's when you get all cosy with someone, and you snuggle up together. I'd have my head on your chest, your arm around me and we would be, well, snuggling. Not that I snuggle with men. Well, I do, but no one in particular.' Holly was not used to feeling so nervous around someone, but with him, she couldn't help it.

'I think you might need to show me,' he said, moving his hand a little closer towards hers.

Holly froze and gulped loudly. Her heart told her to do it, her head was in disbelief, and her body was consumed with nerves. She tentatively placed her hand beside his. Their fingers touched. He slowly stroked the top of her hand before she turned it over and he tickled her palm. His fingers slid in between hers and he held her hand in his. She closed her eyes to take in the moment before bravely turning her head towards him.

As their eyes met, she noticed how they sparkled even without the talc. He bit his lip, and she mirrored his actions by biting hers before closing her eyes. As their lips touched, he squeezed her hand. He raised his other one and pushed his fingers through her hair. Lost in each other, their embrace intensifying, she felt his body against hers. Immersed in the moment, she tried to ignore the niggling thoughts that she shouldn't be letting this happen. The only happy endings that existed were in romance books. One night could end in heartbreak for her, so she pulled away. Their lips parted first, then their bodies, followed by his grip on her hand loosening.

They sat apart for a few moments in silence, no longer facing each other. Holly leant forward and picked up her mug of hot chocolate. Tyler copied. 'Well, that was, erm, unexpected,' said Holly, breaking the tension. Tyler nodded and continued to drink. 'I … erm … I think I'll go to bed. Alone, just to be clear, I am going to bed alone.' Still avoiding eye contact, she stood up, placed her half-empty cup on the coffee table and made her way past him and towards the stairs.

'Goodnight, Holly.'

'Goodnight, Ty.'

*

Holly spent most of the night tossing and turning, reliving every moment of the evening before, from the candlelight walk, to when Tyler held her hand, and to that kiss. Eventually, in the early hours, she grabbed her book and snuck downstairs. Quietly, she set herself up on the dining table in the corner of the room. Laptop, notebook, and a large mug of coffee – ready to turn scribbles into chapters.

As the night turned to morning, sunlight broke through the curtains to hit the sun catcher hanging in the window, and projected a spectrum of rainbows around the cottage. The colours lighting up the room fuelled the inspirational fires that were well and truly burning within Holly.

It was only the aroma of fresh coffee and toast that eventually drew Holly's attention from her screen. Tyler was standing beside her, fully dressed, placing a plate and a steaming mug next to her laptop.

'Oh, thanks. I didn't hear you get up.'

'I'm not surprised. You've been writing for hours. This place really must inspire you.' He relaxed onto the sofa beside the table, eating toast and holding a cup of coffee.

'Yeah, well, no, actually. I've been here nearly three months and have lots of scribbled notes, but nothing that could coherently be turned into a novel. And then, boom! Last night I couldn't sleep, and the story just started writing itself.'

'That's awesome. So, I'm guessing something triggered this wave of inspiration then? Any ideas what? Or maybe … who?' He smiled with the same air of cheekiness she'd seen during the candlelight walk when the woman scolded them for talking.

'Absolutely. I really must thank Betty when I see her this morning. The candlelight walk was the spark I needed.'

Tyler laughed a little as he placed his cup on the table. 'Betty, of course. Nothing to do with the "handsome stranger who gave her hot chocolate in one hand, and stole her heart with the other." Wonder who the handsome stranger was?'

Holly gasped. 'When did you read my story? How rude are you?' She slammed her laptop closed, then saw her notebook next to him on the sofa. She made a dash towards it, but he got there first and held it high above his head, stretched out away from her. She tried to reach over his head but slipped forward, landing with her hands either side of him, her chest against his, and her face inches from his. The book slipped from his fingers as he lost concentration. The heat of his body almost melted her.

'Stay,' he whispered.

'What?'

'Stay another day?'

'With you?'

He nodded.

Pushing herself back up and clambering off him, Holly picked up her book from the floor, pondering the proposal.

'Separate rooms. I may be a cowboy, but you'll learn that cowboys can be gentlemen, too.'

It was not like Holly to take such big risks, but then again, not making her usual safe decisions was the reason she was here in Cringleton in the first place.

'And you're not a serial killer. Are you?'

'No, but I get it if you think it's weird.'

'Well, we already spent one night together, and you didn't try to sneak into my bed.'

'Ha, ha, ha, you sound disappointed.'

Holly shrugged, not knowing whether to admit her disappointment. 'When are you leaving?'

'Christmas Eve. I'll leave the keys with the lawyer or the realtor, and I'll be on my way back home to Fort Worth, Texas. So, you can stay until then if you want, so long as we don't annoy each other. I'm okay sharing my cottage with a pretty English girl for a week.'

Holly walked back over to the dining room table, sat down, and opened her laptop. She smiled as she looked around the small living-cum-dining room, which still had the rainbows flickering from the window. 'Well, this pretty English girl is okay sharing with a handsome Texan cowboy.'

'Well, now that's settled. I've gotta meet with the lawyer to sign some documents or something. Do you have any plans?'

'I might just carry on writing for today. Gotta write whilst I am in the zone.'

'I'll carry your case back upstairs and then I shall leave you to it. I'll let Betty know you'll be staying a few more days. She's the executor of Hope's will, and I think she wants to talk to me about it later.'

'Perfect. I'll just nip upstairs and get showered and changed, if that's okay.'

'Sure, don't let me interrupt you, unless …'

'Unless nothing. You said you were a gentleman. Don't make me regret my decision.'

Tyler stepped back with his hands in the air, laughing. He picked up her case and carried it upstairs as she followed him.

'Have a nice day, Holly.'

'You too. And Ty, I'm sorry about your auntie. I didn't know her, of course, but I'm sorry for your loss. Were you close to her?'

He paused outside her bedroom door. Turning back to face her, he answered, 'Not as close as I wish I had been. When I was little, she was my favourite adult. We would laugh for hours. I used to write to her, but over the years, life got in the way. In any letter she would send me, she would end it with, "remember, my dear boy, everything happens for a reason." I wish I'd made more of an effort to come over when she was alive rather than being here now that she's gone.'

'She must have been a very special lady. I am sure she knew you loved her.' When Holly placed her hand on his arm, he smiled and nodded, but didn't say anything more. He popped into his room to get his phone and keys before heading downstairs. She heard the front door shut and watched him walk down the path from her window. As he got to the driveway, he turned and looked up. He waved. She hid behind the curtain, embarrassed that he had seen her watching him.

Holly quickly sent a text to her agent to let her know that she had started the Christmas novel. After her shower, she settled back at the table downstairs and carried on writing page after page, chapter after chapter. The words flowed easier than a waterfall.

*

Over the next few days, Holly and Tyler spent almost every minute of each day together. She became his tour guide around the village and took him walking through the forests, around local reservoirs and even hiking up

Man Tor. Every now and then, Tyler would have a sense of familiarity. The smell of the Brussel sprouts from the Christmas lunch being served in the café, or the poinsettias in the windows. In the evenings, while Tyler sorted through his aunt's personal belongings, Holly took advantage of the creative stimulation she felt around him. Instead of showers to get her inspiration going, just being in his presence kept it flowing like an endless river. She could almost believe that true love was possible in real life if it weren't for the fact she knew he was leaving, and they'd only known each other for less than a week.

Holly noticed the moments when he thought she wasn't looking, but she could see him watching her. If she was describing those looks in her book, she would say that "Ty was enchanted by her" and she knew no one had ever looked at her like that before. As the days went by, she dreaded Christmas Eve arriving, as that was the day he would be leaving and she was not prepared for it.

The day before Christmas Eve, Holly spent the morning prepping for the last meal together. In the afternoon, Holly was tidying round the bedroom and dropped a pen down the back of the bedside table. When she moved the furniture to reach it, she found an unsealed envelope stuck between the bed and wall. When she peaked inside, she smiled and held it to her chest. Excited by her discovery, she quickly placed it in her notebook and took it downstairs with her.

The turkey was sliced, the vegetables cooked, and the table set with Christmas crackers, tinsel trim, and a bottle of wine. For their last evening together, Holly had persuaded Tyler to let her cook him a traditional Christmas dinner. She wore her one and only little black dress. Tyler wore his usual jeans but with a smart white shirt and bolo tie. When dinner was ready, they set the table together and just before they were seated, Tyler asked Holly to wait for one minute and disappeared upstairs.

'Sorry, here now.' Tyler stood in front of her, holding up a sprig of mistletoe. Holly leant in towards him. Her hands felt the crispness of the shirt against her fingers as her lips touched his. The kiss was gentle and the moment perfect until the memory of Julia and the "camel toe" conversation popped in her mind and she almost spat in his face as she tried so hard not to laugh.

A confused Tyler stepped backwards. 'Well, I ain't had a girl laugh in my face when I kissed her since Mary-Lou in Junior high. You letting me in on the joke?'

'I'm sorry, my sister made a joke about mistletoe and I'm sorry. It's not funny, the kiss I mean. The kiss was … mmmm … yummy.' Holly gulped nervously, now wishing she hadn't laughed. He shook his head and held out the chair for her to sit down first. As they sat down to eat, he was overwhelmed with how much effort Holly had gone to for him.

'This is so kind of you. It's been more than twenty years since I had a Christmas dinner like this. You have no idea how much this means to me.'

Holly reached over the table and held his hand. He squeezed her hand tightly. She never wanted him to let go, but just didn't know whether to admit it.

She desperately wanted to tell him how she felt, but the only words that came out were 'Tyler, I really ... wish ... hope you enjoy it.'

They chatted and laughed, swept up in the Christmas spirit. Pulling their crackers, wearing silly hats, much to Tyler's dismay, and even talked about their favourite Christmas memories.

'Holly, the food was amazing. Except for the sprouts. Not my kinda thing, but the apple pie and custard sure made up for it.'

'You're too kind. Now, let's get this cleared away.' Tyler put the plates in the kitchen before joining Holly, who had moved to the sofa, waiting for him to return.

'Your aunt's spirit will always be around. She is watching over you.'

'Maybe. She kept all these mementos of my visits and even Betty says she used to talk about me all the time. I guess I didn't see how important I was to her, and I realise now how much I took that for granted. I am a grown ass man, but I ain't afraid to admit that I missed getting that card from her this year.'

'Maybe not. I found something today that I think was meant for you.' Holly picked up her notebook, removed the envelope, and handed it to Tyler.

When he opened it, there was a Christmas card that had the words "Happy Christmas Nephew" with a Christmas tree on the front and on the inside were the written words, "My Dearest Tyler, Happy Christmas. I hope this year you get everything you have been waiting for. All my love, Auntie Hope." He sat back on the sofa, holding the card to his chest.

Holly watched as the first tear trickled down his cheek. She slid into his embrace, lay her head on his chest and snuggled with him as his body trembled. She said nothing, but comforted him while he calmed and composed himself.

As he did so, she moved from the arm of the sofa to take the seat next to him instead. She lifted his arm and lay her head on his chest. As she did so, Tyler kissed her forehead before resting his chin on her head. With their arms wrapped around each other, he hugged her tight. She closed her eyes, wanting to remember every second of what was happening.

'Isn't life crazy? A week ago, you walked into my bathroom and I threw a tub of talc at you. Now, I feel like I've known you for years.'

'I know. I came over to sort out my aunt's stuff and sell the cottage. I thought at best I might get to see a bit of England, but you've shown me there is much more to England than tea and biscuits.'

'Would you ever consider moving over here?' Holly mumbled.

'Nothing for a cowboy to do round here.'

'Oh, I dunno. I could probably help you figure out a thing or two.'

'I bet you could.' He reached his hand down the side of the sofa. 'Holly, I want to give you something.'

'Oh, lucky me!'

'Not that,' reacted Tyler, smiling at the innuendo before handing her a black velvet box. She opened the lid and discovered a delicate vintage silver watch with a pearl face. When she turned the watch over, she noticed the word "Hope" engraved on the back. 'It was my aunt's. I noticed it in one of the photos. That's what I had to see Betty about today. She had mistakenly given it to the charity shop and had been trying to track it down.'

'It's stunning, but you should take it with you.' She put it back in the box and pushed it towards him.

'Everything happens for a reason. She would want you to have it. I just know from my boots to my hat it's the right thing to do.' He took the watch back out of the box and placed it around her wrist. He took her hand in his and kissed it. Holly wanted to burst with happiness.

They settled back together on the sofa, snuggled tightly. He squeezed her as he kissed her forehead. They sat in silence for a few minutes, immersed in each other's hold.

'Have you finished writing your book yet?'

Holly shook her head. 'I wish. I can't write that fast, but I am about halfway through, so it's going well.'

'And does the handsome man with the hot chocolate win her heart?'

'Well, you'll just have to wait to find out, won't you?' She paused for a few seconds before asking him nervously, 'Have you checked in for your flight?'

'Yep. All set.'

'So, you're definitely leaving tomorrow, then?'

'I am.'

Holly felt a crack in her heart. She released herself from his arms and placed her hand on his thigh. 'I'm tired. I'm gonna head to bed.' She kissed him gently on the cheek and walked towards the stairs. Hesitating for a second, she turned back towards him and reached out her hand.

'Holly, I don't think it's a good idea.'

'Maybe not, but maybe just lay with me until I fall asleep. If it's our last night, at least we can spend it together.'

They held hands as she led him into her bedroom. As he lay down on the bed, she released the curtains from their ties and watched as the delicate white lace and chiffon surrounded the bed.

'When I saw the photos of this room online, I loved the lace curtains, and I loved this bed. It looked like the most romantic bedroom in the sweetest of cottages. It promised so much inspiration. I think this whole "everything happens for a reason" is true. I guess it just takes more than a bed to inspire. It takes people, and that's something that had never really clicked with me until now … until you.'

As she lay down beside him, he whispered, 'You're amazing.'

He lifted his arm, and she slid perfectly into the nook of his armpit like she was the missing piece of his jigsaw. When she lay her head on his chest, it felt like something they had done a million times, except it wasn't. It was only the third time she had felt his heart beating against her cheek and felt the safety of his arms. She sighed contentedly as he kissed her on the head, a wave of emotions submerging her heart in happiness. She closed her eyes, quickly feeling herself drifting off to sleep but still awake enough to hear him whisper, 'I think I am falling in love with you.'

She didn't answer. If she told him she felt the same, the thought of leaving might break his heart as much as it did hers. Instead, she squeezed him tight and didn't let him see the tiny tears rolling down her cheeks.

As his breathing deepened, she whispered, 'Stay, please. Just one more day.' He didn't reply, but she kept her eyes closed, holding on to a tiny thread of hope that he wouldn't leave. They fell asleep in each other's arms, neither one willing to let go, just yet.

*

When Holly woke in the morning, she found herself alone in bed.

'Ty?' There was no answer. She jumped out of bed and ran into his bedroom. His case was gone and there were no clothes left.

She ran downstairs, but it was empty.

She opened the door. His car was gone.

She looked around the empty cottage. There was a note on the coffee table:

Holly,

I'm no good at goodbyes and I really do need to get home. Sorry.

Aunt Hope would have loved the thought of this cottage inspiring you and I think she would have loved you too. I have arranged for you to stay until January 10th, which I hope is enough time to finish writing your novel.

Everything happens for a reason. Meeting me has inspired you to write one story, but maybe meeting each other has started an even bigger story. Just not the kind you need to write!

If you find yourself wondering what the next chapter in our story might be, then I think I know of a ranch in Texas you might like for your next vacation.

Forever your cowboy,

Ty

P.S. Yes, I wish I could have stayed another day too.

Sarah Shard

Wrapped in Red

Joe Burkett

December 24th 2016

Ah, December. My favourite month of the year. I know it's a cliché, but it really is the most wonderful time of the year. Andy Williams sang about it, so it must be true. It's the month where you can treat yourself to some new high street style for your office Christmas party, catch up with friends for some festive-themed cocktails, and belt out "Driving Home from Christmas" like you've just stolen the car and Chris Rea is providing nothing more than backing vocals, shifting into fifth gear as the concert for one brace's itself for a very merry mixtape of seasonal classics. And, of course, December presents the perfect backdrop for popping a certain question. Who doesn't love a Christmas proposal?

Christmas time in Dublin, you can't beat it. Well, you could, I suppose, if a sunnier climate was your chosen holiday destination. Christmas in Santorini with the sun beating down on you, not a bad thought. A Greek Adonis of a Santa Claus dressed in nothing but a pair of red hot-pants with a fluffy white rim, not a bad view. Of course, it has its pluses, I'm not disputing that, but Christmas at home in Ireland surrounded by friends and family, that's where it's at for me. Now, Clodagh, a dear friend of mine,

191

swears that a December trip to New York is the most magical experience ever; Rockefeller Christmas tree, Saks Fifth Avenue light show and New York Christmas window displays. Again, a Christmas vacation stateside is very special to some people, but I'm not one of them. Look it, each to their own! In my humble festive opinion, you can keep your Times Square; Grafton Street is the place to be to soak up all of your seasonal shenanigans.

Here I am, walking down Grafton Street listening to some young busker murdering "I Wish It Could Be Christmas Everyday". While I agree with the sentiment (my love of all things Crimbo is well-known), I can't get on board with this wannabe Ed Sheeran's version of the classic. However, there is something endearing about Irish Ed and I admire his determination in belting out festive hits in the hopes of making a few bob. Good on you, mate. I remember busking on this very street with Clodagh when I moved to the big smoke two years ago. Our version of "Santa Baby" would have given Tom Jones and Cerys Matthews a run for their money. But, yeah, my move to Dublin, for many different reasons, was the best decision I ever made.

God, I've heard cows in labour sing better than this young fella. And, I should know, being from the country. Good old Roscommon. The best road in Roscommon is very much the road out of it! I'll throw Irish Ed a few euro anyway, sure. Support the arts, that's what I always say. As the coins bounce their way into his guitar case, I see his spotted teenage face light up. His initial reaction is one of thanks for the few euros I've just thrown him, but I think he recognises me on the second glance. I give him a quick nod of acknowledgement, and he straightens his stance before returning to crooning (badly) to the Wizzard classic.

Good lad, follow your dreams. That's what Clodagh and I did. Look at us now, I've had three top ten hits in the Irish charts and Clodagh and her band, The Rigs, are charting all over Europe and are about to crack the US market. God, but I'm only delighted for her. Bless her, she has never forgotten her roots. Always one to support a local cause or duet with a cash-strapped busker trying to break the internet. Heaven knows that this poor busker could do with a duet from a certain famous flame-haired Irish singer at this point. I'd step in myself, but Clodagh is far more famous than me.

I catch sight of myself in the Brown Thomas Christmas window display. Running my fingers through my quaffed black hair with its one lightning strike of grey in the fringe, I can't help but be proud of my little grey streak. I think it gives me an edge!

'Like a silver fox in training.' Lorcan always jokes. It's about the only thing about my appearance he approves of. He hates that I never feel the cold and that even now, with the threat of snow looming, I'm still wearing my shorts, accompanied with some biker boots and a Christmas-themed Marvel t-shirt. I'm the height of fashion; me. It wouldn't be to Lorcan's taste, but I guess that's what makes us work.

Opposites do attract. Well, that's what they say. Lorcan is diary-date driven with meetings, gigs and interviewers scheduled well in advance. A career-climbing guy with his eyes on the prize. I'm more of a "let's head out for a drink on a random Tuesday evening and see where the night takes us". Many a night has ended in a hotel room with a traffic cone and deli-style sausage rolls. Of course, those nights were before I met Lorcan.

I would say I'm a little more on top of my time-management now. He has worked his time-management magic on me, and now, I am mostly on time for things. I guess I'm more conscientious now. I am now *so* conscientious and time-management driven that I've checked Lorcan's diary, and he is at home tonight, in our little terrace townhouse, working on some social media campaign for my new album. Ah, Lorcan, always wanting the best for me ever since we first met.

Lorcan hates it when I tell this story, but I first encountered him on this very street. It was my first Christmas in Dublin and I was busking to buy my bus ticket home to Roscommon. Singing my heart out to Wham's "Last Christmas", I was giving it my all, desperately trying to entice the last-minute Christmas Eve shoppers to part with their loose change. There I was, strumming my guitar and reaching the crescendo of the song, when this tall, dark and handsome stranger wearing a red Santa-shaped diamond earring with a gold rim edge and a scruffy rainbow scarf caught my eye. He had the cutest dimples too. And, he was swaying along to the tune. But for the benefit of the tape, Lorcan was actually standing behind Mr Rainbow Scarf with the cutest dimples.

Lorcan stepped out from behind Mr Rainbow Scarf as I finished my song. As he made his way towards me, I took him in and captured his image in my mind's eye. I've never forgotten how smart he looked that first night we spoke. Tight, skinny-fit, navy trousers sitting perfectly on a pair of brown shoes, accompanied by a knee-length camel coat with the collar pulled up around his neck. Attractiveness oozed from him like a chocolate bomb dessert on Christmas day.

'Best version of that song I've ever heard,' Lorcan said.

'I don't think George Michael would agree with you,' I replied.

'You've got a great voice. George Michael should think himself lucky that you're singing it.'

Lorcan had a twinkle in his eye as he invited me for a drink. As I accepted his offer, Mr Rainbow Scarf threw some coins into my open guitar case.

'It's good to support the arts,' he said as he placed his hand on my upper-arm and for a fleeting moment, we locked eyes. There was an energy there. I could feel it.

'Let's make a move,' Lorcan said.

I nodded my thanks, broke free from Mr Rainbow Scarf and returned my attentions to Lorcan, who was telling me about this bar we could head to. He could get us on the VIP list. How exciting! Me, on a VIP list. Far from my bus ticket to Roscommon my mind was wandering! While Mr Rainbow Scarf had caught my eye, it was Lorcan who stole my heart.

The faint crooning of Irish Ed echoes its way down Grafton Street as he attempts to take on "White Christmas". And with the threat of snow, it's a very apt song choice. I move away from the Christmas window display and distance myself from the off-key singing. The Christmas streetlights dance above my head. Twinkling chandeliers accompanied with the words *"Nollaig Shona Duit"* illuminated and shining bright. *Nollaig Shona Duit* (Merry Christmas to you), indeed. And Merry Christmas to you, Lorcan. This year, I'm not laden down with gifts. I'm not concerned with bus tickets home. I'm not busking on the streets. I've just got the one very special gift, and it's for you. Placing my hand in my pocket, I search around for the four-carat diamond ring, wrapped in red with a gold ribbon. Taking it out, I admire the hope for my future, twinkling under the Christmas lights.

Christmas this year is going to be amazing. I just know it.

December 23rd 2017

Kerry International Airport! A place so small that you could carry it on the plane with you as hand luggage. It's no JFK in terms of size, but getting through security is a hell of a lot quicker here than it is in New York. Speaking of New York, the Kerry crew won't be giving the Rockefeller Christmas Tree any cause for concern this year with their sparsely decorated Christmas one. Purple and blue tinsel hanging dangerously from the branches, baubles flung upon it with careless abandon and an angel sitting on top, falling sideways, she looks like she's had one too many at the bar. I've never felt more in sync with a Christmas tree in all my life. I'll be taking a leaf out of that angel's book and the only thing I'll be decorating is a very large glass with duty-free vodka. If I had a drink in my hand, I would raise a toast to the Kerry International Airport Christmas tree for not giving a shit and owning it! Screw the Christmas tree decorating and any other festive related frolics because this year for me; Christmas is cancelled!

Now, where the hell is my luggage? You'd think, with the place being as small as a stamp that my luggage would be bobbing its way along the conveyer belt by now. "Jingle Bell Rock" begins to play on someone's phone. It's a mother and a little child. The child is dressed in a Christmas jumper, and, of course, Mummy dearest is wearing a matching one. There was a time when I would have loved this, but not now. "Jingle Bell Rock" my eye; give me a vodka-jingle-bell-on-the-rocks over this crap. I scratch my head before massaging my temple as mother and child are now directing a sing-a-long with the other passengers.

I seek solace from the crooning Christmas travellers and hide beside my good friend; the Kerry International Airport's Christmas tree. I take the opportunity to check my emails on my phone. I quickly search for my booking and, by default, my escape from all things festive, and breathe a sigh of relief that my self-catering cottage in the heart of the Kingdom is all confirmed. This Christmas is all about me. After last year's disaster, I've decided to avoid any chance of heartbreak. So, no mistletoe kisses for me.

'Charlie,' a voice calls out from the crowd by the conveyer belt. Oh no. I recognise that voice. Clodagh. But what's she doing here?

'Charlie, boy. Fancy seeing you here,' she says darting towards me like a demented snow plough.

Last Christmas when things spectacularly fell apart with Lorcan, Clodagh was my rock, but I haven't seen much of her since then. Friends like her are rare, and seeing her here and now, I do feel a pang of guilt for not being in touch. Her gut feeling about Lorcan had always been one of mistrust and dislike, but she placed her trust in my feelings for him and supported me. "Listen to your gut," she would always say. And, normally, I would. But where Lorcan was concerned, my heart was so full of love and hope that my 20/20 vision had blurred and become blind to his wandering eye and scheming ways.

'Clodagh, Christ. How are you?' I greet her with a hug. What the hell is she doing down these parts?

'So, what brings you to the Kingdom?' she asks while adjusting her Nutcracker-style hat.

Akin to a Nutcracker, I had retreated from my life like a wounded soldier following Lorcan's betrayal. I had lost the battle for his love, respect and affection without realising I was even in the war. Clodagh, bless her, had tried to reach out to me, but I felt like such a fool. Even though I knew she wouldn't judge me, I was judging myself. She knew I was planning to propose. The feeling of shame and embarrassment would grip me like a vice when she would phone me or send a text. Her concern was genuine, and the nausea I felt from not answering her calls or replying to her texts was all-consuming. I was broken, hurt, and rejected. I couldn't face her sympathy and pity.

I can feel Clodagh's eyes on me, her anticipation to know why I am in Kerry. I must deflect.

'What about you? You gigging down here? Where are the boys?' I change the subject and ask about the Rigs. Clodagh and the Rigs (I know it's a silly name but the lads worked together on the oil rigs and just went with it) were flying high in the US charts last time I had the heart to check.

'Bit of time out. We've got a big tour in the New Year; sure, you know yourself ...' Clodagh pauses.

That's the thing; I don't know, not anymore. I've not gigged since last year. After everything that happened with Lorcan, not only did I lose my relationship and my home, I lost my management. He made sure that all my gigs were cancelled, my new album shelved and, worse of all, my love of singing and creating music has all gone because of him. He did a real number on me.

I need to get away from Clodagh. A friend so dear to me, a friend who has always had my back and now, I can't face her. Another thing Lorcan has taken from me.

'Yeah, sure I know,' I lie. 'Listen, I'm actually rushing. I'm being picked up.'

'Are you staying someplace local? We could try and catch up. It would be good to chat. I've not heard from you in ages,' Clodagh says.

And there it is. From anyone else it would have sounded judgemental, but from Clodagh it's so sincere and heartfelt that I can't help but feel the re-emergence of that pang of guilt. Like a lump in my throat, I swallow down hard to deter it from manifesting into the form of flowing tears. Clodagh means well, but I can't catch up with her. I'm not ready and I don't know when I will be.

'Definitely. I'd love that. Sure, I've got your number.' I see my suitcase appear on the conveyer belt and make a play for it. 'I'll give you a call.' I grab the suitcase and head off.

'Be sure you do. And, Merry Christmas, Charlie,' Clodagh says.

I dodge past her and drag my suitcase along the ground. I can't return the gesture. I can't wish her 'Many Happy Returns' because I don't feel it. My Christmas spirit is somewhere between the Grinch and Scrooge. I don't look back. I don't dare wave. I keep looking forward so that I can stifle the stirring embers of hope igniting within me. I want to run to Clodagh, to talk to her, to cry and laugh with her, to bitch about Lorcan, and then cry some more. With her help, I know I could pick up the pieces of my broken jigsaw heart and put them back together, but for now, it's all I can do to not cry as I make a beeline for the exit.

*

The doors open and I exit the Arrivals Hall into the lobby of the airport. The swell of expectant family members waiting for their nearest and dearest to arrive home for Christmas momentarily overwhelms me. Inhaling deeply, I gather my thoughts and re-establish my reasons for being in Kerry, for not getting in contact with Clodagh and for needing this Christmas to just pass me by. With my steely resolute restored, I exhale and grab my suitcase.

Darting through smiling mothers and excited siblings, I search the crowd for my driver. It takes me a few minutes before I see a guy emerge from the lobbying stampede of Christmas well-wishers. Stepping towards me, I take stock of him. He is handsome yet unconventionally so. His lips are straight and tight and his eyes are dark. His wide smile reveals a beautiful set of veneers and light up the room like a disco ball. God, he seems a bit full of himself. His swagger reminds me of Lorcan as he walks towards me. This guy thinks he's the sexy Santa to all willing wish-list writers. How very Lorcan! Well, you aren't on my wish-list. Not me, sunshine; not this Christmas.

'Hi, I'm Charlie.' I say curtly.

He looks at me bemused, and I feel like such a tit when I see the sign! What a cliché. He is literally holding a sign clearly stating that he is here to pick up a Mrs Winters. My cheeks redden as I make a hasty escape. Rushing from my ill-advised near car-jacking incident, I smash straight into another guy. Christ, I feel like a learner driver with a shining great L-plate wrapped around my neck.

'Hi,' he greets me.

'Hey. So, sorry,' I reply, the heat in my cheeks explode like an inferno. How many more times am I going to embarrass myself before leaving this godforsaken airport?

'Charlie? I'm Jack.' He places his hand on my shoulder.

The touch of his hand on my shoulder ignites a jolt of electricity in my veins as a surge of energy curses through my body. I'm feeling a little light-headed. If I didn't know any better, I would say I was going weak at the knees. But before my knees have the chance to abandon me, he releases his grip, and I am cast afloat with a willingness to reach out and pull him back.

I haven't felt an instant connection like this for a long time. I need to refocus. Good God, Charlie; talk to the man.

'I'm Charlie,' I say before closing my eyes with embarrassment. 'And you've just said that.' I shake my head and offer a weak smile as I reopen my eyes.

Jack lets out a hearty chuckle. His dimples are cute when he laughs. Why do I think his laugh is cute? Old me would have been a sucker for a giggle, but new me? Well, I thought I knew the new me. But his laughter is making my heart rise from captivity, and, dare I hope, to a place where it can heal.

His eyes meet mine and I am completely at peace with falling into his hazel brown eyes. A warm feeling engulfs me as I take in this handsome man standing before me with his strong jawline and subtle hints of stubble. His outfit is fashionably festive. Clearly a fan of the Yuletide holiday as his tatty Christmas jumper with a flashing Rudolph nose has seen better days.

He breaks eye contact and I am transported back to the airport lobby with 'It's beginning to look a lot like Christmas' blasting through the air.

'Aunt Melody asked if I could collect you. I think she was trying to email you earlier, but she couldn't find the code for the Wi-Fi. There may be a small issue with your cottage,' Jack says, while picking up my suitcase.

A small issue with my cottage. What constitutes a small issue in Kerry? Double-booking? No electricity? Christ, this cannot be happening. My Christmas in exile is under threat. I knew I should have just stayed in a hotel. And where the hell is he going with my suitcase? I haven't agreed to being okay with the "small issue" yet!

'I can carry that.' I reach for my suitcase and our hands meet. The quickest, gentlest of touches, but enough for me to feel that spark again. Did he feel it too? What is it with this guy? Is he powering the national grid or something?

We both step back. I'm blushing once again. He must think my complexion is a cross between a cherry tomato and Santa's suit!

'My apologies.' He smiles.

God, but his lips are kissable, and that smile is stretching across his face. I like his face. I like his smile. First, I think his laugh is cute, now it's his face and smile. What is going on with me?

'No hassle. I'll just pay for the parking and we'll head to Melody's. I'll leave you and your suitcase, and I'll meet you at the door.'

I watch Jack as he walks away. He's tall and toned. I wouldn't say he's a gym-goer, but he definitely looks after himself. His dark hair is a different tone to mine, with no hint of grey. Not a bad view from behind, even if I do say so myself. His butt is like two eggs in a hanky. All of a sudden, I can't control my hankering for eggs. My fantasy fry-up doesn't quite get the chance to materialise as he waves the packing ticket and beckons me to follow him to the car park. I diligently oblige and think to myself yes, it *is* beginning to look a lot like Christmas.

*

I've got to say, that while Jack is the best-looking Kerry man I'd ever met (and he might be the only Kerry man I'd ever met), but since getting into the car with him twenty minutes ago, he's managed to hit a traffic cone, narrowly avoided knocking down a cyclist and mixed up the headlights and windscreen wipers on several occasions.

'Is this your first time in Kerry?' Jack asks while swaying the car dangerously over the white line.

'Yes, it is,' I answer, double-checking my safety belt.

'The Kingdom really is beautiful. Full of culture and art, music and dancing. If we could only roof it, we'd be flying it,' Jack laughs.

There's that laugh again. Still cute.

My appreciation of Jack's ever-endearing laugh will have to wait. I brace myself as my chauffeur attempts to overtake a tractor and trailer. I clench the sides of my seat with all the strength of the Incredible Hulk. And, my reddened complexion from earlier is now as green as my bad-tempered hero. Flashing the lights as he passes it by, Jack grinds the gearstick into top gear, leaving the tractor behind in his wake, like a twinkling star in the darkening December skyline.

As Jack steadies the car to an acceptable speed limit, I mentally reassure myself that I have my will made out. I'm pretty sure I have. Or have I? It doesn't matter very much because I don't have that much to leave anyone, anyway. Another thing I can blame Lorcan for. If it wasn't bad enough him cheating on me, he also cheated me out of the royalties from all of my songs. Oh, yeah, cleared our joint bank accounts too.

Like I say, money can be replaced, but passion; how do you recapture something so precious, so intangible, that not being able to do it manifests itself as a physical pain? Since our break-up, I've not been able to sing, play or write a song. He cheated me out of so much more than betraying our relationship. His betrayal of my love, I am learning to heal. Will I ever trust and love a man again? I hope so. But what about my love of music? Will I get that back? God, Lorcan; you really saw me coming.

Unlike me, who doesn't see the sharp turn as Jack swerves the car and we skid into the seaside village of Ard Carraig. I can see a wave of posters plastered all over the main street of the village. "Save Our Hall" seems to be the most common title.

'What's the story with all the posters?' I ask.

'Cutbacks, you know the likes,' Jack berates. 'The hall must close. No funding. Ye must fundraise if ye want the doors to stay open.'

His disdain for the situation is etched on his face. His friendly, carefree smile is replaced with a scowl.

'That is a pity.' I say, relaxing my grip on the seat.

'It's more than a pity. That old hall … it's much more than a hall to the community of Ard Carraig. It's our history. It's where first dates were had, the home of tea dances and where old stories could be told and passed on to the next generations. It's where musicals and plays are held. It's a home for the arts. For our culture. For memories to be made and cherished.' Jack shakes his head. 'I'll say no more.'

'The hall clearly means a lot to you. Are you involved in saving it?' I ask. Silence falls. I shouldn't have probed. Jack's breathing is laboured and I can sense the ache in his heart. 'I shouldn't have asked. Take no notice,' I say.

'Not at all. I'm the manager of the hall and, yes, I'm definitely involved in trying to save it. I've got the entire community willing me to save the old place and I am trying. But …' Jack tails off and the silence returns.

Lesson learned from before, so I decide not to engage Jack any further. God, seeing him so cut up about the possible closure of the hall, my problems pale away. Not that I'm dismissing my own hurt and pain, I would never. But Jack's got the weight of history on his shoulders. His quest to keep the hall open was evident from the number of posters and placards decorated around the village of Ard Carraig. Bless him.

Music tinkers around the car as Jack tunes into some Christmas-themed radio station. I get the feeling that he wants silence for the remainder of the journey. And, that's okay by me! I lean my head against the window and stare out at the night sky: a dark blanket engulfing us but speckled with shining stars and a moon so bright that I am certain I can see my reflection in it. "Christmas Lights" plays through the speaker and my attention turns to the homes we pass by. Christmas trees sparkle in living rooms, fairy lights adorn roofs and inflatable Santas and snowmen wave in the wind. I suppress the urge to wave back at them and instead focus on the song.

I've not listened to music much since last Christmas. The pain is sometimes too hard to bear. I had penned a Christmas song for my album, but I never got to record it. I shake my head attempting to drown out the lyrics, and return my gaze to the stars. I imagine the stars as twinkling baubles of lights and colour that light up Grafton Street during December.

Within seconds, I am transported back to that awful night when I headed home to surprise Lorcan.

What had I just seen? My body was shaking. I couldn't control it. How could Lorcan betray me in such a cruel way? And, at Christmastime. I leaned against the door of our bedroom before I fled. I blinked furiously, trying to wipe my memory of what I had just seen. I bolted from the house without looking back, afraid of bearing witness to his betrayal once more. Stood in the garden, I could feel the snow falling. My breath was short, and sharp and visual on the air. The winter cold engulfed me, but I felt hot and clammy. In a complete trance, I scratched my neck. Fight or flight? What was I to do? I felt the need to run. But I couldn't move. Could I turn back the clock? Could I unsee what I had seen? Could I repair the damage to our life together and erase all evidence of this treachery? I could phone Clodagh. She would rescue me. Then I saw the beauty of the twinkling of the Christmas tree fairy lights visible in the window, and the festive wreath on the front door. Our home. Our safe haven. Our future, gone. I retrieved the little box wrapped in red with a gold ribbon from my pocket and there in the corner of my eye, I saw him. Lorcan. I clenched the box tightly as he slammed the door shut.

The jolt of the car braking is enough to spiral me back, along with the sound of Jack yelling at a cat.

'Meet Whiplash,' Jack jokes. 'She acquired the name because she has a fierce habit of running out in front of cars and giving the drivers whiplash.' He laughs. I do like it when he laughs.

'I can top that, y'know,' I say, thinking that Jack seems to be more like himself again. Nice job, Whiplash.

'Go on then,' Jack challenges me.

'Where I'm from, there is a cat called … Pothole … because everyone tries to avoid him.'

Jack hollers with laughter. I howl with laughter too. He looks at me and nods. I smile, feeling silly. We're laughing about cats. Are we those people who laugh at cats?

'Oh, here we are,' Jack says, as he swings the car into the driveway of a house called Ramble Inn. It appears to be a bed-and-breakfast if the signpost outside the white fence is to be believed. But I don't remember booking the Ramble Inn. And I don't see any cottages of any description in the vicinity. Didn't Jack want to tell me something about my accommodation at the airport? A small issue?

'Home sweet home for the next few days,' Jack says, as he exits the car.

'Ramble Inn doesn't very much look like a self-catering cottage to me! Jack?' I call after him.

The chill of the December air feels nice on my skin and calms my sense of unease as I exit the car. I hadn't realised I needed some fresh air but I guess I was enjoying Jack's company too much to care. I make my way to the back of the car and join Jack as he grabs my suitcase. What is it with this guy and carrying suitcases? Does he think that I've lost the use of my arms? Before I can wrestle my suitcase back, I notice his earring for the first time. Sparkling under the moonlight, a red diamond stud flashes momentarily and catches my eye. The crunch of the wheels from my suitcase on the gravel distracts me and I give chase after Jack, who is making his way towards the Ramble Inn.

'Where exactly is the cottage? My cottage?' I call.

'Ah, about that. I might just let Melody explain that one,' Jack says.

The stone house itself is quaint, with a red door adorned with a homemade Christmas wreath. There are twinkling fairy lights hung along the roof and I can see the shadow of a Christmas tree in one of the bigger windows. The place has a homely feel to it; a sense of warmth vibrates from the house. I feel myself embracing that warmth and my unease start to wane.

Inside, the heat from an Aga is soothing, as Melody places a fresh pot of tea and some homemade gingerbread on the table. She turns to embrace me with a welcoming hug. I tense up ever so slightly but the smell of the home baking evokes a hunger in me. And my thoughts of self-catering cottages are replaced with a willingness to devour festive treats, like a demented Paul Hollywood on Bake Off.

Melody potters away from our embrace and beckons me to join her at the table. She pours a hot drop for all three of us and slides the plate of gingerbread towards me. I smile gratefully at Melody before nibbling away at one of the festively decorated delicacies.

'Now, pet. Did Jack tell you at the airport about the cottage? Awful business, but sure, it is what it is. Can't be helped. Sure, 'tis the time of year, what can we expect?' Melody gives Jack the side-eye. Jack is oblivious to this as he is looking through some papers and not taking any notice of his aunt.

'Not really. He said something about a small issue?' I ask.

'Small issue? Chance would be a fine thing! No, lovely. The cottage has a burst pipe. The whole place is flooded. But not to worry. You can stay here with me and Jack. Isn't that right, Jack?' Melody nudges him.

'Course. Yeah,' Jack replies, but quickly returns to reading through his papers.

'Stay here? With Jack?' I blush, which doesn't go unnoticed by Melody, who gives me a sly smile. 'It's Christmas and I really wouldn't want to impose. And, you guys have got so much going on what with trying to save to the hall.'

'Awe, stop now. Don't be upsetting yourself,' Melody says.

'Honestly, I can go and stay in a hotel. Actually, my friend Clodagh, she's staying nearby, I can call her,' I say.

'Oh, is that the time?' With a wave of her hand, Melody dismisses my suggestion. 'Jack, we better get a wriggle on. I presume you haven't told Charlie about the Christmas concert.'

Jack doesn't react. Instead, he gathers up some papers and, for the first time, I notice that he's holding music sheets. A warm smile creeps across my face. Music sheets. What I wouldn't give to be able to play music and sing again. Any chance of daydreaming such an occurrence is equally as dismissed as my hotel suggestion, when Melody whips up my cup and the crumbs from the gingerbread (which was delicious), and places them in the sink. A bit like Whiplash the Cat, Melody turns around to face me with lightening precision, and looks me up and down. I can tell exactly what she's thinking. Late December and I'm still wearing my shorts and t-shirt. She presses her lips together and I can see the cogs moving in her brain.

'You didn't pack a coat, by any chance?' Melody asks.

'Nope. I hadn't planned on leaving the cottage for the next two weeks.'

'Not to worry. You can borrow one of Jack's. I'd say ye would be about the same size.' She eyes me up once more before heading off down the hallway.

I look at Jack, who is perusing through the music sheets. He hums a familiar tune too as he goes about his task.

'*Silent night* …' Jack sings softly, with a quality to his voice that is both welcoming and charming to the ear. Singing a mere two words, and I am already swaying along.

The urge to sing bubbles in the pit of my stomach. I can hear practically the harmonies between Jack and I. And I desperately want to join in with him. I stop myself. I haven't sung in so long. But my heart is beating so loudly in my chest that I am certain he can hear it, too. I concentrate on his voice; his singing pacifies me. I allow my longing to subside and enjoy the moment for what it is. A beautiful man stood before me on the eve of Christmas Eve, singing "Silent Night".

Melody bustles her way back into the kitchen weighed down with three coats. Jack ceases his serenading of me. Not that he knew he was serenading me anyways. Putting on their coats, they head towards the door as I get to

Joe Burkett

my feet. And just like Whiplash, I grab the coat, which Melody launches into the air at me. Quickly, I put on the coat even though I'm not cold. Why am I putting on Jack's coat? Why am I following them? Why am I not phoning Clodagh to come and get me?

My breath catches under my ribs, and my fingers tingle, wanting to follow Jack. My body pulses with the need to hear him sing again. My impulse to initiate my "home alone for Christmas" plan is slowly vanishing. I'm caught up in the familiarity of music meaning something, maybe everything, to someone. And, I can't help myself.

'... *In heavenly peace.*' I sing.

*

The Ard Carraig community hall comes into view as Jack parks the car and we exit the vehicle. Melody offers to help Jack with his music notes and she heads off inside, while I take a deep breath. The smell of the ocean is fresh and clean compared to the mucky and murky fumes of the congested traffic in Dublin.

'This way,' Jack calls.

I quickly give pace after Jack and follow him to the courtyard of the community hall.

'Wait here. I've got a surprise for you,' Jack says.

'A surprise for me?' I question.

'Close your eyes,' Jack replies.

Having only just met Jack, I trust him, and so I oblige. I close my eyes. Before I have the opportunity to ask Jack any questions, he returns.

'Just making sure,' he says, placing his hands over my eyes.

'Okay,' I say, putting my hands on his hands.

Jack's hands are soft to the touch and I toy with the idea of interlinking our fingers, but I'm hesitant. Why am I hesitant? Jack has been so kind to me since we met. I feel at ease with him, but my hurt from Lorcan; I can't shake it.

Jack removes one of his hands from over my eyes and places it on my upper-arm. I lean back into his hold without hesitation. Maybe not all men are like Lorcan? Slowly, he removes his other hand from over my eyes. Blinking, I take in the view before me.

'Oh my God,' I gasp.

Glittering fairy lights illuminate the night sky as I take in the view of the Ard Carraig Christmas Land Market and Santa's Grotto. Little stalls with wooden, handmade North Pole shaped post boxes, embroidered stockings and Christmas garlands catch my eye. I look to Jack. His face is filled with pride. I rub my hand along his upper-arm before giving his bicep a friendly squeeze. Christ, his bicep is amazing.

'Jack, this place is amazing,' I say.

Before Jack can reply, Melody rejoins us and informs him that the school children are just arriving for carol singing practice. And just like that, Jack and I aren't alone anymore. A bustling group of parents with excited children make their way towards the hall. Little girls wear matching red coats while the boys rock Santa hats. They burst into life with their rendition of "Frosty the Snowman" as they skip through the market. It was never a favourite of mine, but I find myself swaying along to it. Jack is swaying along too, greeting the parents and high-fiving the children as they pass by. The rapport between Jack and the community feels so genuine; unlike Lorcan and his business cronies.

People didn't smile at Lorcan.

'Charlie, I'm gonna head inside. I need to start rehearsals with the kids,' Jack says.

'Cool. I'll come with you,' I offer.

'No need. Enjoy the festivities. I highly recommend Gloria's hot chocolate.'

And with that, Jack darts away through the crowd. Ducking in-between chatting groups of friends and families, he makes his way towards the door of the hall. He steps out from behind a tall, slender man at one point, and I can't shake the feeling of déjà vu. Have I seen Jack somewhere before? He looks familiar, and there is definitely a connection between us. But surely, I would remember him, wouldn't I?

I pass through the market, greeting people along the way. A few of them look at me, and I overhear them saying who they think I am – the remnants of my fame not shining as brightly now as it was with that young busker last year.

I approach Gloria's camper van café, aptly named Gloria's Goodies. As I order my hot chocolate, I take in the happy, smiley faces and I can't help but feel my Christmas spirits starting to lift. I've always loved this time of year; little festive markets, mulled wine, mince pies, and shopping trips. I would always pick up a Christmas themed souvenir magnet, and place on it on my fridge. I didn't do that last Christmas. Lorcan robbed me of my love of Christmas last year. With a sense of renewed determination, I vow that he won't rob me of this Christmas.

Flurries of soft snow begin to fall as I pay for my hot chocolate. Yummy, melting marshmallows, my favourite. God, this place really is amazing. I can see why Jack is fighting so hard to save it. The community spirit evident here tonight is a testament to his fundraising campaign. Happy, smiling faces run through the courtyard.

A wave of sadness washes over me and I can't help but feel mournful for what could be lost. What will become of the Ard Carraig community hall if Jack's fundraising fails?

Before I have the chance to engage in my melancholy, out of the corner of my eye, I spot a souvenir stall. Maybe it's time to get some of my Christmas traditions back?

I purchase a "Christmas tree on the Ard Carraig beach" souvenir, and place it carefully in my pocket, I pop my head through the door leading into the big hall. Slowly, I step inside, hoping not to be noticed as the sound of the music and singing soothes me. My eyes soften as I see Jack conducting the school children in their carol singing. Their upbeat rendition of "Winter Wonderland" is literally music to my ears.

I take in the children and watch the wonder in their eyes as they listen and react to Jack. His manner with the kids is calm and effective. They seem to love him. And, who could blame them? I'm doing it again. What is going on with me? I came here, to Kerry, of all places, to spend two weeks in isolation to rebuild myself, to place a blanket over the last year and to start anew. Yet, here I am, stood in a hall, watching this handsome man conduct his music and my heart is starting to sing. After a year without music in my life, it feels like home.

*

We're back at the Ramble Inn, after what Jack referred to as "a good final rehearsal". He throws some turf into the Aga to get the place nice and warm once more, while Melody is busy hanging up our coats.

'Do y'know something?' Melody says. 'I'm so looking forward to the concert tomorrow night. I think it's going to be a great night and you can be sure there will be a huge turnout.'

I notice that while Jack is nodding and humming along with yeahs; he's not as convinced as his aunt.

'The people of Ard Carraig are great to support and sure everyone wants the hall to stay open so they'll be there. Now boys, I'm going to leave ye at it. I'm off to my bed.'

Melody heads off after telling me that there are fresh towels at the end of my bed if I fancy a shower in the morning. I thank her kindly.

'Fancy one?' Jack says, offering me a beer.

'Sure, why not? It is Christmas,' I say, as Jack passes me the bottle. 'I'm sure you'll get a big turnout tomorrow night.'

'I doubt it. Tickets sales have been slow, and to be honest, the community is tired of fundraising. It's been relentless these past few months.' Jack takes a swig of his beer.

'But there was a huge crowd there this evening.'

'Yeah, and tomorrow is Christmas Eve. What was I thinking having the concert on Christmas Eve?'

'All of the people that were there tonight will still care as much about the hall tomorrow as they did today. They'll take no notice of it being Christmas Eve.'

'I hope you're right, because if you're not and we don't raise enough money to prove the hall's worth keeping open, then it could be game over.'

'I wish I could help,' I say absentmindedly.

I can meteorically see the lightbulb ignite over Jack's head. A flashing neon lightbulb signalling that I'm going to have to deny him. Reject him when he needs my help the most. And I, like a fool, have just offered my help. What was I thinking? He's going to ask me to sing. He must know that I'm a singer. Melody, to be fair, wouldn't have a clue who I am. She would have taken no notice of my name when I booked. But Jack; he knows me. But he never said. Why didn't he say he recognised from my singing days? My heart rate increases. My pulse is ready to explode. I try to concentrate on my breathing. Focus, focus, focus.

Remember what Ben, told you after he lost his partner, Evan, and he started getting panic attacks, I tell myself. He said, "Focus on the present. Don't let your mind race. Just focus."

Melody's Christmas tree will do nicely. Lovely green tree with white snow tipped edges, decorated beautifully with red and gold tinsel. Red and gold. Like the engagement ring box, wrapped in red with a gold bow. Christ, I need a new focal point.

'If you could help, that would be amazing. Maybe you could sing?' Jack asks.

The question has been asked. Oh God, I don't feel well. My mouth is dry. I can't speak. I feel the words in my throat, but they won't come out. I feel dizzy. Everything is starting to spin. Red and gold swirls of tinsel are invading my mind.

'Jack,' I say. 'What makes you think that I can sing?'

'Charlie,' Jack says. 'I know you and I know your music. You are a beautiful singer. So full of soul and life. I just know you would do an amazing job at the concert tomorrow. Everyone would flock to see you. It would be amazing. I could do up some last-minute social media advertising. The concert would be a sell-out …'

Silence falls. I can't speak. My heart is aching because I don't want to disappoint Jack, but I know me. And, I can't sing at the concert.

'I'm sorry, Jack. I can't do it,' I say.

There it is; the disappointment. The one thing I didn't want to do. Jack's face drains of the excitement that had filled it seconds previously. He is pale and pensive. That fiery lightbulb very much distinguished.

'God, no. Charlie, it should be me who's sorry. I shouldn't have asked.'

'No, no. It's okay,' I say. 'I'll probably be leaving tomorrow. I mean, my cottage isn't available, so it makes sense for me to leave …'

'Does it?' Jack says.

His words hang in the air.

December 24th 2017

It's the morning of Jack's big fundraising show. The cottage is silent. I thought there would be more hustle and bustle, but silence is all that I can hear. I'm okay with silence. It's what I wanted from this trip away. Just me and my thoughts. My healing time. But I can't get Jack out of my mind. Things were left up in the air last night. Awkward.

I head downstairs to be greeted by Melody.

'Aw, there you are. Did you sleep well? 'Tis a fine bed. Very comfortable. It sleeps two, you know,' Melody winks.

'Yes, very well,' I lie. 'Very spacious.' That's not a lie, but I tossed and turned all night trying to think of ways to help Jack. 'Is Jack not around? Has he gone down to the hall?'

'Correct. He's at the hall, the poor devil. Sure, he'll be there for the day. He said to say … lovely meeting you, all the best and something about if you change your mind, you know where he is … now, what would that be about will you tell me?' Melody asks.

I'm not embarrassed by what Melody is saying, but something is happening. I'm feeling something. But what? Jack thinks that I am leaving today. Well, I am. That's the plan. But there is an ache in my stomach, I can feel it. It's a physical pain. I'm aching because I don't want to leave. I want to help Jack.

'You never did give me the Wi-Fi code, Melody,' I say.

'A Wi-Fi code? Well, that is news to me …'

'Never mind. I've got data. Just need a signal.' I smile.

'A signal, is it? I don't think you'll need a code for that, my boy.'

Minutes later, I'm waving my phone in the air, desperately trying to get a signal so that my video call will connect. I'm wearing Jack's coat again – not that I need it, but I like the way it makes me feel when I wear it. While standing on an upended bucket beside a stone wall with a cow giving me the side-eye, I finally get a signal.

'Clodagh ...' I say as the screen freezes. 'Hello ... can you hear me? Can you hear me ... now?' God, I sound like that guy off that TV commercial.

I can hear laughter. Clodagh is laughing at me.

'Where the hell are you?' Clodagh asks.

'The middle of the middle of nowhere ... but listen, before the signal drops ... I need a huge favour ...' I tentatively say.

I can picture her eyebrow arching as she says, 'Tell me more, Charlie boy.'

*

The stars are bright in the sky with a full moon beaming down on the village of Ard Carraig. I watch the community head inside the hall. All the little family groups chatting about who the celebrity star turn is going to be. Wrapped up in Jack's coat once again, I smile to myself. I never wore anything belonging to Lorcan. Why would I? His clothes were way too corporate for me. But Jack's coat is perfect: a little bit hipster, with a lot of character. Even though I don't feel the cold, I feel warm wearing Jack's coat.

'Charlie!' Jack calls as he exits the building. 'How did you do it? Clodagh and The Rigs.'

'My data finally kicked in, and I was able to get in contact with Clodagh. And sure, she is always one to support the arts.'

'Well, good on her. And good on you. The hall is packed. We've had to put out extra seats. How did you manage it?'

'I might have gotten access to the hall's social media accounts and thrown up a few teasers about a special celebrity guest attending the concert.'

We smile in sync.

'I don't know what to say. Thank you.'

'I said I wanted to help, and this is my way of helping.'

'I felt so bad about asking you to sing last night ...'

'Please don't feel bad. I would love to sing, but for now, I can't. But one day I will sing for you ...'

'I'd really like that.'

I look into Jack's eyes. He's so close that I could touch him. And I want to. I want to hold him and sing to him – but what if he doesn't want me?

Jack's phone alarm goes off. The moment passes. Jack frowns and presses stop. And then he says, 'Let's go inside. Clodagh's up first.'

Jack leads me into the packed hall. Everyone from far and wide must have heard about Clodagh playing because the place is packed to capacity. If this doesn't prove to the council that the hall is needed, I don't know what will. The curtains open, and the crowd gets to their feet to lead a rapturous applause. A spotlight illuminates Clodagh. The drummer begins his countdown, the guitarist strikes a chord, and Clodagh sings.

'Charlie, this is all because of you …' a teary Jack announces.

'No. This. All of this … is because of you. Your warmth, energy, vision and drive to keep this place alive … this is what you've told me about the hall in Ard Carraig. Where stories begin … tonight, new stories will begin and that's because of you.'

Our eyes lock. It's like an invisible magnet is pulling us together. Propelling us to be as one. I notice Jack's lips. His kissable lips are inviting, and I want to lean forward and take him in my arms, embrace him and kiss him. The smell of his aftershave is a welcoming fragrance as I take a step towards him. My mind is racing and my heart is pumping so much that if I don't get to kiss this beautiful man in the next ten seconds, I am physically going to explode.

I want Jack. And, I haven't wanted someone since Lorcan with his cheap perfume and his uninviting lips. Inconsiderate of my feelings when we made love or when I wanted to be intimate. It was always on his terms. Why couldn't I have met someone like Jack instead of Lorcan?

But I know that Jack will be different. He is different. He is nothing like Lorcan. His warmth and charm radiate from him like a lighthouse guiding a ship safely home. I want to be that ship and I need Jack to be my lighthouse. Please, Jack, guide me home to your arms. Take me and kiss me.

'Jack. You're wanted on stage,' Melody calls.

The moment is gone. What a bitch. Sorry, Melody, but seriously; read the room, girl!

Jack looks at me. I nod. He squeezes my hand before walking away.

The audience applauds as he walks through the crowd towards the stage. I don't want him to go. I want him to stay with me. I want to reach out and grab him and pull him back. I place my hands in the pockets of the coat. It's the only thing I can do to stop myself from giving chase and pulling Jack away from the stage. I feel something in the pockets. As I remove the garment from the pocket, it's a rainbow-coloured scarf. And, then Jack glances back towards me. It hits me like a bolt of lightning. That's it! Back on Grafton Street, two years ago, when I was busking, the guy standing in front of Lorcan. The guy that caught my eye was ... Jack.

A rush of energy surges through my body and I run towards the crowd. Pushing my way through them all, I'm desperate to get to Jack. He can see me, and he's waiting. I reach him, and silence falls. It's just us. Just me and Jack.

'Charlie ...'

'I should have seen you. I did see you. I know I'm not making any sense but ... Grafton Street ... It was you.'

'It was me.' Jack moves towards me, and I feel his hand on the small of my back. I place my hand on his cheek. Leaning forward, our lips touch, and we kiss.

The silence ends as the audience erupts into cheers. Jack and I both laugh.

'It seems that Jack might be a bit busy, so, ladies and gentleman ... let's sing on ... after all ... IT'S CHRISTMASSSS.' Clodagh, channelling her inner Noddy Holder, leads the community in song.

As the community breaks into song and dance, Jack and I share another kiss.

'Merry Christmas, Charlie,' Jack says.

'Merry Christmas, Jack,' I reply.

December 24th 2018

Grafton Street is alive with the sound of festive cheer as drunken friends sing about a fairy tale in New York while I, once again, am walking down the street laden with last-minute gifts.

My phone rings and I look at the caller. It's my friend Ben, and I know exactly why he's calling. He wants to know if I've asked the question, and what Jack's answer was. I cancel the call. I've not asked Jack anything just yet.

I giggle to myself as I pass a young busker. He seems to be singing an original song, as I'm unfamiliar with the lyrics. It's catchy, yet sweet. This guy is giving me a certain ginger superstar vibe. I'll bob him a two euro. Support the arts, that's what I always say!

And it's a good thing I said it to Jack because with the additional funding from the Arts Council, the Ard Carraig town hall has become the local concert venue for plays, musicals, singers, performers and art festivals. I would say that Clodagh and the Rigs also helped the fundraising drive and Jack's little Christmas concert got national coverage. I couldn't have been prouder of him that night last year, standing on stage having saved his community hall, beaming with pride.

As I approach the taxi rank, I place my hand into the pocket of Jack's coat. I've taken to wearing it; not that I feel the cold, but just so that I can feel close to him. It can be tough with me living in Dublin and him down in Kerry. Hopefully, that won't be forever. I fiddle about in the pocket, and thankfully both of his presents are in there. A little mixtape (I know — *very retro*) of songs that we've created memories to over the last year. First up on my little love album is "It's beginning to look a lot like Christmas", which was playing in Kerry International Airport the first time we met. God, how I've grown to love that airport. And, I've added my own Christmas song to the collection. It's the song that I wrote for my album which was never released. I promised Jack that I would record one day. And now I have. But it's just for him. Darting down the street, I see a familiar face in the distance. Jack. He smiles as he makes his way towards me. I glance away for a moment, and look down at his second present which I've removed from the coat pocket. A little box lays in my hand. Wrapped in red with a gold ribbon. It's the key to my apartment. Maybe the key to my heart. Christmas this year is going to be amazing. I just know it.

Santa Baby

Helen Hawkins

When two of her colleagues jumped onto the CEO's desk to perform an ear-splitting rendition of "Fairytale of New York", Ellie knew it was time to leave the Christmas party. She'd suffered through the office secret Santa *(cheers for the umpteenth pair of novelty socks and bog-standard bath bombs)*, noted the irony of drinking gin by the watercooler and turned a blind eye to the trainees debasing the photocopier with their body parts.

   She'd been desperately trying to get hold of Max at the Birmingham office about the last-minute marketing gig he'd tossed her way. She was due to visit the venue on her way back later that evening to introduce herself to the client, but without the brief from Max, she didn't know what to expect and doing a half-decent job would be a miracle. It was difficult enough with the client impossible to get hold of. She'd had one hurried phone call with him and then nothing more for 48 hours. *If he really needed the firm's help, surely he could make himself more available?*

She pushed her way through the crowd and fell through the door into the reception area, cursing as a rogue piece of tinsel wrapped itself around one of her heels. She threw it off in contempt and opened her emails, one hand massaging her temple where a stress headache was forming. *Why didn't anyone else seem to care that the office would close in a few days' time?*

Thankful to be out of the chaos, Ellie checked her email to Max once more before sending it. Frustration surged through her as the phone vibrated in her hand, and a call from "Vicky" filled the screen. She let out a grumble and swiped to answer.

'Hi Sis!' Vicky sounded friendly. *Too friendly.* Ellie's guard went up, suspecting she was after something.

'Hi,' she said uncertainly.

'Look, El, something's come up and I have to go into the office.' Vicky spoke quickly. 'The problem is, I promised Sophia a trip to see Santa at the Christmas Market this evening and I really, really don't want to let her down. I heard from Max that you're heading there for a client introduction … which is a marvellous coincidence!'

Vicky left the comment hanging, and there was a moment of silence. When Ellie didn't answer, she asked, 'Could you take Sophia with you?'

Ellie sighed.

'Vick, I'm super busy trying to get things through before Christmas, and everyone is getting drunk at the office party, which means everything's taking longer. I've not even heard from Max, which is frustrating as he's clearly spoken to your office, and I'm only going to the Christmas Market for business. Isn't there anyone else who can take her?' She nibbled her bottom lip anxiously, hoping that her sister would see sense and let her off the hook.

'El, I know Christmas is hard for you after what happened with Billy … but I promised Sophia, and she was so looking forward to it. She asked for you personally, and isn't it just serendipitous that you're heading over there, anyway?'

Ellie leant her head against the wall. Christmas *was* tough these days, but she knew she wouldn't say no. She might be a grinch when it came to Christmas, but she refused to be a lousy aunt too.

'All right,' she conceded. 'Can I meet you both there? I haven't got time to stop on the way.'

'Ellie, you're a lifesaver. Sophia will be so excited. I'll see you there in fifteen.'

*

Connor turned the page of the ledger and looked again at the takings and balance from the fundraiser he'd put on the previous weekend. He was old-school and liked the feel of a thick, heavy tome for the finances; he didn't like the number of minuses and zeros quite as much though. He rubbed a hand over his face and rested his elbows on the table, chin in hands. What was he going to do? The marketing firm his uncle had recommended had better have some ideas, because he was all out.

One of the grotto elves, Tyler, bounced in, the jingling bell on his hat breaking Connor's reverie.

'Everything okay, Big Man?' he asked.

Connor fussed with the white trim on his Santa suit. He was yet to stuff his fake belly and hoped Tyler's use of "Big Man" wasn't a sly dig at his recent weight gain.

'Ho! Ho! Ho!' he said with a hint of sarcasm.

'No, really.' Tyler ventured a little further into the office, all six foot five of him. 'You look kinda stressed. Is everything okay?'

'Everything's fine.'

Connor shut the ledger and resolved to forget about money for the night. He'd started the charity to help children with dyslexia; children who'd struggled like he had at school. It wasn't about the money, except without it, the charity couldn't provide any support. It was a vicious cycle. *Ugh!*

He was sure the real Santa never had to worry about where the next lot of money was coming from. He was even more certain that the real Santa didn't need the help of a marketing company to keep him from going bankrupt. Over the past two days, Connor had sent a barrage of emails containing all the information the company had requested, but these – and his follow-up phone calls – had gone unanswered. He was losing hope fast.

'Right!' He clapped, then stood and slipped a cushion underneath his suit. 'Santa time!'

Connor's leap to action surprised Tyler, who mock saluted him and marched out the room to happily greet the crowds. Thankfully, the grotto had sold out in advance and there was already a line of eager children and harassed parents waiting to enter.

He grabbed the beard and hat from the back of his chair and fixed them in the reflection of his computer screen. He was fairly sure the event would make enough to cover costs and raise funds for the plans he had in the new year. But fairly sure wasn't sure enough. This event needed to be a roaring success or they wouldn't make it past the new year.

*

'I'll see you later, Sausage.' Vicky crouched to kiss Sophia on her cheek, then straightened up. 'Right El, I'll see you later. I shouldn't be more than an hour and you can reach me on my mobile if there's an emergency.'

Ellie nodded. 'We'll be fine.'

'Love you both!' Vicky said and jumped into her car, pulling away at speed.

Working for the same company, Ellie and Vicky's relationship had been reduced to a smattering of work calls and fleeting conversations over the past couple of years. Ellie hadn't realised quite how she'd allowed it to happen. But ever since Billy had left, she'd sort of pushed everyone away.

Ellie and Sophia regarded each other for a moment, and Ellie wished she'd made more of an effort with her niece over the years. She realised she didn't know what to say to her, this young person whose sparkly unicorn trainers and chocolate-covered fingers said "child", and BTS backpack said "cusp of adolescence". *When had that happened? She was eight!*

'Come on,' Ellie said. 'Shall we go?'

Sophia nodded. 'Mum booked us in for seven-thirty.'

'Great.'

Ellie did the maths. Her 7.45pm meeting with the client should be well timed. Not having children herself, she wasn't sure what the acceptable etiquette was for this situation. Perhaps she could put Sophia on the carousel or something while she did it? Before she could take Sophia's hand, she was already skipping ahead.

'It's this way,' she called, turning to check Ellie wasn't too far behind, her eyes sparkling with excitement.

Despite her aversion to all things Christmas, Ellie had to admit that the Christmas Market was tastefully festive. Nestled amongst the wooden market huts and food stands, there was a small log cabin grotto, decked out with tiny fairy lights, twinkling softly. Instead of snow, great lengths of cotton wool adorned the roof and window ledges, some even artfully fashioned into a little puff of smoke hovering over the chimney. If Hansel and Gretel had popped out to greet the guests, Ellie wouldn't have been surprised.

Elves of all shapes and sizes flitted around the crowd. Ellie was impressed by their costumes and dedication to spreading Christmas cheer. From what she could see of the Santa, he looked well put together too – that was one *very* realistic beard.

Sophia had made her way to the queue and was hopping from one foot to the other in excitement.

'Look at the elves!' she squeaked.

She poked Ellie in the arm, nearly making her drop her phone, and Ellie restrained herself from tutting out loud. *She's just a kid, after all.* Oblivious to Ellie's annoyance, Sophia directed her attention at two of Santa's helpers, who had exploded into an impromptu acrobatic routine, one leaping onto the shoulders of another. She squashed closer to the people in front for a better view while Ellie checked her phone for the time. It was already seven-thirty, and they were not yet at the front of the queue. She fidgeted with her lanyard. This event might not be at the top of her list of priorities, but she always gave the client her best and being late for this meeting wasn't a good start.

'Aunty Ellie?' Sophia said, turning from the elves.

'Yes?' She didn't mean to sound quite as snappy. She softened and added, 'What is it, love?'

Sophia squinted at Ellie as if trying to work something out.

Eventually, she said, 'Why do you hate Christmas so much?'

Her question was like a punch to the stomach.

'I don't hate Christmas,' Ellie protested.

'Mummy says it's because Christmas makes you sad.'

'It doesn't make me sad …' she trailed off unconvincingly.

The truth was, Christmas did make her sad, and it had since the day of her and Billy's non-wedding. It was only now that she realised her sadness was something other people could see. She'd thought avoiding Christmas had been a coping mechanism, something only she felt on the inside while the festivities went on merrily around her. Now, she realised, she'd also been pushing people away. Vicky was family. She deserved better.

Sophia smiled, clearly not believing her, but Ellie was saved from further questions as the people in front of them stepped up to see Santa.

'We're next!' Sophia said.

Ellie sighed with relief to be off the hook.

'Are you excited to see Santa?' the elf at the front of the queue asked.

Sophia nodded. 'My aunty has brought me.'

'Aw, that's so lovely. I hope you've thought about what you'd like for Christmas.'

Sophia smiled and tapped her nose conspiratorially. 'Yep!'

*

'If you're a good boy right up until Christmas, I'll see what I can do.'

Connor thanked the little boy for visiting him and promised he'd speak to his elves about a monster truck for Christmas. The boy had requested a life-sized monster truck, but Connor reckoned he'd saved some of the upset on Christmas morning by haggling him down to something smaller.

He checked his watch. The next slot would have to be the last before his scheduled meeting – if the executive was even going to show!

'This is Sophia.'

An elf led a little girl to the porch of the log cabin, where Connor sat. Cold flushed her cheeks, and she had a smear of chocolate on one of her eyebrows. Her expression brightened as she approached, and a huge smile spread across her face. But it was the woman behind that caught his eye. Her deep brown eyes drew him in.

'Hello, Santa!' Sophia chimed, and Connor returned to the task at hand.

'Hello!' he said, perhaps too enthusiastically. 'And what's your name?'

He stole another glance at the woman, and a feeling travelled through him that he couldn't quite put his finger on.

'I'm Sophia.' The girl pointed at the woman. 'And this is Ellie.'

Their eyes met briefly. Ellie smiled at him and then looked down at her phone.

'Sophia. What a lovely name,' he said. 'And have you been a good girl this year?'

Sophia launched into a monologue about how she'd tried her best to behave and where it hadn't quite gone to plan, how it hadn't been her fault. Connor laughed behind his beard.

'It sounds like you've done your best.'

He watched as Ellie put her phone away and gazed around the market, seemingly taken by the festive ambience.

'What would you like Santa to bring you for Christmas?' he asked Sophia, attempting to clear his throat, which was suddenly dry. He was finding it difficult to focus all of his attention on the little girl.

'Well,' Sophia began, and Connor worried she was about to break into another lengthy soliloquy. 'I was going to ask for the Dreamworld Dollhouse, but I know Mummy is already getting that. I saw her shopping on the computer for it and asking Daddy where his credit card was.'

Connor smiled.

'I also know that you're not the real Santa, just his helper. So, I wondered whether you could speak to the real one for me 'cause this is a big one, and you'll need all the help you can get.' She lowered her voice to a whisper and said, 'I need you to help my Aunty Ellie.'

That caught his attention. Connor raised an eyebrow, intrigued by the request.

'She gets pretty sad because her boyfriend left her alone at Christmas,' Sophia continued. 'Could you use your magic to make her happy? I'd like it if she could come to our house for Christmas dinner and smile again. I know Mummy would like it too.'

Ellie was still looking around the market. For a fleeting moment, a wave of guilt washed over Connor for the secret insight divulged by Sophia.

He returned to Sophia, who was gazing up at him expectantly.

'Well, Sophia, I will definitely see what I can do.'

*

Once Santa had given Sophia her small present, Ellie promised her a hot chocolate while she met with the event's organiser. They rushed to the nearest hot drink stand, but suddenly, Sophia stopped dead in her tracks, yanking Ellie to a halt.

'Can I go on the carousel? Please!'

A large sign read: "£5 per ride". *Bit extortionate!* But Ellie rifled through her purse all the same.

'Here you go. I'll wait right here.'

Sophia chose a pastel pink carousel horse, covered in ornate yellow flowers. She jumped on and grinned as she grabbed hold of the golden pole. She hadn't stopped smiling all evening, and Ellie felt a warmth from her niece that fended off the chilly night. She waved at Sophia, who waved back and then clung on tightly as the carousel started. An odd version of Wham's "Last Christmas" played on the organ, and Ellie smiled to herself. The urge to pull her phone from her bag came over her, but it wasn't to double-check her emails; it was to take a photo of Sophia having a wonderful time and send it to Vicky.

'Hi.'

Ellie startled at the voice next to her.

Leaning on the railing was none other than the Santa from the grotto. His beard obscured most of his face, but his friendly eyes crinkled and Ellie could tell he was smiling.

'Hello again,' she said.

'Sophia is delightful,' Santa continued, nodding to the carousel. 'Very polite. And as Santa, I really do see all sorts.'

'I'll bet.' Ellie smiled.

Over on the carousel, Sophia strained on her horse to see her Aunty Ellie talking to Santa, her eyes wide.

'Are you having a good time?' Santa asked.

Was she? Ellie hadn't actively participated in Christmas for so long that she couldn't tell if what she was feeling was enjoyment … but Sophia's excitement was infectious and, coupled with the romance of the market, Ellie decided that yes, she just might be.

'I am. This place is great.'

'And all the proceeds are going to charity.'

'I know,' she said. 'I'm actually waiting to speak to the organiser. He's a client.'

Santa held out his hand. 'Connor O'Shaunessy.'

'Mr O'Shaunessy?' Ellie stammered, taking it.

'The very same.'

'Did you know it was me when we …' She nodded to the grotto.

Connor shook his head.

'No, I noticed your lanyard just as you left, but I thought it best to let Sophia tell you all about her visit to Santa before we talked business. Have you received my emails? I sent the information over a couple of times but there was no response … from the office.' He seemed to add as an afterthought.

Now it was Ellie's turn to shake her head.

'No, sorry. I was expecting them, but I've had nothing on this end.'

She pulled out her phone and checked her inbox. Still nothing there. Then she thought to check her Junk folder and rubbed a frustrated hand over her face when it showed a mountain of unread emails from Connor. She was usually so organised, but once again, Christmas was here and she was dropping the ball – it seemed to have that effect these days.

'Sorry. I usually remember to check the Junk folder, but it's been a hectic week.' Heat rose to colour her cheeks as she cringed at the rookie error.

'Not to worry. It's been busy here too. I've been putting this together,' he said, gesturing around.

'It's very impressive,' Ellie conceded. 'What is the charity raising money for?'

'Supporting children with dyslexia. We do outreach work in schools and youth clubs, making sure the children get the support they need.'

He pulled at his beard to remove it, along with his hat. Beneath the beard was a friendly face and a shadow of stubble. Ellie caught herself thinking it was a shame the beard hid his jawline and her traitorous heart-rate increased. She banished the thought from her mind: this was business – she couldn't afford to fancy the client. He smiled lopsidedly, and something in Ellie stirred despite her resolve.

'It looks like you'll be making a lot of money for the charity tonight,' Ellie said, forcing herself into work mode. 'So, why do you need our help?'

'We'll be okay for this month … maybe.' Connor played with the beard in his hand, picking at strands that had wound themselves around one another. 'If we're lucky.'

'What do you mean?'

'The charity always does well at Christmas, but fundraising for the rest of the year is tough – I struggle to find the time for marketing as I'm too busy with support work.'

'That's certainly something we can help with.'

Ellie admired his work ethic. He clearly cared about the children his charity helped – unlike her other clients, solely driven by profit and sales. She sensed this job would be different.

She hoped Connor wouldn't be one client too many, though. Work was already taking over her life. She acknowledged the thought – was she really thinking about her own wellbeing for once? She'd not done that since … well, she couldn't remember when.

'So, you're the fun aunt, huh?' he said, breaking the silence.

'Something like that.'

In an instant, Ellie's good mood dissolved. If only she was the fun aunt; she realised she had been anything but fun for the past couple of years. She swallowed the lump in her throat that signalled tears might be on their way if she didn't quickly pull herself together.

'I probably could have done better,' she added.

Before Connor could answer, Sophia climbed down from the carousel and ran over to them, linking arms with Ellie. Ellie stroked Sophia's hair, pleased by the familiarity of her niece despite her own absence over the years.

'How was it?' she asked.

'Great!' Sophia's cheeks were flushed with exhilaration.

'It looked fast!'

'Super fast!' Sophia said.

Ellie realised her meeting would need to end and was surprised to feel a pang of disappointment.

'Mr O'Shaunessy, I think Sophia and I are off to get some hot chocolate before heading home. It was lovely to meet you and I'm sorry we can't talk for longer this evening. It seems we're both busier than we thought we'd be,' she said, realising that she way okay with that – for once. 'Shall we pencil in a meeting for next week? You can come into the office.'

Connor nodded. 'That sounds good. I'll email you,' he added, winking.

Their eyes met, and he held her gaze for a beat longer than she expected him to.

Until a voice from below said, 'Do you want to come with us for hot chocolate, Santa?'

*

'Here.' Ellie handed Connor a cardboard cup and then passed a smaller version to Sophia. The hot chocolates were covered with lashings of whipped cream, and a tiny gingerbread man clung to the sides of each cup.

They moved over to where a group of carollers were singing acapella. A couple of the men in the back row added some creative beat-boxing, and there was armography going on too. At one point, a girl in the middle did a back flip. Quite a crowd had gathered, and Sophia pushed her way to the front, gleeful as she watched the performance. Connor wasn't sure when he'd booked such an avant-garde group of performers, but he made a mental note to keep in touch with them, given their popularity.

'How long have you worked for the company?' he asked Ellie, eager to continue their conversation from earlier.

'I moved back to the area a couple of years ago. I was working in the city before.'

Her dark hair was blowing in the breeze as she watched the choir, and he found himself wanting to reach out and brush it back from her face.

'Oh? What made you come back?' he said, clearing his throat — and his mind.

Ellie bit the arm off her gingerbread man and swallowed it down before she answered. When she spoke, it seemed considered.

'A relationship ended, and I needed to be around family and friends,' she explained.

Her answer surprised Connor. He hadn't expected her to be so open; until now, she had seemed so corporate.

'I'm sorry.'

He didn't know what else to say, but he wanted to know more. He tried to quell the fluttering of hope that she might be single, knowing it would be inappropriate to make a move if she wasn't ready. And even if she was ready, he thought, he was her client — and she probably wouldn't find him attractive in this stupid Santa costume either.

Ellie's expression softened, and she let out a sigh.

'It was a Christmas Eve wedding, and he left me at the altar. He was already married and had got in too deep with me and what he'd thought was an affair. I genuinely didn't have a clue – until his wife practically chased me down the aisle. I don't know what he was expecting to happen once he was married to both of us.' She laughed, then closed her eyes for a long moment. 'Sorry. It's just … it's actually funny when you say it out loud to a stranger.'

'It sounds awful,' Connor said lamely, still stuck for words.

'It was,' she said. 'But it was a couple of years ago now. What about you? What do I need to know about my newest client?' She spoke quickly, perhaps to deflect the attention away from herself. 'You've clearly got a genuine passion for the charity. Have you got people helping you run it or are you a one-man machine?'

'It's just me – which was fine for a while, but it's grown quickly and now it's a lot for me to coordinate by myself.' The zeros from the ledger haunted him again for a fleeting moment. 'There's no Mrs Claus to help me out. I mean, I'm by myself. There's no partner in the business or anything. Maybe I should get one …' he trailed off, mortified that his brain would throw him under a bus like that.

Ellie turned to look at him, her sparkling blue eyes fixed on his. He sucked in a breath and opened his mouth to speak again, but he was interrupted by Sophia, who had left her spot at the front of the crowd to join them.

'Mum phoned,' she said. 'She's back from the office, waiting in the car park.'

Ellie's gaze dropped before she shot Connor an apologetic look.

'I'm sorry, we have to go. It really was lovely to meet you.' She smiled. 'I'll be in touch about a meeting.'

She didn't give Connor more than a moment to lift his hand in a slight wave before they were gone.

*

'It wasn't so bad, was it?' Sophia asked, as they walked back through the market towards the car park. As a final treat, Ellie had bought them a bag of candyfloss to share on the way.

'What do you mean?' Ellie frowned, taking double steps to keep up with Sophia's sprightly half-skip, half-jog.

'I mean, I know you didn't want to come, but I think you had fun in the end? And you got to have your business meeting, which was the main thing.'

When did Sophia start sounding so grown up?

'Hey.' Ellie stopped and reached out for Sophia, another ripple of guilt making her shiver. She pulled her coat around her and knelt down so they were the same height. 'I wanted to come here with you,' she said, looking her right in the eyes.

Sophia frowned. *Didn't she believe her?*

'It might have been because your mum had to work at first, but I'm glad she did. It meant we got to spend tonight together, and it was the best night I've had in a really long time.'

'Really?' Sophia raised her eyebrows.

'Really.' She kissed Sophia on the forehead and stood. 'And I'd like to do it again sometime.'

'Because of Connor?' Sophia smiled.

Ellie's pulse raced. She didn't know whether it was the mention of Connor's name – which made her think about his eyes and that jawline again – or the embarrassment that Sophia had picked up on whatever had passed between them at the Christmas Market.

At least Ellie thought he'd felt something too …

'I think he looooooves you!'

'Sophia, I don't think you understand …'

Sophia stopped in her tracks. Ellie turned to face her, hands on hips. She wasn't going to kneel down this time; she needed all the authority she could muster. She opened her mouth to continue her protest, but Sophia got there first.

'Don't play the grown-up card, Aunty Ellie. Kids are better at picking up things like this. Grown-ups spend all day working or worrying, and they don't see the little things like we do. Every time you were doing work stuff on your phone, he was looking at you. And when we left, he looked sad – and so did you. I think he looooooves you.' She dragged out the word again, discrediting her profound speech. 'Santa's going to be there all night; I think you should tell him. And you should do it now – he'll be busy next week. It's Christmas.'

'Sophia, I really don't think …'

But it was enough to get Ellie thinking. She'd enjoyed herself tonight and, for once, it hadn't been overshadowed by the memory of Billy. She felt a little lighter for it: her shoulders lowered, and she sighed.

'Sophia, sweetie!' Vicky's voice echoed across the car park, and Ellie didn't get a chance to respond further.

Sophia pulled a smug face, wiggled her eyebrows and turned towards her mum. Vicky was waiting by the car as they approached.

'Did you have fun?' she asked.

Sophia wrapped her arms around her mum.

'It was magical,' she said, her eyes sparkling.

'And you?' Vicky asked Ellie.

'Yes, actually. It was lovely. Thank you for inviting me,' she said, looking pointedly at Sophia. She telepathically willed her not to say anything more.

'Was the meeting okay?'

'All good,' Ellie said, tight-lipped.

She ignored Sophia's enormous eyes that harboured her secret. There wasn't a chance they'd go five minutes in the car home before Sophia told her mum everything about her and Santa.

Vicky smiled. 'I'm glad.' She reached for her sister's hand and gave it a squeeze. 'We've got lasagne waiting at home if you want to join us?'

Ellie nodded to accept the invitation – the first she'd said yes to in a while. But before she could formally answer, Sophia interrupted her.

'Actually, Mummy, Aunty Ellie has something she needs to do.' Sophia gave Ellie a huge encouraging smile, accompanied by an exaggerated wink.

Vicky raised an eyebrow at Ellie.

'Something you want to tell me?'

Ellie's heart beat against her chest. Was she really going to do this – race back to Connor like some festive film? And for what – to ask him out on a date? She almost laughed out loud at the absurdity of it all. Whatever happened, she realised she had to do something; she couldn't walk away – she didn't want to. And by the look on Sophia's face, she had little choice.

'She's right,' Ellie said. 'I *do* have something I need to do.'

*

Ellie raced back through the Christmas Market. Finally reaching the grotto, she pushed her way to the front of the queue, trying to avoid the small children waiting patiently. A couple of parents glared at her, but she couldn't stop now; she could see him talking to twins. She stopped and rested against the queue barrier, stepping forward as they left. Her eyes met with Santa's across the grotto's garden, but they weren't the rich hazel she'd been expecting, and a loud sigh of disappointment escaped her lips, visible in the cold air.

What had she been thinking? How ridiculous to assume something good could have come from an unexpected encounter – and at this time of year, too. Her whole body sagged, and she slowly trudged away from the queue. One of the glaring parents tutted loudly, but Ellie couldn't even muster up the energy to explain herself.

Her phone vibrated in her pocket. Checking it, she could see that Max had finally replied to her email. But she didn't care. She swiped to close the app and sat down on a low wall, calling a taxi to take her home to an empty house. She should have accepted the offer of lasagne from Vicky. She'd been offered an olive branch and now she wondered idly whether it was too late.

'I was looking forward to seeing you again. I didn't realise it would be so soon.'

Ellie looked up to see Connor, still dressed in his full Santa costume – beard and all.

'Sophia went home,' she said, instantly feeling foolish. 'I was just contemplating a mulled wine before I call a taxi.'

'I'd invite myself to join you, but I'm not sure how well a Santa drinking on the job would look, and I need all the good publicity I can get.' He chuckled, and the smile reached his eyes. 'I have a rigorous marketing executive trying to sort out my charity and I don't want to do anything to upset her.'

'I've got a few contacts I'm going to speak to on Monday. We can get some publicity going for you and we definitely need to work on your social media presence–' She stopped abruptly, realising that she'd fallen into business mode.

Connor sat down next to her on the wall.

'Do you really want to talk about business?'

Ellie blushed and pulled her scarf up to hide it. She shook her head.

'No. Not really.'

'Why did you come back?'

Ellie's face grew warmer, and she avoided answering the question.

'You've got a great thing here.' Ellie gestured around the market. 'Sophia had a wonderful time tonight.'

'Sophia is a good kid.'

'What did she ask for in the grotto?'

Connor smiled and tapped his nose.

'I'm afraid Christmas wishes are just like any other wish. If you share them, they might not come true. And this one's particularly special.'

'Oh?' Ellie's interest piqued.

'A Santa never tells. Rule number one when we train.'

Ellie laughed. 'You trained for this job?'

'I take my role as Santa very seriously,' he said reverently, but he couldn't keep a straight face.

When he laughed, it was deep and hearty. His knee made contact with hers and something electric passed between them. The butterflies in Ellie's stomach awoke and stretched like they hadn't for a long while.

'Can I buy you that drink?' he said, when silence settled once more. He jumped off the wall and held out a hand.

Ellie realised that she was living one of those important moments in life, where the decision she made in that very second would change the course of things forever. He was a client. And she knew that this one decision could be dangerous – reckless even – when she had to return to the office on Monday and work for him in a professional capacity.

'I'm not sure …'

Connor's smile faltered.

'I understand. I guess I'll see you on Monday.'

He turned, and Ellie felt the moment slipping away. It had been an unexpectedly lovely evening. She'd genuinely enjoyed spending time with Sophia, away from her emails. And then there was Connor. The butterflies in her stomach took flight and hovered expectantly in the air like drifting snowflakes. She knew what she wanted to do, what she had to do, but the words stalled in her throat as she watched him walk away.

'No, Connor, wait …' she called.

He turned back, his beard now in his hand. There was that jawline again, those eyes. Her mind flickered to what other rugged handsomeness might be concealed under the Santa suit.

'Drink?' he asked, smiling. 'And perhaps a fresh start that doesn't involve unanswered emails?'

He held out his hand again.

Around them, the fairy lights continued to twinkle; shrieks and laughs from children caught on the breeze; the carollers sang their merry tune, and the smell of sugar hung in the air. And yet, for all the joy and cheer, Ellie's world stood still. Behind her, the pain of the past was fading, and her determined professionalism melted. In front of her stood Santa, waiting expectantly for her answer.

Ellie smiled. 'A drink sounds lovely.'

She jumped off the wall and took Connor's hand.

'And perhaps our business could wait until the new year,' he suggested.

'Yes, it probably could.' The thoughts of emails, meetings and accounts felt less important now. A cosy Christmas with Vicky and her family suddenly seemed perfect. 'I think I might take Christmas off and spend it with Sophia and her parents.'

'Sophia will be glad to hear that.'

'What do you mean?'

They stopped by the mulled wine stand.

'Let's just say it sounds like one part of Sophia's Christmas wish is coming true.' Connor tapped his nose and winked.

'What about the other part?' Ellie asked curiously.

Connor passed her a cup of steaming wine.

'That depends entirely on how well this drink goes and whether you'd maybe like to see me again?' There was that smile again; this time, slight and bashful.

Ellie blushed, sipping her mulled wine to hide her embarrassment.

She put the cup down and looked up at Connor. He'd not taken his eyes off her, and the way he was looking at her made her heart race.

'I would definitely like to see you again – and not just for business,' she said.

Connor reached out and tucked her hair behind her ear, resting his hand on the side of her face, the past couple of years of hurt melting away as he did. The fact he was a client? She'd worry about that in the new year – that was future Ellie's problem. She covered his hand with her own, and Connor seemed to let out a sigh of relief at her response.

He smiled and said, 'Then I would say there's a very good chance Sophia will get *exactly* what she wished for this Christmas.'

Fairytale of New York

Michelle Harris

Kirsty made a mental note as she pushed open the scruffy, paint-chipped pub doors with full force and stepped into the December evening. *Next time, before you storm out of the pub in righteous anger, pick up your stupid coat.* There was no going back, though, not after this. There was no way she was going back to that table and having to look at Daniel's so-contrite-she-might-punch-it-or-kiss-it face again tonight. Or maybe ever, she wasn't sure. She would work out the finer details when she wasn't ever so slightly gin-drunk and sick with let down and frustration. At this moment in time, she was just trying to stay upright, and not because she was drunk. Her chest was tight, her vision blurred, and her breath came in fast uneven bursts which puffed clouds of warmth into the frosty air.

She pulled her grey cardigan tightly around her and sat down quickly on the adjacent wooden bench before her wobbly legs let her down. The cold engulfed her arse area in seconds as the damp frost soaked into her jeans. Perfect, what she really needed right now was an icicled lady-area. She wiped at her eyes with her shaking hands and breathed deeply.

Don't cry, don't, she willed herself. *If you start, you might not stop.*

Michelle Harris

The frost on the pavement glistened under the streetlight, as a lone fox picked at a discarded box of kebab-shop chips under a table in the deserted carpark that also served as the beer garden of The Drunk Tank.

'Cheer up, love, it might ever 'appen.' From the shadows stepped a familiar face. Barry had been a regular at The Drunk Tank for years. He never arrived with anyone, he just tagged on to groups as the mood took him. Kirsty couldn't remember being in the pub when it was Barry-less; he was part of the furniture. No one really knew if he had a home to go to once the final bell had been rung, but if it he did, he smelled as though there may not be a shower in it.

'It already has happened, so just leave me alone, Barry, okay?' Her voice was shrill as it echoed in the night.

'I'm just saying, love, it's Christmas Eve, you know … don't waste it cryin'. Where's your Christmas Spirit, eh? Where's your fella?'

'My fella isn't my fella, actually, Barry. As of five minutes ago, I am *sans* fella. We were meant to be flying to New York in a week, together on a big, loved up, once in a lifetime adventure, and now, my "fella" has bottled it and I don't know why. So, excuse me, Barry, while I indulge in a little weep, okay?'

As the enormity of what she'd said out loud sunk in, Kirsty found she could no longer hold in the tears. Ultimately, she did not have a "little weep"; she had a massive one. Huge rasping sobs shook her body and tears flooded down her face. Barry surveyed her with some consternation, and even through her tears she recognised in his eyes the expression of terror that always overtook him if he accidentally spoke to a woman for too long. Women scared him at the best of times, but crying women, these were a whole new level of confusion and fear. There was no way he could possibly say anything helpful at this juncture, and they both knew it. Instead, he opted for a quick exit.

'That bloody fox has nicked me chips. See you later, chin up.' And he was gone, leaving her alone to ugly cry into the silence.

*

Inside the pub, Daniel felt close to tears himself, and he was not a crier. He couldn't believe he was doing this to Kirsty, now. What kind of an arsehole ended a relationship like this, on Christmas Eve, and backed out of something so massive at the last minute? Not him. Not dependable, long term, reliable Daniel. He hated himself for doing it, while all the while knowing he had to. Over the soundtrack of festive music and the chatter

230

and drunken revels of the pre-Christmas crowd, he was certain he'd actually heard the moment when Kirsty's heart had broken. Or was it his own? It was hard to tell. Either way, it felt horrible, more than just a breakup, more a physical pain. And he'd had a few days to process this; for Kirsty, it was all brand-new information. He could only imagine how she must feel, and he cursed himself for being the cause of it.

Face in hands, he inhaled deeply and reminded himself that he was doing the best thing for Kirsty in the long run. The best thing for her. And for him? He wasn't as sure, but best or not, it was the right thing. And Daniel had to do the right thing now. Even if the right thing absolutely sucked.

His phone buzzed on the table. Mum's timing was perfect, as usual.

Don't stay for me, darling. Follow your dreams.

They had been over this many times, and each time the outcome was the same: he knew he had to stay with her, not just for her, but for him. He would never forgive himself otherwise. And therefore, New York was just not an option for him right now. Following his dreams would have to wait. But Kirsty's dreams, well, they wouldn't wait. For her it was now or never, so it had to be now, he felt certain. He wished it wouldn't make her hate him, but he couldn't think of another way. He knew he was doing what was best. He knew it. But he didn't feel it.

Daniel sighed, downed the last of his whisky, picked up Kirsty's coat, and headed outside.

'Here, you'll catch your death of cold.' He put the coat around her shoulders. It was all he could do not to pull her into his arms, but he knew that wouldn't be welcomed now. He looked at her, hunched and wet-bummed on the damp, dilapidated bench, and it didn't feel even slightly like the best thing. As he breathed in her very presence, so familiar and so precious to him, he wondered how on earth he was going to cope without her. She was all he had ever known. After twelve years with her on his team, he couldn't comprehend how he was going to get through this next period without her.

'Don't. Don't dare be nice to me when I am this angry.' Kirsty wiped the tear-smudged makeup from under her eyes, and tucked her hair behind her ears, a habitual nervous gesture which had occasionally bugged Daniel, but not today. She pulled her coat around her and sighed. Daniel knew she was gearing up for a tirade, and he didn't blame her at all.

'I just don't understand how you can suddenly just change your mind about it all. Two weeks ago, you were online interviewing for jobs. Last week you were buying new suitcases and helping me with the flat-hunting.' Her voice shook with — what? Was it rage, fear, sadness, betrayal, or a culmination of all four? 'It was happening. We were going to New York, and you couldn't wait! We were almost annoyingly smug about it all – I know at least three people unfollowed my Instagram. That's how self-satisfied we were!' Sarcasm had always been Kirsty's go to emotional protection. 'We were one teensy step away from matching "I heart NY" tattoos, and it was all going to be amazing. And now, just like that, you can't go? You just don't fancy it? I mean, what the hell, Daniel!'

'I'm so sorry, Kirsty. I know how it looks, and I am sorry. I can't explain it properly. But I can't go.'

'Why? What's changed, suddenly? What's so important?'

For a moment, he thought about telling her the truth. He imagined himself telling her why he had to stay, imagined her comforting him, reassuring him that of course he couldn't leave, not now. But he couldn't, because he knew her too well. Her next logical step would be to stay and help him through this. She just couldn't not be there for those she loved, couldn't not show up for her people. If he told her why he had to stay, she wouldn't leave without him. It wasn't her nature, and it was part of what made her so damned lovable.

Daniel knew that if he told Kirsty the truth, she'd immediately cancel everything and pretend that not going was okay by her. She'd smile, make a flippant comment about how, if it was meant to be, it would happen, and selflessly dismantle the dreams she'd worked so hard on for so long. See you later, Billboard magazine, so long editorial career progression, goodbye fanciful notions of walking down Fifth Avenue with armfuls of shopping to pretty up their postage-stamp sized apartment on the Upper East Side.

She'd pretend there would be another chance, when the reality was, that if she cancelled this for him, she might never get another go at this amazing new life she so deserved. Daniel felt certain that she would come to resent him if that happened, so he couldn't let it happen. He loved her too much to steal this from her, whatever the reason. She deserved to have her dreams come true. So, she had to go without him. But how to make sure she did?

'It just doesn't feel right, Kirsty. And … I don't have a job there yet, it's very uncertain …' he tried to fill his voice with conviction, but he knew he sounded faltering and weak.

'You'll get a job, Daniel. There'll be loads of places crying out for your skillset. You'll be snapped up in no time once you can interview in person. Mr Charisma won't struggle to get a job.' She stopped and stared at him, incredulous. Her green eyes bored into his dark brown ones so deeply that he half expected her to suddenly glean the truth and shout at him for lying.

'Daniel, is there something else going on here? I'm just so confused. I can't believe you would do this to me, to us. Is it just a crisis of confidence, or is it something more?'

'It's … complicated. My circumstances – that is, my er, situation, it's just that we …' Could he persuade her with vagueness alone, he wondered? Annoy her with his inarticulate bluster to the point where she'd walk away from him?

'Seriously Daniel, use your words, please, because this is borderline ridiculous. I have to go to New York. I *want* to go to New York, and I thought you wanted to, as well. If you don't want to go, what does that say about us? I thought we were good, you know? There's nothing I wouldn't do for you, sweetheart, you know that.'

He did know that. And that was the problem. He took a deep breath.

'I just … I do love you, Kirsty. You must know that. But I'm not coming. I'm so sorry.' In the end, he decided he couldn't outright lie. Omission was going to have to be the chosen path. 'I have my reasons, Kirsty, but I can't tell you what they are.'

'There's not someone else, is there? I mean, I never had you down as that type, but then, I thought you were moving to New York with me, so maybe I had you all wrong! Is there someone else you want to stay for?'

In his pocket, his phone buzzed again. He ignored it. He knew it would be a reworded repeat of the previous message; they had been coming for days now.

'I have to stay here, and I wish I could explain, but right now I can't, and I'm sorry. I want you to go to New York and do everything we've talked about. Be amazing, be you and never ever settle for anything less than you deserve. Knock their socks off, Pocket Rocket. I love you.'

He didn't trust himself to speak anymore, and he knew if he hugged her or even touched her arm right now, his resolve would crumble. So, he breathed in one last look at her, his beautiful Kirsty, the only future he had ever imagined for himself. And then he turned and walked away.

She didn't try to follow him. As he permitted himself the briefest glance behind him, she was frozen to the spot, staring after him, and he knew he would never forget the expression on her face as long as he lived.

Eleven months later

Happy Hour at Blackwell's was in full swing as Kirsty scanned the sea of people for familiar faces. The mahogany bar was adorned with festive greenery, and the burnt orange walls were ornamented with coloured lights and tinsel. Beneath the lively chatter and clatter, Orla Fallon's "Three Ships were Sailing in", and the whole atmosphere was warm and inviting.

When Kirsty had imagined herself in an NYC bar, she had not envisaged Blackwell's, with its warm Irish welcome and its "When in Doubt, Drink Stout" posters. Instead, she'd seen herself draped elegantly at a lavishly sleek and minimalist cocktail bar, looking achingly and effortlessly sophisticated as she sipped her Cosmopolitan in a one hundred percent Instagram-able location. But she had reckoned without Gina.

A whirlwind in human form, native New Yorker Gina had quickly become so much more than just a colleague. Witty, pretty and with a heart of gold, she had taken one look at Kirsty's tight, drawn face the week after her solitary arrival in New York, and decided she needed a friend. And if Gina decided something, the rest of the world didn't get a choice. Luckily, Kirsty wouldn't have had it any other way; she loved Gina's humour and zest for life, and looking back, she was not sure she could have coped with those early months in New York without her.

Kirsty had still been hard at work when Gina had swung past her desk about forty-five minutes earlier.

'Doll, it's Friday. Will you just let your hair down? I'm off to get me some Irish.'

'Half an hour, G, and I will be there, I promise. I'm on a deadline, but I'm almost done.'

'Okay, sweetheart. Theo and I will start without you. Don't forget your scarf, it's brick out today.' Gina was just the right mix of mother hen and bad influence.

Gina was also a sucker for an Irish accent, most recently, one Irish accent in particular. She'd been on two dates with Eoghan the barman, (if you didn't count the entire evening she had wasted drunkenly trying to work out the pronunciation of his name from his staff t-shirt) and had high hopes for a third, so the gang had been spending a more than usual amount of time at Blackwell's of late. It did have the added bonus of being less than ten minutes' walk from the Billboard Office on Madison Avenue, so Kirsty didn't mind too much. Plus, they served a mean burger.

But although Eoghan was currently mixing espresso martinis at one end of the long bar, the high, patterned barstools were all otherwise occupied, so Kirsty skirted past them to the booths beyond, where she found Gina and Theo deep in conversation, and two-thirds of the way through a bottle of wine.

As Kirsty approached the pair, she already knew what they would be discussing; Theo's tumultuous on-again-off-again relationship with 'Wall

Street Guy' Jack was currently off-again, and there'd been some speculation as to whether Jack had been vibing with their mutual and stunningly attractive friend, Eduardo. Sure enough, as Kirsty got close enough to hear, Gina was gesticulating emphatically with the hand not holding her generous glass of wine, and saying, 'But, Theo, if he wants to go, let him go, right? You can do better, anyways.'

'Can I, Gina? Can I really? Because my dating record reads like a who's who of human garbage, and I just feel drained from it, drained and I–' He broke off as he noticed her approaching. 'Oh, Kirsty honey, that dress is just fabulous on you. Pull up a chair and let me tell you how I'm gonna die alone.'

'You're not going to die alone, Theo. You can't even eat dinner alone. Besides, you're so theatrical, you could never manage to die without an audience.' Kirsty didn't mean to be unsympathetic, but she'd heard a lot of this before. 'Shall I get some more drinks?'

At that moment, Eoghan appeared with another bottle of wine and a glass for Kirsty. 'Another bottle of Santa Rita for the lady, and this one's on me.' He planted a kiss on Gina's cheek as he put down the bottle and passed Kirsty her glass. 'I can't stop, sure, we're jam packed this evening. G, I get off at midnight, so if you're still here, ye can buy me a nightcap.'

Gina flushed slightly. 'Ah, to be sure, I can buy you a wee dram,' she quipped, in a barbarism of an Irish accent.

'I don't talk like that. No one talks like that. Kirsty, will you tell her?' and Eoghan was gone, but he smiled as he went.

Gina poured a substantial glass of wine for Kirsty, refilled her glass and Theo's, and surveyed Kirsty with an expression of deeply melodramatic concern.

'Speaking of dying alone …'

'Stop it!' Kirsty laughed and sipped her wine.

Cold and crisp, it was exactly what she needed after a busy week at work. She still had to pinch herself any time anyone asked her what her job was. 'I'm an editor at Billboard.' It just never got old. But the run up to Christmas was well underway, and her deadlines and schedule were in danger of becoming out of control. To be here in a bar before the end of happy hour had been unheard of for the past month. She'd regularly been the last one out of the office, heading wearily to her apartment via Whole Foods, just scraping in before closing time for her sad little late-night dinner for one. Out on a Friday night, Kirsty felt a little giddy, and as though she was bunking off.

'Dead-ass, Kirsty, you haven't so much as looked at a guy in months. You had like three dates with Eddie and then never answered his messages, what's up with that?' Gina would not be deterred.

'I like Eddie. He's … nice.' Kirsty took another sip of wine. If she was going to be interrogated, she would need it.

'Nice? NICE?!' Theo was incredulous. 'Eddie Mathews is drop dead gorgeous. Eyes so deep you could drown in them. Plus, he cooks. If he wasn't straight, we'd be picking out china right now – I'm serious.' He didn't look serious. His blue eyes danced with amusement, and he flicked his acid blonde hair for extra emphasis.

'I'm sorry, guys, I really am. I suck at dating, and I've let you down.' Kirsty decided to keep things light and hung her head in mock-shame.

'You *shouldn't* suck at dating. You're gorgeous, you're funny and guys really dig that short feisty girl vibe you've got going on. You're not short on offers. Guys are lining up down the block to date you. Sean, Eoghan's friend, says you're an eleven. He's ripped, I'm just saying … You need to let go of "The Daniel Thing".' Gina pronounced "The Daniel Thing" in a faux British accent that rivalled her Irish one for its dismal quality. Kirsty couldn't help but laugh.

'"The Daniel Thing" is ancient history. I'm not claiming life is perfect, but I'm doing pretty well now. I love my job, I love my apartment, I love my little dog, I love my friends, I love my life. I've done all this despite him. I would totally date if the right guy came along.'

Gina was unconvinced. 'Remember, doll, I knew you when you were fresh off the plane. You came from JFK a total mess. You couldn't go a day without crying, and you were broken for a really long time.'

'Honesty is one thing, G, but that's brutal.' Theo interjected.

'It's not brutal, actually. It's a fair assessment,' Kirsty conceded. 'I was pretty broken. I was confused, and let down, and angry and sad. "The Daniel Thing" was the only "Thing" I knew. And the whole twelve years we were together, right from day one when we were kids and we snogged on the dancefloor at the youth club Christmas disco, I was certain of one thing: he would never ever hurt me.'

Theo only interjected to pour the wine. It didn't matter that he probably had no idea what a snog or a youth club actually were; he could get the gist. He'd never heard the full story before, and Kirsty knew he was curious. She took a gulp of wine and continued.

'You know how some people are just, like, yours? Not family, but your people? Daniel was that for me. And not just him, his mum and sister too, and his little nephew. His family was my family because my family are idiots.' She paused for another sip of wine. It was really going down too well.

'Daniel and I, we just fitted together so perfectly, we laughed our arses off, loved each other in a really easy, brilliant way, and if ever I stopped to think about it, like when a friend got cheated on or treated like rubbish by an idiot partner, I knew beyond a shadow of a doubt, he would never ever hurt me. So, when he called time on us and our plans, I just couldn't understand it. I kind of always thought one day, he'd tell me why. I felt like he had to have a reason, a motive, otherwise he'd just hurt me, and he would never do that. I don't *not* want to date. I totally want to find someone, but I just … I feel like I am lacking some closure, and until I get it, I can't be open to anything new.'

Theo perused the bar menu as he considered her words. Kirsty had a strong suspicion he was about to suggest a round of cocktails.

'I don't wanna state the obvious, honey, but you could ask him. There're these darling new inventions you English Roses might not have heard of, called the telephone and the email. Why not try them out?'

'I could, Theo, I know I could. But being honest, I am scared to seek him out. If I heard his voice, or even read his name in an email, I worry I might fall apart like I did when I arrived. I like who I am now. I don't want to go back.'

Kirsty met Gina's eyes as she made the admission, and she saw in her friend a silent understanding. Gina broke the connection their eyes had made, grabbing the menu from Theo to lighten the tone. She could always sense what Kirsty needed.

'Okay, kids, it's cocktail time. What's your poison? It looks like I'm here until midnight, and you're staying until Eoghan's ready for me. No arguments. Does this count as date number three? Because we all know what's acceptable on date three, right?' She burst into infectious laughter.

As she sipped her wine and skimmed the cocktail menu, Kirsty wished not for the first time that she could be a little bit more like Theo and Gina. She envied their casual approach to dating, and she wondered if they'd ever been hurt as deeply as she had. They certainly never mentioned it. But, she told herself, enough was enough. Time for change. Time to be single and ready to mingle, at last. A more relaxed and open attitude could be her Christmas present to herself.

As Kirsty considered that possibility, the jukebox at Blackwell's struck up a familiar and suitably Irish Christmas song. Kirsty sighed. If only Daniel had been a scumbag or a maggot, this would have all been a whole lot easier.

*

Stripped of all the furniture and photographs and knick-knacks that made a house a home, Daniel didn't really recognise this place anymore. It looked naked and alien without all the things that had just always been there, relics of a childhood long ago expired. The world's comfiest sofa where he'd laid and watched daytime tv when he'd had shingles at 16, the ancient dining table that he and Esther had accidentally ruined doing a science experiment, and had never been replaced. The art deco sideboard that his mother had bagged second-hand and loved so much that the children had joked it was her third child and nicknamed it "Bro". Bro was safely relocated to Esther's flat now; they couldn't bear to part with him. Now that the living room was totally empty, he realised that the carpet was threadbare and faded. Somehow before, it hadn't seemed worn out; it had just meant home.

It wasn't just the absence of stuff; the house smelled weird now too. When he'd remarked as much to Esther earlier, she'd pealed with laughter, and shrieked, 'What you can smell is cleaning products, Danny! If she can hear you now, she's flipping livid!'

Esther was kind of right, although it wasn't that the house had been dirty, it had been unfailingly as clean as a pin, but something was always cooking when Juliet had been well. Baking smells from the oven or hearty stews bubbling away on the hob had welcomed them home from school daily, growing up. Even when they were older, and Juliet had worked more hours, and even later still, once they'd both moved out, there had always been something tasty waiting in a cake tin on the side when they let themselves in. In the run up to Christmas, the house would usually be fragrant with homemade mincemeat, fruit cakes, puddings, and pastries.

Gosh, Daniel could really have done with a mince pie and a cuppa with Mum right now. It was hard to believe she wasn't here anymore. It didn't seem possible that eighteen months ago they hadn't even known she was sick again. She'd felt tired, and a little withdrawn, but that shouldn't spell the end, right? She'd been through enough three years previously, with chemo and operations and worry after worry. With the passing of time, they'd started to really believe all that was behind her, and so when it came, the news had hit them all like a wrecking ball. When she'd received her diagnosis and the extent of the spread had been revealed, he still hoped he had time. But when their assigned hospice nurse had gently explained what it had meant, Mum had borne it with a quietly dignified acceptance. 'Nothing to be done. Let me go to Jesus.' Only a slight wobble in her lip had given away her truth. Daniel bowed his head as grief threatened to overwhelm him. How could someone so strong go so quickly?

The clear-up operation at their childhood home had been bleak and nostalgic and beautiful and sad, and about a million other emotions, all in random order and all as raw and rough and harsh as he had expected they would be.

'Well, I guess that's it. All done and dusted. Are you okay?' Esther stood in the living room doorway and Daniel remembered when she'd stood exactly there seven years previously and told Juliet she was pregnant with Rudi. A defiant, scared, and scrawny sixteen-year-old, her voice had betrayed the fear behind her "grown up" words as she explained to their mum that she was keeping the baby, that she could do this on her own. Esther had chosen that spot, he was sure, in case Mum had hit the roof and chased her out into the street! But in that instance, she should have known better. Instead, Juliet had listened the whole thing out, and then stood from the sofa and hugged Esther so hard.

'Now it begins, child. It's not my first choice for you, but you don't have to do it alone. I am here.'

I am here. This had been her go-to phrase. Juliet's standards were high. She was driven and had high expectations of herself and her children. As a single mum, she had been both parents to Daniel and Esther, and she'd worked hard her whole life to make sure they had everything they needed. She had always instilled in them a drive to do what was right, and to be the best version of themselves they could possibly be. But she had never judged, and she had always been there when they needed her. When Esther had been a confused, scared, pregnant kid, Mum had been everything to her. Looking at his younger sister now, Daniel felt nothing but pride. Rudi was a fabulous kid, and Esther had her own flat, her own job, and no intention of settling for any man that didn't meet her standards. That was Juliet, right there. She *was* here.

Esther shifted uneasily in the doorway. 'The thing is, Danny, I've got to go and pick up Rudi, but I have something for you. Mum made me promise to wait until now, and I couldn't not do what she says, because you don't argue with cancer patients. It's frowned upon. She said it had to be the day when everything was dealt with.'

She handed over a white envelope, addressed to him in his Mum's handwriting. It was a little more haphazard than usual, but unmistakably hers. Out of the blue like this, it made his breath catch in his throat – so many birthday cards had been addressed the same way – "To my Danny Boy."

'I had one too. I got mine early. I cried for literally a whole day, but I plan on doing as I was told, because that's what we always did, right? Call me and tell me all about this. I have to go, it's a quid a minute at after school club after half-six.' Esther kissed him briefly on the cheek and made her way out.

He ripped open the envelope with no idea what to expect. Why was his hand shaking? He wasn't sure.

My Danny Boy,

If you're reading this, I guess I am finally off your hands. I'm glad to go, you know? I'm ready to. And I don't want you to worry about me. I know you're not big on God, sweetheart, and I don't mind, because I went to Church enough for both of us. I know that where I am beats where I was, and that's enough for me.

I want to write you pages, but I am tired, and I think you will be here at home to see me soon, so I will try and tell you to your face instead, how proud, and happy I am that you made me a mother. You made my life, you and Esther. I was proud of you, every single day.

Thank you, my darling son, for everything. You are the only man I have ever known who has never let me down. But now you must think of your own happiness. You know what I mean, Danny Boy: you must go get your Kirsty. You put me before her, and I never wanted that to happen. But now I am gone, and I don't want you to wait one second before you go and try to get her back. I love that girl, and you do, too. You owe this to yourself, sweetheart.

I asked you not to stay for me, but I am so very grateful that you did. You were here. I love you all the world, my Danny. And I want every happiness for you. It's time to take some risks.

Love always,
Mum.

PS I tried to look for a bible verse to convince you, but Esther says I should just threaten to haunt you if you don't do what I have said. Go to New York, or I will "woo hoo" outside your window with a sheet over my head, make no mistake about it! The enclosed is just to help you on your way before the house is sold. Please make sure Esther doesn't blow all of hers on Rudi; you both need to make a change. I have big dreams for you both.

PPS Look after Bro. He's very special.
x

A cheque for ten thousand pounds was neatly paper-clipped to the letter. A cheque, how very Mum – he had always teased her that no one wrote cheques anymore. Daniel's chuckle-turned-shudder escaped his throat as his eyes filled with tears, and he allowed them now to spill down his cheeks. Her signature on the cheque was her final goodbye and her final instruction. It was all just so tragically unfair. He should have twenty more years with her yet, at least. She should be hugging more grandchildren, and clapping at Rudi's graduation, and a million other big and small things that she would now forever miss.

He wiped his eyes with the back of his hand and wondered what on earth Mum had demanded from Esther. He suspected it might involve some studying; Juliet was big on studying. Esther, too, although she worried that if she pursued her own dreams, she'd miss out on being a mum. But clearly, she intended to do as she was told now. It was just so very hard to say no to someone who was dead, and he got the feeling Mum was fully aware of that. *Fair play, Mum.*

Daniel took a deep breath as the realisation of what this meant sunk in. It looked like he was going to New York, then.

*

As the plane cruised at 36,000 feet above the Atlantic Ocean, most of the passengers were snoozing. Daniel, however, couldn't settle to sleep, book or film. Now that he was finally going, ghosts of his past exciting plans for New York with Kirsty occupied his mind front and centre, and it all felt a lot longer ago than it actually was. So much had changed, he supposed, and all the joy and possibility that had been, was now replaced with doubt and uncertainty.

Daniel tapped his phone to life and scrolled through, for the thousandth time, all the information he knew about where Kirsty could be. He knew her office address at Billboard, and he knew the address of the tiny apartment they had secured for rental. But almost a year later, would Kirsty be there? In a city of over 8 million people, how on earth would he find her if she'd moved on? He guessed he would have to call in transatlantic reinforcements in the form of Esther the super-cyber-sleuth – he was rubbish at that stuff himself.

He sighed, and idly flicked through the in-flight magazine, with its festive gloss and sparkle. Broadway stars revealing their favourite Christmas songs, and a Macy's holiday gift guide really didn't fit with Daniel's mood. But then an article caught his eye: "Top Ten Romantic Things to do in NYC this December". Carriage rides through Central Park and ice skating at the Rockefeller Center, both of which had featured in the animated late-night discussions he had Kirsty had enjoyed about life together in New York, jolted Daniel's mind to the sudden realisation that he had no idea what he would say to Kirsty when he finally saw her. No romantic gesture, no plan. How did you attempt to win back someone who had no idea that you had never truly let them go in the first place?

He knew he owed her a full explanation if she would let him. But he just didn't know how she would react. A year was a long time. What right had he to assume she would want to listen to him? And what if he had come too late? Although he hated to admit he, he knew there was a strong possibility that Kirsty would have moved on, even if he did get to see her. Resolving to remain optimistic, Daniel sat in the muted light, and continued to read the romantic countdown, hoping against hope that Kirsty was not currently "snuggling up against the cold in a rooftop igloo for cocktails at 230 Fifth" with somebody else.

Restlessly, he shoved the magazine back into the slot in the back of the seat in front of him and decided that as soon as the plane had landed, he was heading straight to Billboard. He had to find Kirsty straightaway.

*

As she sat bundled in blankets and spooned a generous heap of Rocky Road ice cream directly from the tub into her mouth, Kirsty wondered, why all did sitcoms have such rubbish endings? Why did Rachel have to give up her dream job for Ross? Why did Will and Grace fall out? Why did the Mother that Ted Met have to end up dead? And why on earth did the program writers not understand that Robin should have ended up with Barney, comedy genius, instead of Ted, the wet blanket?

'Because TV is pants,' she declared, switching off the TV with the remote control, and reaching for her glass. Her beloved cockapoo, Broderick, had been asleep on her lap, but as she leant forward and threatened to topple him onto the rug, he murmured his dissent in typical dog fashion, jumped off and made himself comfy on the other end of the sofa.

On his end of the FaceTime call, Theo replied to this declaration. 'Sweetie, TV mirrors life, that's why. People make dumb choices, people leave, people die, people settle … it blows, basically.' Resplendent in lilac silk pyjamas, he slurped his gin and shook his blonde bed-head in disgust. Jack and Eduardo had recently gone public, and Theo was taking it characteristically badly.

'Jeez, Theo, Merry friggin' Christmas.' On her end of the video call, Gina was applying her make up for a date with Eoghan. They were going well, and it showed; Gina shone, and it wasn't because of her expertly applied Dior cosmetics.

'I'm serious, G. Kirsty and I are cases in point. We're pathetic.' Kirsty wasn't sure that a couple of dubious dates on her part made her pathetic, but it seemed Theo made the rules, and they changed quite often, so she didn't bother to interject. Theo pouted and gulped his gin again. 'It's Christmas Eve and I'm gonna die alone! Kirsty, do you wanna come over and watch while I die alone on Christmas Eve? I've got Ben & Jerry's.'

Kirsty considered. 'Nah, me and Broderick have some stuff to do. But thanks. Maybe you could die alone after we have lunch tomorrow? 'Cause if you bail on me on Christmas Day, I'll be sad.'

'Ah, fine. I guess you and lunch are now my reasons for existing. I'm such a giver. See ya later.' And Theo was gone.

'Enjoy your date, Gina, and I'll call you tomorrow.' Kirsty made to end the call, but Gina interjected.

'Kirsty, honey, I think you need to fix that hair. And wash your face. And show me the apartment. Is it tidy?'

Kirsty was confused. 'It's fine. And why would I brush my hair? Broderick doesn't care what my hair's like, do you, Broderick? He loves me just the way I am.' Gina tutted, and Kirsty continued, 'Why are you being weird?'

'I'm not being weird. Just … I think your luck is changing. So, fix your hair, ok? I gotta go. Have a good one.'

Kirsty looked at her watch. It was 7.15pm on Christmas Eve and all she had to look forward to was more wine, more Rocky Road, and more TV. Maybe Theo was right, maybe she was pathetic. *No*, she inwardly asserted. *Dates or lack of dates do not define me. Men do not define me. I am a strong confident woman, and I happen to like Rocky Road and wine. Take that, female repression.*

She could smash the patriarchy and still feel lonely though, right? It would have been nice to be with someone for Christmas Eve, especially since last year had turned out so spectacularly horrendous. After things had fizzled out with Eddie a month or so ago, Kirsty had been on several dates, but none had led anywhere. Richard had mansplained every joke at the comedy club, Anton had clicked his fingers at the waiter, and Simeon had revealed he didn't like dogs. What was a girl to do?

Picking up her phone, Kirsty took another gulp of wine and opened Instagram.

'Broderick, avert your eyes, please. I'm not proud of what's about to happen.'

She didn't know why, but suddenly she had to see Daniel's face again. Annoyingly, she'd unfollowed him on all social media from the airport while waiting for her flight, inconsolable and bitter. She had regretted it ever since. At the time, the idea of seeing updates from him was too painful to comprehend, not that he posted much, anyway. But recently, she'd let thoughts of him creep back into her mind, and she just wanted to look at him. *Christmas makes people do weird things*, she decided. But the tiny thumbnail that greeted her above his private Instagram profile was not enough. She could see his smile and imagine the sparkle in his eyes, but she needed more.

'Broderick, my boy, we are falling down the rabbit hole.' This called for a bigger screen, so she put her phone on the coffee table and picked up her laptop. She wasted the best part of an hour looking at mutual friends' Facebook photos – not that anyone posted anything on Facebook anymore – and then remembered Esther's Instagram, scrolling frantically for photos of the only face she really wanted to see.

Goodness, though, Rudi had got big. His sweet face and cool corn-rows, the pure joy he radiated, beamed out of her screen and touched her heart. She loved Daniel's family. She'd always felt so welcome. Esther wasn't a prolific Instagrammer, but her photos reminded Kirsty of the love that had always emanated from them all. No references to Daniel for the last year or so; he'd always been a bit sceptical about appearing on social media. Kirsty scrolled further back, searching for a mere mention of him, and eventually came across a photo that featured them both. Daniel, smiling that gorgeous open smile, with one arm around her and one around Juliet, with Esther to her other side, holding Rudi on her lap. Esther hadn't written any caption, just "#family". Kirsty's breath caught in her throat and she decided she just had to go for it. One more gulp of wine for luck. What time was it in London? Late. He'd be asleep, probably. Oh crap, she was doing this.

She opened her messages and typed; it didn't matter that she had deleted his number; she knew it by heart – please God it was still the same.

- *I know it's been ages, and I just want to say … Merry Christmas. I wish I could see you.*

Send.

Oh god, oh god, oh god. She cringed at her own desperation. She could hear Theo in her head saying, 'Damn girl, you so thirsty,' and found herself blushing, even though only Broderick was there to witness the shame spiral. She hid her phone under a cushion – the only sensible adult course of action, obviously. Covering her face with her hands, she took several deep breaths, and then retrieved it.

Sweet Lord, he'd read her message. Clearly, he wasn't asleep. Maybe he had someone with him, keeping him awake. Shame spiral level two activated. Kirsty stared at her phone screen, barely even blinking.

The tell-tale "…" while he typed had her heart in her throat – would he be mad? Sad? Dismissive? She didn't know what she was hoping for, but when the reply came, she was totally blindsided.

- *On my way. Give me fifteen minutes. (Seriously!)* Xxx

She spilled her wine, and emitted a sound she had never made before, a sound so confusing that Broderick sat up and cocked his head at her as if to say, *what's up with you, human?*

'Oh my god, Broderick!! I need to fix my hair!' Damn Gina. There was no doubt now what she'd been referring to, but why couldn't she have told her?

She couldn't believe he was here in New York. It was too much to process. Was she angry with him or pleased to see him? Was he going to be contrite, or defiant, or what? Was he even here for her? He had to be, right? A Christmas Day business meeting just happening to bring him into her neighbourhood was just too unlikely a coincidence, she felt sure. Daniel, her Daniel, was finally here, and despite everything, despite all that she'd felt, or done or said, she could not wait to see him.

In the fifteen minutes that followed, Kirsty did her hair, hid all the evidence of her ice cream and wine binge-flop, brushed her teeth, applied some lip gloss, speed-cleaned everything she could think of, changed out of her pyjamas, and into some jeans and a non-try hard sweater. After a squirt of perfume for good luck, she just found time to message Gina, *You could have effing well told me.*

Gina replied, *I met him at work earlier. He's hot. I think you should let him be your Christmas present. xoxo*

By the time the entry phone announced Daniel's arrival, Kirsty wasn't sure how she would be able to keep her hands off him.

*

When Kirsty's message buzzed his phone into life, Daniel felt almost as though he had willed it there. It seemed too perfect, too coincidental, too fairy tale. Or was it the universe? If you believe all that nonsense. He smiled inwardly; or maybe it was Mum, woo-hooing like she promised.

Now he came to think about it, everything since his arrival in New York had had a hint of the fairy tale about it, kind of hazy around the edges, but exciting and pleasant – could this be jetlag? He was half inclined to cast Gina in his mind as some kind of overly blunt fairy godmother figure in Jimmy Choos. She'd been leaving work when he'd arrived at the Billboard building and asked her if she knew Kirsty, and she had immediately cancelled her afternoon plans, escorting him to a local bar before he could protest, and instructing him to 'spill all of the tea'.

Daniel wasn't one to talk about emotions and feelings much, but in the space of one drink, Gina's warmth had drawn all the truth out of him, and he found he felt better for it. Gina had then directed him to a couple of stores where he'd picked up some gifts to surprise Kirsty with. He'd been on Fifth Avenue when the message came through, and had jumped in the nearest taxi, heart racing, holding a huge bouquet of red and white peonies, and feeling ever so slightly like he'd jumped into some film plot. If only he had a script!

Now he was finally outside the door, Daniel realised he had no definite plan, despite the flowers and present. When Kirsty opened the door, her eyes shining, Daniel moved towards her without even registering what he was doing, pulling her into the hug he'd been waiting for since last Christmas Eve in The Drunk Tank. She hugged him back and said into his chest, 'I can't believe you're finally here.'

'Me neither,' he replied, and he couldn't. Time seemed to freeze as they embraced, breathing in each other along with the scent of the peony bouquet, still caught in Daniel's hand. As they stood locked together, Daniel became aware of the little black and white dog, jumping up at their legs, its tail wagging enthusiastically. He pulled back and bent down to ruffle his ears, as he did so, awkwardly giving the flowers to Kirsty with his other hand.

'Who's this little guy? Is he yours?' He didn't know why he was talking about the dog instead of them, but it seemed safe.

'He's mine. I got him from an Adoption Centre on Ninety-Second. He's called Broderick.' Daniel got the feeling that Kirsty was happy to keep things light, too.

'Hi, Broderick!' He fussed over the cute little dog, who pawed his knees and yapped his greeting. 'Hi, little guy, aren't you just adorable!'

'Can you believe some people call them cockerdoodles here, instead of cockapoos? It's like they're trying to make them even cuter.'

'I should have known you'd get a dog; you always said you wanted one when we got here – ' He broke off. The elephant in the room had trumpeted loudly. There was no going back, and they both fell silent.

'Yeah, well … I guess Broderick and I, we sort of rescued one another.' Kirsty placed the flowers carefully on a side table, crossed her arms over her stomach, and dropped awkwardly into the armchair. Broderick settled himself at her feet.

Daniel moved towards the sofa. 'May I?' Kirsty nodded, so he sat down.

'I am so sorry, Kirst. I never, ever wanted to hurt you.' His voice was slightly hoarse with emotion.

Kirsty's lip wobbled as she whispered, 'Then why did you?'

Daniel took a deep breath, and out it all came. All the pain of hearing that Juliet had been back to the doctor in secret, worried about her tiredness and discomfort, recognising from her previous illness that this was more than just the everyday aches and pains of aging. The frustration that she had not told him that she knew the cancer was back, and only admitted it once she realised how little time she might have left. The sadness of knowing that his time with his mum would soon end, and the realisation that the shitty, shitty timing of it all meant he couldn't leave his family.

As he told her about Juliet's illness, Kirsty's eyes streamed with steady, silent tears, which she wiped with the back of one hand, reaching out with the other to hold the nearest of Daniel's. She didn't interrupt him, but as he tried to explain why he'd let her go without her knowing about Juliet, she stiffened slightly, and the expression on her face changed. He paused in his story, not sure what the change in her demeanour represented.

'You understand why, Kirsty, don't you?' He squeezed the hand he'd been holding, but she pulled it away and clasped hers together in her lap, fidgeting slightly with her jewellery.

'You know, I'm not sure I do.' She paused for a second to gather her thoughts. 'I just wish you could have been honest. I could have been there for you. I could have helped. I just can't believe she's gone. I'm so sorry.' She reached out to him. 'Your Mum was amazing.'

'Thank you. She was.' He couldn't bring himself to say any more.

'But Daniel, I still don't fully understand *why* the dishonesty. I mean, I would have understood why you wouldn't come. I wouldn't have felt so-betrayed.' A note of coldness crept into her voice.

'You say that now, but I think you would have stayed for me and missed your chances here. I didn't want you to grow to resent me.'

'So, you broke my heart instead, and wanted me to hate you? Don't you see how messed up that is?'

'I didn't see it like that. I –'

'Of course you wouldn't. Why would you? You had bigger things to think of. I get that, truly. But I just wish that I had known back then why you backed out of it all. If I had known it was bigger than us, then maybe I wouldn't have been so … and I wouldn't have felt so … and you wouldn't have seemed so …' she trailed off, and as had always been their way, they caught each other's eyes unexpectedly and all the depth of emotion gave way to misplaced mirth. Seeing her smile gave him such joy. 'Since you arrived, I seem to have trouble finishing a sentence.'

'I can see why they pay you to write. You really are quite the wordsmith.' They laughed, the tension broken. Momentarily, at least. Maybe, it would be okay, after all?

'Oh my God, Daniel, I hate you. Do you want some rocky road? And wine. I need wine. Today's been a lot.' She headed to the kitchen, and he suspected she was as glad of the mood change as he was.

Maybe the jetlag had well and truly kicked in, but Daniel felt very "fairytale" and hazy around the edges again; they sat together on the sofa and ate and drank and chatted. The peonies he'd arrived with lay abandoned on the table and the other surprises he had planned were forgotten for now. Broderick humphed and sat moodily in the armchair, as if affronted that another human was in his place. The reservation for dinner he'd been so pleased to bag last minute, in hopeful expectation that Kirsty might join him, came and went and he didn't even realise. They talked themselves around in circles, reminiscing about old times and discussing old and new friends, sharing the life developments each had missed. She explained about her work, and Gina and Theo. He regaled her with Rudi's adventures and the revelation that Barry from the pub had got a girlfriend.

Daniel loved how Kirsty's eyes shone when she was telling him about her life in New York. Sure, it came with a pang of regret that he'd missed it, but still, to him she had never looked more beautiful. He wanted to kiss her so much, but for now, he just wanted to just take in her presence and not ruin the closeness between them. As the wine kicked in though, and Kirsty went to open another bottle, he mentally checked himself; *don't fuck this up. Don't push your luck.*

Kirsty returned from the kitchen with a bottle of Merlot and a sudden sadness in her smile. She wore her emotions on her sleeve, and he loved that about her. But what could possibly have happened on the journey from the sofa to the wine rack and back again?

'What is it, Kirst?'

Please, he inwardly implored, *don't let this be this moment she tells me that it's over.*

'It's just – I – it's a lot, as I said. Earlier today I was pathetic, on my couch in my PJs with nothing to look forward to for Christmas but lunch with Theo. Now I have you here, and I feel like it's old times, but it isn't, is it? It's new times, and I don't fully understand them. And I feel uncertain, because it's not like you moved here, is it? You still have to go back home at some point, so I have to lose you again, and I just don't know if I can do that again …' She broke off and turned away.

It killed him that she seemed almost embarrassed talking about her feelings with him; once upon a time there had been nothing they couldn't say to each other.

'I ruined us, didn't I? Whether I wanted to or not.' The unfairness of it all flattened his voice, despite the depth of feelings for Kirsty. This was so difficult.

'I'm worried you may have, yeah.' She was crying now.

It seemed to Daniel that all he ever did now was make her cry, and he hated it. They'd always been so happy.

'I don't want it to be the end, but it feels so strange. I want you so much, but I am still so confused. I mean, you turn up after a year with a bunch of flowers, and suddenly, we're fine? How?'

She sat down again on the sofa and fiddled with her hair absentmindedly as she continued.

'Are we back to normal? Are we back together? Are we happy ever after? Do you have an engagement ring in your pocket?' She checked herself at the sudden change of expression on his face.

'Please, don't panic. I don't need you to have an engagement ring in your pocket! I just feel like so much is still uncertain …'

Broderick intervened, jumping from the armchair, and stretching front and back legs in turn and settling on the doormat, head cocked to one side, expectant.

Daniel was beginning to love this dog – he didn't like where Kirsty might have been headed. 'This guy knows how to break the tension. What does he want?'

'He needs to go out – he's overdue a walk.' She checked her watch. 'How is it this time already?! We usually go to the park in the evenings. Actually, *I* need a walk. My head is all over the place. Are you coming?'

Michelle Harris

He felt like Broderick had thrown him a lifeline. A walk, some fresh air, a fresh outlook. Maybe it wasn't over yet. He stood up and picked up his thick woollen coat. Kirsty layered on her coat, gloves, hat, and scarf. She gestured to the coffee table. 'Pass me that roll of poop bags.'

'Poop? You're so American.'

'Shut up, Daniel.' Her smile was a blessing, a relief, a chance.

*

When he realised that "the park" meant Central Park, Kirsty could sense Daniel's excitement; he'd always wanted to go there. They walked in silence, and despite the tension, she made sure they entered the park through a footpath slightly further from her apartment, in sight of the iconic "Alice in Wonderland" sculpture, artistically lit, even at this late hour. She was gratified to see his handsome face come alive with recognition and pleasure, and she wished for the thousandth time that they could have gone on this journey together. Cold air whipped their cheeks as the snow swirled around, glowing under the streetlamps dotted around the park. Kirsty walked briskly and breathed in the cold as an antidote to the heat she'd been feeling inside since Daniel had arrived. God, she wanted to kiss him. But she didn't dare, because her feelings were all over the place.

Once they were a safe distance into the park, she bent down and unclipped the little dog from his harness, and he skipped off into the dark.

'Will he be okay out there?'

'Yeah, he's fine. He always comes back, and the good news is, he doesn't take a year.'

The chill in her voice matched the chill in the air, and she wasn't even entirely sure why she had said it, why she kept going back and picking the scab. She wasn't sure she even blamed Daniel anymore, but she couldn't seem to get over the hurt. She felt the grief of Juliet's passing like a physical blow; she'd been like a bonus mum to her, and she couldn't believe she had not heard the news; from somewhere. Juliet would have hated to hold Daniel at home; she could hear her voice admonishing Daniel, telling him to put himself first, but he never would have. He was rock solid.

Daniel stopped walking and put his hand on her shoulder to stop her, too. She turned to face him and found the chocolate brown eyes staring into hers intently. She didn't look away.

'Kirsty, I want to say something. I feel like you're talking yourself out of us. And I want you to just stop for a minute, please.' His tone suggested this was a "now or never" type moment, so she didn't interject.

250

'Okay, so I don't have all the answers. Us now looks a lot different to us then. But I love you, I have always loved you, I just wanted you to live the life you wanted. Maybe I went about things wrong, but –'

'All I wanted was a life with you.' She spoke in almost a whisper.

'What is this, the 1930s? Giving all this up for me wouldn't have made you happy. You wanted big things, and you deserved them.'

'But I want you … I mean, I wanted you.'

'"Wanted" or "want", Kirsty? Because if it's "wanted", I'll go. I've no intention to make things harder than I already have, believe me. But if it's "want" … well, then, you've got me. You've got me one hundred per cent, for as long as you want me. I might not know the details yet as to how, but if you say it, I'll stay, and we will figure it out.'

Kirsty couldn't believe her ears! Daniel, the ever practical, ever sensible, ever dependable, had just declared his intention to move to New York and be with her right now, without a plan. She had honestly never seen anything sexier in her life than this beautiful man, spot lit under the streetlamp in the snow, smiling broadly at her as the enormity of what he had just agreed to set in. She suspected in his head he was already planning how he might let out his flat and hand in his notice, and the juxtaposition of the practical and the fantastical made her laugh out loud.

The question hung in the freezing air, and Kirsty was silent. Daniel reached out and pulled her towards him, stroking her cheek gently.

'"Wanted"? or "want?"' she could hear the need in his voice, and she felt the same need flare up from the pit of her stomach like a fire.

'It's "want".' She couldn't have said any more at that moment.

Daniel kissed her with a force that took her breath away. She put her hand on the back of his neck, and breathed in the scent of him. He felt like home. She allowed herself to get lost in the kiss, as his hands on her back warmed her even through her thick coat. She knew then, without question, that he'd never truly let her go. If it were possible, she loved him even more for putting her first, even when he hadn't wanted to. She didn't know what their happy ending might entail, but she knew that they would get one.

*

Breathless, they pulled away from the kiss after what seemed like forever, and yet at the same time, not long enough. She smiled giddily at him, and he back at her. He pulled her back into a hug, but just as his lips were about to meet hers again, she became aware of movement in her peripheral vision.

'Drop it,' she said with severity.

'What?!' Daniel was nonplussed, to say the least.

'Not you, silly. Broderick. He's bought something out of the bushes. He eats everything. Urgh, it looks gross …'

Kirsty ran towards the puppy. The little dog did indeed have something hanging from his teeth, and he was clearly very pleased with it. Kirsty chased him around in the frosty grass as he dodged her and refused to give it up. Daniel watched in amusement, squinting to see what the dog had found, until Kirsty cried, 'Oh holy shit, it's a condom! Broderick, you absolute filth monger, drop it. Drop it!'

Any remaining romance in the situation fell away at that moment. A condom in the bushes. In New York. In December? Daniel didn't know whether to be disgusted or impressed; these winter tourists clearly meant business; it was bloody freezing. This had *not* featured in the magazine list of "romantic things to do in NYC" this holidays.

He surveyed the situation with amusement, as Kirsty, clearly used to Broderick's non-discerning treasure-hunting, donned a poo bag on each hand and wrestled with the small dog in the lamplight as the snow continued to fall in earnest.

'Can I help at all?' He didn't want to appear ungentlemanly.

'No – I can do it. Broderick, drop it. I said, drop it, Brody, you're disgusting.' Each declaration was accompanied by a shake of the dog's head, or a dive from Kirsty as she attempted to grab the offending article hanging impotently from Broderick's mouth. 'Brody – boy, let go, let go! I don't want a puppy with gonorrhoea!' She had snow in her hair, and her cheeks were flushed with exertion.

'Bro – drop it, drop it! Bro, will you let it go? Thank you!' She was jubilant. 'Bro-bro, good boy. Good boy. You dirty little beastie, Broderick.'

At the mention of the shortened name, Daniel couldn't hold in his laughter and his shoulders shook with mirth, his booming laugh echoing in the silent park. Had he known when he'd got into the cab like a Hallmark movie hero, that just hours later Kirsty would be wrestling a condom from the mouth of a puppy named after his departed mother's favourite sideboard, well, maybe he wouldn't have been musing about fairy tales.

Triumphantly, Kirsty skipped to the waste bin where she deposited the condom inside the poo bag gloves and clipped the harness back onto an unrepentant Broderick.

'Sorry about that,' she said with a wry smile. 'Dirty little bugger.'

'You're hilarious. But you're a fantastic date. So refined. Bro, by the way?'

'Haha, yeah, that nickname just kind of happened. Bro is very special. I hope he's well.'

'He is under new management, but he's all good.' He loved how much she understood him. 'So, what are your plans for Christmas Day?' Daniel knew he had to spend the day, and every day that followed, making Kirsty happy.

'Well, if we don't have lunch with Theo, he might die alone on Christmas. You don't mind, do you?'

'Of course not. I would love to meet him. It sounds like he and Gina have been great friends for you.'

'Cool, I'll message him in the morning and let him know. But right now —' Kirsty's eyes gave a devilish flicker as she continued, '— I'd really like to get you back to the apartment and have my wicked way with you, please.'

'Apartment? You're so American.' Daniel smiled widely at her. 'I can think of nothing I would rather do.'

As Kirsty slipped an arm though his, music began to play in the darkness. Startled, they looked in the direction it came from. On the steps of the Metropolitan Museum, a choir had gathered. "Silent Night" rang out across the park, and as the harmony swelled, Kirsty snuggled into Daniel and sighed. 'Just like a fairy tale. You being here has been just like a fairy tale. STI-riddled dogs aside …'

Daniel smiled again. 'I know what you mean.' No proposals, no huge declarations, but they had found a touch of Christmas magic in their own unique way. *Talking of proposals*, he thought, as he put his hand in his coat pocket and felt the small, robin-egg blue box he'd picked up on Fifth Avenue earlier. Encouraged by Gina, and discombobulated by jetlag, this had seemed a necessary purchase; a big romantic gesture designed to win back his princess. He decided to do things their way – that particular fairy tale ending could wait until a later chapter.

For now, he pulled Kirsty close and kissed her again. As the choir sang, and somewhere in the distance, the bells rang out for Christmas Day.

Michelle Harris

Biographies

Jenny Bromham is a freelance writer, developmental editor and creative writing teacher. She writes both romance and children's fiction and her published stories can be found in The Christmas Collective's anthologies, the online 2022 National Flashflood, and within Milton Education's material for students learning English.

Jenny was a winner of the *Montegrappa First Fiction* competition and was shortlisted for both the *Retreat West Opening Chapters Competition* and the *Penguin Michael Joseph Christmas Love Story Competition*. She is hoping to complete two romance novels over the next year, "The Empty Nest Club" and "The Prepact Christmas".

Currently living in Madrid with her husband and three daughters, Jenny loves reading, travel, wine, cheese and, of course, Christmas! Follow her on Twitter for editorial reflections, writing updates and general bookish discourse @JennyBromham

*

Marianne Calver is a primary school teacher from Greater London. She believes ordinary is beautiful and likes to explore the magic of everyday moments in her writing. A place on the shortlist for the *Penguin Michael Joseph Christmas Love Story* competition 2021 led her to the Christmas Collective. "Christmas for Two" was her short story debut.

Marianne lives in happy chaos with her husband, three children, a needy dog, a murderous cat and some fish. When not teaching or writing, Marianne is most likely to be found walking, researching her family history or making wonky costumes for her children that she could probably buy cheaper online. You can find Marianne on Instagram @mariannercalver

*

Bláithín O'Reilly Murphy is the author of "Distinctive Weddings: Tying the Knot without the Rope Burns", "The Meaning of Purple Tulips" and soon to be published "It Started with a Gift" as well as the short stories "Sealed with a Christmas Kiss" and "Sausage Rolls for Everyone". In addition to writing fiction she also ghost-writes non-fiction works for discerning clients. Bláithín retired from her award-winning wedding planning career in 2017 to start a family and is mum to two beautiful angel daughters in heaven and one personality-filled little dude!

She loves to write festive-filled romances that keep the readers on their toes featuring female characters who haven't yet realised their own strength. Her latest story, "Sausage Rolls for Everyone" is a festive filled tale of accepting oneself and love in all its forms and can be found in the Christmas Collectives second publication *The Mistletoe Mixtape*. Bláithín's first short story "Sealed with a Christmas Kiss" found in the Christmas Collectives first publication *More than Mistletoe* is the enticing prequel to her festive novel "It Started with a Gift" which was shortlisted for the *Penguin Christmas Love Story* Competition in 2021. She is obsessed with Hallmark Christmas Movies and Korean Dramas which she says gives her writing an emotional edge!

Bláithín is never far from a toasted scone or glass of Prosecco and she tries her best not to kill her plants in her spare time. She lives near the Irish coast with her darling husband, adorable son, and 4 cute furbabies. Her great ambition for later life is to be the crazy cat lady living on the corner of your street that everyone secretly loves and to own a bookstore, where everyone gathers for readings, and signings, and socialising; and hopefully buys a book or twenty. She can be found oversharing in her IG stories and trying to sound witty and relevant on Twitter as @WhatBlaDidNext

*

Karl King lives in Co. Kerry in Ireland with his wife and three children. He moved over just as lock down happened. To take some of the lock down boredom (we all felt it!) away, Karl joined up with fellow author Joe Burkett to write a proposal for the *Penguin Christmas Love Story* Competition. He was shocked to find out that their little story, created in less than a week, was shortlisted for the final! (Spoiler alert!) they didn't win, but it did ignite a creative passion in Karl to write more. He was invited into the Collective and is super excited to be releasing his debut short story with them.

Karl works in film and TV as a Location Manager and has read hundreds of scripts, as well as written a few himself. He was part of a small team that wrote the comedy play "At Your Services" which premiered in 2016 in the UK. When he's not location managing large productions, he is also on the Board of the Kerry International Film Festival, self-building his dream home and presenting on a podcast all about Formula 1.

*

Cici Maxwell is the chosen pen name for Amy Gaffney, and is taken from her two cats, Cici, a rather spoilt dame, and Max, who was a fluffy white bundle of madness until he went missing. His antics from the middle of the Christmas tree are hugely missed. Amy is a graduate of UCD's Creative Writing MA. A lover of all things Christmas, Amy was thrilled to discover she was shortlisted for the *Penguin Michael Joseph Christmas Love Story* competition in May 2021. She was also shortlisted for the *Dalkey Creates* Short Story Competition in 2020. Her latest poem appears in *Washing Windows Too*, a collection of poetry by Arlen House. Amy's short story "Mother May I" was shortlisted for the *An Post Book of the Year* Award 2019 in the writing.ie Short Story of the Year category.
Her first novel, *The Moonlight Gardening Club* will be published in May 2023 by Avon, Harper Collins, under the name Rosie Hannigan.
Follow her on Twitter: @gaffneyamy or Instagram @amy_gaffney24

*

Hayley-Jenifer Brennan is from Ireland but currently lives and works in South Korea. She is an ESL teacher and a graduate of University College Cork's Creative Writing MA programme. She was shortlisted for the *Staunch Book Prize for Crime Fiction* in 2020 and the *Penguin Michael Joseph Christmas Love Story* in 2021. She has published poetry in several online journals and in the "Analogies and Allegories" anthology. She also writes essays and articles for various online sites. A festive achievement was having one of her short stories published in Cork's "The Holly Bough" in 2020.

Hayley-Jenifer is an avid musical attendee and a cosplayer in her free time. She loves Christmas, her favourite pillow, and hoodies with sweatpants and fluffy socks. You can find her on Twitter @hayleyjenifer and on (cosplay) Instagram @hpdlfdl

*

Donna Gowland is a writer and teacher who lives with her husband and two daughters by the seaside in Merseyside. When she isn't teaching, writing, or daydreaming she loves reading romances and walking her dog Darcy. Donna has written for *The Guardian, Seren Poetry Press* and *The Female Gaze* and as well as being a prize winning short story writer, she is also a proud member of the RNA New Writers' Scheme.

Her story "Dominick the Donkey" is a fish out of water story about a woman (Sam) who finds herself stranded in a Welsh village on Christmas Eve – learning that her boss's Christmas invitation wasn't quite the romantic declaration she'd hoped for! Cast into a starring role in their nativity, will Sam be able to put her long standing crush on her boss behind her and snuggle under the Mistletoe with handsome stranger, Digger?
You can connect with Donna @DLGowlandWrites on Twitter and @donnagowlandwrites on Instagram.

*

S. L. Robinson is an author from Liverpool who writes broadly across fiction genre. She is currently developing her shortlisted novel "The Last Christmas" for release but has several other works in the pipeline across different genre (because who wants to be pigeon holed?). In her spare time she enjoys crochet, cooking and DIY.

Follow her on Tiktok for random ramblings, bookish thoughts and lip sync challenges @slrtheauthoress

*

Sarah Shard As with the heroine in her soon-to-be-released debut novel "Then There was Two" (working title), new chick-lit author Sarah Shard's world shattered when her father passed away suddenly in 2015, triggering a sequence of events which turned her world upside down. Amid the chaos, she found solace in the magic of the written word, thus beginning the start of an unexpected new chapter. Away from her award-winning career in project management, Sarah spends as much time as she can immersed in the fictitious villages she creates from the balcony of her home in Saddleworth, England. When she isn't writing, she loves to go on hiking adventures with her boyfriend, Lee.

Sarah is a lifelong fan of chick-lit and romantic comedies, and she hopes to bring moments of joy, frustration, laughter, surprise and love to her readers. She writes as she reads, creating the (almost) perfect book boyfriends she would love to fall in love with, but as in real life, love doesn't come easy. Her stories take you on the ups and downs in the search for that happy ending every reader hopes for.

As well as her shortlisted work in progress Christmas novel, "December for Dad", Sarah is also working on a new series of books which she calls 'chick-lit with a sprinkling of magic' set against the backdrop of the fictitious Cornish seaside village of Beacon Hope. To keep up with Sarah you can follow her on Instagram (@inspiredlifeclub) and Twitter (@sarahshard2) or check out her website at www.sarahshard.com

*

Joe Burkett lives with his husband Tom in the Kingdom of Kerry located in the idyllic west coast of Ireland. A doting uncle to his six nephews and nieces, he enjoys spending time with his extended family and creating life long memories. Joe adores spending time with friends! Be it hosting an impromptu barbecue, chasing down the perfect 99, planning a scenic holiday in Greece or weekend getaway in New York, he is always on board for a good catch up!

"August in December" Joe's short story featured in the Christmas Collective's debut anthology and he is thrilled that his latest festive tale "Wrapped in Red" will feature in this year's outing. Joe was immensely proud to be shortlisted for the *Penguin Christmas Love Story* Competition in 2021.

When he's not writing, creative director Joe is extremely busy with his stage school and events business 'Joe Burkett Theatre Company'. His childhood hobby formed the basis of his career and he adores training the next generation of aspiring dancers and actors in all things theatre. Joe is also embarking on a Licentiate diploma in drama teaching this year as part of his continuous professional development. With ambitions to continue his writing career and an increased focus on short stories, Joe is always on the lookout for new stories. Taking inspiration from his everyday observations, overheard conversations and witty side of life.

If you want to connect with Joe on all things writing, drama, dance or his utter devastation at the cancellation of Neighbours, you can follow him on IG @JoeWritesStories

*

Helen Hawkins is a writer, editor and English teacher who loves all things Christmas and romance. Her debut novel, "A Concert for Christmas", was shortlisted for the *Penguin Michael Joseph Christmas Love Story* Competition and highly commended in this year's *I am in Print Romance* Competition. "Santa Baby" is her short story debut and she is thrilled to finally be venturing into the world of publication.

When she's not writing, Helen can be found editing, singing and dancing with her local operatic society, or running around with her toddler and partner at their home in Oxfordshire.

You can connect with Helen about all things writing, editing and romance on Twitter or Instagram @helenwritesit.

*

Michelle Harris is a former secondary school English and Drama teacher who recently made the transition to Primary teaching, which she loves. Her new answer to every single ailment is 'put a wet tissue on it.' She has also worked in social media marketing, so if she is spotted hanging around scrolling Instagram, please understand it is Very Important Research. She lives in Greater London with her husband and two children.

Michelle's novel "Queen of Christmas" was shortlisted for the *Penguin Michael Joseph Christmas Love Story* Competition, and she hopes to release this in 2023. Her debut short story "The Ghost of Christmas Past" was included in 2021 Christmas Collective anthology, and she's thrilled to be back with the Collective again. When she grows up, she's going to be Judi Dench.

Twitter @MichelleBHarris
Instagram @michelle_b_harris